# THE
# IMPERIAL
# WAY

# THE
# IMPERIAL
# WAY

James Melville

ANDRE DEUTSCH

First published 1986 by
André Deutsch Limited
105 Great Russell Street London WC1

ISBN 0 233 97819 4

Phototypeset by Falcon Graphic Art Ltd,
Wallington, Surrey
Printed in Great Britain by
Ebenezer Baylis and Son Ltd,
Worcester

The Japanese characters which appear on the
title page mean The Imperial Way
Calligraphy by Mie Kimata.

## AUTHOR'S NOTE

Western writers on Japan frequently adopt in English the practice of rendering proper names as they are written in Japanese, with the family name first and the given name second. There are two reasons why I have chosen not to follow their example, of which the more compelling to me is that for documents in English the Japanese authorities themselves reverse the order and give names in the western manner, even though this practice has in recent years excited some controversy in Japan. Furthermore although I believe my reconstruction of the February 26 Incident to be historically accurate both as to essentials and to a great extent in detail, *The Imperial Way* is a novel and not a work of scholarship; and I believe that the great majority of its readers will find the familiar western form of the characters' names both acceptable and readily comprehensible.

# PRINCIPAL CHARACTERS

*In* 1936 Fiction

Yukichi Shimada
*His wife* Chie Shimada
*Elder son* Lieutenant Hideo Shimada
*Elder daughter* Yoko Shimada
*Younger daughter* Teruko Shimada
*Younger son* Jiro Shimada

*Tokyo correspondent,* Dwight Rogers
*New York Times*
*Lecturer, Waseda* Mr Nagai
*University*

*In* 1936 Fact

His Imperial Majesty The Emperor of Japan
Major His Imperial Highness Prince Chichibu
Viscount Saito, Lord Keeper of the Privy Seal
Joseph Grew, American Ambassador to Japan
Courtiers and members of the government
Seihin Ikeda, President of Mitsui Holdings
Generals Mazaki, Kawashima, Honjo and Sugiyama
Colonel Aizawa

*Rebel Officers* Captains Ando, Nonaka, Yamaguchi and Kono;
Lieutenants Kurihara, Takahashi, Yasuda,
and Nakahashi

*Their civilian* Ikki Kita and Mitsugi Nishida
*associates*

*In* 1986 Fiction

| | |
|---:|:---|
| *President, Shimada Trading Corporation* | Jiro Shimada |
| *Retired professor of librarianship* | Yoko Nagai |
| *Retired professor of Japanese* | Dwight Rogers |
| *Writer* | Lesli Hoshino |
| *Tokyo bureau chief,* Newsworld *Magazine* | Charlie Goldfarb |

*Note*: The writer Lafcadio Hearn lived and worked in Kumamoto and in Tokyo during the periods indicated.

# 1. *Tuesday 31 December, 1935*

Lieutenant Hideo Shimada of the Third Regiment of the First Division of the Imperial Japanese Army marched with an air of assurance into the Arden Beauty Salon in the Ginza and almost at once recoiled, blinking several times under the impact of the hot, perfumed atmosphere of femininity which engulfed him and made him prickle with sweat under his heavy serge uniform and greatcoat. Before he could speak to the receptionist at her little desk, her own hair a marcelled miracle of advertisement for the salon, all heads had turned in his direction and he confronted a hostile vista of curlers and face packs. Then he focused on the agonised face of his younger sister Teruko as she made timid shooing motions, and after a second or two of hesitation turned on his heel and retreated smartly through the door without having spoken a word.

As he stood there wondering what to do next he saw Teruko's indistinct figure loom up against the misted glass of the window in her white smock. She held up one open hand and four fingers of the other and pushed them briefly against the glass, and he nodded in comprehension before she scuttled away again into the recesses of the salon. Hideo had been under the impression that his sister finished work at eight in the evening, knowing that the elegant western-style establishments of Tokyo's Ginza affected a very different trading style from the open-fronted neighbourhood shops around the Ueno area near which they lived. These stayed open until ten or eleven, for the little shops merged visibly with their associated living quarters. But it was New Year's Eve, and perhaps the management of the Arden Beauty Salon with its clientele of foreign and rich Japanese women felt obliged to recognise the fact that even in these hard times it was important to the ladies that they should look their best on the following day.

Hideo intensely disliked being kept waiting, but on this occasion shrugged philosophically as he turned away. He looked at the big clock on the Mazda Building opposite, visible over the top of the tramcar clanging and swaying along the bustling street. Ten past eight. It was a pleasant evening, crisply chilly but dry, and he set off at a brisk march in the direction of nearby Hibiya where most of the cinemas were. He supposed that when Teruko did at last emerge she would be bursting with all the latest Hollywood gossip, although she knew he disapproved of her frivolity. He had been to the cinema a few times but only to see Japanese films reflecting, even if in extravagantly heightened ways, the world he knew and fiercely cherished: he disliked foreigners on principle and felt nothing but distaste for their ways.

There were a good many soldiers and sailors in uniform on the noisy streets and Hideo saluted as necessary like an automaton, his thoughts elsewhere until he came to the Shochiku Theatre with its gaudy poster advertising *China Seas* with Clark Gable, Jean Harlow and Wallace Beery. He paused to look at the photographs in the showcase outside: the platinum corrugations of Jean Harlow's hairstyle both fascinated and repelled him, but she was remote and not really credible to him, whereas the receptionist at the Arden Beauty Salon had been essentially Japanese under her alien permanent wave. The forthcoming attraction was *Top Hat*, and Hideo's eyes were drawn as if by magnetism to the stills in the next showcase and the brazenly exposed legs of Ginger Rogers as she whirled at the side of Fred Astaire smiling, smiling, smiling in the arrogant awareness of her female power.

Hideo huddled himself into his greatcoat and dragged himself away from the bright warmth of the entrance. He was hungry, but that was a familiar state which bothered him only a little. His funds wouldn't run to a meal in a proper restaurant and it would be unseemly for an officer of the Imperial Army to patronise a cheap noodle bar: noodles must by all means be eaten late on New Year's Eve but he planned to take Teruko to the great Kannon Temple at Asakusa on the way home and they could enjoy them there at an open-air stall without a single eyebrow being raised.

He wandered back past the huge pile of the Imperial Hotel and under the railway tracks to the alien glitter of the Ginza, the familiar indignation rising in him. Even the papier-mâché models in the windows of the dress shops had been given European features and colouring, and the ugliness of the roman script everywhere testified to the snobbish craze for English and French words and phrases. Foreign ways had eaten corrosively into the very heart of Japan while small farmers couldn't afford to eat the rice they grew. Hideo was not yet a Company Commander with all the fearsome responsibility of a father towards his men, but he had seen enough half-starved recruits to share the sense of anger and shame so often expressed by the captains when they spoke of hearing from their men of famine in the north-east, and tales of sisters sold to brothels for a few hundred desperately needed yen. Yet here in Tokyo wealthy politicians and capitalists spent that and more weekly on trinkets for their mistresses.

The only bright, glorious light in the darkness of corruption and folly was the Emperor in his great palace behind the moat across the expanse of Hibiya Park, inexpressibly blessed at last by the birth two years earlier of the infant Crown Prince. Hideo had been shocked by the rumours going around at the time that His Majesty had made it clear that even if his young Empress were to produce yet another daughter he would not take concubines to his bed. It was incomprehensible, for was not the Emperor himself the son of a concubine? His divine Imperial forebears had never scrupled to ensure the continuance of the line – but all was well, and the regular Imperial Household Agency reports indicated that the little Prince Akihito was comely and robust.

It was a few minutes after nine when Teruko at last tripped out of the Arden Beauty Salon on her high heels and joined her brother. She had never in her life presumed to address him by his given name, but only in the conventional fashion as *O-Ni-san* or Elder Brother; but during the years of her apprenticeship at the salon her manner towards Hideo had become more and more cheeky and disrespectful.

'I could have died with embarrassment when you came in,' she began, then broke down in giggles. 'What must you have thought of those ugly old hags?'

'I hardly noticed them,' he said haughtily. 'In any case, you made it very clear that I wasn't welcome.'

Teruko became at once conciliatory. 'I'm sorry. I was just taken by surprise to see you. We all thought you were going to be on duty over the holiday.' Hideo had been transferred from Nagoya to the Third Regiment's barracks at Azabu in metropolitan Tokyo towards the end of November 1934 on his promotion at the age of twenty-five to First Lieutenant, Second Class. The jump in pay from 850 to 1020 yen a year had seemed enormous until he discovered how much more expensive the life of an army officer in the capital had become since his days as a cadet at the Military Academy there.

'I was, but a friend of mine volunteered to exchange orderly officer duties with me and the Major agreed. His home is in

Shikoku and he wouldn't have been able to get there in time anyway.' This was not the real reason for the switch, but Hideo had no intention of letting his family become aware of his reactivated membership of the Young Officers' Movement, dormant from the time of his recruitment to it as a senior cadet until his return to Tokyo. He was proud to have been able to collaborate in this first, small way to enable one of the leaders of the faction to have access to all the confidential papers in the Adjutant's office over the most important holiday period in the year, when there was virtually no likelihood of any senior officers putting in an appearance.

'Anyway, it was nice of you to telephone the salon. It'll be a surprise for the others.' The Shimada family could not easily have afforded to buy a telephone through a broker, even had the thought of such a luxury held much attraction for them. Hideo could have sent a telegram to warn his parents to expect him, but that would have cost money and probably frightened his mother. Instructing the military exchange operator to connect him with the Arden Beauty Salon on Ginza 57–4393 had been simple if a little embarrassing: he only wished he had thought to ask the receptionist there not only to give a message to Teruko but also to let him know what time the place was due to close that evening.

'I thought we might go to Asakusa first.'

Teruko shrugged prettily. Her cloth coat wasn't very warm, but the approach to the temple with its stalls and shouting hucksters would be crowded with people all night long. At nearly twenty Teruko considered herself a *moga* – the fashionable contraction of *modaan gaaru* or 'modern girl' – too sophisticated to take part in such common festivities as seeing out the old year in the traditional way, but she felt a flicker of anticipatory excitement all the same. 'All right. We can get a tram at the corner.'

A great many people were heading in their general direction and the tram was crowded. Teruko and Hideo had to stand, squeezed into a corner as it jolted along, and all at once Teruko stood on tip-toe to whisper to her brother. Hideo experienced a hot, shameful pleasure in her physical proximity and the moist warmth of her breath at his ear. 'Try to guess which people are going home, which ones to Ueno, which ones to Asakusa – and which ones to Yoshiwara!' Not only the soft pressure of Teruko's body, but what she said, was giving him an erection, and he twisted away from her in a brief violent movement, grateful for the concealment provided by the voluminous folds of his greatcoat. It was not the first time he had been aware of a new, flaunting sexual awareness in Teruko, in sharp contrast to the modest, serious and respectful attitude of her elder sister Yoko. Yoko would have pretended ignorance of the very existence of the Yoshiwara brothel area while blushing scarlet at the mere mention of its name, and certainly would not have invited her elder brother to guess which of their fellow-passengers might be on the way there. 'Really! Behave yourself!' he hissed.

Teruko was unabashed. 'I'll bet *you've* been to Yoshiwara,' she whispered jauntily, her eyes sparkling under her rakish beret. 'Come on, what's it like?' The fact that she was right made Hideo more rather than less indignant. He had been there two or three times in the company of brother officers, most of whom came from well-to-do families and had very much more money to spare than Hideo, who could not afford to spend a whole night with a whore but had to make his way alone back to barracks after a short half-hour. 'Mind your own business,' he snapped, and stared in silence at the window, opaque with steam from the breaths of the full load of passengers.

They had nearly reached their destination before he trusted himself to speak again. 'How's Mother?' he asked her then.

'All right, I suppose.'

' "All right, all right," all you ever seem to say is "all right".'

Teruko raised one thin, plucked eyebrow. 'My, my, you *are* touchy tonight, aren't you? She's getting dottier all the time, if you ask me. Doesn't listen to what you're saying, mutters her prayers and forgets to clean the house. I feel quite sorry for Father. Yoko's doing the cooking for tomorrow and the next day, then I suppose we shall have to get food sent round from the noodle shop as per usual. Talking of noodles, I'm famished. Can we have some, please?'

Hideo nodded. Their mother had always been vague and dreamy, and had become steadily more withdrawn during the past year. It was as well that Yoko had a good job as a library assistant at Waseda University and that their brother Jiro, the youngest member of the family at seventeen, was apparently so self-sufficient and doing so well at school.

The tram jolted to a stop and almost everybody got off and headed for the great stone *torii* gateway which marked the entrance to the precincts of the Kannon Temple. The approach to the main temple buildings was lined with stalls selling everything from cheap clothes to New Year talismans, and the reek of paraffin lamps mingled with the mouth-watering smell of chicken kebabs grilling over charcoal and noodles being fried up in huge round-bottomed pans. The noisy, cheerful mood of the jostling crowd was infectious, and Hideo had no inhibitions about ordering fried noodles at the first stall they came to and standing there to eat them with throwaway wooden chopsticks like everybody else. Two generous helpings in paper containers cost far less than a single small bowl would have done anywhere downtown, and the food cheered him up considerably. Then Teruko insisted on treating them each to a tumbler of warm *sake* which put him into a distinctly good mood and made her helplessly giggly. 'I expect everybody thinks I'm your girlfriend,' she spluttered, and could hardly contain her amusement even when they arrived at the huge incense container in the temple forecourt and symbolically washed their hands and faces in the sweet-smelling smoke before climbing the steps, tossing a few *sen* into the great offertory box in front of the altar and bowing their heads in brief petition.

As always for the past couple of years, Teruko made a wish for an American husband; while Hideo was momentarily solemn again as he prayed for the opportunity to be of service to the Emperor in the coming year. Then they made their way on foot to their home in the Hongo district a couple of miles away, enjoying each other's company.

## 2. New Year's Day, 1936

'Happy New Year!' 'Happy New Year!' Yukichi Shimada responded to his children's greetings briskly enough, and looked at them in affection as they knelt on the *tatami* matting, their heads bowed very low. He had been in bed when he heard Teruko and Hideo arrive home but had risen eagerly at the sound of his eldest son's voice, and even persuaded his wife Chie to get up as well to greet him. Yoko was still busy in the kitchen at well after eleven, but joined the others for green tea and a brief chat; and after a while Jiro emerged in his *yukata*, heavy-eyed and yawning but smiling even as he pretended to complain about the noise. After what seemed only a few minutes it was midnight, and time to exchange formal congratulations on the death of the old year and the beginning of the new.

The smell of incense clung to Hideo and Teruko's clothes, and they had brought a bottle of *sake* in with them. 'We won't open it yet,' Yoko said. 'I've prepared some spiced New Year *sake* for tomorrow – I mean today – so let's just have one cup now for a toast and then we really ought to go to bed. Mother? Will you have just a little?' Chie looked round the crowded little room, smiling timidly, her eyes darting about in her white moon face. She spilled a little of the drink as they all raised the shallow, almost saucer-shaped red lacquer cups used on special occasions, but managed to drink most of it.

'Well, a very good start to the year,' Yoko said after the toast, gently taking her mother's cup from her. 'How nice that you could get leave, Elder Brother.' Yoko was twenty-three years old, but often looked more: this was one of those occasions. She had removed the voluminous apron she had been wearing over an old *kimono*, but her hair was still protected by a white cloth, which she now touched self-consciously. 'Oh dear, what must you think of us all?'

'Never mind. We shall all be dressed up in a few hours' time,' Yukichi said, his eyes still fixed on Hideo. 'You'll come with us to the Meiji Shrine I hope, Hideo?'

'Of course. It looks as if the weather will be good. There will be tremendous crowds there. You won't mind, will you, Mother?' Chie looked at him directly for the first time, her smile now anxious. 'I feel very well,' she said timidly, and her husband reached out to her and patted her arm.

'She'll be fine,' he said. 'All the same, I think we should all go to bed. You'll have to make room for your brother, Jiro.' Yoko scrambled to her feet in haste. 'I'll put some bedding down for you. I'm sorry the bath water isn't hot, but perhaps we'll celebrate by heating a fresh one in the morning.' The younger Shimadas were proud of their tiny bathroom with its wooden tub and the wood-fired boiler at the back of the house. Most of their neighbours in the Hongo district not far from Tokyo University had to use the public bathhouse, and one or two had let it be known indirectly that they considered the Shimada family's acquisition of two years previously to be not only a wanton extravagance but also a fire hazard. Teruko enjoyed it most, even though as the younger daughter she was strictly speaking last in line to enter the water to relax after soaping and rinsing in the evening, after her father, brothers, mother and elder sister.

It seldom worked out that way, even when Jiro remembered to light the firewood on arriving home from school. Hideo was hardly ever there, their mother still preferred – when she felt well enough – to take her wooden bowl and tiny towel round to the public bathhouse and talk to Mrs Toda and the other women in their half of the big sunken bath, and even if he had already arrived home by the time she got there, more often than not her father would tell Teruko to use the bath first. He was old-fashioned enough to believe that a woman's body 'softened' the water.

It was well after one in the morning before they were all in bed. Yukichi lay in sleepless silence beside his wife in the larger of the two upstairs rooms, listening to her whispered prayers. It was the first time for months that Hideo had slept at home, even though he had managed to visit the house for a few hours two or three times most months since being posted to Tokyo. Yukichi's colleagues at the vast Mitsui headquarters office were properly respectful about the fact that he had an Army officer son, and repeatedly told Yukichi how proud he must be. 'But then you come of samurai stock yourself of course, Shimada-san.' Yukichi could not remember ever having told anybody at the office this, but it was pointless to try to keep anything secret from other members of the great

Mitsui 'family'. Except one thing. Nobody at the office must ever find out that his wife Chie was going mad. Yukichi sighed and turned over.

Yoko and Teruko shared the adjoining room. It was only four and a half *tatami* mats in size, about nine feet square, and had been designed to be used for the tea ceremony; but although the girls' bedding covered most of the floor area when they spread it at night they had no feeling of being cramped for space. On the contrary: very few of their acquaintances enjoyed the luxury of so much personal privacy. Yoko was hunched in the sleep of exhaustion, but Teruko was wakeful, stimulated by the noise and flaring lights of Asakusa.

1936 at last. She was certain that it would be an exciting year. Soon she would become legally an adult, on her twentieth birthday at the end of January. She would no longer be an apprentice at the Arden Beauty Salon, but a fully qualified beautician who could, if she wished, almost certainly get a job at the Imperial Hotel or even move to Yokohama or Kobe where most of the wealthy foreigners lived. She already knew enough English to greet foreign ladies in that language and to understand most of their instructions: she resolved to buy a phrase-book from the Maruzen Bookstore, study it diligently and become fluent. Only in that way could she become really attractive to Americans. Slowly and lazily she opened her *yukata* and slid her right hand up her smooth thighs as she opened them, her left hand going to her breast. Tonight, she decided, Spencer Tracy would be her dream lover.

Downstairs Jiro slept dreamlessly amid a clutter of books and discarded clothes. He was alone in the cubby-hole which he had in practice if not yet in theory inherited from Hideo. After one look at the mess in his old room Hideo had told Yoko to put down bedding for him in the living room instead. Sleep did not come easily to him, and when it did, it was troubled.

It was like a river gathering breadth and majesty as tributaries of people joined the thickening mainstream to pass under the mighty unpainted *torii* gate of the Meiji Shrine and move inexorably towards the sanctuary, and only at the edges of the path was it possible for individuals to go at their own pace, to dally or to overtake. A noisy river, with the mutter of thousands of human voices underlying the crunching clatter of wooden *geta* sandals on the gravelled surface. On this day of days most girls, every woman and the majority even of the adult men were wearing kimonos, though Hideo's army uniform attracted approving nods and there were many other naval and military men among the crowds. Jiro, like most of the other boys his age, was dressed in the black, high-buttoned uniform tunic and trousers which differed from school to school only in minor details of buttons and cap-badge. A cheap box camera was suspended from his neck by a thin leather strap, and he cradled it in his hands with a fierce protectiveness.

'Father looks very handsome in his kimono, doesn't he?' Yoko murmured to Teruko. It was only in recent years that Teruko had begun to think of her father as a man like other men, rather than as an awesome background presence, grave and uncommunicative; authority to be placated rather than a person to know. She looked ahead and to their right where he walked between his two sons, a slight, elegant figure lent added dignity by the flowing lines of the traditional dress, less dandified than in the dark suit and stiff-collared shirt he wore to go to his office. 'Yes, I suppose he does,' she said in some surprise. 'It's all right for men though, they don't have to hobble along like us.' A brief inclination to rebel had sparked in Teruko as she and Yoko had helped each other to tie their stiff *obi* sashes, but she had suppressed it. To have appeared on New Year's Day in the western dress she infinitely preferred would have precipitated a major family row, and in any case she possessed neither a coat new or smart enough nor any suitable shoes. As usual and in spite of her strange, withdrawn manner, their mother had dressed quite competently without assistance, and even allowed Teruko to apply a touch of rouge to her cheeks. She walked in silence beside Yoko, looking around her wide-eyed, as though surprised to be there.

It was quite chilly still in the shade of the great trees which lined the approach, but the sky was a pale egg-shell blue high above, and as the Shimadas reached the open forecourt at last they came into the warm sunshine which bathed the massive roof of the shrine. There was more elbow-room there, even though people had to crowd five and six deep before the sanctuary in order to make their acts of reverence to the sacred memory of the Emperor's grandfather; to him in whose name political power had been retrieved from the last of the Shoguns. Only a lucky few were able to reach the ropes attached to the invocatory bells, but they clanked continuously anyway above the chink and clatter of coins in their hundreds being flung into the offertory boxes which extended across the whole frontage of the sanctuary within which priests moved in their archaic Court robes and head-dresses, attended by shrine virgins in white kimonos with scarlet over-skirts, their long hair enclosed at the back in golden tubes.

Enough people made way respectfully for the army lieutenant and his family for them to approach the barrier rail itself, and Jiro was within reach of a bell-rope which he shook vigorously before clapping his hands and bowing like the others. Only Mrs Shima-da's lips moved in what looked like becoming a lengthy prayer: her husband had to shake her arm gently and lead her away as others pressed in on them to take their places at the front. Yoko found herself at her father's side when they escaped from the crush and stood at some distance to watch the scene.

'We can relax now. What did you wish for, Father?'

Yukichi looked at his elder daughter, a slight smile on his pale, lined face. 'The usual things,' he said. 'A good husband for you, for one.' A dark flush mantled Yoko's neck and cheeks. 'It's all right, I'm not going to talk about it today,' he reassured her. 'I made other wishes too.' For an insane moment he wished he could confide to Yoko what they were. She was his favourite child, and the only one who might begin to understand.

'Let me take a photograph now. There are two left on the roll.' Jiro spoke loudly enough to command fairly general attention, and officiously began to pose everybody against the background of the shrine buildings. His mother stood obediently where she was put, and his father and Hideo automatically took the central positions. Teruko was slow to respond. 'Come on, over here beside Elder Sister! What are you smiling at?' The other members of the family had already assumed the preternaturally solemn expressions considered seemly when being photographed.

'Look over there. It's a foreigner and he's watching us.' Teruko spoke in an intense undertone, still staring to her left, then smiled again in that direction. 'Oh, no! He's coming over here!' she added in delighted embarrassment as a tall young man approached. The Shimadas stood as though rooted as the stranger smiled at Jiro, bowed and volunteered in courteous, perfectly intelligible Japanese to take the photograph for him so that he might be included in the family group.

Jiro hesitated but soon entrusted his precious camera to the young man, who handled it with easy familiarity, politely re-grouped his subjects and took the picture. Then he handed the camera back with another smile and was just turning away when Teruko found the boldness to speak. 'Why don't you take the gentleman's photograph now, Jiro? With us,' she added even more daringly, ignoring the scowl on Hideo's face and the uneasy shuffling of her sister Yoko.

'Good idea,' Yukichi said, and approached the young man. 'Good morning, sir,' he said in careful English as Yoko and Teruko listened with admiring awe. 'My son likes to take your picture, please.' He gestured towards the others and the tall foreigner smiled and moved towards them obediently. Jiro took rather longer to compose the group to his satisfaction and Teruko who had firmly placed herself at the foreigner's side edged a little closer to him. He smelt a little, but of eau de cologne, not the 'butter-stench' characteristic of most westerners, and Teruko experienced a delicious frisson as his hand brushed the back of hers.

The photograph was taken at last and Jiro was sternly winding the roll on, peering intently at the little red window, when inspiration came to Teruko. 'We will send you a copy of the photograph,' she said rather breathlessly, 'if you will tell me your address.' Her heart thumped as the young man grinned directly at her. 'You are very kind,' he said, and took a slim leather wallet from his inside pocket. 'My name is Rogers. Dwight Rogers.'

'Shimada is our name. You speak Japanese very well.' Yukichi said genially, with a half-bow. It was pleasant to be able to air his English once in a while. 'You live here in Tokyo?' Rogers took out a name-card and hesitated for a moment, wondering who to give it to and which language to use. Then he replied in Japanese out of courtesy to the majority as he placed the card in Teruko's out-stretched hand. 'Oh. Yes. That's my card. Japanese on one side and English on the other. Yes. I've lived here in Tokyo for almost three years. I'm a – ' 'Newspaper reporter!' Teruko squeaked delighted-ly, having been studying the card. *'New York Times!'*

'You are an American? A Happy New Year to you.' It was Mrs Shimada, speaking shyly but clearly, and looking up at him. 'I hope that you will be blessed and that there will be peace. Peace in the world, peace in China – ' 'It's time we were going, Mother.' Hideo's voice was harsh, his manner angry as he interrupted her. Throughout the encounter he had ignored Rogers, and only the pressure of his father's hand on his arm had kept him in place for the second photograph.

'Please. I mustn't detain you,' Rogers said. 'It has been a great pleasure to meet you. I wish you all a very happy and prosperous 1936.' He smiled round at them all, his teeth very white beneath his neatly-trimmed moustache, then turned and walked away, his height making him visible above the crowd from a considerable distance.

'You ought to be ashamed of yourself,' Hideo stormed at Teruko. 'Throwing yourself at a foreigner like that.' Then he wheeled round. 'And as for you, Mother, I know you aren't very well, but you should know better than to talk politics to an American – '

'That will do, Hideo.' A touch of colour had come into Yukichi's face and his voice had thickened. 'The young man was courteous and friendly. Much more so than you. Teruko may have been a little forward, but I am not upset with her. As for you, you owe your mother an apology.'

'It doesn't matter. He didn't mean it, I know.' Mrs Shimada seemed unaware as she spoke of the teardrops trickling down her cheeks until Yoko dabbed them away with a handkerchief she took from her kimono sleeve, as though her mother were a child.

'I thought he was very nice. And he was only trying to be helpful,' Yoko said quietly.

Teruko said nothing at all. She was used to Hideo's sudden rages and aggressive ranting, and not bothered in the least by her father's mild reproof. She had Dwight Rogers' name-card in her possession, and thought it quite likely that the others had already forgotten its existence. She doubted very much if Jiro would raise any objection when she offered to take the film to the big chemist's shop near the Arden Beauty Salon to be developed, and since she would be paying, nobody need know how many extra prints she ordered for the American. If it came out well, she wanted him also to have a copy of the photograph Jiro had taken of her alone the previous week, in western dress and wearing proper make-up.

Hideo muttered what passed for an apology to his mother, and cheered up a little at the prospect of the festive meal Yoko had prepared for them to eat when they got home. They went by way of the big public open space which lay between the shrine precincts and the military parade grounds at Yoyogi, and lingered for some time to watch boys and men flying gaudy paper kites, many of them vividly and humorously decorated with grotesquely staring painted eyes and grimacing mouths. Other boys played with little elastic-powered model aeroplanes made of cardboard which hopped and swooped short distances before plunging to the coarse brownish turf. They bore crudely-printed Army or Navy markings, and were a recent fad.

## 3. *Saturday 4 January, 1986*

Slightly flushed, Lesli Hoshino watched as the immigration officer eventually, and with a new respect in his manner, stamped her passport and entered the code number for a three-month 'cultural' visa. It was a good many years since she had last been in Japan, and the first time she had arrived at the new international airport at Narita, a full eighty kilometres east of the capital. She had never had the least trouble before: on the contrary, Japanese-Americans like herself usually attracted a special word of welcome, particularly when they spoke good Japanese.

As she made her way down the open staircase into the customs hall Lesli reflected that it must have been the fuss at the next counter involving a little group of Filipino women which had made her own inquisitor look her up and down with obvious suspicion and quiz her at such length about her plans. Spotting her suitcase already on the carousel restored her good humour: after all, it was almost flattering in a way, at thirty-seven, to be taken even temporarily for a hooker coming to work in a bar, turkish bathhouse or strip show. Anyway, the mention of Jiro Shimada's name had done the trick, as indeed it should.

Lesli spotted the sign as soon as she was nodded through customs and the automatic doors opened before her. It was done on card with a green felt-tip marker and read WELCOME MISS LESLI HOSHINO NEWSWORLD MAGAZINE. It was being held somewhat diffidently to his chest by a short, middle-aged man whose eyes were flickering anxiously from a photograph he held in his other hand to the faces of the arriving passengers. His face lit up as Lesli approached him. 'Ah! Welcome Miss Lesli Hoshino Newsworld Magazine!' he intoned in English, beaming. Lesli grinned. 'Word perfect. Hello. I'm Lesli Hoshino.' Dropping his sign, the little man produced a card from his top pocket and proffered it with a bow. 'I am Kazuo Yamada, Shimada Trading Corporation. International Liaison Department. I am very happy to meet you, Miss Hoshino. You must be very tired after your long journey.' 'Oh, not too bad really. Nice meeting you, Mr Yamada. I really appreciate your coming all this way out to the airport.'

A younger, good-looking man in a dark suit approached, bent to retrieve the fallen sign and took command of Lesli's luggage trolley. 'Ah. Yes. This is Mr Hatano, President Shimada's personal driver. He will take your bags to the car.' Lesli bowed and greeted the chauffeur politely in Japanese. He looked as surprised as he was gratified, and Mr Yamada switched to that language himself as all three headed for the exit.

'How beautifully you speak Japanese, Miss Hoshino! I had been informed of this, of course, but had no idea that you were so completely fluent.' He stopped short, and fumbled in his breast pocket. 'Forgive me, I am forgetting the most important thing. President Shimada gave me this personal letter for you. He is so sorry not to have been able to come to welcome you himself.'

Lesli took the creamy envelope and ripped it open as she smiled a little ruefully at Yamada. She had uttered no more than a few words to the driver, and those a cliché of the most conventional kind: the Japanese could be so patronising with their ludicrously extravagant compliments. By contrast, Jiro Shimada's letter was pleasant courtesy itself, and she found herself almost believing that he really had intended to make the journey out to Narita but had been detained by some tiresome chore. She stuffed the letter in her handbag and smiled again. 'I'm overwhelmed, Mr Yamada. It's more than kind of Mr Shimada to ask me to be his guest indefinitely at the Okura Hotel. I remember it from the old days, but never dreamed that I would ever stay there. It'll be marvellous to unwind there over the weekend, but I'm sure Mr Shimada will understand that I couldn't dream of imposing myself on his generosity for more than a few days. I'll explain when I meet him on Monday afternoon. He writes that he'll be expecting me around three p.m.'

It was chilly outside the terminal building, and Yamada made no comment as he led her quickly towards the big black Nissan parked immediately opposite the doors, the driver Hatano waiting by the passenger door. 'We should be at the hotel in less than an hour today,' he said as he joined her in the back. 'There's hardly any traffic on the expressway, because of the holidays.'

Lesli nodded as the car picked up speed. 'Crossing the date line always did confuse me. It's hard to get used to the idea that there never will be a third of January 1986 as far as I'm concerned. It's nice for people to have an even longer New Year holiday than usual on account of the weekend . . . I hate keeping you and Mr Hatano here from your families this way.' Lesli sat back and looked at the familiar green motorway signs as both Yamada and

Hatano politely demurred. She knew she had said the right things so far, and helped the two men overcome their embarrassment at dealing with that most un-Japanese phenomenon, a professional woman travelling alone.

Yamada remained silent for several minutes before reverting to his halting but quite serviceable English. 'When were you last in Japan, Miss Hoshino?'

'Let me see, I left just over six years ago. I lived here for three years at the end of the seventies. I expect you know I was with the Tokyo bureau of the magazine.'

'Yes, of course. All of us staff at the Shimada Trading Corporation were very honoured when our President was named *Newsworld Magazine* Achiever of the Year a couple of weeks ago. The first Japanese to have that distinction, I think?'

'That's right. And richly deserved. "Japan's Ambassador to the World" – that was my phrase, Mr Yamada. I'm rather proud of it. We started researching the cover story some months ago, of course, before it was finally decided that none of the other contenders for 1985 matched up to Mr Shimada.'

'And was that when you decided that you would like to write a full-length biography? When you were working on the cover story in New York?' Mr Yamada seemed to be gaining confidence.

'Why, yes, it was. I became convinced that Mr Shimada must be a truly remarkable man: not just a highly successful business leader, but someone who cares about the world and who represents a new kind of Japanese success. Human success.'

'Yes. Our President is very successful. You are also very successful, Miss Hoshino. Many times suggestions have been made that Mr Shimada's biography should be written, but he always refused, until your letter arrived. Now he seems very pleased about the project, and has asked me to make sure that you have all the help you need with your research. It will be my pleasure.'

Lesli recalled Yamada's words a couple of hours later, when she had bathed, eaten a light meal, unpacked and tidied away her belongings in the spacious double room reserved for her at the luxurious and expensive Okura Hotel. She felt tired enough to sleep for a week, yet hopelessly wide awake, and waltzed a little unsteadily around the room in the crisp cotton *yukata* provided for her, eyeing the orchids which had been waiting for her there, with a hand-written card attached repeating her host's words of welcome. They were wonderfully decadent, and Lesli thought them entirely appropriate to the splendour in which she was being accommodated at the expense of the tycoon of tycoons, the respected member of the Club of Rome and the Brandt Commission, the world-renowned patron of the arts and maker and breaker of Japanese governments. She had never met him, but had in a sense lived with him for many weeks, and felt that she already knew him well. She looked forward to Monday afternoon with real excitement.

It was just before midnight Tokyo time when Lesli finally clambered into the big bed, and in fact she slept very well.

## 4. Monday 6 January, 1986

'I *am* sixty-seven years of age, Miss Hoshino, after all,' Jiro Shimada said in easy, mid-Atlantic English and with a warm smile. Lesli assumed that he must be wearing contact lenses, and he had certainly spent thousands of dollars on dentists. His white hair was abundant, and even his skin colour suggested a Californian tan rather than oriental pigmentation. Photographs didn't do him justice, she decided. In the flesh he looked a little like Cary Grant made up for some weird reason as a Japanese.

During her successful career as a journalist Lesli had met many of the great and famous, and was well accustomed to the fact that such notables tend to seem physically smaller than expected when encountered in person. Unusually, Shimada came across as being rather larger than life, and had a thoroughly un-Japanese air about him. He could easily have been a *nisei* or *sansei* – a second or third generation American of Japanese ancestry – like Lesli herself, retaining the facial characteristics of the race but bigger in bodily stature than ordinary Japanese as well as notably more outgoing and uninhibited. Judged by appearance and manner alone, Shimada might well have been a U.S. Senator, Wall Street financier or president of a media conglomerate rather than a Japanese industrialist and public figure.

'It's hard to believe, Mr Shimada,' she replied with professional courtesy. They were sitting in his office on the twenty-seventh floor of the Shimada Trading Company building which reared up like a glass fang among the other skyscrapers in the newly fashionable Shinjuku area. Not that the bedlam of the Shinjuku railway and bus terminus complex or the raunchy entertainment area of nearby Kabukicho had gone away: the old two-storey shops and alleys of cheap snack bars huddled tenaciously and garishly around the skirts of the glossy new hotels and office towers, like a froth of cheap and tawdry lace trimming tacked amateurishly to the skirt of a couturier evening gown.

No such vulgarity marred the expensive simplicity of Shimada's office, whose only decorations were a Joan Miro painting on one wall and a Shoji Hamada pot in a niche between two bookcases. Two of the remaining walls were almost wholly of glass, and through one of them the snow-capped summit of Mount Fuji was visible in the dry, sparkling winter sunshine. 'Well, there's nothing to be done about it,' Shimada said cheerfully. 'And you know as well as I do that practically every male Japanese in my age group must have been caught up in world war two. So I've not the least objection to your writing about my time in the Imperial Navy. I regard those years as having been the real beginning of my education. Anyway, you'll find a few bits and pieces covering those years among my personal papers. All in Japanese of course, but I understand that won't bother you.'

He looked at Lesli appraisingly: a confident man well aware of the usually aphrodisiac effect on women of his fame and wealth, but she met his steady gaze coolly. 'No. My father and mother brought me up to be bilingual. They were interned during the war and were still bitter about it when I was born. I've been grateful to them for making me sweat over reading and writing Japanese ever since I started earning money from being able to handle it.' She sipped the coffee which had been brought in for them both by a girl who could have made a good living as a model, yet whose remote, unreal beauty was in marked contrast to her shy, deferential manner.

'It's strange, Miss Hoshino. Forgive my being personal; but it is always strange to meet someone like yourself. You look completely Japanese, yet your expression and manner are those of an American woman. I look forward to getting to know you better in the next few weeks.'

It was an all too familiar line, and Lesli's smile stiffened slightly as she remembered the orchids in her hotel room. 'I hope I won't be bothering you personally very often, Mr Shimada. It's very good of you to make your personal archives available to me. The *Newsworld Magazine* bureau here has a mass of material, of course, far more than we could use in the Achiever of the Year story. Besides, I know what a busy man you are, and how much you travel.' Shimada's answering smile was rueful, and Lesli wondered briefly if she had misread what she had thought was a sexual signal. It was disconcertingly easy to forget that Jiro Shimada was a man in what her father used, in his quaintly-accented English, to call the sunset years.

'The fact is, I'm flattered, Miss Hoshino. First to join the select company of *Newsworld Magazine* Achievers of the Year. Secondly that you are interested enough to write a full-length book about me. Why, if I had my portrait painted I'd have to make myself available for, what, up to a dozen sittings? You're entitled to at least as much. Do you really think there may be a market for your book?'

'I do, sir, and so do the publishers. Enough to give me an advance equal to the six months' salary I'm losing by taking a sabbatical to write it. They're already talking to *Reader's Digest* about a condensation deal.'

Shimada sat back in the deep leather sofa, one arm along its back. 'Are they indeed? You know, I've always resisted approaches from Japanese publishers and writers who've wanted to do something similar. Does that surprise you?'

Lesli shrugged. 'In a way. May I ask why?'

Shimada straightened up, and for the first time since she had arrived spoke in Japanese. 'I am a private man, Miss Hoshino. A public figure, I know but still . . . I have always taken a lot of trouble to keep out of the Japanese media as much as possible. But on the whole I've welcomed publicity in the west, because I've tried over the years to get rid of some of the misconceptions there about Japan and the Japanese. Your book may help that process along. Maybe on the other hand the real reason is that old age is getting to me at last and making me vain. At all events, I hope researching the story of the founding and growth of the Shimada Trading Company won't bore you too much over the next few weeks.'

Lesli sensed that the interview was being brought to an end, and began to gather her belongings together as she replied in the same language. 'I'm very grateful, President. Of course, I want to start from the beginning, so if you can spare me a couple of hours next week as you've promised, I'd like to ask you about your childhood: hear about some of the experiences and influences which have made you what you are.'

Shimada rose from the sofa with the ease of a much younger man and went over to the window. 'Pollution isn't as bad as it was ten or fifteen years ago, you know,' he said with his back to Lesli. 'The Kasumigaseki Building was the first real skyscraper in Tokyo, about as tall as this building. In the late sixties, it must have been. In those days Mount Fuji was visible from its top floors on four or five days in the year at most. Now it's more like fifty or sixty. It's eighty miles away, you know.' He paused as Lesli joined him at the window, then went on with no change in his tone or manner.

'My childhood was of no interest or consequence. A couple of paragraphs will cover it comfortably. I'm afraid you're in for a disappointment if you expect me to ramble on about early experiences and influences which may have made me what I am. I am firmly of the view that I made myself what I am, you see. That's what the existentialists used to argue, isn't it?'

He turned to her with another warm smile, reverting to English. 'You must still be tired from your flight, Miss Hoshino. I make the trip to and from the States so often that I sometimes feel I'm commuting, but it doesn't get any easier. Have a good rest and take your time. I think you'll find that Mr Yamada will be able to turn up all the material about me that you're likely to need. He should be waiting to show you the room I've had prepared for you to work in whenever you feel like coming here.'

The office several floors below to which Yamada escorted her was quiet and pleasantly furnished, and only two doors along from the registry, in which Yamada explained the main company records were stored electronically, adding that since computerisation, printout copies were made of all Jiro Shimada's own correspondence, and filed manually also. He pointed to the new-looking IBM electronic typewriter on its stand near the desk provided for Lesli. 'There are only a very few of these left in the building now, Miss Hoshino. I hope you will find it suitable, but of course I can have a word-processor brought in instead if you would prefer it.'

Slightly over-awed, Lesli insisted that the IBM would be fine, and turned her attention to the two filing cabinets in the room as Yamada handed her keys to them and explained their contents. These proved to be box files, each neatly labelled. There was one called simply, 'Imperial Navy', and then a series labelled '1945–50 Personal', '1951–5 Personal' and so on in five-year groupings right up to 1981–5. Other files had names like 'Shimada Trading Corporation (Policy)', 'Club of Rome', 'Brandt Commission', 'Federation of Economic Organisations', 'Real Estate', 'Legal' and even 'Medical'. Each of the boxes she opened contained what looked like beautifully organised original papers, and a large envelope full of photographs, mostly of Shimada in the company of others. The cabinets were a gold mine of material, and Lesli itched to start going through the papers at once, constrained only by the need to make polite conversation with Yamada.

'Have you been with STC long, Mr Yamada?'

The little man blinked behind his glasses, seemingly surprised at being an object of interest. 'Oh. Yes, a long time now. More than twenty years.'

'You must know Mr Shimada very well, then.' Yamada had a smile of singular sweetness, but Lesli sensed a slight withdrawal on his part as he shrugged.

'Not really, Miss Hoshino. You will surely know him much better than any of us when you have seen all these papers and had many interviews with him. The President is not very – how shall I say – forthcoming with any of us.'

Lesli smiled in return. 'Well, we shall see. I really feel that I've made a start this afternoon, even though Mr Shimada doesn't seem to be very interested in talking about his childhood. These papers seem to date from his joining the navy in 1941. I know he was at Tokyo University immediately before that, but we didn't try to go into the earlier years for the *Newsworld* cover story. He was born in Tokyo, wasn't he? I seem to recall that.'

Yamada nodded. 'Yes. On the twenty-seventh of May, 1918. I know the date well, because he always gives a big party for the staff on his birthday. Oh, by the way. My telephone extension number is on the list beside the phone on the desk there. Please never hesitate to let me know if there is anything I can do to help you. You may perhaps find some of the older documents in Japanese a little difficult to read, especially the hand-written ones . . . I know of course that you are fluent, but many of the Chinese characters have been simplified since the war . . .' His voice trailed off in some embarrassment, and Lesli hastened to assure him that she almost certainly would need help.

Eventually Yamada left her alone, and Lesli became so absorbed in the '1956–60 Personal' file that it was nearly six before she left the Shimada Trading Corporation building and returned to the Okura Hotel, to be handed a note of a telephone call from Charlie Goldfarb, *Newsworld* magazine's Tokyo bureau chief. Lesli sighed to herself as she entered her room and laid the note on the dressing table. So Charlie wanted her to drop by the bureau the next day around eleven-thirty or noon and then lunch at the Press Club, did he? Lesli hoped she wasn't going to have trouble with him: it had all been a long time ago. Still, she needed to get at their Shimada material so she would have to try to be nice. Not too nice, though. She decided to wear a high-necked blouse.

## 5. *Monday 6 January, 1936*

'Happy New Year, Miss Shimada!' 'Oh. A Happy New Year,' Yoko squirmed in her chair as she replied, embarrassed by the strength of her mingled surprise and pleasure at hearing his voice and looking up and seeing him. She had lost count of the number of New Year greetings she had already exchanged on that first morning back at the Waseda University Library, including the ceremonious formal word with the titular Director, a professor of economics whom she had hardly ever seen in the six years she had worked there, first as a clerk and then, having completed the course at night school and secured her qualification, as one of the library assistants.

After the Director had left the library at the end of his lightning visitation the professional Chief Librarian had taken command of the proceedings and delivered a short speech of congratulation, encouragement and exhortation to his staff, gathered as they were in a wide semicircle facing him, and then had come the time for general and even timidly frivolous conversation over green tea. Officially the library was open, but nobody seriously expected any students to appear on the first day after the holiday. Although they would normally have reassembled on the fourth of January had it not fallen on a Saturday, the first day back was by tradition an occasion for getting ready to get back to work rather than actually doing so. Students would certainly not show up for a day or two, and it was surprising for an ordinary member of the academic staff to put in an appearance. Most of them, like the professorial Director, kept those of the library's books which interested them for months and years on end in their offices anyway.

'I know it's the tradition, but it's a surprise all the same to see all you ladies in your kimonos. They must be rather uncomfortable to work in.'

Yoko uttered a brief deprecatory sound, only part of the way to intelligibility, and smiled at Mr Nagai as he stood with one hand in his trouser pocket on the other side of the broad information desk. He was dressed in his usual suit, with the unconventional soft-collared shirt she thought became him so well, and Yoko was pleased that he seemed to be in good spirits. It had been several months since she had first seriously analysed her feelings about him and concluded that she felt a warm regard for the young history lecturer; perhaps something more, although she hardly knew what her sister Teruko meant when she talked so often in bed at night about 'love' and 'romance'. Yoko knew only that a sweet sadness flooded her consciousness when she thought about Mr Nagai, and that she had felt nothing but shock and dismay the previous evening when, after suggesting to her that they should take a short walk, her father blurted out even before they reached the corner of the street that he wanted her before long to meet formally a prospective husband, a young man at his office.

As a respectable middle-class girl Yoko had never consciously questioned the inevitability of marriage, and took it for granted that in due course one would be arranged, but until she turned twenty the prospect had seemed comfortably distant. Now she had to face the fact that within a year or two she would be on the shelf, and her father's remark during their visit to the Meiji Shrine was by no means the first allusion to the desirability of finding a suitable husband for her well before she reached the watershed age of twenty-five. It was really her mother's job to explore possibilities, but over a period of several years her and Yoko's roles in the family had gradually reversed themselves, and neither Yoko nor Yukichi had attempted even to discuss such matters with her. Now there was at last a specific person who wished to be introduced to her at an *o-miai*, a carefully chaperoned mutual appraisal encounter, and although deeply reluctant to take even that preliminary step Yoko knew that she would not be able to put her father off for very long. Today she looked at Mr Nagai in the sudden, bleak awareness that she loved and wanted him.

Except that he visited the library often and almost always stopped to exchange a few words with her, Yoko had no reason to think that Mr Nagai's attitude to her was evidence of anything more than simple friendliness and awareness of their shared love of western classical music, for he had spoken to her at length at a meeting of the University Music Appreciation Club, after listening to Fritz Kreisler's recording of the Beethoven violin concerto.

It was bold on Yoko's part to attach herself to the club, for even members of the university administration greatly senior to her were not eligible to join student societies, most of which were fiercely hierarchical. The music-lovers were different, though, and after an initially startled reaction the secretary accepted the quiet girl's fifty sen subscription. In the ensuing months the weekly record recitals held in the dreary, draughty room which was the only one available had been a source of deep and secret joy to Yoko. Nagai almost always went along, and towards the end of the previous year had begun to choose a seat near or even next to her, speaking quietly, during the frequent changes of record and needle, about Mozart and Haydn, Bach and Schubert.

'Well, I wonder if the club will be able to afford one of the new "Auto-Electone" gramophones I've been reading about? It can play up to twenty twelve-inch records automatically, imagine that!'

Yoko smiled shyly. 'It would be wonderful, wouldn't it?' The cheap model which constituted the club's only physical asset frequently gave trouble, and there were moves afoot to replace it.

'It would. I dare say people will accuse us of extravagance if we do get one, though. We shall have to calm them down by promising only to play Wagner.'

Yoko looked at him apprehensively. She wished Mr Nagai wouldn't jest so freely about the people who, even in Waseda University with its liberal traditions, frowned on such groups as the Music Appreciation Club and the dramatic and poetry societies, regarding them as effete and verging on the unpatriotic. He was in enough trouble already. He had spoken openly in support of the disgraced Professor Minobe of Tokyo University, who had been charged with *lèse majesté* a few months earlier for having argued in a textbook published over thirty years before that the status of the Emperor was that of an 'organ of the State'. Even though the Emperor himself had let it be known that he did not disagree with the eminent jurist, Minobe had been compelled to resign from the House of Peers, and the controversy still raged.

Nagai grinned cheerfully. 'Don't look so worried, Shimada-san. Nobody heard what I said except you, and you aren't going to report me, are you?'

Yoko shook her head vehemently, a lurching fear gripping at her stomach now that he had come out with it. 'Of course not. Never . . . but you will be careful, won't you?'

His eyes held hers in silence for a few seconds, making her blush. 'Thank you for your concern,' he said at last. 'Don't worry, though, things aren't as bad as all that yet.'

\* \* \*

'Time is *not* on our side, comrades.' Mitsugi Nishida almost hissed the words as he thumped the table and glared in turn at each of the two dozen or so young officers gathered before him. They were in a training room in one of the more isolated buildings in the grounds of the Military Academy at Ichigaya Heights, not far from the spacious parade grounds of Yoyogi on the western outskirts of Tokyo. Nishida was thirty-four, and had himself resigned his commission as a cavalry lieutenant ten years before on health grounds in order to devote himself to politics. 'I said this many times fifteen years and more ago when I founded our movement as a cadet in this very Academy, I have continued to say it and I say it to you today with an even greater sense of urgency.'

Captains Nonaka and Ando who flanked him at the table facing the rows of desks both nodded. 'The rumours we have all been hearing during the past few weeks are based on fact, gentlemen,' Ando said quietly, his bespectacled, normally cheery face solemn. 'The decision has been taken to transfer the First Division to Manchuria.' He glanced at Hideo and nodded almost impercep-tibly at him. 'We have very recently been able to gain access to certain General Staff meeting minutes which confirm the in-formation passed on to us informally by ... I need mention no names.' One or two of the young men grinned at this and glanced at their neighbours knowingly. 'The effective date is likely to be some time in April.'

Nishida nodded, a bitter smile on his thin lips, then abruptly stood up, commanding their attention. 'So you have three months at most if you aren't to be led away by the nose by your aristocratic masters as soon as they condescend to tear themselves away from the arms of their *geisha*. The situation in the Palace as we enter this eleventh and crucial year of His Majesty's reign could hardly be more dangerous. You all know that Saito was appointed to be Lord Keeper of the Privy Seal on 26 December last, less than ten days ago. We know what he was like as Prime Minister, let alone as Foreign Minister: *and* he was a Navy man. Now this traitor, this corrupt, degenerate dotard of an admiral not only has daily access with his lies and schemes to the very Throne, but is also the chief offical interpreter of His Majesty's sacred will and intentions. All the advantages of Colonel Aizawa's splendid, selfless action last August in assassinating the two-faced General Nagata, and the excellent sounding-board his forthcoming court-martial will pro-vide for our ideas to be laid before the people, are in jeopardy.' He glared round the room. 'Who are our two finest leaders?'

'Mazaki!' came the shout from one side of the room, while from the middle one of the youngest men countered with 'Araki!' Nishida's wolfish smile flashed again. 'My old friend Kurihara is right . . . but so also is our young comrade here. General Mazaki must lead the next government, and at his side as an equal must stand our good General Araki, moustache and all! Never forget, it was Araki who first spoke of the "Imperial Way", that great cause to which we stand committed with our blood and our lives. And where are these two fine men? On the sidelines as mere members of the Military Council, without commands and without responsibilities, while the Imperial Army must endure the snivelling Watanabe as Director General of Military Education: a man who last year brazenly and publicaly declared his sympathy with the blasphemous rantings of the insane communist so-called Professor Minobe. The Imperial destiny cannot, must not be frustrated; and it is YOU who have the high honour of leading the march along the Imperial Way.'

Nishida's voice had been rising as he spoke, and flecks of saliva appeared round his lips. Hideo gazed at him in awe and reverence, tinged with a bitter regret that this noble man, this seer was no longer himself one of the officers on whom the liberation of the Emperor from those who surrounded him depended. Many officers at all levels of seniority more or less openly supported the 'Imperial Way' group which opposed the pragmatic policies of the General Staff, but Hideo was one of less than three dozen lieutenants and captains in the Young Officers' Movement who had met in secret at a restaurant just before the year-end holidays to pledge themselves to take direct action. Mitsugi Nishida was revered by them all as their founder and ideological adviser: his and their inspiration was another civilian, the visionary radical rightist Ikki Kita, the uncensored version of whose *Outline Plan for the Reorganisation of Japan* was required reading, which Hideo frequently and dutifully pored over.

'What news about where Prince Chichibu stands? He's on our side, and he's His Majesty's *brother*. Can't he warn him? Have Saito dismissed?' It was his friend, bright-eyed Lieutenant Yasuda who spoke, and Hideo wished it had been him, until Captain Ando turned on the young man and withered him with an angry glare.

'Be slient, Lieutenant,' he snapped. 'Some of us have the honour of His Imperial Highness's personal friendship: we are old comrades. It may have escaped your attention that the Prince is no

longer attached to the General Staff. Last autumn he was transferred to the Thirty-First Regiment where he is serving as a major.
Indeed he is one of us, a "comrade" in the sense in which we in
the Movement use that word, but do not be presumptuous. He
remains an Imperial Prince.' Captain Ando was one of the most
popular officers in the regiment, and his rebuke was all the more
effective for that.

Nishida was still on his feet, and his glittering eyes now swept
along the rows of officers again. 'Captain Ando's words are, as
always, wise and timely,' he said. 'Remember our slogan: "Revere
the Emperor – Destroy the traitors". We revere not only His
Majesty personally, but even more the very Throne, to which our
comrade the Prince is very close. But it is the traitors who
surround His Majesty's person, and other dangerous men in
influential positions, whom it is our duty to remove. Prime
Minister Okada above all, then Lord Keeper Saito. His predecessor
Count Makino. Grand Chamberlain Suzuki. Takahashi the senile
Finance Minister who schemes and intrigues to starve the Army of
funds. General Watanabe. A few others, perhaps; not many. We
mean no harm to the innocent, and intend no civil war. With the
guilty purged from the body politic by their blood, we may go
straight to the Army Minister and make him demand the forma-
tion of a new cabinet under Mazaki and Araki, pledged to the new
Restoration of the Emperor and to the reforms the people yearn
for.' It all seemed to Hideo not only possible but straightforward,
even inevitable, and a prickling sensation swept over his entire
body at the thought of the cleansing of the State in which he
would be privileged to play a significant part.

'It will not be easy,' Captain Nonaka cut in, not questioning the
proposed orgy of political murder but sounding quietly rational
about it. 'There will inevitably be several hours of confusion. We
shall need enough men to control a number of key points in
Tokyo –'

'No! We should act alone! That is the samurai way; the clean and
sincere way.' It was Lieutenant Kurihara of the First Regiment on
his feet, and not alone in his opinion, for several of the others
growled their support.

'We know your views and respect them, comrade,' Nonaka
replied. 'But we do not share them.' He looked round at the
expressions of flaming dedication on the faces of his associates,
feeling no serious doubts about the loyalty of any of them, but
seeing the project in terms of practicality and efficiency. 'We plan

a military operation, not a romantic gesture, and Ando and I with our civilian comrades are convinced that we must not only "destroy the traitors" but must also seize effective control of the centres of government. Now let me say something else. Some of us will die, gentlemen. Perhaps all of us. If any one of you has the slightest doubts about his commitment to this enterprise, let him inform me in confidence within the next twenty-four hours. He may withdraw in honour, provided only that he keeps silence about anything he has heard up till now. I shall say the same thing to those of our group who are not able to be with us today.'

Hideo felt the blood pounding in his body and a dark joy growing within him. Irrelevantly, the recollection of his tram ride with his sister Teruko on New Year's Eve and the pressure of her body drifted into his mind. 'For those of us who go forward,' continued Nonaka, 'total secrecy will be the rule. When the time comes there can be no farewells. In the meantime those of you who are married will not speak of this affair to your wives; none of you will allow your parents or acquaintances outside this group to suspect that anything beyond your routine military duties engages your minds.'

'Captain Nonaka is right.' Nishida dipped his shoulder in a curious, jerky movement and regained the initiative. It was almost as though he resented the authority and dignity of Nonaka's words. 'We want nobody half-hearted. Nobody who will not give his life with joy for the Emperor. We shall not meet again as a group very often, if at all: it is too dangerous. You will receive your individual instructions through Captain Nonaka or Captain Ando. When the word does come it will be at short notice. Meantime, search your hearts and consciences and remember this. The future of Japan rests with you.'

## 6. *Tuesday 7 January, 1986*

'You haven't changed, Charlie.' Charlie Goldfarb winked, gulped at his martini and said, 'Aw, shucks' in his funny mountaineer voice, taking Lesli's remark as a compliment. They had been in the bar at the Foreign Press Club, high above the airline offices and cinemas, restaurants and shops of the fashionable Hibiya area for less than fifteen minutes, but already Lesli had been greeted by two people she knew from the old days. Not that she cared one way or the other if people jumped to the wrong conclusion, except for Charlie himself, of course.

She removed the hand with the heavy gold ring on the hairy little finger from her thigh. 'It's good to see you, Charlie. But it's just professional this time. Okay?' She spoke lightly.

'Sure, sure. It was great fun, but it was just one of those things. Like in the old song, huh?' 'That's right.' Lesli could see that Goldfarb didn't really believe it. Although his manner was easy, warm and friendly, the shrewd eyes were assessing her, taking in the absence of a wedding ring, the good but not expensive clothes, the grey here and there in her thick mop of short black hair. Wondering, no doubt, how long it would take him to get her back into bed again and whether her brief marriage had taught her any new tricks. Word of her divorce from David would certainly have reached the Tokyo bureau months before.

In many ways it was true, Charlie hadn't changed. As Lesli raised her own glass with a smile and sipped her kir she wondered what circuit in her had been switched off. The six intervening years melted in her consciousness and she saw herself as she had so often been, frantically clawing at the mat of curly hair on Charlie's chest, biting and sucking in a mad sweetness of frenzy before mounting him and bucking and heaving until she shuddered to sweating, panting, heart-hammering oblivion. The recollection was vivid, but the woman on the bed was another person, not the Lesli Hoshino who sat looking at a dapper New York Jew with bright, slightly protuberant eyes glistening like decorations on a Christmas tree, and a lopsided grin; a devoted family man who indulged his overweight wife and worried about his married daughter in Rochester and his son at Columbia University, and the most extraordinary lover she had ever had.

'Just professional,' she repeated. 'Although I'm not even on the payroll for the next few months.' 'Aw, come *on*. You just go right ahead and treat the office as a second home, Lesli. Anything we can do. You know that. Hey listen, what's with this Okura Hotel deal? You win the state lottery or something?'

Lesli shook her head as Charlie pointed at his empty glass and then at her own with eyebrow raised interrogatively. 'No, I won't have another. Thank you. You go ahead, though.' She waited while he ordered his second martini before continuing. 'I'm at the Okura for just a week. Guest of STC. Shimada offered to pick up all the tabs for as long as I'm in Japan, but –'

'You mean you turned it down? Lawdy, Miz Mary-Lou, you is one crazy woman, you heah?'

Lesli shook her head with a slight smile. 'If I'd been ghosting an autobiography for him I'd have stuck him for every dime, believe me, Charlie. But it isn't like that. This is going to be my book. Authorised, sure, but my book. If I get too beholden to him it's going to cramp my style. So I'm moving to the International House of Japan in a few days. They aren't full at this time of the year.'

'Among all those professors from the States? Dullsville.'

'A lot more interesting than a bunch of businessmen and well-heeled tourists, and I can get a room there for the price of lunch at the Okura. *And* there's no muzak in the lobby or the elevators, so far as I recall.'

A waiter brought menus and loomed over them until they had ordered, and within five minutes was back to escort them to their table in the huge, noisy dining room. 'God, I'd forgotten how busy this place gets at lunchtime.' Charlie was busy waving and calling greetings to acquaintances all over the room, but his other hand was cupping Lesli's elbow in a proprietorial way. 'Sure. Great place. I'll fix you up with temporary membership while you're here.' They sat down and food was brought, but Lesli hardly noticed what she was eating, there were so many breezy interruptions from Charlie's friends, explanations by Lesli of her presence in Tokyo to those she knew and introductions to those she didn't. It was not until they had drunk their coffee and the room was emptying rapidly that she became aware that the decibel count around them had diminished and that Goldfarb was looking at her quizzically.

'Why are you doing this book, Lesli? Shimada's a big wheel, sure, but is he *interesting*? Worth months of your time?'

'You're not the first to ask that question, Charlie. I may say that I have several different answers to it, depending on the circumstances. I think you might understand the real reason, though. I'm a *nisei*. I'm not half Japanese and half American. My genes are *all* Japanese. My parents don't speak English too well even now. But I'm also *all* American. I was nearly thirty years old when I first came to Japan, to work with you in the bureau. Okay, I knew the language, but in many ways it was worse than being a regular foreigner, the kind they call "blue-eyes". I *look* Japanese, but I don't *act* Japanese and I sure don't *feel* Japanese. Am I making sense?'

'Sure.'

'Well, I did my best to say and do all the right things when I met distant cousins and stuff like that, but it was a total waste of effort. To them I was alien, and all the more so for my Japanese blood. And they were utterly alien to me too. My Japanese relations are in a cultural prison of their own construction, and they just love it in there. I thought all Japanese were like them, and on the whole I still think that. Except for Shimada. Shimada has somehow broken free. He's a Japanese who's out here in the big world, easy and assured. He wouldn't fascinate me at all if he had a background like mine, but he's not a *nisei*. He's a hundred percent Japanese, brought up in Japan. I want to know how he got to be the way he is. It may help me to come to terms with my own people, my parents' and grandparents' people.'

'Shimada's not unique, Lesli. Look at Akio Morita, the man who created the Sony Corporation. Morita has charm, style, huge ability, all the rest of it. And he goes down as well in the States as he does here. Better, if anything.'

'All that's perfectly true. But Shimada has more. He's not just an international business leader, he's an international political figure, too. He is, quite simply, the most famous Japanese in the world, and has been for years. Outside Japan, ninety-nine people out of a hundred couldn't tell you the name of the premier here, but everybody's heard of Shimada. And people like what they've heard.'

Goldfarb produced a solid silver Cross ballpoint pen and scrawled signatures on the bar and restaurant bills which had been placed folded on a plate beside him. 'And you're going to show the world what he's really like, warts and all, is that the expression?'

'Strange you should put it like that. Shimada himself said he could hardly spare me less time than he would if he were sitting for his portrait. I'm going to have to dig around to find out anything about his boyhood, though. It looks as though he's going to be as tight as a clam over that.'

Goldfarb winked at her before pushing his chair back. 'We'll have to see what Uncle Charlie can do to help,' he said as they started to make their way out of the room. The hand resting lightly on her shoulder irritated Lesli, but she let it stay there. At least his touch didn't make her hot and bothered any more, thank God.

## 7. Wednesday 8 January, 1936

Sword in white-gloved hand, Hideo Shimada stiffened as he heard the section commanders far away to his left begin to bring their men to attention, and stamped his booted left heel as he came up from the 'At ease' position himself. Then he screamed out the order. 'Number fourteen section! Atten-SHUN!'

It was a beautiful crisp morning out there on the Yoyogi Parade Ground, and although Hideo and his men with the rest of the ten thousand troops of the Imperial Guard and the First Division had been in position since soon after eight and it was now nearly ten o'clock, the time had passed quite quickly; for the Imperial New Year Review called for a whole series of preliminary inspections, beginning with his own and followed by those of the company commander, the battalion commander and the regimental commander. Hideo's section had survived them all without rebuke, and now at last from the corner of his eye he could see a small group of mounted officers entering the parade ground. He risked a more direct glance at them. Yes! The leading horse was pure white: it was Shirayuki, White Snow, the most famous horse in the Empire, and the favourite mount of His Majesty.

It was not easy for Hideo to keep his head amid the blare of the band and the bellowing of orders and remember the timing and sequence of the commands he had to shout to the men behind him, but he somehow contrived to play his part and in what seemed like no more than a few moments he was rigidly presenting his sword in the Imperial Salute as the horsemen clattered and jingled past no more than a few yards away. The sweat ran down his face and he dared not raise his eyes, but even so the image of Shirayuki's creamy white flank, the chrysanthemum emblem on the saddle-cloth and one glossy boot seared his vision before the Emperor, General Uyeda the parade commander and their staff officers had vanished into the distance again, and the sound of the band once more became audible as the roaring of the blood in his ears abated.

Then there was new, and external, roaring, and all at once the

sky above the parade ground, which on the first three days of the
New Year had been filled with kites and model aeroplanes, was
darkened by the Fifth Air Regiment, flying past in salute in
seventy-three aircraft from the military aerodrome at Tachikawa
just west of Tokyo. This time Hideo raised his eyes, respect and
pride replacing awe, and as he watched the planes and saw the
tiny figure of the Son of Heaven in the far distance sitting
motionless on the white horse he felt purged, uplifted, unreal. He
lost all sense of time: it could have been ten minutes or all eternity
later that the Emperor and his suite rode off the parade ground,
and he heard his own voice as though it belonged to some other
person shouting the commands which resulted in his moving off
with his section towards the dismissal point. He was still in a state
of exaltation, but moments after he had handed over command of
the section to his sergeant Hideo felt limp, exhausted and for some
reason he could not understand close to tears. It was eleven-
fifteen.

'What?' He became aware that Lieutenant Yasuda was talking to
him. 'What did you say?'

'The eclipse of the moon. Tonight – well, between 2.30 and 3.30
tomorrow morning, actually. Are you going to watch it?'

'Oh. I'd forgotten all about it. I doubt it. Why?'

'I don't know. It seems like a kind of omen, but I can't think
what it might mean.'

'You wanted to see me, Director?

'Ah. Section Head Shimada. Good. Yes. I hope you had a
pleasant holiday?'

'Thank you, yes. My son was able to get a few days' leave and
join the rest of us.'

'The army officer? You must be very proud of him, and happy to
know that he is for the present at least here in Tokyo.' Yukichi
stood quitely and deferentially in front of the desk. He had been
expecting the summons, and dreading it. 'He's back on duty now,
of course?'

'Yes. In fact at this moment he should be on parade at Yoyogi.
For the Imperial Review.'

'I see. A great honour for him. Well, Mr Shimada. We must all
hope that this will be a year of accomplishment in every way. Our
fine Crown Prince already two years old – how time passes! But
healthy and strong . . . and who knows, perhaps he will have an
Imperial brother before long. And the news from Manchuria is

encouraging, I suppose. The emigration programme is progressing, though I must say that to settle as many as one million Japanese households there within twenty years is by any reckoning a massive undertaking . . .'

Yukichi said nothing. Following the assassination of Mitsui's managing director, Takuma Dan, by a right-wing nationalist four years earlier, and in the face of continued widespread allegations that the leaders of the huge Mitsui industrial empire manipulated the political parties and sought only ever-increasing profits regardless of the national interest, the men at the top of the company had for the past two or three years taken certain defensive measures. A number of members of the Mitsui family itself were eased out of senior posts through the introduction of a mandatory retirement system, and others began to involve themselves conspicuously in 'patriotic' voluntary organisations and charities. Even so, senior executives of Mitsui like their opposite numbers in the other great industrial and financial conglomerates known as *zaibatsu* were still inclined to give voice in confidence to what might be considered 'dangerous thoughts' about the policies of the government, especially in relation to the puppet state of Manchukuo. It was not wise for people at Yukichi's level to risk doing so.

Director Nishi passed a hand over the strands of hair pasted with brilliantine across the bald crown of his head as Yukichi looked down at him with distaste. There was a heavy brass paper-weight on the desk between them, and Yukichi was briefly and insanely tempted to kill the younger man with it. The impulse was so strong that when Nishi looked up Yukichi feared that he must be able to read his murderous thoughts in his eyes, and rapidly glanced towards the window, through which could be seen the red-brick facade of Tokyo Station in the middle distance. 'Yes. It could be a momentous year for the Empire and for us all, Mr Shimada. And of course, it will inevitably be a significant one for you personally. How I look forward to my own retirement! But unlike you, I must labour on for some years yet. Your birthday falls in July, I believe?'

'That is so. Yes.'

The institution of the new retirement code had come as a shock to Yukichi, who would be fifty-five on the ninth of July and would be obliged to go at the end of that month. Before the Mitsui reorganisation retirement arrangements had been flexible, and Yukichi had always supposed that even though it seemed unlikely that he would advance beyond junior management status he would be able to carry on until the age of sixty or so, by which time both Yoko and Teruko would be married and even Jiro at least half-way through his university course – if he were lucky enough to gain a place.

Yukichi, with his hundred and fifty yen a month, was not badly paid, and the girls now earned enough to buy their clothes and meet their own expenses. All the same, food prices had been alarmingly high for years, and he had accumulated only a meagre sum by way of savings for the years to come. Hideo would presumably marry within the next few years and bring a wife into the house to take care of Chie and himself in their old age after Yoko and Teruko were gone, but only the most senior colonels and generals were well paid, and Yukichi saw no glittering future for his passionate, headstrong son.

'I thought so. I have been asked to make a recommendation about the question of a retirement bonus for you, but there is no great hurry about that since you will be with us for six months or so yet. Your work over the years has always been very satisfactory, Mr Shimada, and I hope to feel able in due course to suggest to the head of the Establishments and Salaries Department a figure which you would not regard as ungenerous. Incidentally, my wife and I hope soon to make the acquaintance of your charming daughter. Young Sato is rather hoping that the *o-miai* can take place before the end of the month. We thought that the tea lounge at the Imperial Hotel would be a pleasant setting for it.'

Yukichi felt himself beginning to tremble. He had expected something like it, but the crudity of the combined threat and offer of a bribe was still unnerving. It was all so ridiculous: the young man Sato was unrelated to the Director. Indeed, if he *had* been, Nishi would certainly have aimed socially higher than the Shimadas after undertaking to find a suitable wife for him. Sato was bright enough, Yukichi supposed, even though the cast in his left eye made him look unprepossessing. He might do quite well with Mitsui: he had certainly exploited the conventions cleverly by asking the Nishis to act as his go-betweens within months of having been assigned to work as the Director's personal assistant. Bound by custom, the Director could not refuse, and now that he had hit upon the idea of marrying the young man off to Yukichi's daughter Yoko, he and his wife would lose face intolerably were the plan to fall through. It was quite enough to make him completely ruthless.

'I have spoken to my daughter, Director. I shall raise the matter again with her when she has had a little more time to think about it.' The proposed bargain was clear now. He was being offered a purchase price for Yoko: a lump sum of perhaps three years' salary, calculated on the basis of a month for each of his thirty-three years of service. He had even heard of some favoured Mitsui staff at his own level of seniority getting twice that amount. If on the other hand he failed to deliver Yoko, the Director would exercise his undoubted discretion to recommend a minimal terminal gratuity. They would have to give him something, but it might be as little as a derisory three months' pay.

'I shall look forward to hearing from you very soon, Mr Shimada. We shall need a week or two to make the arrangements for the meeting, which I am sure will go off splendidly. Sato was most taken with the photograph of Miss Shimada, and I imagine that she is well aware of the advantages of marriage to a rising young executive in a company like ours. In peace or in, er, conflict, Mitsui will prosper. Do take a cigar with you, Mr Shimada. You will enjoy it after lunch, perhaps.' He pointed with a smile to the open box of 'Alhambra' Manilas on his desk.

'Thank you, Director. Another time, perhaps.' Yukichi bowed, retreated to the door and bowed again before leaving the room.

'Somebody to see you, Rogers-san.' Dwight Rogers was not pleased when Osamu Miwa the office boy put his head round the half-open door of his cubby-hole and made his announcement. 'Jeez, Sam, it's the lunch hour. I'm not expecting anybody.' There was a broad grin on 'Sam' Miwa's spotty face, and he winked stagily. Sam was a keen movie fan who particularly enjoyed Hollywood representations of life in newspaper offices. Although the entire personnel of the Tokyo Bureau of the *New York Times* consisted of Rogers, old Mr Eguchi the clerk-accountant and Sam himself, he tried hard to create the right atmosphere. 'She's a real cutie-pie, sir. She could sure interrupt *my* lunch hour any time.'

Rogers groaned gently, closed his eyes and placed his hand on his forehead in the way that always delighted Sam. Then he opened his eyes again. 'What does she want?' He had been working hard to finish a carefully worded background report on a serious clash between police and over a thousand farmers in Nishi Temma-gun on the outskirts of Tokyo on the thirteenth of December. Rumours about the incident had been rife before the year-end holidays and he had sent a short cable to New York two weeks earlier, but only on the previous day had he been able to talk off the record at some length with the economic affairs officer at the American Embassy and put together a longer piece about the continuing distress in the agricultural sector. Cash income and outlay still accounted for only a proportion of the economy of a farming household, but an astonishing seventy percent of spending in cash went to pay electricity bills, and the taxes on textiles and *sake* were cripplingly high. 'Wants you, boss. Says she has something for you.' Another wink, and Rogers capitulated. 'Okay. Have her come in.'

He was still in his waistcoat and shirt-sleeves and reaching for his jacket from the peg behind the door when Teruko Shimada edged her way in hesitantly and bowed. Then she swallowed, bowed again and spoke in formal Japanese, in a very small voice. 'I am disturbing you.' Rogers hurriedly struggled into his jacket and returned her bow. 'Not at all.' Then he quietly but firmly closed the door in Sam's interested face.

'Thank you for the other day,' Teruko then muttered, her face aflame with embarrassment. It was a conventional enough greeting between people who know each other, for all Japanese judge it wise to assume that they are obligated in some way or another to each and every one of their acquaintances; but Rogers could not recall ever having set eyes on the young woman in the neatly tailored navy-blue costume worn over a white blouse with a little blue bow-tie and a jaunty beret perched on one side of her head. 'On the contrary, I am in your debt,' he replied to complete the polite formula, desperately trying to place her. 'Won't you sit down?'

Even in his tiny office it had been necessary to squeeze in a low table with two easy-chairs for the use of visitors. Rogers was normally embarrassed by the proximity the lack of space enforced, but on this occasion watched with open admiration as Teruko tucked herself tidily into one of the chairs with a momentary flash of petticoat as she arranged her pleated skirt over her rayon-sheathed knees.

'I have brought the photographs,' she said uncertainly. 'The photographs taken at the Meiji Shrine on New Year's Day.' Rogers beamed as she opened her handbag and enlightenment came to him.

'How very kind of you. How different you look in western dress!' Although it had taken place only a week previously his recollections of the encounter with the Shimada family had already faded to vanishing point, though he could still recall the shaven head of the boy in student uniform and the hostile scowl on the face of the young army officer. He would certainly not have recognised either of the middle-aged parents again if he saw them in the street, and the two young women in their kimonos had made little impression on him.

'You very kindly gave me your name-card, and since your office is quite near where I work, I thought I would bring these for you. They aren't very good, but . . .' Teruko handed him three small photographs. The uppermost showed him with all the Shimadas except Jiro, who had taken the picture quite competently. 'Now do you recognise me? Standing beside you.' The American's friendly informality began to subdue her jitters, and she leaned forward. Rogers became more aware of her perfume and noticed the nail varnish as she indicated herself in the photograph with a slender finger. 'The other one is the picture you took of all of us. I thought you might like a copy.'

'You are very kind. Thank you so much.' Rogers looked at it and came to the third, which showed her smiling roguishly in spite of having had to half-close her eyes against the direct sunlight in which Jiro had posed her. 'Oh dear, that's a mistake – it must have stuck to the other one.' Teruko half-heartedly reached out to take it back, but Rogers continued to scrutinise it. Then he looked from the picture to her. 'You look very pretty in the picture,' he said. 'But then you *are* very pretty.' Sam had been quite right: his unexpected visitor was a welcome interruption, even in the lunch hour.

Teruko felt the colour rising again up her neck and cheeks, but forced herself to smile boldly at the tall young foreigner with the wavy hair. She knew quite well that she looked her best, and had enjoyed fending off the curious questions of the other girls at the salon when she slipped out for her lunch break all dressed up. It was just as well that the bright noon sunshine was quite warm enough for her to do without a coat, for the one she owned was entirely unworthy of the rest of her turn-out. She was entitled to only half an hour, but could probably stretch it to forty-five minutes without getting into trouble, because she had contrived her absence to overlap the manageress' own lunch break and the other girls frequently conspired to cover for each other. 'Thank you, Mr Rogers,' she said shyly in English.

The name for which Rogers had been racking his brains suddenly popped into his head. Shimada. He was sure that was it. 'Why didn't you say you can speak English, Miss Shimada?' The look of terror and incomprehension which at once came into her eyes made him realise his mistake at once. 'Just a little. *Sukoshi*,' she faltered, and Rogers came to her rescue by reverting to Japanese. 'You have a charming accent,' he said. It was true: she did have a very cute way of talking, and he liked her slightly cheeky face and the fact that the natural line of her lips was rather full even though the Cupid's bow of her lipstick partly disguised it. 'You say you work near here?'

'Yes, very near. In the Ginza.' The *New York Times* outpost in Tokyo was housed within the Asahi newspaper building, itself two minutes walk from the fashionable stores and smart restaurants.

'May I ask what you do?'

'I'm a . . . a beauty consultant,' Teruko said. 'With the Arden Beauty Salon. I expect your . . . wife knows of it.' She had made very sure that there was no Mrs Rogers among the regular clientele of the salon, but one never knew. It was the one point she had been absolutely determined to clarify during her call on Rogers, and she felt a little faint with relief and excitement when he grinned at her. 'I don't have a wife, Miss Shimada. But if I did, I'd certainly have her consult you.' He had in fact heard of the Arden Salon: it would be difficult to go to parties and meet the wives of diplomats and expatriate businessmen without hearing them admire each others' permanent waves and mention the Arden as one of the two or three reliable hairdressers in town; and as a single man Rogers was in brisk social demand.

'I'm sure you must have lots of lady friends, then. Japanese lady friends, perhaps?' Rogers was both intrigued and startled to realise that the girl's manner had changed from one of seemingly agonised bashfulness to something approaching flirtatiousness. It was by no means a new experience, but so far as Japanese women were concerned one restricted to waitresses in traditional-style restaurants in Tokyo and the old-fashioned inns which he was often obliged to stay at for want of a western-style hotel during his occasional trips to the provinces. In country towns the maids at inns would usually cheerfully double as sleeping partners for a consideration, whereas in the larger cities and Tokyo itself it was necessary to head for the licensed quarters to find professionally complaisant women. Yet this girl's family was manifestly respectable to a degree, and she herself was fashionably dressed and well spoken, even if the perfume was unsubtle.

'Oh dear, no. I'm just a lonely reporter,' he said. 'I'm too busy for lady friends.' Then he smiled again. 'But since you work just around the corner, perhaps we could meet some time and have a cup of coffee? Or do you by chance have time to eat lunch with me now?'

Teruko was afraid he would hear her heart thumping, and the words came out with difficulty. 'I'm afraid I have to go back to work now.'

'Well, what time do you get through this evening?' She lowered her eyes and fidgeted with her handbag.

'It depends. Usually at eight o'clock, but on Thursdays I have my short day and finish at five.'

It was clearly time to strike while the iron was hot, and Rogers quickly took out his diary. 'Well, how about tomorrow, then? At five o'clock? If you have time, we could go to the movies. There's a new Shirley Temple at the Imperial – *Curly Top*. Or we could just eat and talk. Come on, say yes!'

Nothing could have induced Teruko to say no, and she nodded, speechless with delight. 'It's a date? Wonderful. I'll come by the Arden Beauty Salon to pick you up, then. Tomorrow, a little after five. Okay?' Teruko nearly panicked, then saw herself in a sudden vision, tripping out of the salon in full view of the other girls, to be greeted politely with raised fedora hat by the tall, smiling, unmarried and more than adequately handsome American. She might even dare to keep him waiting for a minute or two.

'Okay,' she whispered as she stood up. The photograph of herself lay disregarded by Rogers with the others on the table, and she willed him not to try to give it back to her. Next time she would ask for a picture of him, she decided as Rogers escorted her through the outer office and to the door past the admiring gaze of Osamu Miwa, who deliberately dropped a box of paper clips he was holding but failed to attract the attention of either of them.

## 8. Thursday 9 January, 1936

Two or three miles away from the Shimada house, a light snow had powdered the stubby rectangular tombstones in the huge Nakano cemetery at Nippori by the time Chie began dimly to become aware again of her surroundings, and she wondered how long she had been there. The cemetery was a good place to perform the hand movements of the salvation dance service and to pray to the Mother who had not died, but merely withdrawn into a spiritual state; so that they still placed her meals before her sanctuary every day at the head temple in Tenri where she had been born as Miki Nakayama a hundred years before, and where God had commanded her to become herself his shrine and found the Tenrikyo sect.

Chie believed with all her heart that just as the Mother had taught, God had created human beings to delight in their life of joy and harmony, but at home there was only distress and perturbation of spirit; misunderstanding of her obligations to the Mother and resentment of the simple rites and prayers which she had learned with such joy when being received into Tenrikyo a few years or all eternity before.

That was why she came to Nakano. The Lord Buddha did not begrudge her space and quiet in which to perform her duties before his image, or that of the compassionate bodhisattva Kannon, in any of the several temples whose precincts formed one boundary of the vast cemetery; so big that even by day she was rarely interrupted, and in the evening never.

She tried again to think how long she had been there. The ecstasy of prayer and communion made her oblivious to cold, hunger or thirst for as long as the Mother granted her access to her spirit, and to her secret and inexpressible delight Chie knew that this access had become more frequent and protracted within recent months. Tonight the Mother had seemed to want Chie to tell her about her girlhood, and for a long time she had roved in her imagination about the Kyushu village in which she had been born. Pale as she had always been, but freed with joy from the shapeless prison of her sluggish, fifty-year-old body, young Chie wandered again in and out of the studio of the old man, the master potter who talked to her about her dreams. Sometimes he would take her hands in his thin, stained fingers as he showed her how to shape the clay, to mix and apply the glaze; and when he was not very well he would tell his young student-apprentice to help little Miss Dream-maker as he always called her.

She remembered and whispered in the darkness about the wonder of seeing the colours transformed after the mystery of firing, and the heartbreak when the master decreed that this or that pot was not worthy to be kept. She whispered about the thudding of young Chie's heart as she crept after dark to the potter's rubbish heap and retrieved a few condemned pieces, and hid them in the recesses of the cave behind the little waterfall by the wayside shrine outside the village.

That was forty years ago, back in the reign of the Meiji Emperor, and less than twenty years after the great battle of Kumamoto Castle a few miles away, in which Yukichi's father escaped death by a hairsbreadth and her own was gravely wounded in the furious fighting between the conscript army of the government and the samurai forces from Satsuma Province, led by the great General Saigo who fought the Emperor's men in the name of the Emperor.

Chie could remember wonderingly tracing the long lines of the scars on her father's thin forearms with timid fingers as he told her about the melée, and wincing in terror at the thought of the noise and the blood, and the blue-white curving sword-edges flashing murderously in a haze of gunpowder smoke beneath the massive walls of the castle. At ten years old she could not understand why her father's smile was twisted as he murmured several times the words *kateba kangun* – which side wins is the Emperor's army. She knew only that Kumamoto Castle lay in those days half in ruins, its courtyards taken over by farmers and turned into rice fields.

Chie whimpered quietly as she rubbed her hands together in the bitter chill of the early dawn. It had grown unaccountably dark at some stage during her hours of prayer, as though she had been transported into the blackness of space behind the moon and the stars; but now the outline of the temple roof was etched black against blue-grey, and there was a stirring in the stillness about her.

It was when she was fourteen that Chie first met Yukichi Shimada: not one of the 'main house' Shimadas who were one of the leading families in Kumamoto and had been for generations, but a member of a minor branch. He was nineteen, and surrounded with an aura of romance, for he was about to make the long journey to Tokyo to enter Waseda University on the recommendation of the strange Englishman Lafcadio Hearn, who had long since left Kumamoto to teach at the Imperial University in Tokyo.

Chie met the famous Mr Hearn herself in 1893 when he called one day at the workshop of her friend the master potter: at first she tried to scuttle away, frightened by the foreigner's walrus moustache and even more by the awful blankness of his blind left eye; but the potter called her back and made her bow in respectful greeting to the English professor who had come with his Japanese wife and their baby son to teach at the Number 5 Higher School, the most respected academic institution in all Kumamoto. He spoke Japanese quaintly and smelled strongly of tobacco, but soon took his leave, and Chie then listened in awe as the potter explained that the *sensei* was a writer famous throughout the world and that he loved Japan so much that he had become a Japanese citizen with a Japanese name, Yakumo Koizumi. She thought his first name very pretty, for it meant Eight Clouds, but quite failed to understand how a foreigner, the first she had ever met, could become a Japanese.

The meeting with Yukichi Shimada was much more terrifying, for it was an *o-miai*, a formal introduction with a view to marriage. Chie's father was by then the stationmaster at Uto to the south of the city, a responsible post for Uto was a junction, with the Misumi Line winding away from the main southbound Kagoshima Line to the south-west, along the coast of the Ariake Sea. As a government official, even a minor one, her father was a man of consequence in the village, and his thoughts turned naturally towards Kumamoto when her mother reported to him that Chie had begun to menstruate and should therefore be betrothed before long. His former platoon commander was now the Assistant Chief at the Kumamoto Police Station, and he genially agreed to act with his wife as go-between.

Before long he suggested the name of Yukichi Shimada, the son of an old comrade who had died ten years after the great battle of 1877, leaving a young widow and the five-year-old lad who had done so well at school and who had, while still only ten or eleven, attracted the attention of the English writer. Yukichi was of solid samurai stock, with good if rather remote family connections, and above all a young man with excellent prospects thanks to the patronage of Professor Hearn who continued to take an interest in him after leaving Kumamoto, corresponding with Yukichi's teachers and securing him a place at the highly-regarded Waseda University.

Dressed in a scratchy new kimono, Chie knelt in silent trepidation on the *tatami* matting of the best room in the house of the Assistant Chief of Police in the company of her own parents and of the police officer's wife, listening to the sound of male voices as the master of the house arrived with Yukichi and his mother and jovially urged them to enter. Then they were inside the room and all at once it was crowded, with a maid even younger than Chie bringing green tea and small, hard sugar cakes.

Chie bowed repeatedly but could not bring herself to speak even when directly addressed. It was only from beneath half lowered eyelids that she cast occasional sidelong glances at the thin young man in his new black, high-buttoned student uniform; but that was enough for her to decide that he was impossibly smart and good-looking for a girl like her. Besides, he was going to Tokyo, where her friends told her that girls often showed their legs in western dress and reddened their cheeks with rouge. For her the meeting passed in a daze of speechless embarrassment, and she remained mute throughout the short train ride back to Uto, astonished to gather from her parents' brief remarks to each other that they considered the *o-miai* to have gone off quite well.

Both the Assistant Chief of Police and the stationmaster at Uto had access to telephones, and one evening a week or so later Chie's father casually remarked that he had spoken that day to his acquaintance, who confirmed that Yukichi had found Chie's appearance and manner satisfactory. Chie could consider herself betrothed. She saw Yukichi once more before he left for Tokyo, when he called at her house and she was encouraged to walk the length of the village street with him unchaperoned; and three times more at intervals of a year before their marriage, which took place in 1904, the year after his graduation, when she was almost eighteen. There followed the exhausting journey to Tokyo; over thirty cramped and uncomfortable hours by train and ferry in those days, while in 1936 it could be covered in twenty-two or so. After becoming a Shimada Chie had never returned to her native village, and as she turned away at last from the Buddha image and weakly, tremblingly moved towards the gateway, a fleeting picture returned to her mind of the wayside shrine and of herself as a young girl caressing one of her treasured, stolen pieces of pottery.

She did not get far. The steps up to the gateway were too much for her and she clung to one of the uprights which supported its roof of rice-straw thatch, her head spinning. Then she remembered nothing until the sound of his voice penetrated the fog and brought her back to consciousness. '. . . very worried about you. Come along, now. I'll help you. I've brought a little *sake*. Drink it first.' The little flask clattered against her teeth and some of the liquid ran down her chin as she began to drink, but then a tendril of warmth wound its way round her stomach and Chie became aware that it was day. Her voice was no more than a cracked whisper at first.

'Thank you, Jiro,' she said. 'But you shouldn't have come all this way to find me. I've been so happy here.'

'My, you look like a million dollars!' Teruko did not understand the American expression but had no difficulty in interpreting the look on Dwight Rogers' face as she stepped shyly out of the front door of the Arden Beauty Salon and smiled up at him. In spite of the crisis at home the previous night when her mother had failed to return from her customary visit to the public bathhouse, and the chaos when she was brought back soon after dawn by Jiro, Teruko knew that she looked her best. One of the other girls had done her hair specially during the lunch break, with finger curls at each side of her forehead: she had to be very careful not to spoil them when putting on her saucy felt hat. She wore her best shoes with the narrowest of straps buttoning at the instep, and a new pair of rayon stockings which she could ill afford. The rest of her outfit unfortunately had to be the same as she had worn to call at Rogers' office, but her best friend at the salon had lent her a marvellous coat with fake astrakhan at the collar.

To her relief he then switched to Japanese. 'Well, what's it to be? The movies, or dinner?' Teruko shrugged helplessly: she could not possibly choose between such delights. 'In any case, we have time for a cocktail at the Imperial Hotel, don't we?' Rogers led her to the edge of the sidewalk and masterfully hailed one of the taxis which were parked outside the Mazda Building opposite. It was one of the flat-fare type which would go anywhere in the metropolitan area for one yen, and Teruko was overcome by the thought that Rogers would spend such a sum on a journey of less than half a mile to the Imperial Hotel.

She had been in a taxi perhaps seven or eight times in her life before, and as she climbed awkwardly in and settled into the pleasantly smelling leather upholstery it occurred to her for the first time that the American she had now quite firmly decided was very handsome indeed might well take her home in one at the end of the evening, and she experienced a moment of by no means disagreeable panic at the thought that he might kiss her.

Scenes showing film stars kissing never occurred in Japanese films and were always excised from those imported from Hollywood, but the censoring was so clumsily done that it was perfectly obvious to Teruko and her friends what was about to happen or had just happened at such moments. Indeed she and the other girls often talked about it in the little room at the back of the salon where they changed into their smocks, and Teruko and her particular friend Haru sometimes gave demonstrations at popular request, with Haru in the Clark Gable role and herself batting her eyelids seductively and fluttering them closed as Haru enclosed her in her arms and kissed her passionately on the lips. Being kissed by Haru always made Teruko's nipples stiffen and she used to feel funny and rather breathless afterwards, even as the pair of them joined in the delighted giggles of the other girls. During her delicious nightly sessions of masturbation Teruko sometimes imagined Haru kissing her with no clothes on, but more often concentrated on film stars like Don Ameche, Preston Foster, or Jushiro Kobayashi.

She was too excited to say anything as the taxi pulled away and headed for the Hibiya area, and Rogers simply sat and smiled until they were almost there. 'Miss Shimada, excuse my asking, but is there a particular time you must be home by? Do you live far away?' Teruko had been dreaming about America and it took her a moment or two to come down to earth. 'Oh. Oh no. Not far away really. We live in Hongo, not far from the Imperial University. Trams and buses both go there. And I am almost twenty, you know. On ordinary working days I usually get home by about nine, but I often stay out *much* later.'

'I see. Good. Well then, why don't we have cocktails, then dinner, and then maybe go dancing for a while? Would you like that?' Teruko did not trust herself to speak, so she merely nodded vehemently. She had never been to a dance hall and never danced with a man, though she spent hours poring over the black and white footprints, dotted lines and arrows on the pages of the ballroom dancing primer she had bought from the big Maruzen bookstore a couple of years before, and sometimes persuaded her reluctant sister Yoko to shuffle about the *tatami* matting at home with her during one of the very rare broadcasts of dance music on the wireless. None of the half-dozen records Jiro possessed was any use. Mostly Teruko danced alone while humming to herself. Her favourite was the fox-trot, though she also liked the quick-step and of course the waltz.

Teruko enjoyed it when the uniformed doorman flung open the door of the taxi outside the Imperial Hotel, enjoyed watching Dwight Rogers pay the driver with a note taken from a well-filled bill-fold, enjoyed it when he ushered her through the great doors *ahead* of him, and enjoyed it most of all when he led her to the cloakroom boy in his pillbox hat at a counter on one side of the huge lobby with its exotic brown and ochre brickwork and stood behind her slipping her coat off to check it in. Did his big hands linger for a moment or two on her shoulders? Was there the slightest pressure there?

Rogers for his part was in something of a quandary as he took off his own overcoat and handed it to the boy. On the one hand Teruko was the easiest pick-up he had ever come across in Tokyo, and indeed he was well aware of the fact that she was throwing herself at him; while on the other it was as clear as crystal that she was naive and inexperienced, for all her expert make-up and stylish clothes. He had not given her a thought since her visit to his office, but having glanced at the photographs again from time to time he still found it difficult to credit that this pretty girl with the finger-curls was the same person as the kimono-clad child of the previous week who had admittedly made the running, with the rest of her family seemingly following her lead. Except for the glowering young army officer, of course. He had obviously hated every minute of the whole encounter.

Well, he was fancy-free at the moment, and though this puzzling Shimada girl seemed to have rather less to say for herself than she had at his office, nobody could say that she seemed in any way reluctant to accompany him to the bar. 'Oh, anything you like,' she said with a sudden sophistication of manner to match her appearance when he led her to a corner table and asked her what she would have as the waiter approached. Rogers looked at her a little dubiously before ordering a crème de menthe frappé for her and a gin and French for himself. It was tempting to fill her up with alcohol and see what happened, but something held him back and he was relieved that he had exercised restraint when she coughed and her eyes watered even after sipping the diluted, sickly sweet drink he had chosen for her. Her second attempt was more successful, and she smiled at him bravely as she put the glass down.

Something similar happened when he took out his cigarette case and politely offered it to her. She took one without hesitation and leant forward to enable him to light it for her as if to the manner born, but then nearly choked on the first puff. 'You probably don't have your cigarette holder with you,' he suggested courteously, gently removing the cigarette from her fingers and stubbing it out. 'If you're used to one I don't recommend smoking without it. The smoke will get in your eyes.' Ashen-faced, Teruko nodded at him gratefully.

'Tell me about yourself, Miss Shimada. For a start, what's your first name? You know what mine is – Dwight. We Americans like to use first names. It would be nice if you would call me Dwight.'

'*Dowaito*. It's a very nice name,' Teruko whispered. Rogers smiled.

'I'm not sure about that, but it's certainly a lot nicer the way you say it. And you?'

'My name is Teruko.'

'Now that really *is* beautiful. "Little Shining One". May I call you Teruko?' Teruko blushed, wide-eyed and nodded before taking refuge in her drink.

'Well, that's settled. Good. Were you born here in Tokyo, Teruko?'

'Yes, I was. You speak Japanese very well.' Rogers suppressed a sigh. It was heavy going, but he manfully braced himself to confirm before long that he liked Japanese food – even raw fish – and that he could use chopsticks. This curious girl might look like a model or even an actress, but her conversational clichés were no different from those of any other Japanese confronted with that terrifying phenomenon, a westerner.

He took her to the Prunier Room soon after that and chose carefully for them both, selecting much against his own inclination a bottle of Sauternes to go with their trout and gesturing to the wine waiter to keep away after Teruko drank her first glass rather quickly. Its effect on top of the crème de menthe was to give her confidence, and she began to talk more freely. 'I like this wine,' she said abruptly, after wrestling clumsily with the unfamiliar knife and fork. 'It's nice and sweet. Does it come from America?'

'No, from France. I'm glad you like it, though. We do make wine in America, of course. In New York State and in California.'

'In *New York*? But New York is a city.'

'Of course, but I said New York State. It has many cities in it apart from New York itself, and goes all the way up to Lake Erie and the Canadian border.'

Teruko tried again without much success to dismember her trout as the wine waiter approached once more, and this time Rogers allowed him to refill both their glasses. 'You come from New York, don't you? Is it far from Hollywood?' she asked then.

'I wasn't born in New York, but I used to have an apartment there when I went to work at the *New York Times*. I was born in another state called New Hampshire. Hollywood is clear across America on the west coast, thousands of miles away. Why, come to think of it, Hollywood is half as far away from New York as it is from Japan.'

Although the words he used were perfectly intelligible Teruko could not begin to imagine what he was talking about, so she drank some more Sauternes. The second glass tasted even better than the first; smoother, and it didn't burn her throat going down. The spacious, elegant room looked if possible even brighter and more gorgeous, and she was no longer frightened by the loud voices of the many foreigners at the other tables or the ostentatious swoopings of the waiters. It was, in fact, just like being in the movies, and she looked around smiling, noting with pleasure that among the handful of other Japanese women diners none was as young or as pretty as herself. If Fred Astaire had appeared in person and danced from table top to table top with tailcoat flying she would not have been in the least surprised.

Teruko finished the last of her apple pie and ice cream. She had no recollection of beginning it or indeed of its being placed in front of her, but it tasted wonderful, and a spoon and fork were reasonably easy to cope with. 'Seven fifteen,' Rogers was saying, looking at his watch. 'Too late for the cinema, I'm afraid. Would you care to come dancing?' He was more than a little bored, but there was no doubt that Teruko was a peach of a girl, and having spent quite a lot of money on her already he felt justified in taking her into his arms for a while. Teruko nodded happily, and at once began to stand up. She lurched a little as they left their table, but recovered quickly when Rogers took her arm and led her towards the door of the Prunier Room. 'I'll just settle the bill here,' he said. 'The ladies' room is right across the lobby there. I'll meet you by the cloakroom in a few minutes.'

Half an hour later Teruko sat again blissfully at Rogers' side, at a

small table not far from the dance floor at the Ginza Premier
Ballroom. The furnishings were marginally less elegant than those
of the Imperial Hotel but even more spectacular, while she thought
the sight of the band on the platform in their dinner jackets
behind the monogrammed music stands was indescribably splendid. Then Rogers was on his feet and smiling at her, hands
extended. 'Let's dance,' he said in English, and led her to the
glossy floor where he drew her close to him.

It was a fox-trot, and Teruko's initial nervousness was dissipated within seconds as Rogers led her so confidently and
skilfully. She forgot about her feet: they floated through the
movements she had practised so earnestly. She was conscious only
of the music, the warmth of the hand holding hers and the
pressure of the other against her back, the smell of his eau-de-
cologne and the smart green and purple stripes against the silvery
grey background of the necktie a few inches from her nose.

It seemed to be over in no more than a few seconds, and then
they were sitting at their table again. Teruko would have liked
some more of the smooth wine that made her feel relaxed and
excited at the same time, but Dwight Rogers explained that they
didn't sell it there. So they danced some more and Teruko asked
who were the girls who sat in a row at one side of the hall with
numbers pinned to their pretty dresses, and were sometimes
approached by men who handed them a little piece of paper, after
which they stood up and danced with them. Rogers explained that
they were dance-partners for hire, called in English 'taxi-dancers',
and that they sometimes earned as much as twenty yen in a single
evening at one yen a dance. He admitted that he knew this
because he had sometimes danced with them: Teruko did not
much like to hear this.

Later Teruko spoke to one of the taxi-dancers in the ladies' room
which was fitted with pink mirrors but otherwise nothing like as
luxurious as the one at the Imperial Hotel. The girl was perhaps a
year or two older than herself and not particularly good-looking,
but her stockings were of pure silk, as was her dress. They had a
little chat while Teruko deftly helped her to re-fix a vagrant
kiss-curl, and after some initial hesitation the girl agreed that the
money was good, though only rarely as much as twenty yen in an
evening. She explained that girls were forever leaving for one
reason or another and that new ones were being taken on all the
time; and even told Teruko the name of the manager.

By the time Teruko returned to Dwight Rogers she thought he

was looking rather impatient so she smiled at him especially seductively and contrived to brush her breasts against his arm as they made their way between the chairs for one last dance. He *did* take her home in a taxi, and he did kiss her on the way. Teruko responded too eagerly and he missed her mouth, landing instead at the side of her nose and tickling her with his moustache. Then he tried again and she opened her mouth as she sometimes did when Haru kissed her, but this time their teeth clashed together quite painfully.

All too soon they were nearly at Hongo, and separated hurriedly when the taxi-driver turned round in his seat to ask for directions. Teruko asked him to stop at a corner a hundred yards or so away from the house and quickly pecked at Rogers again while the driver was walking round to open the door; and he responded by squeezing her hand. When Teruko thanked him fervently his teeth showed white as he grinned in the gloom of the taxi. 'I'll be in touch,' he said in English, and then repeated it in Japanese. 'Goodnight. Sleep well.'

Rogers waved as the taxi drew away to take him to the Tokyo Station Hotel where he rented a room on a long-term basis which with breakfast cost 75 yen a month. On balance he didn't regret the amount he had squandered that evening, because her eagerness in the taxi left him in no doubt that Teruko Shimada was potentially hot stuff. He might indeed renew the acquaintance, and arrange a little privacy next time. There was another thing: he had the receipt from the Prunier Room and could charge their meal to expenses as a business lunch. Associated with an interview for a piece about the hopes and dreams of young Japanese women at the beginning of 1936.

Teruko watched as the taxi disappeared from view. She was in love, and knew who would shortly join her in her imagination in bed.

## 9. *Friday 10 January, 1986*

'I'm anxious that you should not misunderstand me, Miss Hoshino. There is no secret about my childhood. My father was what we should nowadays call a "salaryman": a section head in the Mitsui head office in the days when it was a true *zaibatsu*. You are familiar with that word, I'm quite sure.'

Lesli nodded. 'Of course. Wasn't it originally some kind of political slogan, something like "wealthy clique" in English?'

They were using that language, and interested as she was by Shimada's sudden outburst of candour about his origins, she had been reflecting as she spoke that, fluent as he was, he had at least retained the Japanese characteristic of formality. Any American of whatever ethnic origin would be calling her 'Lesli' by now: probably would have done so from the time of their first meeting.

'Over the years,' she went on, 'it came to mean financial/industrial conglomerate. Then MacArthur tried to break them up after the war, but a lot of people think he didn't succeed too well.'

'That's right. More or less. Except that it wasn't MacArthur's own idea to try to break them up. That was cooked up in Washington long before the war ended, largely on the initiative of the economic advisers to the State Department. The political experts who knew Japan argued that the family-owned *zaibatsu* – the Big Four as they used to be known – had always supported parliamentary democracy in Japan and had done their best to oppose militarism in the thirties. I mean the Mitsui, Mitsubishi, Sumitomo and Yasuda concerns. MacArthur's staff labelled another six conglomerates as *zaibatsu* too, after the war. Incidentally, if you're thinking of the Shimada Trading Corporation as a latter-day *zaibatsu*, forget it. My business operations are small-time compared with the Mitsuis, Mitsubishis or Sumitomos, even of today. The Yasuda group was always mainly in finance and insurance, and what's left of it still is.'

'The Fuji Bank, you mean?'

Shimada nodded approvingly. 'You've done your homework,' he said.

'Your father must have been very able to have gotten a senior job with Mitsui – or was there a family connection?' Shimada's expression remained calm and friendly, but Lesli sensed a reaction of controlled irritation to her question in a momentary clenching of the fists resting on the arms of his chair.

'No. No family connection.' He raised one hand to rub his nose, then appeared to come to a decision and bestowed upon her a warm smile. 'Let's just get this all straightened out and done with, shall we? My father came from the city of Kumamoto in Kyushu. *His* father – my grandfather – was a samurai until the system was abolished. Not a very important one, let me add. My father came to Tokyo when he was lucky enough to get a place at Waseda University, and good jobs – at least, what were considered to be good jobs – weren't too hard to find for Waseda graduates in his day. He graduated around 1902 or 1903, I think. Mitsui were already big, and they'd started moving into heavy industry in the nineties, but they went on growing fast right up to world war two. They needed bright young men in those early days, and my father did reasonably well. But you know as well as I do that to stick at section head level is no very big deal.'

Lesli spread her hands in a rather helpless gesture. What he said was true enough, assuming that pre-war section heads carried roughly as much weight as their successors in the eighties did. Junior management. Nothing to be ashamed of, but nothing to get excited about either.

'Right. We were a conventional middle-class family. No worse off than a lot of Tokyo people at that time, and a hell of a lot better off than the great majority in the provinces and the countryside. My father died in 1940. My mother died before him, in 1936. She was from Kyushu originally, too. I had a sister; now also dead. After senior high school I passed the entrance examinations to Tokyo University, graduated and went straight into the Navy. An unremarkable boyhood. End of story.' Shimada spoke very quickly, almost gabbling the last few phrases, then sat back and took two or three deep, slow breaths, looking fixedly at Lesli. She thought he looked all at once much older: a man in his late sixties, as he really was rather than a vigorous executive in his fifties as he seemed to be on television, in photographs and, indeed, face to face at their previous meeting.

'Thank you, Mr Shimada. I didn't want to seem unreasonably intrusive, but I'm very grateful for that information. It must have been tough to be a teenager in the thirties.'

The luxuriant eyebrows rose. 'Oh? Why? They weren't such bad days. I had a camera, I remember. And a wind-up gramophone. Not a Victrola, but a copy. Would you believe I was a jazz enthusiast? Bix Beiderbecke especially, although he was dead by then. And Louis Armstrong, of course. Their records were hard to come by, but I managed to collect a few. And there was a Japanese group, Ray King and His Band they called themselves. They were good. I don't know what became of them.'

Having at first been so unforthcoming about his early years, Shimada now seemed to be indulging in nostalgia, and Lesli warmed to him. 'It's kind of you to let me tape-record all this,' she said, and he waved a hand airily. 'An old man's ramblings,' he said. 'Go ahead, but spare me the embarrassment of seeing any of this in print. I meant what I said before. I had no traumas, no formative experiences as a boy. Why, I didn't even fall in love until I joined the Navy.'

'Would you care to tell me about that? I had thought of a chapter on "Love and Marriage", something like that.'

Shimada's smile was one of genuine humour, and his chest heaved with silent laughter. 'Do they really go together like a horse and carriage, as Doris Day used to sing? How I used to enjoy those pictures of hers in the forties and fifties when I was working too hard and building up the business! You're a real American, Miss Hoshino. I keep forgetting. We Japanese regard love and marriage as two quite separate and distinct things. I fell in love many times during the war and after. I got married in 1950, when I was twenty-nine. We had no children, and my wife died of cancer three years ago. I was desperately sorry for her when she was in pain, and very sad when she died. It was a successful marriage, and I miss her very much. But love – what you would call love – has nothing to do with all that. And it is hardly relevant to a serious work of biography, I should have thought.'

'I'm sorry, Mr Shimada. I – I –'

'No need to apologise. I am a public person, Miss Hoshino. My career is open to inspection. My private life, such as it is, is not. Maybe you and your publishers feel that a biography has to be, how shall I say, spiced up with personal revelation. That my public life is of little interest –'

'No, no, it isn't like that –'

Shimada raised his hands a few inches: it silenced her like a slap in the face. 'Or that my ideas, my philosophy of business, my thoughts about the future of the world economy or about Japan's present and future role as a great power are banal. I am quite prepared to accept that possibility. But I have to make it clear that these are the kind of topics I had looked forward to discussing with you.'

'May I say something now?' Lesli's tone was sharp and Shimada looked at her in some surprise.

'Of course. Go ahead.'

'Mr Shimada. Perhaps I should try to make my own position clear, too, especially as I've been accepting your very generous hospitality for the past several days. I'm a serious writer, not a gossip columnist. You are an outstanding person, a world figure. *Of course* it's your extraordinary business achievements and your wide-ranging involvements in public and international affairs which I plan to describe and analyse in my book. But a biography is above all the story of a human being – in your case a particularly fascinating human being – and people who read it will want to know not only what you have done and how you have done it, not only your philosophy of life, but also what makes you tick, what sort of things you delight in or hate . . . and yes, what you eat for breakfast, too, but only to be reassured that you are a *person*, with hopes and fears like everybody else. Even perhaps somebody who is sometimes lonely, bewildered or frightened.'

'*Hammu eggu.*'

'I beg your pardon?'

'I said, I eat a very conventional sort of breakfast. Ham and eggs, or as we Japanese put it, *hammu eggu*. Toast, marmalade or jam, coffee. And I've already told you that I miss my late wife very much. Bewildered? Yes, often, but it doesn't do to let it show, does it? And I have many times been frightened during the course of my life, Miss Hoshino. There, haven't I answered all your questions?'

'Come in!' The tap on the door had been hesitant, and Lesli was not surprised when it was opened to see Yamada's head peeping round it.

'Am I disturbing you, Miss Hoshino?'

'Oh, hi, Mr Yamada. Come right in. I had a great session with Mr Shimada today – I've just been enjoying myself playing the tape back.' Yamada hovered near the door, smoothing his thin hair back with one hand while jingling keys in his pocket with the other. Lesli had discovered that he did this whenever at a loss for words, and waited patiently enough for him to react. In the meantime she indicated the easy-chair near her desk, and after some hesitation Yamada sat down.

'The President had no objection to your making a tape-recording?'

'No, none at all. He was in great form. You know, Mr Yamada, I'm beginning to like the man, even though the mask of the tough charmer did slip a little now and then. Am I shocking you?'

Yamada shook his head with a brief smile. 'No, Miss Hoshino. Some of the staff here might be surprised to hear you say such things, but I've already come to appreciate your frankness. May I ask what you talked about . . . that caught Mr Shimada off-balance? Is that correct English?' he added with a trace of anxiety. Although Lesli's Japanese was rather better than his English, they had reached an unspoken agreement to speak English together. Lesli had decided that she liked Yamada. He was helpful without being fussy, and now that he was more relaxed in her company revealed now and then a wry sense of humour which she suspected was too thoroughly suppressed in his normal work at the head of the International Liaison Department.

'Sure, "off-balance" is fine, although you'd hardly have noticed. We were talking about his boyhood, as a matter of fact. His hobbies, and things like that. I was beginning to think I wouldn't ever get that far, but he was surprisingly forthcoming. He told me about his family background, his parents and when they died, and his late wife, and mentioned he'd had a sister who was killed in the war.'

'Really? You must be a very persuasive lady, Miss Hoshino. In all the years I have worked with the President I have never heard him mention a sister.'

'Well, I mustn't give you the wrong impression. He didn't exactly open up to me. It was more a question of giving me just enough to keep me quiet in future, I think. It was like a kind of challenge at the end when he more or less made me admit that he'd answered all my questions. Well, in a way he had, and yet he hadn't. He's pretty sneaky, but certainly I know a whole lot more about him than I did. And I really don't want to pry for the sake of prying, Mr Yamada. I'm writing a biography, not carrying out a security check.' Lesli all at once felt slightly ashamed of herself, and at the same time resolved to guard her tongue more carefully. For all she knew Yamada might be closer to Shimada than she supposed, and be retailing their conversations back to his boss.

'Of course. I understand.' Yamada seemed to sense her embarrassment, and handed over the plastic folder he was carrying. 'I've put phonetic equivalents beside the old-style Chinese characters used in these Imperial Navy documents for you, and suggested English translations of some official terms you might not be familiar with.'

Lesli smiled at him gratefully. 'Mr Yamada, you're wonderful. Thank you *very* much. I suppose it was lucky for me that my mother and father could not get hold of new-style schoolbooks when they started in to teach me Japanese. Two thousand characters were more than enough to master, let alone a couple of thousand more. You must have been among the last to have to learn the old ones.' She riffled through the papers, wondering if she had said the right thing. Yamada could be anything from fifty to sixty, she thought, but one could never be sure with Japanese men.

'You know, some of these papers ought to be in a museum. A complete dossier, from the notification of the date and place of his physical to his service record. Basic training, commissioned as an ensign, special training in communications, ended up as a lieutenant serving aboard troop transports, I see . . . oh, by the way, Mr Yamada, I'll be checking out of the Okura Hotel tomorrow. I have a study-bedroom reserved at the International House of Japan. I explained to Mr Shimada that I really can't justify free-loading like this, and he was very understanding.'

'Of course, Miss Hoshino. Whatever you prefer.' Yamada stayed and chatted for a while longer, but Lesli thought he seemed a little uneasy, and worried again after he left about the way she had talked to him about Shimada. On the way back to the Okura she reflected also that there had been no word from Charlie Goldfarb since their lunch together, and wondered whether he really was going to behave as a perfect gentleman towards her. There was no message for her at the reception desk, and Lesli smiled at her own momentary irritation over being neglected. She decided to dine expensively in the hotel on her last evening as Shimada's guest. He would probably never even see the bill, which would undoubtedly be charged to corporate expenses. As for Charlie, it was more likely that some other lucky girl was getting the treatment and that he was simply too preoccupied to bother with her, she thought.

## 10. *Sunday 12 January, 1936*

General Jinzaburo Mazaki was wearing a kimono when he received the six young officers in a *tatami*-matted room flooded with sunlight, and Hideo thought he looked calm and relaxed. His house, not far from Yoyogi, was quite large but not in the least ostentatious, and Hideo felt ashamed of the clutter of the Shimada house as he looked round at the austere furnishings. The others had been there before and were eagerly boisterous in their manner towards the General, like favoured schoolboys in the company of a popular teacher: indeed one or two of the older among them had trained at the Military Academy while it was under Mazaki's command in the mid-twenties and that was almost exactly their relationship to him. For Hideo it was the first time and he hung back until pushed forward by the others.

'Lieutenant Shimada, eh? And where do you hail from, young man?'

'He's all right, General!' It was the lively and articulate Lieutenant Takahashi who answered for Hideo. 'His father was born in Kumamoto – and his mother, so he's a good Kyushu man, like you. Samurai stock. One of us.'

Mazaki clapped Hideo on the shoulder. 'Well, there are Kyushu men and Kyushu men, and I'm from Saga myself, practically a neighbour. You're very welcome. Which regiment?'

'The Third, sir.'

'Splendid. Well, don't let that rascal Ando lead you astray!' Hideo was delighted and bewildered in equal measure by the General's bluff informality: his training made him want to stand stiffly to attention, yet his comrades were sprawled around the room laughing and joking with each other as though they were in a teahouse, and Mazaki beamed round at them like nothing so much as an indulgent uncle.

'It continues cold at night, gentlemen,' the General said affably after a maid had brought them all tea. 'I understand that there were four degrees of frost on the night of the eclipse. And icicles formed on the fountains in the Hibiya Public Park in central

Tokyo. The sunshine is agreeable, though.' His visitors had fallen silent and were hanging on his words, so he sipped his tea and spoke again.

'The New Year pine, plum and bamboo decorations have been removed from the entrances to people's houses. I wonder if you are aware that by tradition in the family of the new Lord Keeper of the Privy Seal only one of these is placed at his gate, rather than the customary pair? I understand that this peculiar practice recalls an occasion some three hundred years ago when an ancestor of Admiral Saito was summoned to battle on New Year's Day, having had time to place one only in position, and left immediately without bothering about the second. An instructive story. I wonder if the Admiral is under-equipped in any other respect at this time?' A roar of sycophantic laughter greeted the General's elegant jibe and the deputation relaxed again.

Mazaki knew all about the conspiracy. He had watched Mitsugi Nishida create the Young Officers' Movement while under his command at the Military Academy, and had kept in touch with him after he resigned his commission to promote the ideas of the intellectual Ikki Kita, whom Mazaki also knew. As a leading member of the 'Imperial Way' school of strategic and political thought in the Army, he had insisted that the curriculum at the Military Academy had strongly emphasised patriotic 'Japanism', and what he called spiritual training. Mazaki was completely in sympathy with the conspirators' aims: he was moreover angry over having been manoeuvred out of his influential post of Inspector General of Military Education some months previously; but it was necessary for him to play his cards very carefully. If these young officers who hero-worshipped him were to succeed in their enterprise they could help to make him Prime Mimister; but he must be in a position to repudiate them if they failed. He therefore had no intention of encouraging the young radicals openly, but did not want to forfeit their loyalty or cause their faith in him to be eroded either.

'I am truly heartened that a group of such fine young officers – a *representative* group, I am sure – should take the trouble to call on an old man entering his second childhood at nearly sixty, and one relegated to the sidelines of the Military Council, to express their good wishes,' he said sententiously, and there was a roar of eager dissent. Captain Kono was the ranking officer in the delegation and it was he who spoke in hot indignation.

'The General is far from being an old man! The General has been the victim of a criminal intrigue, but the day is not far off when justice will be done and we shall look to him to lead the way in establishing a New Order! We bring not only good wishes, sir. We bring an expression of faith, an expression of hope, and an assurance that the Army awaits only a word from you to deal with the traitors who obstruct justice and corruptly frustrate His Majesty's intentions!'

Captain Kono was always rather more fiery in his style than the other leading spirits, and Hideo felt the familiar goose-pimples rising on his skin as the words exalted him, even though their idol was raising a hand in gentle rebuke. 'I appreciate the sincerity of your attitude, Captain,' he said. 'And I am touched that your comrades appear to share your generous point of view. But these are complex times, and the way ahead is not always perfectly clear, even to those who see what must sooner or later be done.'

Hideo was not quite sure what the General meant, but his words sounded encouraging, and merely to be in the presence of a man he revered was an inspiration to him. 'The course of events is not wholly unsatisfactory,' Mazaki continued. 'I have reliable information – and I tell you this in confidence, for it will not be generally known for several days – that our delegation will shortly withdraw from the Naval Conference currently taking place in London. This in spite of the treasonable attitudes of most of the politicians and the weakness of some – I say *some* – even of our senior naval colleagues.' He smiled silkily. 'Don't forget that my younger brother is an admiral. So is our friend General Araki's. Spines have been stiffened at last. The Americans and the British have been told that their precious ratios, which we have protested against for years and which have led to the present intolerable discrepancy between the size of the Imperial Fleet and those of the other two Powers, are repudiated. They refuse to accept our equality thesis: so Japan will leave them to their own devices.' His voice had risen and he was gripping the closed fan in his hand tightly. Then he breathed deeply and reverted to his former controlled manner.

'As I say, there are encouraging developments. You gentlemen for your part are probably gratified by the great public interest stimulated by the forthcoming public court-martial of Colonel Aizawa. Needless to say, none of us can approve of the Colonel's action in killing a brother officer. A senior officer. A general, and a prominent member of that group of so-called pragmatists who deride the necessity for spiritual discipline. Why, unworthy as I am, I have the honour to be a general officer myself. We certainly wish no harm, for example, to my successor as Inspector-General of Military Education, General Watanabe. Do we? He must not be disturbed while composing more speeches in support of his great friend the learned Professor Minobe.' Mazaki's expression was unreadable, but Hideo joined in the general grinning and laughter of the others.

The General's voice rose commandingly above the din, which immediately subsided. 'All the same, there is already widespread recognition of the fact that Colonel Aizawa's sincerity is unquestionable, and that he was motivated in what he did by the highest considerations of patriotism, some of which will without doubt receive welcome and timely publicity during his trial. That trial is due to begin later this month, gentlemen. I ask you to bear that in mind.'

In fact Mazaki had already been warned that he would himself be summoned to give evidence at one of the court-martial sessions planned to take place according to a leisurely timetable agreed by the General Staff. In spite of the gravity of the offence and his open admission of guilt, nobody seriously expected Aizawa, when convicted, to suffer more than a disciplinary posting to the provinces with some loss of rank. His trial, like that of other military men in previous years, would constitute something of a discussion meeting, with the accused permitted to make long speeches in defence of his action; and these speeches would be widely reported. Mitsugi Nishida who was organising his defence would see to that. Aizawa was an eloquent man who could be counted on to harangue those sitting in judgment on him and accuse them and their superiors of being the truly guilty men.

As they left General Mazaki's house Hideo and one or two of the others were for proceeding straight to the home of General Watanabe and confronting him, and Captain Kono hesitated for a few minutes, briefly tempted by the suggestion. Then, with some reluctance, he decided that so decisive a move should not be made without the knowledge and approval of Nishida, Captain Ando and the other leading conspirators, and ruled against it.

Hideo was not particularly sorry to be overruled, but spent a long time when back in his spartan quarters at the Azabu Barracks thinking about what General Mazaki had said. Hideo and his friends had several times discussed their possible fates. Many expected to die in the course of their coup d'etat. Others quite freely considered the possibility of failure and subsequent court-martial, but had faith in the justice of their case and confidence that it would be sympathetically heard if it came to that. On the whole Hideo thought that if they could not succeed in what they hoped to achieve, he would prefer to die in the attempt: he knew he lacked Captain Kono's stirring way with words.

It was miserably cold again that night, and Hideo's insomnia was as troublesome as ever.

## 11. *Monday 13 January, 1986*

'Why don't you ask him what high school he went to? You know how it is in Japan: alumni associations in the States can't hold a candle to the network here. You get these old guys meeting once a year to talk about when they still had teeth . . . and they even keep the hierarchy going. You know? Being respectful to upper classmen and so on. Even when they're company presidents or something big in politics. You'd be bound to find somebody around who'd remember him from those days. Or you could try Tokyo University. Maybe they could dig up some old class lists. Or hire a private investigator, the way people do when they're arranging a marriage for their daughter. Why, there's all kinds of ways, especially for an approved biographer. You could find out who his cronies are in the Federation of Economic Organisations, for example. That's it, the Keidanren. The big bosses' mutual aid club. There's bound to be somebody there who hates Shimada's guts and will tell you the dirt if you give his knee a squeeze.'

'Right. And within ten minutes or less Mr Jiro Shimada would hear about it and down would come the shutters. This man has *connections*, Charlie. Later on, perhaps. But I can't afford to make him mad at me so early on by being too obvious about digging into the prewar years.'

'So. Well, you're the boss. You could be right at that.' Charlie Goldfarb looked around the huge, lavishly furnished lounge of the Tokyo American Club and chuckled. 'Here we sit in capitalist splendour, right next door to the Soviet Embassy. Always kills me when I think about it. I wonder what Ivan Ivanovitch makes of us when he peeks out of his top floor window?'

Lesli smiled. 'He's probably listening to our conversation right now, Charlie. Talking of peeking, maybe if I were to stop by he'd let me glance through their file on Shimada.'

'He might at that. You can be sure as hell he has one.' He looked at her steadily for a long moment. 'What's with you, Lesli? Why are you making such a big deal over these early years?'

She shook her head and shrugged. 'I wish I knew. There's

*something* there, and it's bugging me. Even when he's making a show of being candid and informative, he's holding back. It doesn't make sense for a Japanese with his money and influence to be such a solitary person. Parents dead –'

'For God's sake, kid, that's hardly surprising – they'd have to be in their nineties to be alive still.'

'No, you didn't let me finish what I was going to say. Parents dead – of course – wife dead, sad but not so very surprising either, sister dead, no children. None of these things significant in itself, but adding up to a curious degree of isolation. And then this repeated insistence that life began for him when he entered Tokyo University.'

'Aw, come on, Lesli! You suggesting he bumped his folks off? The Lizzie Borden of the Orient? And used the family jewels to pay for his tuition? And maybe years later his wife found out and started blackmailing him so he fixed her too? You writing a biog aphy, or a movie script?'

'Don't be silly, Charlie. Of course there may be nothing to it. And Shimada has a perfect right to hold back any details he cares to – he's not in a confessional. All the same, I'm not writing a history of the Shimada Trading Corporation; I'm writing the story of a man's life. Ye gods, his grandfather was a samurai, imagine that! With a top-knot and two swords stuck in his sash!'

'That's nothing. My grandaddy was a rabbi in Odessa, with the greasiest long black coat you ever saw.'

'Charlie, you're impossible.'

'Nope, just realistic. Look. Either you really want to find out about this guy's early background, in which case go ahead and do it, or you're scared to, in which case there's not much point in sitting around on your adorable fanny speculating about it.'

Lesli sighed. 'I suppose you're right. It's been less than two weeks so far, but I have enough notes and photocopies of Shimada's papers to fill a trunk already, and I've looked at zillions of photographs. All courtesy of the man himself. The book's already beginning to shape up, and I have a feeling that once I get properly started it'll write itself. And it's going to be good. He really is an extraordinary man, you know.'

'You bet. And he got his start during the Korean war like a lot of others, no doubt. Good old Uncle Sam's procurement requirements, right?'

'Only partly. He started in before that. Buying up prime real estate for peanuts.'

'And black marketeering? Maybe that's why he's buttoned up about the early days.'

'No, you've got it wrong, Charlie. He's quite frank about those years. It's his boyhood that's largely a closed book. Except I know he used to be a Bix Beiderbecke fan.'

'Then he can't be all bad,' Goldfarb said solemnly, then twisted his rubbery face into a grin. 'Look, honey, I have to go. I'm due to meet Rachel at the Jewish Community Centre at Hiroo in ten minutes. I have to grab a cab.'

'How is Rachel?' Lesli enquired dutifully as they walked out of the brightly lit entrance lobby and Goldfarb waved for a taxi from the line of half a dozen waiting to one side of the spacious forecourt.

'Oh, she's okay. It's aerobics now, would you believe it? I keep begging her to wait till the Jane Fonda Workout Book for Fat Yiddisher Mommas comes out, but she won't be told. Can I drop you off some place?'

'No, Charlie. Thanks though. It's just ten minutes walk to the International House from here.'

'If you say so. Listen, Lesli, if you're really serious, let me know. I can ask around here and there for you. Might come up with something.'

He kissed her quickly and dived into the taxi, and the driver operated the mechanism which banged the door closed. The red tail lights of the taxi were disappearing round the bend into the main street as Lesli left the forecourt and walked along beside the high, barbed-wire-topped wall of the Soviet Embassy compound, past a silent, incurious Japanese riot policeman in full protective gear standing outside his semi-permanent sentry box. On an impulse Lesli blew him a kiss and enjoyed the expression of surprise which swept over the face behind the plastic visor of the helmet. Then she swung into the busy thoroughfare in which a drab grey bus containing several more riot policemen was parked, turned away from the Tokyo Tower direction and headed for the bright lights, bars and restaurants of Roppongi.

Part of her wished that Charlie Goldfarb hadn't kissed her. At least, not on the lips, though even that could have been interpreted as no more than a friendly salute from an old friend: there had been no prolonging of the contact, no probing tongue. Yet Lesli knew quite well that her sudden mood of elation had something to do with that kiss which she had so capriciously blown away in the direction of the riot policeman on watch outside the Russian Embassy, to cheer the young man during his lonely vigil.

It was as though she could still taste Charlie's lips just as surely as she could still in her imagination smell the cologne he had always used and which had once been more familiar to her than her own favourite perfume. She was in no doubt that she was cured. Neither the thought of Charlie in his taxi on the way to meet his plump Rachel at the Jewish Centre, nor that of Rachel herself with her weakness for cheesecake and all those rings slightly embedded in the flesh of her fingers, even ruffled her tranquillity; hard to believe that once she would have been consumed by guilt and jealousy. She smiled as she tried to visualise fiftyish Rachel in a leotard, puffing her way through her aerobics classes.

Charlie really hadn't changed. His good humour was never far from the surface and so often bubbled up to fracture the solemnity even of serious conversations; and he retained the ability to make her see that so many of the issues she framed in her mind as dilemmas were really capable of quite straightforward resolution. In spite of the hand on her thigh and later on her shoulder at the Press Club, and now that kiss, he seemed not to be quite so indefatigably randy as he had been six years earlier; so charged with unforced sexuality that even their final, tearful breaking-off encounter had turned into a protracted, achingly sweet act of love. It was good to feel simply affectionate towards him, and to sense that he was glad to see her again.

Occupied with her thoughts, Lesli had made more rapid progress than she realised, and was surprised on looking around to get her bearings that she had missed her turning and was almost at the Roppongi crossroads. Retracing her steps she passed the MacDonald hamburger restaurant and was briefly tempted to eat quickly there, but then decided that her luxurious drinks with Charlie at the American Club merited a slightly worthier postlude. The food in the downstairs restaurant at the International House was nothing special, but the atmosphere was spacious and tranquil, and the view out to the Japanese garden even on a winter's evening was always a delight.

She turned off into the narrower, quiet and comparatively much less brightly lit street leading to the International House and two or three minutes later entered the lobby and went to the small reception desk, to be greeted by name as her room key was handed to her. 'One message for you, Hoshino-san,' the clerk

added in Japanese, and handed her a folded slip of paper torn off a
message block. She took it with a smile, then fumbled in her purse
for a hundred-yen coin which she put in the plastic box beside the
pile of copies of the *Asahi Evening News* on the desk, helping
herself to one. Then she went over to the nearby lifts, unfolding
the slip of paper as she did so.

A Mrs Yoko Nagai had called. She would like Miss Hoshino to
call back, before ten this evening or after eight in the morning. A
Kamakura number. Lesli couldn't imagine who Mrs Nagai might
be, unless she was yet another distant Hoshino family connection
emerging from the Japanese woodwork. Well, there was no hurry.
Mrs Nagai could perfectly well wait until she had eaten and read
the paper.

## 12. *Kamakura,*
## *Thursday 16 January,*
## *1986*

'Oh, yes. I shall never forget that camera. Jiro took it with him when we went to the Meiji Shrine on New Year's Day in the eleventh year of Showa. That is, let me see, nineteen thirty . . . six, I think.' Lesli sat quietly on her cushion in the neat little *tatami*-matted room and let Yoko Nagai reminisce with as few interruptions as possible. Although this was their second meeting, she was still trying to adjust herself to the idea that the sister Jiro Shimada had described as having died was not only very much alive, but seemed to share his own quality of durability: certainly she looked a lot less than seventy-three.

Mrs Nagai was again wearing western dress: this time a tailored wool skirt and jacket of navy blue over a simple blouse with lace at the collar. Her abundant white hair was drawn back in a plain style but without severity. The small, old-fashioned house on a hillside in the northern part of Kamakura had a southern aspect, and although the electric heater in a corner of the room was not switched on, it was comfortably warm in the sunshine streaming in through the sliding glass doors which gave on to a tiny garden of moss, a stand of slender bamboo which grew to no more than four or five feet in height, and a few azalea bushes. An ancient stone lantern stood in one corner of the garden, its upper surfaces softened with lichen.

'I still go into Tokyo on the train to teach one day a week at Ochanomizu Women's University, you know,' Mrs Nagai said abruptly and with a touch of pride. 'I was the first woman Professor of Library Science, and when I retired formally they invited me to carry on as a part-time lecturer. I am lucky enough to enjoy good health, you see. Would you like some more tea, my dear?' Lesli made a polite gesture of refusal, willing her to go back to 1936 and the subject of her brother Jiro.

Their first short telephone conversation had left Lesli bewildered but intrigued, for Mrs Nagai merely said that she had heard that Lesli was engaged on writing the biography of Jiro Shimada and might be able to be of some assistance to her. That she lived in

Kamakura, an hour's train ride from Tokyo, and would be pleased to meet Lesli in either place; but that if it would not inconvenience Lesli too much she would prefer to welcome her at her house in the ancient city where, Lesli might perhaps have heard, there were many beautiful temples as well as the famous Great Buddha . . . Lesli was polite, for the voice and manner were clearly those of an elderly lady, but her hesitation must have communicated itself to Mrs Nagai. 'Do come, Miss Hoshino,' she said. 'I knew him a very long time ago, you see.'

The idea of revisiting Kamakura had its attractions anyway, but the last thing Lesli expected as she stepped from the train at Kita Kamakura Station was to be approached by a trim, bright-eyed old lady who introduced herself briskly and explained that she had feared her description of the whereabouts of her house would prove to be inadequate, and that she had therefore decided to meet Lesli at the station instead of waiting for her at home.

The hour that followed was agreeable enough, but Lesli realised towards the end of it that by then Mrs Nagai knew a great deal more about her than she did about Mrs Nagai. The old lady had a deft way of extracting information, whether it was about Lesli's family background and career in America, her experiences as a member of the Tokyo bureau of *Newsworld* magazine a few years earlier, her relatives in Japan or even the fact that she had been married and divorced since her Tokyo years. They strolled round the spacious precincts of the Engaku Temple, reached the house where they drank green tea and nibbled at small bean-jam cakes, and Lesli had begun to glance surreptitiously at her watch before Mrs Nagai dropped her bombshell.

'You must forgive my having been so inquisitive,' she said. 'But I found everything you told me so interesting. I do hope that now we have met you will come back to see me often. I can tell you a lot about Mr Shimada, you know. I really can. But before I even begin, you must promise me that you won't say anything about me to him, or to any of his staff. Will you promise?'

The cheerful, gossipy good humour of Mrs Nagai's earlier manner had been replaced by a look of great unease, and the thin, blotched hands which were the only obvious indicator of her age were tightly clenched. Rather startled, Lesli had given the promise sought of her, supposing as she did so that the old lady might be about to confess to having once long ago had a love affair with Shimada. Lesli would have been delighted if this had been the case: as it was she was dumbfounded when Mrs Nagai quietly but

firmly and with complete conviction stated that she was Jiro
Shimada's elder sister and then almost at once courteously but
unambiguously indicated that it was time for Lesli to take her
leave.

The ensuing twenty-four hours of speculation had brought Lesli
to a state of confusion, suspicion and irritation, and she had
arrived at the house in Kamakura to keep their second appoint-
ment in a mood of mingled excitement and scepticism, only to be
disarmed by the warmth of the welcome she received and the
unmistakable look of pleasure in Mrs Nagai's eyes. Now she sat
there, believing what she was being told and trying to assimilate
its implications.

Jiro Shimada was a liar. He had stated in plain terms to Lesli that
his sister, like his parents and his wife, was dead. Mrs Nagai for
her part had been at pains to extract from Lesli a promise that she
would not tell Shimada that they had met. At the very least,
therefore, brother and sister must be estranged from each other,
and it might be that she would not be particularly surprised to
hear that he had claimed she was dead. Lesli certainly had no
intention of mentioning it. Yet Mrs Nagai spoke of Shimada
without obvious rancour, and had indeed just been spending
several minutes describing him as a teenager. His passion for jazz
led her to consider other enthusiasms of his boyhood, culminating
in his acquisition of a camera; and as she spoke of this her
expression softened even more.

'Yes. Nineteen thirty-six. Of course. It began so happily. It was
the day I met Dwight.' Mrs Nagai blinked once or twice, then
smiled determinedly. 'He was a journalist, like you. Dwight
Rogers, Tokyo correspondent of the *New York Times*.' Lesli dared
to interject a question. 'You met him on New Year's Day? Actually
at the Meiji Shrine?'

'Yes. It was quite by accident. He never said why he was there, I
suppose it was to get some background for a despatch about the
New Year celebrations. Jiro was getting ready to take our picture
and Dwight came over and offered to do it for him so that he could
be in the group.'

'Dwight Rogers. Of the *New York Times*.' Lesli repeated the
name to fix it in her mind: she had not yet dared to take out her
notebook in Mrs Nagai's presence, still less ask her if she might
tape-record her.

'Dwight, yes. It was silly of me, I know, but in the fifties, the
time of President Eisenhower, I always felt a little bit shivery

whenever I heard that name. And I was a middle-aged woman by then.' Lesli had brought a box of imported English chocolates with her as a present, and unusually for a Japanese, Mrs Nagai opened the package immediately after thanking her for it and sampled one. She now reached out unseeingly towards the open box on the low lacquer table and took another.

'You . . . met Mr Rogers again after that occasion then?' Lesli knew that the question was stupid: it was transparently obvious that Mrs Nagai had been in love with him.

'Oh, yes. Many times . . . but that was later.' Her face was transfigured, and the young woman she had been looked out at Lesli through the old one's eyes. 'He hardly noticed me on that first day, I'm sure. It was Teruko who was "making eyes" at him.' She used the English words of the old-fashioned expression, and pronounced them in a quaintly formal way. Then she made a sound half-way between a sob and a giggle. 'Poor Teruko! She was convinced from the first that Dwight must be related to Ginger Rogers . . . she was quite put out when he told her he wasn't.'

'Excuse me for interrupting you, Mrs Nagai . . . but who was Teruko?'

'Teruko? Why, my sister, of course.' Lesli thought she might have a headache coming on.

'You have a sister?'

The dreamy half-smile faded and the young woman receded, leaving pain in the old eyes. 'Teruko was our sister. She died. In the war.'

'I'm so sorry.'

Lesli was quite surprised when Mrs Nagai leant across and patted her hand. 'There is no need to apologise, my dear. You obviously didn't know. Jiro hates even to hear her name mentioned, so naturally he wouldn't have told you about her. Once I believe he dismissed a secretary who had been engaged by one of his managers when he discovered that her first name was Teruko.'

'Could you . . . ?'

'No. Please forgive me, but I would rather not talk about my sister's death. I will be happy to tell you about her "crush" on Mr Rogers if you like, though. She was such a happy-go-lucky girl in those days, and really thought at first that she might persuade him to marry her and take her to America! She made very sure that she stood beside him when my father asked Mr Rogers to stand with us so that Jiro could take his photograph in return. As a matter of fact I rather fancy that she suggested the idea in the first place. I

have a copy of that picture somewhere. I'll look it out and show it
to you next time you come. Teruko looked very pretty that day, but
then she usually did. She worked in a hairdresser's shop, but
always told people she was a beauty consultant. And you'll be able
to see Jiro in his high school student uniform, that will interest
you.'

'There were just the three of you at the shrine, then? Your
brother, your sister and yourself?'

'Oh, no. We were all there. The whole family.' Mrs Nagai
touched a finger to the corner of her eye. 'The photograph Dwight
took of us was the last one of us all together.'

'Your parents were there too?'

'Yes. Mother was feeling quite well that day. I think she was
happy that Hideo had been able to come home for a few days'
leave.'

'Charlie? Oh, hi. No, no, nothing special. It's nice of you to call. As
a matter of fact my head's in a spin. I just got back from Kamakura.
Listen, do you have a minute? Yes, *Kamakura*. You remember I told
you about the old lady who called me? A Mrs Nagai? I've just been
to see her again. Yes. Well, the first time, she told me she was his
sister. You-know-who's sister. What? Oh, for God's sake, Charlie,
of course I'm not getting paranoid. *Shimada's* sister then, is that
better?'

Lesli kicked off her shoes and curled up on the bed. Talking to
Charlie helped her to clarify her own thinking. 'Right. It certainly
was a bombshell, and after today I'm beginning to wonder how
many more skeletons are going to come tumbling out of my
smooth friend's closet . . . oh, she's a real sweetie, even though it
was pretty traumatic. I thought for a while she was going to tell me
she couldn't face any more talking about the family after all, even
though she was the one who asked me there in the first place.
Charlie, dear, if you'd just *listen*, I *am* explaining. Mrs Nagai is
another sister, not the one who died in the war. That was Teruko.
Mrs Nagai is Yoko. No, I don't know which of the two Shimadas
decided to turn into an unperson. Hold the line a minute, Charlie,
I have a drink on the desk.'

As she went to fetch it Lesli realised she was not making a lot of
sense, and decided to start again from the beginning. 'Charlie?
Are you still there? I'm sorry. Sure, it's giving me a headache too.
Okay, there were *two* sisters, right? And I'm going to take it as
definite that the younger one, Teruko, is dead. Until I get a phone

message from some other little old lady who wants to talk, that is. So now as of New Year's Day 1936 we have Dad, a section head working for Mitsui. We have Mom, who was maybe some kind of an invalid but was feeling pretty good that day. We have Jiro of course, and then moving up we have Teruko and Yoko, and finally – brace yourself, Charlie, we now have another brother, the mysterious Hideo, who springs from nowhere as an army lieutenant and was twenty-five or so, Yoko said. The girls were somewhere between the two boys, so that makes them anything from say eighteen or nineteen to around twenty-three.'

Suntory whisky with chilled water was not Lesli's idea of a perfect drink, but in her present mood anything alcoholic would do, and she drained half the glass while Goldfarb reacted. 'Right, exactly what I thought. Why in the world would Shimada want to keep completely quiet about a brother and one sister and mention only the other, conveniently dead? Yoko and Shimada both say that their sister died in the war. Well, an awful lot of people died in the war. This young lieutenant would still have been only thirty or so when it started, so he was surely involved. Probably killed in action. Why not say so? Oh, yes, definitely. You'd feel the same if you could meet her, Charlie. She really is a pretty impressive person. Used to be a professor of library science . . . I guess that would be information science nowadays. Looks real good for her age. Sharp, wits about her.'

Lesli closed her eyes as she listened to Goldfarb. His voice was resonant, and the vibrations tickled her ear. 'Yes, I'm curious about the late Mr Nagai, too. It should be easy enough to find out. No problem to sniff around Ochanomizu University without ruffling any feathers. And I'm sure there must be some kind of archive where I could track down what became of the lieutenant, at least. The Defense Agency probably keeps records. I wish I could figure out why Yoko became so emotional when she mentioned him. It's tough to lose a brother you're fond of, but it ought to be possible to talk about it something like forty-five years later, for heaven's sake. No, it looks like a blank wall as far as Teruko's concerned . . . what? Nice idea, Charlie, but I seriously doubt if the Federation of Japanese Hairdressers or whatever kept a record of beauticians who died for their country. The way things stand, I obviously can't ask Shimada. That's what bugs me about this whole thing. *Why* won't he talk about these things? *Why*? Sure. There's nothing else I can do. Mmm, you too, Charlie. I'll call you soon.'

## 13. *Monday 20 January, 1986*

'Okay, okay. Stop looking like a kid waiting for a birthday present. He is still alive. Living in retirement in Vermont. No Sun Belt for these tough New Englanders, you know.' Charlie Goldfarb momentarily rearranged his mobile features into those of a craggy puritan, then grinned at Lesli. She had just arrived at his office in the Mainichi newspaper building at Takebashi overlooking the moat of the Imperial Palace, and he got up from behind his cluttered desk and hugged her. She hugged him back and kissed him on the cheek. 'Charlie, you're a marvel.' He breathed nonchalantly on his fingernails and polished them on his shirt front. 'We endeavour to give satisfaction,' he intoned. 'Sit down. Want some coffee? Or would you rather stand there smiling at the swans?'

Lesli had drifted over to the window and was looking down at the familiar view from the huge fifth floor window across a broad boulevard to the timeless tranquillity of the moat beyond, still against the vast but still graceful granite slabs of the gently curving bastion walls topped with pines, which in their frozen contortions could only be Japanese. It was a view she had never tired of during the three years she had worked in the big general office next door, and one which she would always be happy to see again.

She shook her head slightly as though to wake herself up and turned away from the window. 'I'm sorry, Charlie. Yes, I'd love some coffee, please. Then tell me how you traced Dwight Rogers.' Goldfarb crossed the room to a low glass-fronted bookcase on top of which was a tray with a huge thermos flask and two or three mugs on it. 'I don't have any cream. There's some of that powdered junk some place. "Creap" they call it. Oh, mother, when will they learn?'

Lesli shook her head. 'Black's fine. And no sugar. Thanks.' She was glad of the coffee, for she had more than a trace of a hangover, the consequence of having finished off the bottle of Suntory whisky in her room at the International House without noticing while working on her notes the previous evening.

During the past week she had become aware of a curious

sensation, as though her consciousness had been neatly split into two parallel streams. As a professional writer she had been efficiently organising the wealth of material about Shimada's extraordinary business career and burgeoning international interests made available to her at the offices of the Shimada Trading Corporation, and had largely sketched the skeleton and sinews of what she was now confident would become a well-made, illuminating and successful biography of an undeniably remarkable man. The fact that she continued to be obsessed with the enigma of his early years and fascinated by the revelations of Yoko Nagai seemed, oddly enough, not to interfere with the steady progress of this work: it was as though she could watch herself calmly and systematically doing the job she had set out to do while finding quite separate resources to fuel her determination to unravel the meshes of Shimada's formidable defences.

Lesli took the mug of coffee Goldfarb handed her and sank into the only comfortable chair in the room. 'Well? Give,' she demanded.

Back at his desk, he studied her over the rim of his own coffee-mug. 'It wasn't exactly difficult,' he said. 'Last time I spoke with Marv in New York I asked him if he knew anybody over at the *Times* who owed him enough of a favour to check on Rogers with their personnel and pay staff. Telex was on the machine when I got here this morning. Kinda embarrassing.' He rootled among the papers and found the top copy, which he folded neatly into a paper dart and launched in Lesli's direction. It came to rest in the region of her navel. 'Geronimo! Bulls-eye!' he crowed, but she had already snatched it up and begun to read.

PERSONAL FOR GOLDFARB DWIGHT ROGERS LEFT NY TIMES JOINED US NAVY 1943 RETURNED TO TIMES 1947 BUT QUIT AGAIN FOLLOWING YEAR TO BECOME FACULTY MEMBER COLUMBIA UNIVERSITY STOP HE RETIRED 1974 NOW RESIDES ROUTE 3 ALDERTON RUTLAND VERMONT STOP WHY NOT TRY LOOKING HIM UP IN WHO'S WHO IN AMERICA YA LAZY BUM MARV

Lesli looked up and saw him regarding her gravely. 'I'm sorry, Charlie,' she said humbly. 'It just never occurred to me that . . .'

'Me neither. No sweat, honey. You'll find *Who's Who in America* right there in the bookcase; but suppose I tell you what it says. Dwight Arthur Rogers taught modern Japanese history after he became an academic and wrote a study of Prince Konoe who was Prime Minister right before Tojo, the lovely man who gave us Pearl Harbour. I guess it was probably his Ph.D dissertation. The humble prewar hack ended up as a full professor, did his stint advising John F. Kennedy like everybody else we know, past president American Association of Japanese Studies, pretty big wheel. There's hope for you and me yet, sweethearts. How about this – Dr Charlie Z. Goldfarb, Professor of Burpology at the Stars and Stripes Bar and Grill, Peoria. Like it?'

'Love it. With tenure, of course.'

'Natch. Play your cards right and you could be Dean.'

Lesli got up and crossed to the window again. The traffic was heavy on the boulevard but most of the noise was cut out by the double glazing of the windows. Even through them however the sound of martial music was clearly audible and she looked down to see a khaki-coloured loudspeaker van held up in a temporary jam immediately outside the Mainichi building. Close wire meshing protected the windows, and Japanese flags decorated much of the bodywork. Hideously noisy and conspicuous as the truck was, it seemed to be completely ignored by pedestrians passing by. Lesli sighed, her mood all at once sombre, and turned to look at Goldfarb.

'I think I have to talk to him, Charlie,' she said. 'Do you think he'd see me if I flew back to the States for a few days?'

'Anybody who *wouldn't* see you would have to be out of his mind. Sort of expensive, though. Couldn't you call him instead? He'd be a pretty old man by now. From what you told me I figure he'd have been around twenty-eight back in 1936. That would make him close on eighty. Face it, Lesli. He may be frail, or misfiring on a few cylinders. Even dead by the time you get there.'

Lesli nodded. 'Of course. I realise that. I'll call anyway, naturally. And decide after that.'

'When's your next date with Shimada?'

'I don't know. He's in the States himself, as a matter of fact. Left at the end of last week. You may not believe it, but I'm getting along just fine with the main part of the work. Having access to his files is like being turned loose in a candy store. I'd just as soon not talk to him again while this other aspect is on my mind, though. Last time it was pretty difficult to act naturally, knowing even the little I've learned from Mrs Nagai.'

'I can imagine. You seeing her again soon?'

'Yes. I think she likes me to go there and ask questions and listen. She doesn't seem so scared any more, now that she thinks she can trust me . . . and there's no need to look at me like that, Charlie. She *can* trust me. I wouldn't think of letting Shimada know that I'm so much as aware of her existence.'

'Uh-huh. I believe you. But it's going to be sort of difficult to keep the stuff about his family out of the book, isn't it? And this old dame must have had some reason to be scared in the first place. Come to that, how in the world did she hear about you? Unless she's in direct touch with her brother? I don't get it.'

Lesli found herself becoming irritated with Goldfarb. He was right, of course, and she had already gone to elaborate extremes to keep the notes of her conversations with Mrs Nagai well apart from those she was amassing in the course of her authorised researches. 'Neither do I, yet. But I've been a professional writer for a long time, Charlie,' she snapped. 'I think I'm capable of handling this situation. I don't have a shred of objective verification for what she's been telling me, anyway.'

What Lesli said was almost true, but not quite. During their third meeting Yoko had shown her the photographs which she said had been taken at the Meiji Shrine on New Year's Day, 1936. Looking from the lined but lively face in front of her to the solemn features of the young woman in the kimono shown in both pictures, it was not difficult to see the resemblance. To find the lineaments of the expensively tailored, white-haired tycoon who was the Jiro Shimada she knew in the face of the shaven-headed boy in the black student uniform who appeared in only one of them was harder, though, and Lesli was still asking herself whether it was the will to believe rather than incontrovertible evidence which has persuaded her to accept Yoko's claims as the truth.

Goldfarb held up a hand palm outwards in a pacific gesture. 'Okay, okay. Sorry, ma'am. You're the boss, like I said before.' Lesli's irritation subsided as quickly as it had arisen in her and she smiled at him apologetically. 'No, Charlie. You're the boss here, and I've already asked far too much of you for old times' sake.'

'Hoo boy, what old times they were, too! Any time you'd like to re-run a few of those scenes . . .'

'Don't think I'm not tempted, Charlie. And flattered. But no, thanks all the same.' She stood up and began to gather her belongings together. 'I must get out from under your feet. May I keep this telex? Then I don't need to write down Dwight Rogers' address.'

'Sure, Lesli. You can call him from here if you want to save yourself a heap of yen. The charges for outgoing calls are criminal in this Land of Wa but I guess good old *Newsworld* magazine can bear it.'

'Thanks a lot Charlie, but the Shimada Trading Corporation can bear it with even less effort, and I figure that friend Jiro owes me for giving me the runaround the way he's doing. Thanks for the coffee – and for the help.' She turned towards the door but Goldfarb was already there. He put his hands on her shoulders and looked into her eyes. 'Now whatever happens, don't go rushing off on the next plane without telling me. Okay?'

'Okay,' she said, and skipped away before he could kiss her again.

## 14. *Thursday 23 January, 1936*

Humming to herself and with instruction book in hand, Teruko swayed and slid in her slip and stockinged feet about the room she shared with Yoko, practising the slow fox-trot. It was disappointing that Dwight Rogers had not been in touch to invite her out again on her early evening off: she would drop in at his office again pretty soon. Then there was no sign of Jiro, so it had been up to her to light the fire to heat the water for the bath. All the same she was glad enough to have the house to herself: it was a rare treat and put her in a cheerful mood.

There was no form of heating in the room except what little filtered up from the kitchen and from the stove which was warming the bath-water, but Teruko was not aware of being particularly cold. When Yoko was in the tiny room with her the warmth generated by their two bodies soon made it quite stuffy, and even now that she was on her own the dancing was keeping her quite comfortable. The sliding *shoji* screen over the window was in place and the dim light from the forty watt electric lamp hanging under its enamel shade from the low wooden ceiling struck her as softly romantic. Teruko was quite put out when she heard the rattle of the sliding front door downstairs, but brightened when she heard the ritual shout of '*Tadaima*! I'm home!' The voice was that of her brother Hideo. '*Okaeri nasai*,' she called back. 'I'm upstairs. Won't be a minute.' She looked around for her *yukata* and found it, but was still putting it on when the door of her room was slid open without warning. 'Where is everybody – oh. Sorry.' Hideo made to withdraw. 'It's all right,' Teruko said, adjusting the *yukata* in a leisurely way. 'I'm reasonably decent. You can come in.'

Hideo was in uniform. 'I've got a few hours free. Don't have to be back till midnight. Are you the only one home?'

'I seem to be. Father often doesn't get home till after me even on ordinary days, and it's my evening off on Thursdays. Yoko's gone to her highbrow music appreciation club, I expect. I've no idea where Jiro is.'

'What about Mother? She should be here.'

Teruko shrugged and fluffed the back of her hair up with a languid hand. 'You never know with her these days. She's probably gone round to the public bathhouse, but she might be anywhere. Do you know what she did last week? Spent all night praying at one of the temples in the Nakano Cemetery at Nippori. Jiro found her in the end, practically frozen stiff. He's probably gone to look for her now. She's off her head, if you ask me.'

Hideo stared at his sister angrily. 'She's not well, that's obvious. You might show a bit of sympathy. Has she seen a doctor?'

'I don't know. I shouldn't be surprised. Anyway, what do you expect me to do? I work hard and pay my own way. It's all very well for you, coming back for a few hours now and then and having Yoko fall over herself to look after you. You don't have to put up with her crazy mutterings morning and night. I tell you, if it weren't for Yoko and me nobody would ever get anything to eat in this house. I suppose you're hungry? There's some miso soup I could heat up. Or you could go round to the noodle shop and ask them to send the boy with some later on. The bath water should be hot in half an hour or so.'

Hideo shook his head. 'I had something to eat before I left barracks. I might have a bath when it's ready.' He sat on the *tatami* matting in a corner of the room and idly picked up the ballroom dancing manual Teruko had been studying. 'What's this?'

'What it says it is, silly. An instruction book for ballroom dancing.'

Hideo snorted. 'Ballroom dancing! Another stupid American craze. Don't you ever think about anything else?' He flung the booklet away from him in disgust: it fell in such a way that one of the pages was crumpled, and Teruko pounced on it in exasperation.

'If you don't like it, keep your hands off it! We're not all fanatics like you around here, you know. Thank goodness there are some gentlemen about who don't behave like boors when they're with a girl.'

'Oh? So you have *gentlemen* friends already, do you? Such as who?'

The sneer in Hideo's voice made Teruko really angry. 'Such as Mr Rogers, for a start.'

'*Misutaa Rojazu*? And who the hell might he be?'

'The American we met at the Meiji Shrine on New Year's Day, that's who.'

Hideo rolled back on the *tatami* simulating helpless laughter. 'Oh, that's rich, that is!' he crowed. 'She meets a *gaijin* for two minutes and suddenly he's her "gentleman friend"! When are you going to grow up, Teru-chan?' The false laughter died away and he looked at her, the expression in his eyes changing as he took in the complacent smile on her face.

'Well? What are you looking so smug about?'

'Mind your own business.' Teruko turned her back on her brother and pretended great interest in her fingernails, pushing the cuticles back and then holding them out with the fingers curved slightly backwards to scrutinise the results. The violence with which Hideo seized her by the shoulders from behind almost made her bite her tongue. She whirled round and tried to push him away, fury in her face. 'Take your hands off me!' she whispered savagely, but he grabbed her shoulders again more tightly than ever.

They glared at each other in silence for a moment, then Hideo shook her again, conscious even in his anger of the warmth of the flesh under his fingers and the bones and muscles beneath. 'You'll explain yourself,' he said thickly. 'Now.'

'I'll explain nothing to you, you clod. Not till you let me go, anyway.'

He pushed her violently away and she collapsed on the floor, tears of pain and anger in her eyes. Hideo stood over her, trembling. 'All right. What's all the mystery about the American?' He found it difficult to control his breathing, and the words came out jerkily.

'There's no mystery,' Teruko said at last. She had regained control of herself comparatively quickly, and was experiencing a sense of power as she looked up at her brother, physically so much bigger and stronger than she, yet so childish in his petulance. 'Mr Rogers is a very charming man. When I visited his office to take him the photographs –'

'YOU VISITED HIS OFFICE?'

'Don't shout. I just told you I did. We had a very pleasant conversation and he invited me to spend the evening with him a week or so ago. We had cocktails and dinner at the Imperial Hotel and then went dancing – STOP IT!'

His face contorted with anger, Hideo had grabbed her by one arm and wrenched her up to her knees and now crouched over her. 'And then let him do what he liked to you. Is that it? You dirty little slut! You're nothing better than a whore! No wonder you were so interested to find out what goes on at Yoshiwara ... wanted some ideas to try out with the first *gaijin* you could get your disgusting varnished nails into ISN'T THAT IT?'

Teruko squealed in pain as he smacked her viciously across the face, then became almost blind with anger herself and managed to wrench free, the loosely-stitched sleeve of her *yukata* ripping clean off and remaining in Hideo's hand. Then she was up and attacking, her nails drawing blood from his cheek and narrowly missing his right eye. Hideo's hand was crushing her face as he tried to push her away: she seized it and bit the fleshy part at the side below his little finger as hard as she could and heard him grunt with pain. Then Teruko went for one of his ears, scrabbling and dragging at it as though she was trying in truth to tear it off, but Hideo had her by the wrists at last and flung her down on her back with such a force that she missed a breath.

Before she could recover he had pinned her down by both wrists and knelt over her, one knee between her open thighs as she struggled ineffectually. It was impossible for Teruko to free herself and after a few seconds she gave up trying; at once Hideo's expression changed. 'I'm sorry,' he gasped, 'I'm sorry.' Then he released her wrists and straightened up, remaining in a kneeling position as he took a dirty handkerchief from his trouser pocket and began to dab ineffectually at the blood on his cheek. Teruko lay there staring up at him as she regained her breath, enjoying the contemptuous anger welling up in her at the sight of the hangdog expression spreading over her brother's face.

'Say it again,' she commanded after a while. 'Apologise again.'

'I'm sorry, I'm sorry, forgive me.' Their eyes were locked together and it seemed to Hideo that Teruko's were growing larger and larger and that he was drowning. Her *yukata* was gaping open and her petticoat had ridden high up her thighs, above the stockings which he had never seen in their entirety on a woman's legs before. All at once he slumped down, his head on the warmth of her belly, the perfumed rayon of her cheap petticoat slithering under his bleeding cheek. He was not conscious of his hand groping at Teruko's thighs, and his heart was thundering as waves of blackness and redness threatened to engulf him until he was flung violently off her and she struggled to her feet, hampered by his clawing arms and his face now buried between her thighs as he knelt and blindly nuzzled at her mound of Venus.

Teruko looked down at him as though from a high place, exulting in his contemptibility and humiliation, and in her sudden awareness of her own sexual power. This was quite different from the tickling eroticism of her friend Haru's embraces; different even from the frustrating excitement on the back seat of the taxi with the American. She was breathing hard and her legs were trembling, but her lips twisted in a humourless smile as she slowly dragged the slippery apricot-coloured petticoat upwards through Hideo's clutching fingers and then up and over her head. 'Pull them down,' she ordered, her voice thick and unsteady.

Teruko's moist, warm animal smell flooded his awareness and Hideo stopped breathing for several long seconds until a dry, choking sob forced air into his lungs and he scrabbled first unavailingly at an unyielding suspender belt before finding the waistband of her french knickers and pulling them down over her thighs. He could not, dared not break contact, but mouthed at the warm, springy curls as his sister stepped free of the encumbering material and then spread her legs wide, bracing her naked back against the rough plaster of the wall and groaning obscenities she had never uttered before in her life.

It was as though the choking voice she could hear belonged to someone else who was in possession of her mind and wanted only to degrade and humiliate the panting man on his knees before her; yet at the same time Teruko was clutching her brother's head and grinding herself against his mouth, racked by wave after shuddering wave of the most intense and overwhelming physical pleasure she had ever experienced. Her words became a meaningless babble, rising to a whimpering scream as the terrible power of her orgasm rose, blossomed and shuddered through her. Then she collapsed, almost grateful for the burning pain in the skin of her back as she slid down the wall and lay crumpled on the *tatami*

Panting and exhausted, Teruko was only dimly conscious that Hideo was now standing, ripping off his shirt and fumbling at his trouser buttons, but she tried feebly to protest. It was no use. All her strength was gone and it was Hideo who was now filled with an exultant fire as he dragged her to the centre of the tiny room, spread her unresisting legs wide and forced half the length of his jerking penis into the hot throbbing wetness. He came almost immediately but remained erect and soon began to move again, penetrating a little more deeply with each thrust.

It was then that Teruko began to cry, and then that Jiro Shimada noiselessly closed the sliding door which Hideo had left ajar by no more than three quarters of an inch. Jiro had crept up and positioned himself outside when the sounds of quarrelling rose to a crescendo. He now made his way thoughtfully downstairs and was working quietly at his textbooks in his own room by the time he heard the door upstairs slide open again. He quickly turned the light off. The tread on the stairs was too heavy to be Teruko's. Jiro waited until he heard his elder brother go into the bathroom and quickly slipped out of the house. He was habitually silent and unobtrusive in his comings and goings, but thought that in view of the circumstances it would be sensible for him to come home again, noisily, after about half an hour when Teruko too had had time to take a bath and dress herself. There was no sense in frightening her. Yet.

## 15. *Friday 24 January, 1936*

'It's nothing but a scrawl,' Yukichi said miserably. 'Barely readable, and what little I can make out makes no sense. I'm sorry to have disturbed you, but quite frankly I'm at my wits' end. She talks to you more than to me. What do you make of it?'

Her head aching and her eyes puffy with sleep, Yoko peered again at the scrap of paper her father had found on top of the bedding in his and Chie's room. It was indeed almost indecipherable. Her mother had been taught an old-fashioned cursive style of writing which, when done properly with a brush, had a dancing, graceful charm quite out of keeping with her slow, dreamy manner; but this note had been scribbled with a blunt pencil on paper which seemed to have been crumpled and then smoothed out again. 'It's very . . . confused, Father. I can make out something about "going home", and "very tired", but the rest doesn't mean anything at all to me. I'm so sorry.'

Yukichi rocked slowly back and forth on his cushion. He still had his overcoat on, and the fact that his necktie was askew disturbed Yoko almost as much as her mother's second disappearance: he was usually so fastidiously groomed. 'At my wits' end,' he muttered again, then looked up and saw tears in his eldest daughter's eyes. It was after one in the morning, and the chill in the downstairs room seemed to have a sullen, malign quality. Yoko was huddled in her *yukata* with a padded *tanzen* jacket over it, but still shuddered uncontrollably from time to time. 'You'd better go back to bed, Yoko,' he said dully. 'I'll go out again and try some other temples. I've been all round the ones in the cemetery at Nippori where Jiro found her last time. We had a talk before I made him go to bed. He's sleeping now and I can't bring myself to wake him to ask if he can think of anywhere else. The boy needs his sleep with all the studying he has to do for his examinations. I hope I didn't wake Teruko when I roused you.'

The profound silence outside the house was broken by the hollow but obscurely comforting sound of the wooden clappers of the night fire patrolman making his rounds, and father and daughter both waited until the periodical clacking had faded into the distance. 'No,' Yoko said then. 'I think she must have been very tired. She went to bed early.' There was no need to mention to her father the fact that Teruko had already flung the bedding down anyhow and huddled herself up in it when Yoko arrived home at about nine-fifteen after the gramophone recital, to find her elder brother Hideo emerging from the bathroom.

He was in such a talkative and extravagant mood that she thought at first that he was drunk. It was a relief when Jiro arrived home and composedly joined in the conversation, and an even greater one when not long afterwards, after drinking the remains of a bottle of *sake*, Hideo buttoned himself into his tunic and took himself off back to his barracks at Azabu. Yoko was by then already worried about her mother's absence but Jiro persuaded her to have a bath while the water was still hot and then go to bed, saying that he would wait up for their father.

Yukichi seemed not to notice what Yoko had said. 'I've tried to get her to see a doctor. She's . . . you know, well, it's her age, you see,' he said awkwardly.

'The change of life. I know. I talked to Mother about it a few weeks ago.' Yoko's manner was quite matter-of-fact. 'It seems to give far more trouble to some women than to most. She told me she'd got some powders to take from the Chinese pharmacy near Ueno. I suggested she ought to go to a gynaecologist myself, but she insisted it wasn't necessary. Mother can be very stubborn.'

Yukichi nodded his head gently, his eyes nearly closed. 'You're a good girl, Yoko.' He seemed almost to drift off into sleep, then swayed back and forced his eyes open again. 'Well, I can't just sit here. I must try to find her. She'll do herself real harm if she's standing in the cold somewhere again.' Yoko yawned miserably and clutched her *tanzen* closer to her. 'I'll get dressed and come with you, Father.'

'No, no, you mustn't do that, it's bitterly cold and I don't even know where to start. They told me at the bathhouse earlier that they didn't remember seeing her there . . . Yoko!' He reached for the note again and studied it with painful intensity. 'This phrase about "going home". Could it perhaps mean Kyushu? She's never been back since we were married, you know. What do you think, Yoko? Has she mentioned the possibility at all to you? Has she?'

Yoko's heart went out to her father as he sat there, a tentative expression of hope fighting to gain possession of his drawn features. 'Of course it's possible, I suppose,' she said falteringly.

'Mother hasn't talked to me much recently, either. But she does seem to have been thinking about her girlhood quite a lot, and I've heard her talking to herself sometimes about her mother. Such a long journey, though . . . would she have had the money to buy a ticket?'

Yukichi wanted to believe. 'I think so, yes. I'm sure she has always put a little on one side: I never enquire about that sort of thing. I'll go to Tokyo Station, that's what I'll do.'

Yoko reached a hand across the lacquer table and placed it on her father's. 'They'd never remember, Father,' she murmured. 'One woman among so many people? And surely the ticket office will be closed at this time of night anyway? Wouldn't it be better to send a telegram to Uncle and Aunt in Kumamoto first thing in the morning if Mother isn't back by then? Ask them if they've heard from Mother?'

Her father seemed not to be listening. 'If she is there I shall have to go and bring her back, you see. And that will mean having to be away from the office for several days. The Director . . .'

'For goodness sake, they *must* give you time off in case of illness, Father,' Yoko said, anxiety, exhaustion and irritation giving a shrill edge to her voice. 'The Director might not be so keen to marry me off to this man Sato if he knew my mother's wandering in her mind, anyway. Insanity in the family isn't much of a recommendation.'

Shock and anger made Yukichi go rigid and a touch of colour appeared in his face. 'That is a dreadful, unpardonable thing to say, Yoko! Especially at such a time.' he said chokingly.

She was unmoved. 'It's true, though, isn't it?'

Father and daughter glared at each other across the table for several seconds, and then Yoko's shoulders slumped. The moment of capitulation when it came was banal and unmemorable. 'I'm sorry. All right, for what it's worth you can tell him I'll meet Mr Sato,' she muttered.

Only a matter of hours earlier, as she had left the dreary room at the University exalted by the grandeur of Brahms' first symphony and the proximity of Mr Nagai, Yoko had been quite settled in her mind that come what may she would never yield to her father's pressure to agree to a formal introductory meeting with the Director's assistant. She had no idea whether Mr Nagai cared for her or not: he dominated her consciousness not as a potential lover but as a representative of a finer, clearer-sighted, more generous order of humanity than the other people around her. He seemed to move about in serene, spacious uplands of freedom and detachment, his concerns noble, his pleasures subtle and refined. The hours Yoko spent sitting behind the library desk were hardly ever tedious to her, for books were all around her and the desk was like a magic carpet lifting her effortlessly into Nagai's world of spirit and intellect, a place where music and art were food and drink, and the imagination could ride moonbeams of speculation.

When her head had still been full of Brahms' soaring but majestic architecture the idea of marriage to a superior clerk in the Mitsui organisation, of children, of scrimping and saving to keep up respectable appearances and the deadening chores of house-keeping was unthinkable to her: now as she raised her eyes again and looked dully at her father she realised that the unthinkable was in truth the inevitable. Her spirit wept as she contemplated the shrivelled tatters of what she had dared to cherish as a vaulting dream, but now in retrospect recognised as having been simply a ridiculous schoolgirl fantasy.

'I mean it, Father. Even if you don't need to ask for time off. But I think you may be right about Mother. I think you should send a telegram anyway.'

Yukichi patted her hand. 'Thank you, my dear. Thank you. I'll go to the main telegraph office at Marunouchi. They're open all night. I must be careful what I say to your aunt and uncle. They have enough to worry about looking after your grandmother, and telegrams can be frightening things for people like them. And in any case, it's most unlikely that Mother could have gone all that way. I may be making too much fuss about very little.' He raised himself slowly, leaning heavily on the table-top, then stood looking down at her as he rebuttoned his overcoat and then, almost as an afterthought, bent down, picked up his wife's note and stuffed it in his pocket.

'I expect she's all right, you know,' he said. 'She'll come home soon, no doubt, and this time I'll call a doctor myself. Perhaps arrange for her to go to Kyushu if she'd like that. For a bit of a rest.' He took a step towards the door, then turned and spoke again. 'I'll send that telegram anyway. You go back to bed, Yo-chan. Get some sleep. You know, there's absolutely no question of your marrying Sato if you don't take to him. Lots of *o-miai* never actually lead to marriage.'

Yoko wept quietly after he had stumbled out into the night. It was the first time for many years that her father had called her by her little girl's name.

'Our temporary command headquarters will be at the Sanno Hotel until we have undisputed control of the War Ministry,' Captain Ando said. 'We can seize and hold it with a small force – fifty or so men – and there will be more than enough food in stock there to see us through the inevitable early period of confusion. We're in no doubt that within a day or two at most we shall get full backing from Tokyo District Headquarters and have the whole army behind us. Then our job will be largely over and it will be up to men like Mazaki and Araki to lead the way forward.'

He took his glasses off and rubbed his eyes. 'There's still a lot of argument about timing. We all want General Mazaki to testify at Colonel Aizawa's court-martial so as to get maximum publicity for our ideas, but that's unlikely to be before late February. Nishida-*sensei* in particular has a lot staked on the court-martial, and he and Kita-*sensei* and the other civilian comrades are asking us to delay action till then. Kono, Kurihara and some of the others in the First and Third are for moving sooner, and on balance I'm inclined to agree with them. Anyway, we shall have to come to a decision within a very few weeks and then move fast.' It was just after one forty-five in the afternoon, and Hideo sat bolt upright on the plain wooden chair which was the only moveable item of furniture in Captain Ando's simple room at the Third Regiment's Azabu Barracks a mile or so west of the National Diet Building and the Prime Minister's official residence. Ando himself was sitting on his bed in his shirtsleeves, a litter of papers spread out at his side.

'Another factor in all this is that as you probably know, National Diet elections are due to be held on the twentieth of February. We aren't optimistic about the outcome, but there might be advantage in making our move shortly after the results are known and while the political situation is fluid. Whatever we decide, the exact date and timings won't be communicated to you until two or three days beforehand at most. Meantime I want you to discuss our transport requirements with Lieutenant Yasuda on the basis of this list.' He handed Hideo a single closely written sheet of paper. 'A very simple code has been used which I will explain to you and you must memorise later, but I cannot too strongly emphasise now that you will be held personally responsible for the security of this document and must never allow it out of your possession. Now listen carefully. Movement of the troops who will be needed to secure control of the Imperial Palace itself, the metropolitan police headquarters, the Prime Minister's and War Minister's official residences and various other public buildings will be organised by the officers in command of each detachment through the responsible NCOs: you and Yasuda are required simply to ensure that enough staff cars and drivers are available for command liaison work and that their petrol tanks are full. This is basically a matter of common sense and you must work out the details between you.'

Captain Ando yawned mightily. Hideo Shimada was the sixth of the conspirators to be briefed by him that day, and he was bone-weary. Hideo for his part was still drunk with the excitement of the previous evening. Intimations of shame drifted into the edges of his consciousness from time to time, only to be dissipated almost at once by the vivid excitement of the recollection of the smell and taste of Teruko, of the dark pleasure of abasing himself on his knees before her while obeying her harsh, obscene instructions, and of the yielding, velvety heat of her body and her shuddering weeping as he broke his way into her and through levels of excruciating pleasure into a new, fierce awareness of his own power. He was purged of petty doubts and inhibitions, utterly confident, and quite unaware of the insolent half-smile which had appeared on his face as with part of his consciousness he attended to Captain Ando's unromantic talk about staff cars and petrol.

'The requirements for the special action forces are more complex and are itemised on that sheet of paper. I now turn to your own specific assignment. Are you paying attention, Shimada? I shall not be repeating any of this, you know.'

'Sir.' With an effort Hideo banished the vision of Teruko sprawled beneath him and fixed his attention on Ando.

'We are few in number, comrade, and our main task is quite specific. To destroy the traitors. In other words, to deal with certain guilty individuals. You know who they are because we have often talked about them, but for the present I shall name only one. The one you will be required to kill.'

'I have been – ?'

'You, Lieutenant Shimada, have been selected to command the Special Group Six which will have the honour of killing Saito.'

'Admiral Saito? The Lord Keeper of the Privy Seal?' Hideo's exalted mood was interrupted by a moment of cold horror as he grasped the significance of Ando's words.

'Who else? It's a high honour, comrade. And a heavy responsibility. You will probably have the support of two or three other officers and up to two hundred men, but you will be in command.'

Hideo nodded dumbly. He was not only reconciled to the possibility of being killed in the course of the coup but had even begun to welcome the thought of laying down his life for the Emperor. Nor did the idea of killing in the course of combat trouble him particularly. Like all his brother officers, Hideo had been through brutally harsh, desensitising training, screaming mindlessly while hacking and slashing with his sword at straw dummies: it had not been long before he had begun to enjoy losing himself in the waves of red, murderous fury that sent the adrenalin surging through his gangling body, and to listen and laugh sycophantically when officers who had returned from service in overseas garrisons boasted of testing their blades on Chinese, Taiwanese or Koreans. These were mere animals, creatures of no account.

Admiral Viscount Makoto Saito, on the other hand, was a distinguished Japanese aristocrat with a long record of service to the Empire. He had held the offices of Navy Minister, Governor-General of Korea, Foreign Minister, and even Prime Minister; and now at seventy-eight was His Majesty's principal courtier as Lord Keeper of the Privy Seal. General Mazaki had singled him out for special mention during his allusive, carefully worded New Year remarks to the officers who had called on him, and made him the first object of his polished insults.

Then, as so often, Hideo was uncomfortably aware that although his samurai breeding and Kyushu origins had gained him entrée to the elite Young Officers' Movement, he was something of an odd man out. Many, perhaps most of his fellow conspirators came from much more elevated social backgrounds than he did. Several were the sons of senior officers and moved easily in privileged circles: they were gratified but not awed by General Mazaki's jovial informality. Hideo had often heard them speaking scornfully, almost flippantly about the most eminent people in the country, and had even once or twice overheard near-blasphemies concerning the Emperor himself.

Such scoffing on the part of men who were unquestionably as committed as he was himself to the Imperial Way ideal puzzled and disturbed him. He was prepared to believe that some of those closest to the Throne were guilty of self-seeking, corruption and even treason, but nevertheless he regarded them as superior people. To be charged formally with the duty of putting the Lord Keeper of the Privy Seal to death in the name of the Emperor they both served was an awesome experience.

'A heavy responsibility,' Captain Ando repeated, his tired eyes fixed on Hideo. 'Have you any reservations about accepting it?'

There could be no hesitation: thinking was for later. 'No, sir. None whatever.'

Ando nodded. 'Good. As I have explained, you will not be alone. You will of course pick your own NCO and within reason your own team of men to give you immediate support. I will remind you again that at this stage we are few in number, Lieutenant. There are no more than about sixty or seventy of our comrades in the movement in the Tokyo area at present, and not all of them will be available immediately. We have no access to the Army's normal administrative and other resources, and individual officers cannot look for help in planning the details of the specific operations for which they are responsible. Until we actually launch our coup you must be your own intelligence officer, your own supplies officer, and your own adjutant. That means that it is up to you to reconnoitre the ground. I can tell you one more thing, though. When we do move it will almost certainly be by night. You will therefore probably be dealing with Saito at his house. His office is within the precincts of the Imperial Palace and access would be particularly difficult. You must nevertheless devise a contingency plan.'

Captain Ando sighed heavily. 'Questions?'

Hideo could not remember ever having felt so lonely, exposed and terrified before. He had done quite well to secure a regular commission in the Imperial Army, was conscientious and reasonably efficient, and was fiercely proud of his status as an officer. Throughout his training, and subsequently, there had been much talk of initiative and responsibility. In practice he had always functioned within a framework of clearly defined military conventions, standing routine orders and specific instructions from above; and been supported from below by unquestioning obedience and skilled technical assistance. When he was in the company of the other activists of the Young Officers' Movement faction he was full of excited confidence. Now, alone with Captain Ando in his bare, unheated room, and facing the challenge of his weary, seemingly disparaging stare, he felt stripped, inadequate and unprepared.

'No questions, sir,' he replied.

'Very well. That is all for the present. You will be told the date in time for you to make your detailed preparations.' Ando nodded in dismissal and Hideo jumped to his feet, bowed and reached for the door handle. 'Lieutenant. One last thing before you go. We –

you and I, all our friends in this enterprise – are of no consequence. Do not expect to survive. You will be surprised how much
strength will come to you if you adjust your attitude accordingly.'

'Ow! That hurt! Watch what you're doing, young woman,' Mrs
Wheeler yelped angrily in English as Teruko pulled at her sparse
grey hair while clumsily taking out one of the array of curlers.
Teruko had no need to understand every word to be very clear that
she had offended. She apologised humbly and tried to concentrate, painfully aware of the sharp look directed at her by the
manageress who was standing well within earshot beside the
receptionist's desk.

It was mid-afternoon, and Teruko was in pain and very tired,
even though she had struggled late from the deep pit of sleep into
which she had slumped the previous evening after dragging
herself to the bath and cleansing herself of the blood on her thighs
and the smell of her brother, and washing away the stains of her
own tears. That morning the household was in chaos over their
mother's disappearance and Yoko herself was drawn and ill with
anxiety, but even so had shown concern over Teruko's puffy face
and obvious discomfort, asking if anything was wrong.

One thing at least was not wrong, and in her distraction and
physical misery Teruko returned every few minutes to the crumb
of comfort provided by the knowledge that her period had arrived
during the night. The cramping pains were much worse than
usual, though, and combined with a dull, hot throbbing in the
depths of her vagina to make it painful even to walk. The other
girls at the Arden Beauty Salon were sympathetic as always when
one of them had the monthlies, and Yukiko – the sensitive one
who always had a bad time and was just coming to the end of
her own period – gave her a couple of the 'Agomensin' tablets she
took herself and swore by. It was hard to tell whether or not the
tablets did any good, but Teruko managed to get through the
morning somehow. Fortunately the wife of the French Ambassador
arrived with a great flurry and occupied the full attention of
the manageress for well over an hour, and then it was time for
the lunch break and the relief of being able to sit down for half
an hour.

The rest of Mrs Wheeler's curlers came out without mishap and
Teruko took extravagant care not to allow the comb to catch in the
fat old woman's hair. Mrs Wheeler was absorbed in a six-month-
old copy of *Vogue*: in spite of its costliness the management of the

salon had a standing order for it at the Kelly & Walsh foreign bookstore in Yokohama, who sent their errand boy to deliver copies to all their Tokyo subscribers as soon as supplies arrived and cleared the Custom House. One of the Arden Beauty Salon's clients, the wife of a German professor of medicine, regularly stole the latest issue until the manageress posted one of the girls near the door towards the end of every visit with instructions to laughingly 'remind' the Frau Professor as she left that she must have slipped the magazine into her shopping bag 'by mistake'.

When Teruko had finished, Mrs Wheeler grimly studied her reflection in the mirror and nodded curtly before embarking on the lengthy and complicated ritual of departure. She had been coming regularly to the salon for almost two years; for the past six months always insisting that Teruko should attend to her. Her husband was a senior official of the Hongkong and Shanghai Bank and they occupied a fine house at Meguro. Teruko's friend Haru found this out from the chauffeur who invariably held the door of the salon open as Mrs Wheeler sailed in and discreetly enquired of the nearest girl what time it would be advisable for him to return for her: seemingly it never occurred to Mrs Wheeler to tell him.

Normally Teruko speculated about the Wheelers as she worked, and even shyly offered a comment in English about the weather: while Mrs Wheeler for her part was usually affable even in her imperiousness. Teruko's numb silence that day seemed to have rubbed off on her client, who stood like a statue while Teruko helped her into her coat and finally swept out with an air of queenly displeasure.

When the door had closed behind the English lady the manageress beckoned Teruko into the cramped little room where the girls kept their coats.

'What happened?' she asked. 'Why was Mrs Wheeler angry with you?'

'It was just one curler,' Teruko said miserably. 'That's all. It caught in her hair as I was taking it out. I'm very sorry.'

'It's not like you to be clumsy. You're not yourself today, Shimada-san.'

'I'm sorry,' Teruko muttered again, hanging her head.

'It's your period, I presume. Well, we all have to put up with that.' The manageress was plumply good-looking, in her late thirties and rumoured by the girls to have been the mistress of a member of the National Diet even before her husband's death from tuberculosis, and to have blossomed greatly since. It was hard to believe that menstruation could ever be more than a minor inconvenience to her.

'It's not usually as bad as this time.'

The older woman looked closely into Teruko's white, drawn face and nodded not unkindly. 'You can sit in here for half an hour,' she decided. 'There's some green tea in the kettle. It's probably still quite warm. Have a cup; it might help your cramps.'

Left to herself Teruko lowered herself gingerly into the one chair in the tiny cubby-hole. It had wooden arms and a stuffed seat, and had been transferred from the salon because of a long tear in its light brown rexine cover, but was initially cool against her soreness and she sat still for a long moment before reaching forward to the tray on the small table beside her and pouring herself a cup of the tepid tea. It tasted insipid but was welcome all the same and it did seem to dull the awful pain in her belly. There was a copy of the February edition of *Women's Club* on the table and Teruko leafed through it in an attempt to take her mind off her misery. The contents page was illustrated with a two-colour drawing of a smart girl in slacks and a boldly-checked, tight-fitting jacket. Her hair was done in bangs over her forehead and she was on skis, pointing a stick at a distant mountain range.

Teruko listlessly leafed through the feature article on winter sports. Before the initial wild, depraved excitement and subsequent degradation and pain of the previous evening she had daydreamed about being invited by Dwight Rogers to go with him to learn to ski somewhere in the Japan Alps – to a resort like Kamikochi perhaps, which she had seen advertised on a poster at Ueno Station. She had even worked out elaborate stratagems to deceive her employer and her family. Slumped in the chair, ravaged and aching, she found that the dream had faded and that she could think of nothing but the shattering experience with Hideo in the upstairs room, her own shameful pleasure in dominating him and then her terror when the tables were turned and she saw the blind, triumphant lust in his eyes and smelt his acrid sweat as he tore and invaded her.

It was unthinkable that anything of the kind should ever happen again ... yet her brother had *kissed* her afterwards and smiled down at her with a kind of tenderness before stumbling out of the room. The thoughts tumbled chaotically round in Teruko's head and she moaned as another spasm of pain shot through her.

She dropped the magazine and clutched at her belly. There were still hours to go before the shop closed and she didn't see how she could possibly get through the day, let alone go home to face a family conference about her mother. Teruko had never got along with her even before she became so strange, and had troubles enough of her own without worrying over what the mad old creature had got up to this time.

## 16. *Vermont, Saturday*
## *25 January, 1986*

'You should have been here two, three months ago,' Dwight Rogers said. 'You wouldn't believe how beautiful the leaves are in the fall.' The old man was settled comfortably in a cane chair in the glassed-in patio, looking out over a garden which seemed to Lesli more like a spacious clearing in a forest, and all the better for that. 'Had it all turfed over seven years ago when Anna passed away. I'm too old to fuss with flower beds and you can't get help these days. I like to watch the squirrels. Pesky, but sort of cute.'

'It's beautiful now,' Lesli said. She had not been in New England for many years and had forgotten the simple pleasure of driving along minor roads through neat towns dominated by white-painted churches.

'Mrs Parsons fixed us some sandwiches when she came in to clean the place up this morning. She's a good soul. Mind, it'll be all over the neighbourhood by now that I'm entertaining a young lady. Are you hungry yet?'

'No. No, thank you. This coffee's fine. I just drove from Rutland, after all. It's good of you to let me come here, Professor Rogers.'

'My pleasure. Lady calls all the way from Japan to make a date, I'm not about to turn her away. Help yourself to a cookie.' Rogers gestured towards the plate between them and took one himself. He looked, Lesli thought, a little like former Secretary of State Dean Acheson, with his military-style moustache and bushy white eyebrows: or Hollywood's idea of a crusty but liberal justice of the Supreme Court. It was an enormous relief to discover that although he leaned heavily on a stick and hobbled about in obvious discomfort, he was lively-minded and even bravely gallant in an old-fashioned way.

'*Nisei*, are you, young lady? Or *sansei*?'

'*Nisei*. My father came to America as a student in the early thirties and my mother joined him a few years later: an arranged marriage of course. It took them a long time to get around to me. My real first name is Harumi, but I picked the name Lesli myself when I first went to grade school and it sort of stuck, even though I spelt it wrong then and still do.'

'Pretty name, Harumi. I never could abide the way so many Japanese girls' names end in "-ko". Though now I think about it I suppose I shouldn't really say that . . . well, well, pay no attention to me, Miss Hoshino.' All at once he looked slightly ill at ease. 'Is "Miss" okay? Or should I say "Mzz" like an old coloured woman? Oh, gee, I just remembered we're not supposed to say "coloured" either . . .' He looked so comically distressed that Lesli couldn't suppress a smile.

'I'd be happy for you to call me Lesli, Professor. But "Miss" is fine if you'd prefer it.' He nodded emphatically. 'I would. I always insisted on addressing my young lady students that way.'

He sipped his coffee and replaced the cup on the saucer with a big hand that trembled and was blotched with liver spots. 'Thank the Lord that's settled. So you're a New Yorker, but you live in Japan now. Right?'

'No, sir, wrong. I did for several years in the seventies when I was assigned to the Tokyo bureau of *Newsworld* magazine. Right now I'm just spending a couple of months there researching the book I told you about when I called you.'

'Book? What book is that, young lady?' Lesli blinked two or three times in dismay. The old man was smiling at her encouragingly, but no longer seemed so alert. Even the cheap excursion ticket she had bought for the trip back to America had cost her over a thousand dollars. Not bad with a week's car rental thrown in, but it was money she could ill afford and it remained to be seen whether the Internal Revenue Service would agree with her that it was tax-deductible. It would be a disaster if Dwight Rogers was in fact about to start misfiring on several cylinders as Charlie Goldfarb had suggested he might. She forced herself to keep calm, and aimed at a note of gentle insistence when she spoke again.

'You remember, sir. When I called you from Tokyo, I told you I'm working on a life of Jiro Shimada. *The* Jiro Shimada. You told me you'd met him in Washington over twenty years ago.' The vaguely benevolent expression was replaced all at once by one of tetchy impatience.

'Shimada. I know a thing or two about Jiro Shimada, let me tell you. Why, I was called in to brief JFK one time when he was due to see him. Sat there right in the next room on the President's instructions listening in while he was in the Oval Office, too. Smart guy, Shimada.' He relaxed again and chuckled.

'Pair of 'em charmed the pants off each other. I didn't take to him, though.' The animation in his eyes dimmed again and Lesli willed him to continue. After a few moments it seemed to work. 'Smart guy. Pierre Salinger took him and me out for a fancy dinner after JFK got through with him. Another thing. He came up to New York, must have been a couple of days later, and talked to some of my area studies majors. Made quite an impression on them, I can tell you. Works at it, I'd say, like this new fellow they have for a premier. And now you're writing a book about him, that right? I don't hear so well on the phone these days, guess I must have missed that bit. Or forgotten. I had the idea in my head you wanted to talk to me about Tokyo in the thirties. I was a newspaperman, you know.'

'I know. It must have been a fascinating period.' Lesli paused to consider tactics. Yoko Nagai had said in as many words that she had known Rogers well in 1936; that he had met the other members of the Shimada family on at least one occasion and that her sister Teruko had – what was the phrase – 'made eyes at him'. Yet he referred to his Washington encounter with Jiro as though it had been the first and only time he had met him.

On the one hand it could mean nothing. The Japanese VIP in Washington in the Kennedy era would certainly not have been physically recognisable to anyone who had once met him casually as a schoolboy at the Meiji Shrine in 1936. Then again, Shimada is not an uncommon Japanese family name, and second sons are often called Jiro. Rogers might not even have known what Yoko's younger brother was called, for Japanese hardly ever use people's given names in conversation. Unless he had got in touch with Yoko again after the war, or had otherwise taken a particular interest in the fortunes of her family in the years following their separation, there was no particular reason why it should ever have entered his head that he was linked in a curious way with the tycoon whose call on the President of the United States was regarded at the time as significant enough for an expert from Columbia University to be called in to provide a preliminary briefing and to act as a concealed witness to the conversation between the two men.

On the other hand Rogers might be dissembling, though Lesli could think of no particular reason why he should. It was worth at least a little probing. 'I guess you were frequently called to the White House as a special adviser, Professor Rogers?'

'Beg your pardon?' The old man shook his head guiltily and hauled himself into a more upright position. 'You were so quiet I believe I got a little drowsy there.'

'I'm sorry. I was thinking about your meeting with Mr Shimada at the White House. President Kennedy consulted you about Japanese affairs pretty often, I suppose?'

Professor Rogers smiled slowly as he shook his head. 'I wouldn't say that. I was on various advisory boards and commissions. Pretty chic they were, too. But just how much of all the paper we generated got as far as the President I shall never know. Not a lot, most likely. I was sat around a table with him a few times, that's all.'

'But he wanted to talk to you personally about the Shimada visit. Why was it so important, Professor?'

'Seemed important at the time, Miss Hoshino.' Rogers was once more wide awake. 'You're too young to remember the fuss and bother over the US-Japan Security Treaty. Caused a lot of argument in Japan right from the first when Premier Kishi raised the idea late in fifty-eight, but we were happy enough on the whole on our side, and it was signed in Washington in January 1960. Eisenhower was set to visit Japan in mid-1960 for a back-slapping celebration, but it backfired on Kishi when he tried to get the treaty ratified by the Diet in Tokyo. Plenty of Japanese were more than dubious about getting into what amounted to a formal alliance with Uncle Sam, not to mention our indefinite military presence in their country. Am I boring you, young lady?'

'No indeed. Please go on.'

'Okay. You asked for it. Well, Kishi was desperate to get it all stashed away tidily before Ike's visit, and he rammed it through a so-called plenary session of the Diet around midnight late in May without the opposition parties knowing what he was about. Well, all hell broke loose; not a lot short of civil uproar, let me tell you. I know, I was there. The student federation organised it, but an awful lot of ordinary folk were good and mad. Not only about the treaty itself, but about the sneaky way Kishi had behaved. Hundreds of thousands of people took to the streets to protest. I never saw anything like it in Japan in all my experience.'

'I was just a girl at the time, but I remember my father talking to my mother about it. And we saw some of it on TV, I think. Eisenhower had to cancel his visit, didn't he?'

Rogers nodded. 'That was when Kishi really lost face, when he had to tell our Ambassador that he couldn't guarantee the President's safety. He nearly got assassinated himself before he flew off to Washington in a hurry, exchanged the instruments of ratification and then went back home and resigned.' He sighed. 'All that was in mid 1960, remember. Six months or so later JFK was in the White House. The situation in Japan had calmed down surprisingly quickly, but the left and the students kept the issue alive right through the sixties. It was still regarded as an exceedingly hot potato in Washington. I don't recall who dreamed up the Shimada meeting, but I know our Ambassador in Tokyo pushed the idea hard.'

'Why?'

'You mean why did JFK agree to see him? Well, you have to realise what a phenomenon Shimada was then. What was he, forty or so. Just a kid by Japanese standards. Already rich beyond imagination, personable and full of ideas. He was being begged to go into politics: touted all over the place as the kind of leader Japan needed in the second half of the twentieth century in place of the old men like Kishi and his cronies.'

Lesli saw that the old gentleman was beginning to sag again. 'I'm tiring you. I'm sorry,' she said with a flicker of genuine remorse.

'No, no. I'm okay. Getting a little hungry is all. Why don't you fetch the platter Mrs Parsons left in the refrigerator, huh? And a couple of cans of beer.'

By the time she returned to the patio with the film-protected plate of sandwiches and the beer, Rogers was sound asleep. She put the tray down quietly, helped herself to a sandwich and sat down to contemplate Yoko's former friend and to reflect on what he had said.

Nearly twenty-four hours after boarding the special express train
'Fuji' at Tokyo Station, Yukichi watched the guard enter his
compartment, stand at the end and salute the passengers before
announcing in a loud voice that the train would shortly arrive at
Kumamoto Station. Only a few of his fellow-passengers had come
so far, leaving the express at the port of Shimonoseki at the
extreme westernmost point of the main island of Honshu and
transferring to the ferry which plied the straits between there and
Moji, with its own rail terminus at the tip of Kyushu. Work had
begun the previous year on the grandiose project to construct a
tunnel to connect the two islands, and along with the other ferry
passengers Yukichi had been urged through a megaphone to
observe and admire the lofty wooden towers above the coffer-
dams which marked the route of the tunnelling, and to praise the
heroic efforts of the men burrowing their way under the sea-bed.
A few had been killed in accidents already: the tunnel would claim
thirty-one victims by the time it was completed.

As the train pulled hissing and panting into the station, Yukichi
dragged himself to his feet and reached up for a small bundle of
belongings wrapped in a knotted silk *furoshiki* square which
constituted the whole of his luggage. He had a sour, metallic taste
in his mouth, his legs felt like lead and his head ached abomin-
ably, but he looked around with a flicker of hope as he clambered
wearily down from the train. Kumamoto Station was a long,
single-storey building of no great distinction; a far cry from the
red-brick splendours of Tokyo or even the lofty dignity of Moji
Station with its two or three motor buses in the forecourt. Yet
Yukichi saw it with a distant pleasure, the feeling that he would at
some stage in the future look back and be glad to have seen the old
place again after so many years.

Several dozen people milled about beyond the ticket barrier,
waiting to greet arriving passengers, and Yukichi scanned their
faces anxiously. His wife was not there. He had not really expected
her to be, but had taken it for granted that one of her relatives

would be there to meet him. He saw nobody he knew and nobody came forward as he pushed his way through the crowd and emerged into the dull chill of the late afternoon, to stand indecisively as his fellow passengers passed by chatting busily to those who had come to meet them.

Ever since he went to Tokyo so many years before, Yukichi had been at pains to suppress the distinctive Kyushu accent of his boyhood, and he was pleased that his children spoke good standard Japanese, but Chie had never attempted to disguise her origins, and he now derived some small comfort from the echoes of her familiar tricks of speech in the homely voices on every side. It was little enough after such an exhausting journey, though, and he stood there forlornly in his loneliness, crushed under the weight of his responsibility for his wife. He had only a vague idea of the whereabouts of the home of Chie's brother where her widowed mother now lived, having at the back of his mind only the half-remembered idea that it was a shop with living quarters attached. The three decrepit taxis which he had seen lined up outside the station had all disappeared. Another train must be due sooner or later, but it could well be a long time before the taxi drivers returned looking for new fares.

He did not at first see the boy who approached hesitantly and stood a few feet away, but then became aware of his intent stare and returned it, at which the boy immediately began to bow repeatedly. He looked to be about twelve, and was wearing a kimono, with a man's trilby hat and rather high wooden *geta* sandals on his feet. When he spoke it was in such a low, timid voice that Yukichi could scarcely understand him. 'Excuse me. I apologise for disturbing you. I am looking for his Honour Shimada. His Honour Yukichi Shimada. There is no excuse for my rudeness . . .'

Recognising his own name at least, Yukichi smiled in weary relief. 'I am Shimada,' he said. 'Thank you for coming to find me.' Then a thought occurred to him. 'You must be my nephew by marriage,' he said, desperately trying to remember the lad's given name.

'I am Masao,' the boy muttered, bowing again. 'Please show your favour to me. My father is busy and my mother can't leave the shop, you see, because Grandmother is very ill. I will take you to our place.' Clearly consumed with embarrassment, he abruptly seized Yukichi's bundle and set off at a great pace, so that Yukichi had to make haste to catch him up.

It was dismally cold, and getting quite dark as Masao led the way across the station forecourt and along a street of shops. One or two had the new-style glass show-windows and were fitted with proper display lighting, but most were open-fronted and lit dimly, if at all, with single dangling low-wattage electric bulbs, gas or oil lamps, their proprietors bundled up in padded outer kimonos and hunched beside clay *hibachi* filled with ash, a few pieces of glowing charcoal on top over which they flexed their mittened hands.

Even in his exhaustion Yukichi noticed how poor and ill-stocked most of the shops were, and how shabbily dressed the few people out shopping. Most were women and the majority of them wore drab kimonos, but a good many were in the *mompei* tunics and leggings of countrywomen; the clothes that women even in the cities were nowadays being encouraged by the authorities to wear as a mark of frugality and dedication to the national interest. It was all a far cry from the bright lights and the perfumed, rouged and lipsticked women of Tokyo's Ginza in their short skirts and high-heeled shoes, their furs, rings and bangles.

After a hundred yards or so Yukichi could not contain his impatience for news. 'And your aunt Chie – my wife – how is she now?' The reply to Yukichi's telegram had simply said 'Chie ill come at once'. Director Nishi was not at all pleased when Yukichi went to him on the Saturday following Chie's disappearance to beg for compassionate leave of absence for several days, but the news of Yoko's agreement to the proposed *o-miai* introduction to his personal assistant mollified him, and serious illness in the family constituted a powerful claim to special treatment, even in the new Japan of the thirties. Yukichi had been able to set out that afternoon.

Masao hung his head as he walked on and said something Yukichi couldn't catch. Yukichi seized him by the arm and forced him to stop. 'Your aunt Chie. How is she?' Masao's eyes flickered everywhere except in the direction of Yukichi's face. 'Speak up, lad. What do you mean, you don't know? She's staying at your house, isn't she?' Yukichi began to shake the boy fiercely as a sick foreboding grew in him, and Masao began to babble apologies again. 'I don't know sir I'm very sorry sir Aunt went away sir she was ill and went away sir there's no excuse Your Honour . . .'

Yukichi slowly released his arm, unaware that he was himself now shaking all over as he confronted Masao. 'She went away? When did she go away?'

'It was in the night, sir. We don't know.' The boy's peaky face crumpled. 'Please come to our place, sir. My mother and father will explain.'

## 18. *Rutland, Vermont,*
## *26 January, 1986*

Lesli turned off the generous hot cascade of the shower, towelled herself thoughtfully and put on the cotton *yukata* which travelled with her everywhere. As motels went, it was a good one, and her room was spacious and comfortably furnished, though at that moment she would have liked to be back in the comparatively more austere surroundings of her study-bedroom at the International House in Tokyo. Switching off the TV, she sat down in front of the make-up mirror and set about doing something with her freshly shampooed hair.

Lesli had never been overly concerned with her appearance, even though in high school and college she had been much sought after by young men bewitched by the combination of her exotic features, perfect skin and gamine charm, and had never thereafter been short of male attention. Now she pulled a face at herself, realising how totally Japanese she looked in her *yukata* against the all-American background of the motel room. It was a thought which rarely came into her consciousness, but as she combed her thick black hair and spotted even more silvery strands than last time, she went on to wonder whether old Professor Rogers had been as struck by the difference between her appearance and her manner as Jiro Shimada claimed to be on each occasion they met.

She was now quite certain that Rogers did not connect the Shimada he met in Washington in sixty-one or two with the family he had known in Tokyo in 1936, and that it wasn't just a question of forgetting. It was obvious to her that the old man drifted away from the subject now and then when he became tired, but also that he was perfectly clear-headed the rest of the time.

She was glad that she had waited around while he napped, and reflected that old people are strange. She must have been staring at him for a good half hour after she walked around the garden, but it didn't seem to disturb him. For her part, Lesli always sensed when somebody was watching her while she slept, and woke up immediately. She sighed and began to apply her simple everyday make-up. It was unfair: men were so lucky. Rogers was a good-looking old gentleman, almost certainly more impressive than he was as a young man, but Lesli could quite see how he must have bowled both the Shimada sisters over. He had delighted *her* when he woke up as bright as a cricket and began to reminisce about life in Tokyo in the thirties. She reminded herself again to get hold of that book he mentioned, Ambassador Grew's memoirs; and to find out more about the master spy, Richard Sorge.

It seemed extraordinary that a communist German journalist could get himself officially attached to his embassy and become not only a crony of the top Nazi diplomats but also in effect a colleague of theirs, and it suddenly occurred to Lesli that she had no idea how close Rogers had been to the American Embassy during his Tokyo years. In those days there was no CIA to lean on working newspapermen and women in the way it did nowadays, as she well knew, but it seemed quite possible that Rogers might have been asked occasionally to do little jobs for the State Department – jobs that the political atmosphere of Japan in the thirties might have put beyond the scope of an accredited diplomat. Indeed, cooperativeness on his part might account for his having later being made a consultant to the Kennedy White House. On the other hand, of course, he might have built up such an academic reputation at Columbia by then that he had simply been hauled in along with all the other egg-heads.

Her face in a reasonably satisfactory state, and her short hair drying rapidly in the centrally heated air, Lesli stood up, stripped off her *yukata* and began to dress for her second call on Dwight Rogers, thinking that the tricky thing was going to be getting him to talk about Yoko and Teruko without his catching on about Jiro. Then she paused while pulling on her tights, thankful as always that her otherwise unremarkable Japanese body was blessed with untypically straight, slender legs. Why was she worrying? What would it matter if the professor did make the connection? It might surprise him, but it would hardly be likely to give him a heart attack. It was the possibility of finding out more about Jiro Shimada that had brought Lesli half-way round the world to see Rogers, after all, and a surprise might jog his memory.

As she glanced at the news section of the enormous Sunday paper she bought on her way through the lobby Lesli smiled to herself, struck again by the way one's current preoccupations always seem to be reflected in the media. Years before, when she thought she was in love with crazy Laszlo Marik and he preferred her friend Judy, there had seemed to be nothing but Hungary, Hungary, Hungary in the papers day after day. Features on Hungarian restaurants in New York, recipes for chicken paprika, rave reviews for art movies made in Budapest . . . the wretched country had haunted her. And now it was Shimada. Shimada's speech to the Japan Society of New York, New York Stock Exchange gives reception for Shimada, Shimada donates funds for extension to the Harvard Yenching Institute and massive purchase of Japanese language materials for the library, and picks up yet another honorary doctorate. It was as if the man was pursuing her. Lesli half expected the next batch of Presidential hopefuls to be reported as begging him for his endorsement. At least Shimada was keeping busy. Lesli was committed after leaving Vermont to a brief duty visit to her parents which would consume a couple of days. Then she would lose a day in flying back to Tokyo, but even so would still be back with the Shimada archives well before the great man would have time to see her again. She was honest enough with herself to realise that she was looking forward to their next meeting quite eagerly.

'No,' Dwight Rogers said firmly. 'I never met the man in my life before that afternoon at the White House. Darn it, Miss, I ought to know. He was almost as famous then as he is now. And I'd been watching his career since pretty soon after take-off. I'd been one of the smart guys who began to notice him at the beginning of the fifties and mention him in articles, you know, "Whither Japan?", that kind of stuff. And I sure wasn't acquainted with him then. I might be getting a little creaky at the joints, but I'm not entirely senile. Far as I know, the man has no kin. I read some place he's a widower like me, and I never heard of any children. You must have gotten ahold of some other Shimada family. It's not such an uncommon name. Or you're mixing it up with Shimazu or Shimizu or something similar.'

Lesli looked at him intently, suppressing her urge to shake the old man as he sat there in apparent contentment. In contrast to the occasional vagueness and drowsiness of the previous day, Rogers seemed to be feeling very spry, and not in the least impressed by her claim to have met Jiro Shimada's sister. His reaction of slightly tetchy disbelief and his insistence that he had met Shimada for the first time at the Kennedy White House were not only frustrating but seemed positively unkind to Lesli when she remembered how carefully she had been considering his feelings before raising the matter.

'Let me try putting it another way, Professor Rogers. May I?' The white bristles of his eyebrows stuck out like frosted twigs from a rocky outcrop high on the slopes of his face as he wrinkled his forehead and nodded at her sternly.

'You must have had a very wide circle of Japanese acquaintances when you were in Tokyo before the war.'

Another nod. 'Pretty wide, I'd say. You should know how it is in the newspaper business.'

Lesli held her breath for several seconds and then came out with it. 'Are you quite sure you don't recall any Shimada among them? I think you may have met two sisters of that name. One was called Teruko and the other –'

His forearm came up as though in defence and trembled as he lowered his head into his hand and closed his eyes. His colour looked bad and Lesli started forward in alarm, but Rogers soon lowered his arm, and after taking several deep breaths opened his eyes again.

'Yoko. Teruko and Yoko Shimada. I just don't believe it,' he murmured at last as though to himself.

'Are you feeling okay, sir?'

'Uh huh.' He waved a hand at her absently. 'Ghosts. You made me see ghosts. I'm okay.'

'So you *were* acquainted with two girls called Teruko and Yoko Shimada back in the thirties?'

'Yes. I was. And you're telling me they have some connection with Jiro Shimada? That's not possible.'

He still looked pale and shaken and Lesli hated herself for pressing him. She waited for some time until she sensed that he had himself under control again. 'I'm pretty sure I'm right, sir. The lady I met is called Yoko and her former name was Shimada. Forgive me if I seem to be intruding into personal matters, but . . . I think she's the Yoko you knew.'

The old man stared at Lesli but it was as if he did not see her, and when he spoke there was much tenderness in his voice. 'Yoko. After all these years.' There was a long silence before he began to speak again. 'American President Lines. The *President Cleveland*. I could hardly force myself up that gangway at Yokohama. We had this farewell lunch, you see. I'd gotten really slewed the previous night with some of the fellows at the Press Club. My last night.' Rogers seemed not to notice the tear that welled up in the corner of one eye and trickled down his leathery cheek. 'But young Sam – did I tell you about Sam? He was the office boy. Crazy kid. And old Eguchi-san. My staff. The bureau personnel, the New York office used to call 'em. There they were when I arrived at the pier. And there was Yoko.'

He was now weeping openly, and without a word Lesli rummaged in her bag and found a Kleenex tissue. When she put it into his hand he dabbed ineffectually at his eyes but then disregarded it as he continued. 'Terrible. I'd said my goodbyes before going to meet the boys at the Press Club and made her promise not to see me off. Same thing with the other two. No stopping the Japanese though, is there?'

The old man had dropped the Kleenex, but produced a huge old-fashioned handkerchief from his voluminous trousers and blew his nose violently. 'Chinese. There was too much time, you see? Couldn't figure letting the damn fools stand there for a couple of hours till we sailed. And I knew they wouldn't leave until the ship did. The *President Cleveland*, it was. So we had this Chinese meal at the first place we found in walking distance. Didn't taste a thing. Sam ate most of it. And Yoko's eyes on me all the time. So quiet. And the poor kid going through hell at home, on top of whatever she may have felt about me.' Two squirrels had boldly approached the glassed-in patio and he turned towards them with a half smile. He seemed to have forgotten all about Lesli and to be talking to himself.

'Went through customs and passport control and dragged myself up that gang-plank somehow. Found my cabin, then back up on deck. There they were. Yoko still with the others, but a little apart. Steward passing out those coloured paper streamers . . . insisted I should take a couple. Red and blue, they were. Sam caught them, handed the blue one to Yoko. Then the pull on them as the ship began to move. Sam held on until his broke, but Yoko just bowed and let go her end.'

Roger's voice had become choked and unsteady, and Lesli hardly dared to breathe for fear that she would stop him. As it was he gave a deep, shuddering sigh and paused for a very long time before looking directly and consciously at her again, the faded old eyes full of remembered pain. 'I knew she'd watch the ship clear out of sight. Couldn't take it. Know what I did? This'll probably sound crazy to you, but I went and took a bath. The bathroom had no porthole, and I switched off the light and just lay there in the hot water in pitch darkness for the Lord knows how long, crying my eyes out. Is that any way for a grown man to behave?'

Lesli reached out and took his hand. 'You must have loved her very much,' she said quietly.

'I guess I did. Yes. And she was never wholly out of my mind in all my waking hours for months afterwards. It was hard to imagine what she must have been going through on account of her brother. In my case I reckon it was mostly self-pity and just plain missing her. Once or twice I came darned close to dropping everything, quitting my job and going back to Japan to find her and marry her. But what I started out to say was that eventually I could think about her without tying myself in knots. I wrote to her once. A stupid letter. She never replied, unless you count a Christmas card she sent me that first year. Lord knows where she found it. Nothing after that, and by then it didn't hurt so much. And then before any of us knew what had happened, it was the war. I wondered about her and Teruko now and then, but until you mentioned her name I guess I hadn't thought about Yoko at all for years now, may the good Lord forgive me. How can an obsession just evaporate like that?'

'People grow. People change. The world moves on. Your ways separated.' Lesli realised that there was nothing sensible she could say. Her words were just comforting noises, but they seemed to help all the same; he reached out with his other hand and patted hers. She was emboldened to try another question. 'Professor Rogers, what did you mean about her brother? Her brother Hideo? He was an army officer, wasn't he?'

Rogers ignored the question. 'You've really met Yoko? Truly? Tell me about her, Miss Hoshino. She's well? Why, she must be over seventy – it's hard to credit. She was so beautiful when she was young, even though she never made very much of herself. Not like her sister Teruko. Yoko was a little taller than most Japanese girls of her generation, and held herself like a queen. Solemn, she was, but when she smiled it lit up the whole room. She had these gentle eyes, and a terrible sense of responsibility, as though she had to take care of the whole world.' Tears were again welling up in the old man's eyes, and Lesli knew that the questions jostling for priority in her mind would have to wait. She owed it to Dwight Rogers to tell him first about Yoko.

'Well, she's living in a pretty little house in Kamakura. She's a widow, and her married name is Nagai. She's an emeritus professor at Ochanomizu Women's University and still does a little part-time teaching even now. She's very vigorous for her age, and . . .'

## 19. *Monday 27 January, 1936*

'She came here, yes,' the master potter said, absent-mindedly picking tendrils of clay from behind his fingernails. His face gave the impression of being as deeply stained as his hands, so that no amount of soap could ever remove the ingrained traces of his craft. The sparse, tangled hairs of his wispy beard and the faded blue kimono he wore gave him the look of a Chinese sage in an old scroll painting, and he had only a few discoloured teeth left in his mouth. Yet Yukichi's brother-in-law and his wife had said that he was about Yukichi's own age, and that he had known Chie as a girl, when she used to haunt the pottery in the days of the old master. 'The day before yesterday. We had a long talk. I don't know where she might be now, though. I'm sorry.'

'I apologise for troubling you with such matters, Master,' Yukichi said humbly. 'If I might just ask, though . . . how did she seem when you saw her?' It was deeply embarrassing for him to have to discuss his wife's condition with a stranger: such matters should be kept within the family. It was clear to him after a tense, miserable evening and a wretched night's sleep in the cramped living room behind the little haberdashery shop that he would get little help from his relatives by marriage, though. He had been obliged to share the room with Chie's brother, his wife and the boy Masao: there was another small room, but this was given over to the sick old woman, his mother-in-law. He had not seen her since his wedding day, had never spoken to her and now never would, for she was almost blind and muttered to herself day and night. Yukichi's own mother was dead and he had no close family connections of his own left in Kumamoto, but he had no intention of passing another night under Chie's brother's roof: he would go to an inn unless it seemed more sensible to set off again on the long journey back to Tokyo.

'You see, Master, her brother and his wife were able to tell me very little. It seems that my wife arrived at her place in . . . a state of confusion, and would say almost nothing to them. It was really a guess on their part that my wife might have come here. Is there anywhere else near here that she might have gone?'

The potter looked at Yukichi. 'I am very sorry,' he said again. 'I wish I could help you. I can only say that when she first came here Chie-san seemed to be ill and unhappy, but after we had talked for a while she became more calm. I didn't recognise her at first, and I am sure that she thought I was my father, but then I remembered the little girl who used to come here so often when I was still his student and before he adopted me as his son and successor. And she remembered me too, and began to laugh and talk about the old days. It was very moving if I may say so: almost as though she were reliving them.'

Yukichi nodded. 'She was so happy here always. It was the place she used to talk about more often than any other, before . . . before she became ill. I think that even if her relatives had not suggested it I should have come here in search of her.' He sighed. 'But it seems that I'm too late. All the same, I must thank you with all my heart for talking to her.'

He made the customary preliminary movements with a view to taking his leave, but the potter reached out and touched his sleeve. 'Don't go yet,' he said. 'Chie-san talked continually about somebody called the Mother. I assumed at first that she meant her own mother, but –'

'No. It has to do with religion. My wife joined Tenrikyo some time ago.'

'Ah, that would be it. I've heard of Tenrikyo, of course. I don't know of any branch around here, though. You could try asking the priest at the main Shinto shrine, I suppose. Tenrikyo is a kind of Shinto, isn't it?'

'I think so,' Yukichi said awkwardly. The sect to which Chie belonged was so designated by the government, but from its earliest days had seemed to attract trouble to itself, and Yukichi knew well enough that it was still suspect, and tolerated only under the close supervision of the official Bureau of Shrines. 'Well, I suppose Chie-san might have gone to visit the nearest Tenrikyo shrine. What do you think?'

Yukichi rubbed his eyes, his shoulders sagging. There might well be something in what the potter said, but the prospect of trailing round the Kumamoto area looking for congregations of the Tenrikyo faithful to whom his wife might have attached herself filled him with a sense of exhausted hopelessness.

'I have another idea,' the potter said suddenly, and started to get up, then looked at Yukichi dubiously. 'Would you come with me? It isn't far. I . . . well, we ought to go and look, I think.' All at once his kindly serenity seemed to have been replaced by an air of unease, and he rose quickly and led the way to the entrance to the old wooden house, slipping into his wooden *geta* sandals at the entrance way and waiting while Yukichi tied the laces of his western-style shoes. Then he headed for a stone-flagged path which led through a bamboo grove. The bamboos were fully mature, their stems as thick as a man's arm, their matt, silvery greyish-green mysteriously beautiful against the high blue of the winter sky. There had been a hard frost overnight, which still sparkled on the moss between the bamboos where it was dappled by the sunlight which penetrated the grove.

After a few hundred yards the bamboos yielded to cypress trees, and the pathway degenerated into a rough, stony, uphill track. The potter paused in a patch of sunlight and caught Yukichi's eye. 'Do you know about the cave?' Yukichi shook his head. 'I'm taking you to it. Chie-san kept referring to it the other day, and it just occurred to me that . . .' There was no need for him to say more, and he hurried on again as Yukichi tightened his lips and stumbled forward with a new sense of urgency.

The potter's wooden *geta* clattered on the stones of the pathway, and Yukichi's own shoes crunched and slithered as he blundered on, but otherwise it was very quiet there on the hillside, and before long Yukichi could hear the sound of water cascading from a height. The two men were in full sunshine now, and the chill which had seemed to grip Yukichi's very bones from the moment of his arrival in Kumamoto the previous afternoon had passed off. Instead he was conscious of a slime of sweat all over his body, and it was almost a relief when they turned sharply and passed into the shade again.

The modest waterfall was directly ahead of them, in a fold of the mountainside, and the pathway had been widened to form an area roughly paved with large stones, big enough for two or three people to stand in. The water poured down no more than twenty feet or so from a crevice in the rocks, and in a quantity amounting to an endless bucketful, cascading into a pool a few feet across, at one side of which stood a roughly-carved image of the bodhisatva Jizo, which like most such statues had round its neck several little aprons of red material, like babies' bibs. Yukichi found himself wondering whether they had been placed there by mothers giving thanks for the recovery of their children from illness, or more likely in entreaty that Jizo should take their souls under his protection after their death: it suddenly seemed important to know.

A narrow path extended beyond the Jizo image and the potter sidled along it, momentarily dampened by the spray, and then disappeared. Yukichi scarcely had time to register the fact before he was back, brushing drops of spray from his kimono and shaking his head in mingled disappointment and relief. 'She isn't there,' he said. 'Come and see.'

The same two reactions contended in Yukichi's consciousness as he edged behind the curtain of water after the potter and found himself at the entrance to a fair-sized cave. The last words his companion had spoken previously had convinced him that they would find Chie in the cave, and that she would be dead. Yukichi was almost, but not quite, ready to admit to himself that it would be for the best if she were. Then quite unexpectedly his thoughts about her were suppressed as for the first time in many years a vision of Fujiko rose up unbidden in his imagination and he stood stock still, stunned by its impact.

Yukichi had never thought of himself as having been in love with any woman, and certainly not with his wife. In his university days there had been this girl, though, met at the house of his patron, Lafcadio Hearn. The old professor had long since become disillusioned with the Japan he had once loved and irrevocably committed himself to, but even in his bitterness never ceased to take a kindly interest in the young man from Kumamoto whom he had picked out as a boy.

Graduation was in sight for Yukichi when Hearn was made briefly happy again by an invitation to deliver a series of lectures at Cornell University and began to work on *Japan: An Interpretation*, which he completed but did not live long enough to take to America. Yukichi's last memories of the old man were pleasant; of weekend visits, of Indian tea with milk and sugar, of his own halting English and the smell of the professor's tobacco. Naive as he was in those days, Yukichi sensed nevertheless that his first encounter at the Hearns's house near Tokyo Imperial University with the brilliant medical student Fujiko was no accident, and for many weeks she dazzled him with her sophistication and her beauty. Even after several years in Tokyo he was still pleasantly disturbed by the sight of young women in western dress, and almost fainted with shocked delight on the first occasion when Fujiko abruptly kissed him and deliberately drew his hand to her breast. She could be kind, too, and for a time appointed herself his instructor in Tokyo ways, helping him to improve his appearance and his manner of speaking, and endowing him with a certain *savoir faire* which served the young provincial well as the years went by. Yet her exotic glamour intimidated as much as it attracted him, and in any case his betrothal to Chie presented itself to him as an insuperable obstacle to serious consideration of the possibility of marriage to Fujiko. After a while Fujiko grew bored with his timidity, turned to smarter young men and began to distance herself from Yukichi. Although he continued to trail after her rather forlornly for some time longer, their ways diverged after a few months and they saw no more of each other.

Tears pricked at Yukichi's eyes and he shook himself back into the present, embarrassed by the awareness that the potter was looking at him intently. In spite of the gloom it was possible to see that the back wall of the cave was something like eight feet away from the entrance and that its roof was about as high, though it was no more than five feet or so across at its widest part. Although the curtain of water which concealed it was so close, the air in the cave smelt dry and clean, and the ashes of a small fire which someone had built near the entrance were soft and powdery. The cave was empty except for a rickety wooden chair, which creaked as the potter gave it a gentle push.

'People occasionally come here and stand under the waterfall as a spiritual discipline while reciting Buddhist *sutras*,' he said. 'They probably leave their clothes in here to keep them dry.' He looked around as though getting ready to leave, but then moved to the rear of the cave and scrutinised the tumbled rock closely.

'There must be a crevice of some kind somewhere,' he said as he fumbled about. 'Chie-san made a confession to me, you see. It seems that when she was a girl she salvaged a few pots my father was dissatisfied with and threw out, and hid them here. I never thought to ask her what she did with them later. If she still has them they'd be worth a lot of money now . . . Ah! I hope there isn't a snake asleep in here.' He had found a small opening in the cave wall and slid his arm into it as Yukichi looked on. 'It feels quite spacious inside. A sort of natural cupboard. Empty though . . . wait a minute.' Yukichi heard a dull clinking sound as the potter withdrew something from the crevice and carried it to the better light of the cave entrance.

It was a small, shallow bowl decorated with a delicate grey-green bamboo design against the rich blue of the glaze, and the potter looked at it with tenderness as he turned it this way and that. 'I suppose I can see why he threw it away,' he murmured. 'But the fault is really so unimportant . . . Chie-san did well to preserve it.' Then he held the beautiful little object out to Yukichi. 'Take it, Shimada-san,' he said peremptorily. 'Give it back to her when you find her. And give her my thanks.'

## 20. *Friday 31 January, 1936*

It was a raw evening, with a wind that chilled the skin of the face like ice-water, and Hideo hunched himself into his greatcoat as he rounded the corner for the third time, checked that there was nobody else about in the quiet residential street and then again walked the length of the tile-capped and plastered wall behind which sheltered the private residence of the Lord Keeper of the Privy Seal. He slowed down as he passed the high wooden gates of the main entrance with their built-in wicket door, remembering General Mazaki's anecdote about the Saito family tradition of placing only one New Year pine, plum and bamboo decoration outside instead of the usual pair. It was obvious to Hideo that neither the wall nor the gateway would present any difficulty for him and his supporting team, and although no doubt police patrols kept a regular eye on the place it had no permanent guard. In this respect at least Hideo was conscious of his good fortune: armed police protected the Prime Minister's imposing western-style official residence round the clock.

Hideo could see little of the house itself, for like most residences of the well-to-do it was effectively concealed from the view of casual passers-by, only the roof and part of the upper storey being visible from the roadway. He had concluded that he could do no more under cover of darkness and was about to wind up his reconnaissance when he heard the crunch of wooden *geta* on the gravel behind the gates, followed by the dull rattle of metal against wood as somebody unbolted them. Thinking quickly, Hideo sprinted a few yards and then turned and began to walk back past the gates as one of them was opened, pausing as he met the wide-eyed and untroubled gaze of a maidservant carrying a paper lantern which illuminated little more than her own face as the candle flame swayed with her movements. She could hardly have been more than fourteen or fifteen, and had the apple-red cheeks of the country girl. She wore a simple kimono, the sleeves caught back with long tapes tied around her body to bare her arms.

The girl peered at Hideo without alarm, then held the lantern up to get a better look at him. 'Oh. Sorry, sir. I thought you was the policeman. It was your hat, see. Nasty cold night – I shall be glad to get back inside, I can tell you.' Although he could barely understand her, Hideo recognised her accent at once. The child was from the northern part of the main island: her employer came from there, and she no doubt belonged to one of the families who worked the ancestral Saito estates.

'No, I just happened to be passing,' he said, trying to strike a note of patronising affability appropriate for an army officer addressing a pretty enough young skivvy. 'Why should you be expecting to see a policeman, if it comes to that?'

The girl shrugged, put the lantern down and began to open the gate wide. 'Cause Master's on his way, that's why. They always rings up on the telephone when they sees his motor-car. We got a telephone here.' The pride in her voice was unmistakeable. 'And one of them generally nips round the back way on his bicycle and gets here first to see Master inside safe and sound. Told you so, here he comes now.'

Hideo glanced in the direction in which she was looking, to see the dim beam of a bicycle headlight in the distance wobbling towards them. It seemed well worth while to wait and see what happened next. 'Why all the fuss?' he asked in a casual tone which proved unexpectedly difficult to sustain. 'Who is your master, then?'

'Why, he's the Viscount,' she said importantly, then stumbled a little over his resounding new title. 'The Lord Keeper of the, um, Per-Privy Seal.'

'Oh, really? Well, I'd probably better be on my way, then,' Hideo was saying when the policeman was upon them, looking at Hideo with dark suspicion as he dismounted carefully from his bicycle, propped it against the wall and then saluted him with evident reluctance. Hideo returned the salute with careful courtesy. The patrolman was about his own age, but shorter and burlier, and like the servant girl he had a rustic look about his blunt features. 'So it's you again, is it?' the girl said cheekily to the new arrival. 'I was just saying to this here gentleman that if he was to hang about for a minute he'd be able to see Master.'

'You get that other gate open, my girl, and not so much gab,' the policeman said sternly. 'I can hear the car.'

'I just happened to be passing,' Hideo said to him, too, as the maid set her lantern down on the gravel and pushed open the other gate. 'Had no idea the Lord President lives here. It will be interesting to see what he looks like.'

The policeman still looked distinctly put out. 'Better stand well back, sir,' he said grudgingly. 'Wouldn't do to have a crowd in his way.' The sound of the approaching car was now clearly audible, and as Hideo stepped back obediently the road was lit up by its headlights as it rounded the corner.

Now that the gates stood wide open the house was in clear view. The sliding front door was open and light spilled out on to a gravelled forecourt just about big enough to accommodate a car. As Hideo watched, an old lady came from inside the house and knelt in the raised part of the porch: it must be the Viscountess Saito preparing to welcome her husband home. Then the car had arrived and was sweeping through the gates, and Hideo came to attention and snapped into a salute, remaining rigidly in position until the engine was switched off and he heard the car door being opened.

The passenger in the back seat had been virtually invisible as the car had passed him, but as he lowered his arm to his side Hideo could see clearly that it was the policeman who had opened the door. He was now saluting in his turn as a shiny shoe, white spat and striped trouser leg were extended from the car and an old gentleman slowly worked himself out, nodding to the policeman and to the chauffeur who had sprinted round the back and was handing him a walking-stick. Admiral Saito was well muffled up in a long black overcoat, a white silk scarf at his throat and a trilby hat wedged squarely on his head, and Hideo scarcely saw his features. In any case he had by sheer good fortune learned much more than he could have hoped to do that evening, and it was time to be on his way. He decided that the gods were with him and that he wouldn't be late if he made haste.

At the end of the road he turned back for a last look. The main gates were closed again but the little wicket was open, and the paper lantern which had evidently been left inside cast enough light through the opening for Hideo to make out the figures of the maidservant and the policeman. Even at a distance it was perfectly obvious that they were furtively fumbling each other, and Hideo smiled to himself as he made himself scarce. It was a relief to realise that the policeman had not been suspicious of him after all, or at least not in relation to Admiral Saito's security. He had simply been put out at the thought that his little girl-friend might have found herself another male acquaintance. It accounted for the chit's cheeky forwardness, too.

Hideo preened himself as he quickened his step and headed for the main road. He wouldn't waste his time over an empty-headed servant girl, but had no doubt whatever that as an officer with an Imperial commission he was a much more glamorous prospect than a patrolling policeman for all the awe and fear in which the police were held by citizens who knew what was good for them. He savoured the thought that he could have bowled the girl over in a matter of minutes if he had cared to take the trouble.

As he turned into the main road Hideo saw a one-yen taxicab approaching. He possessed a wrist watch but it was cheap and unreliable, and though he could probably have got to his destination in time by tram it would be intolerable to be late. In the glow of his self-satisfaction and confidence he decided to splurge and hailed the cab; even after paying the fare he would still have enough money left for what he had in mind. After giving his instructions to the driver who was delighted to acquire a fare headed for the Ginza at that time of the evening, Hideo sank back into the comfortable rear seat with a lordly sense of satisfaction, mingled with burgeoning excitement.

The sight of the Lord Keeper had not intimidated him after all, and though the old gentleman had looked harmless enough Hideo could already feel a satisfactory sense of indignation rising in him at the thought that this decrepit aristocrat was in a position to whisper poisonous advice directly into His Majesty's ear, and to keep from access to the Throne those like Generals Mazaki and Araki whose expert and disinterested guidance alone could ensure the security and prosperity of the Empire and the wellbeing of the people. The sick feeling of apprehension which had seized him every time he thought about his assignment had, he decided, gone for good. The time had come to think more specifically and calmly about ways and means, and he had made an excellent start that evening.

As the taxi entered the Ginza Hideo compared his watch with the big clock on the Mazda Building. It was a minute or two to eight, and he came to a quick decision. 'When we get to the Arden Beauty Salon I want you to wait a few minutes. We're picking up a lady, then I want you to take us to, er, just beyond Ueno.' He was too embarrassed to say the word 'Yoshiwara', and could easily give more detailed instructions when they were nearer.

'It'll cost you another yen,' the driver said.

'This is a one-yen taxi,' Hideo said hotly. 'You know perfectly well that you're supposed to go anywhere in the metropolitan area for that. I can report you to the police if you refuse.'

The driver was a wizened, elderly man who made no reply until he drew up in front of the salon. Then he climbed out, walked round and opened the passenger door. 'You booked me to bring you to the Ginza. I wrote it on my work sheet. And here we are. One yen, please.'

In his fury Hideo lunged out of the cab and nearly struck him for his insolence, but then realised that one or two passers-by were pausing and looking curiously in their direction, and somehow regained precarious control of his temper. His hand was shaking as he pushed a one-yen note at the cabbie, and he turned aside without looking at him again and stared at the window of the jewellery shop next door until he heard the cab drive away.

Hideo was still furious when his sister emerged from the beauty salon a few minutes later, but his anger was by then cold and settled, and he had no intention of being crossed again. It was the first time they had met since he had kissed her and stumbled out of her room just over a week earlier, and Teruko shrank back when she saw him. 'What are you doing here?' she faltered.

Hideo reached out and grabbed her by the arm. 'I have to be back by midnight,' he said. 'How much money have you got on you? I need two or three yen. I'll pay you back.' Without waiting for her reply he waved across the road at the first cab in line at the taxi-rank and pointed in the direction they needed to go, bundling Teruko inside as soon as the taxi drew up beside them.

This time there was no embarrassment. 'Yoshiwara,' he snapped. 'An inn called Suisen-ro near the Kikusui-ya.' Teruko opened her mouth to make a horrified protest, then sank back trembling as she saw the cold glitter in her brother's eyes. 'Be quiet.' He mouthed the words at her without a sound, and Teruko for her part was too shocked and terrified to speak, but sat rigid and immobile as the taxi-driver caught Hideo's eye in the rear-view mirror and slowly and deliberately winked at him. She had never heard of a Daffodil Inn but could easily guess that it was one of the places in the Yoshiwara that rented out rooms by the hour with no questions asked: her friend Haru had boasted about going to them sometimes with a student from Keio University.

The scene in Yoko's and her room flashed back into her mind and she closed her eyes and hung her head in shame and horror as the taxi gathered speed. What was happening to her was frightful, unbelievable; and the man beside her was a menacing stranger, not the big brother she had known all her life.

The worst thing of all was that she gradually became sickeningly aware that she would not resist Hideo when they arrived at the inn. The worm of lust was uncurling in her belly, and her breathing began to quicken with the realisation that she wanted it all to happen again.

## 21. *Wednesday 29 January, 1986*

Lesli reached for her carry-on holdall gratefully as her flight was announced at last, delighted to be leaving the bustling impersonality of Los Angeles International Airport and to be on the last lap of the return journey to Japan. She never minded being alone, but felt most vulnerable where the crowds were thickest. The tedious wait between planes hadn't been so bad once she had managed to free herself from the attentions of two relentlessly smiling Moonies and subsequently a bearded follower of Bhagwan, and found her way to a deserted departure gate where she could sit and look through her notes in relative peace.

She was now very eager indeed to get back to Japan. Her second conversation with Dwight Rogers had left her twitching with frustration, and determined to find out what the crafty old man had kept from her. She could try to tease it out of Yoko, or else ask for Charlie Goldfarb's help after all, reluctant though she was to do so. She had been over her notes of the conversations with Rogers again and again, but found no other reference to Hideo, however oblique, in anything he had said. What the old man *had* told her was fascinating enough by any reckoning, and Lesli found it hard to decide who she felt the more sorry for, poor silly Teruko with her head full of romance and Hollywood, or big sister Yoko with the weight of the world on her shoulders, a crazy mother and an elder brother in deep trouble of some unknown kind. It had been nothing short of infuriating when Professor Rogers sighed and hummed and hawed and finally said that if Yoko hadn't seen fit to tell her about the matter, he must respect her confidence.

At least Lesli was now convinced that he really hadn't had the least idea that Jiro was Yoko's younger brother. Coming to terms with the revelation had certainly shaken him, and Lesli hoped that he would in fact write her the letter he had promised to put together, after getting his thoughts straightened out, as he put it. Meantime she should be grateful to the old gentleman for what he had given her. All that first-hand stuff about the Tokyo of the thirties was pure gold-dust . . . Lesli would have given a lot to be able to have just one day's worth of time travel and wander about the city as it had been half a century before, with Shinjuku still more or less a suburb and only just starting to be built up. It would be fascinating to see what used to stand where the Shimada Trading Corporation tower block now rose up, for a start.

Lesli found it hard to understand her own parents' deep-seated reluctance to talk about prewar Japan, and thought it sad that she had been given a vivid picture of the sort of things they must remember perfectly well by an old American professor and one-time newspaperman rather than by her own mother and father. They had made it pretty clear that they thought Lesli was wasting her time on the Shimada biography, and obviously had not the slightest interest in what might have happened to his army officer brother.

Lesli settled into her seat with a feeling of optimism: it looked as though the economy class would be no more than half full, and that she would be able to spread herself over at least two seats, if not three. So, the trip had cost a week of her life and between twelve and thirteen hundred dollars. The first thing Charlie would be bound to ask was whether the exercise had been cost-effective. Lesli had no doubt in her mind that it had. She might not be going back to Tokyo with many answers, but had been able to put together an impressive list of interesting questions to ask and lines of enquiry to pursue. The only problem was that most of them would sooner or later have to be raised with Jiro Shimada himself, and Lesli knew that the prospect scared her at least as much as it excited her. She fastened her seat belt and looked out at the smog-laden sky as the plane began to move slowly backwards under tow.

'Come in!' By the sound of his response to her timid tap at his door, Mr Nagai was not allowing his troubles to disturb his habitual good humour, and when Yoko opened it and entered his room in the History Department, the broad smile which lit up his face as he saw who it was almost made her forget her own, and the solemn purpose of her unprecedented visit. 'Miss Shimada! What a delightful surprise! Come in, come in and have a seat.'

It would have been a grim, ill-lit cell of a room had it not been for the books which occupied most of one wall and lay about in piles over much of the floor, leaving a narrow ravine providing access to Nagai's littered desk and the one spare upright chair available for a visitor. Even this had a stack of papers on it, and Nagai picked them up and looked around him with a comical expression of despair before balancing them precariously on top of the pile of books nearest him on the floor.

'I'm having a tidy up,' he explained to Yoko's bafflement. 'I'm expecting a much less welcome visitor before long, you see, even though even they are still a bit hesitant about coming on to a university campus.' A cold hand clutched at her stomach as she took in what he said, and Nagai grinned briefly, his eyes not involved this time.

'I see you've guessed who I mean. Yes, our friends from the Dangerous Thoughts department of the police. They're interested in my reading matter, it seems. Do sit down, Miss Shimada. Oh dear, though, they're rather ignorant fellows, I'm afraid. They've already been to my lodgings while I wasn't there, looking for communist literature. My poor landlady had no option but to let them in, and do you know what? They ignored Engels but took away my Dostoevsky! Well, of course I went down to the police station and demanded it back. The inspector wasn't a bad chap at all actually, gave it to me straight away and laughed it off. Said his men automatically assumed that any author with a name ending in "-sky" was a communist, but weren't too good at recognising even other Russian names, let alone other foreigners.'

The grin was relaxed and whole-hearted again, and terrified as she was for him, Yoko couldn't help smiling too. 'Anyway, I have a feeling my new friend the inspector may drop in here for a look round, so . . . most of these books belong to the library anyway, as I'm sure you already suspect. I expect you'll be glad to have them back.'

'They wouldn't find anything . . . like that . . . here anyway, would they?' Yoko asked nervously. She had heard of Engels in connection with Karl Marx, but had no idea what inflammatory literature he might have produced. It seemed most unlikely that they would have any examples of his work in the Waseda University library, at least.

'No Dostoevsky, I'm sure,' Nagai said airily, turning to the shelves behind him and reaching down a dusty volume. 'Engels, definitely. Here you are, *The Origin of the Family, Private Property and the State.* Seditious stuff. You'd better have it back, then they can arrest your Director instead of me.'

Yoko took the book gingerly and with extreme reluctance, as though expecting it to burn her. It was indeed clearly marked as library property and she gazed at it in horror until Nagai leaned over and gently took it from her again. 'Don't worry,' he said quietly. 'I'll return it myself later on.' To her great embarrassment, tears suddenly welled up in Yoko's eyes, and one trickled slowly down her cheek as she fumbled for a handkerchief.

Nagai turned away tactfully and looked out of the small, grimy window. He coughed once, and then spoke wihout looking at her. 'Please don't worry about me, Miss Shimada. It's silly of me to try to pass it off as a joke, I know, but I really don't have anything to hide, nor the least trace of a guilty conscience. Japan still has a parliamentary government, and a lot of us expect the democrats to do rather well in the elections this month. I'm sure we'll be able to go on listening to Tchaikovsky at our Club recitals. Professor Minobe won't be in disgrace much longer, and his unimportant supporters like me won't be of the slightest interest to the authorities.'

'But I do worry about you,' Yoko whispered. 'I . . . I care about you, Nagai-*sensei*.' The words slipped out of her mouth quite unintentionally, and she flushed scarlet with horror as the lecturer looked at her fixedly, then scrubbed at her eyes with the handkerchief to avoid his gaze.

'Why did you come to see me, Miss Shimada?' he asked at last. 'I'm deeply honoured by what you have just said, but I think you have other things on your mind. Isn't that so?' Eyes closed, Yoko nodded repeatedly, grateful to him for giving her the chance to start again even though he now knew she loved him, and was much too perceptive to be confused by what she had to say.

Nagai waited patiently for Yoko to compose herself, and sat back quietly when she at last began to speak. 'I am so sorry to disturb you in this way,' she began, and he waved the apology away, gently dismissive. 'I came to say that I won't be at the next meeting of the Club, and that I shall probably not be attending any more. I have had to ask for special leave for a time. My mother is ill, and I have to take care of her. I may have to resign from my job in the library.'

Yoko's voice was now fairly calm and Nagai looked at her in silence, his own embarrassment over her earlier outburst mingled with admiration for her. He liked her, and was attracted by the air of almost childlike solemnity about her even when she was obviously deeply happy, transported by music which always gave him pleasure but seldom touched his emotions. She was beautiful, too, with unusually large eyes beneath the simple fringe of hair which curtained her forehead and contributed to the effect she gave of being a grave and responsible child, seemingly unaware that she inhabited the generous body of a mature woman.

That day Yoko was wearing a dreary blue knitted jumper and cardigan over a plain woollen skirt: Nagai was something of a ladies' man and it was clear to him that the shy librarian cared little about clothes and had no fashion sense; but he had never seen her wearing make-up before, and was touched to notice that she had put a trace of rouge on her cheeks and reddened her lips, obviously for his benefit. He was perfectly well aware that he had been enjoying flirting with her delicately for several months, and was now disconcerted to realise how much the prospect of her absence and possible final departure from the university upset him. 'I am so sorry,' he said. 'I shall miss you very much.'

Silence fell, and Yoko knew that it was for her to choose whether to make her farewells and leave Mr Nagai's room, or to protract the painful pleasure of being in his company by volunteering more about her mother. The etiquette of conversation about illness in a family was delicate: the outsider could and should express sympathy, as Mr Nagai had very properly done, but it was not for him to put questions about the nature of the illness, and there was nothing more he could say without encouragement from Yoko.

'My mother has suffered a nervous breakdown,' she blurted out at last. 'She had been under strain for some months, and then worried us all by disappearing for several days.'

'How dreadful for you.' The kindly concern in Nagai's voice made Yoko want to cry again, but she controlled herself with a huge effort.

'We discovered that she went back first to her mother and brother in Kyushu. My father went there to bring her home, but she had already gone again before he arrived. He arrived back in Tokyo on Thursday and we had no idea what to do next, but a few hours later a telegram arrived, from Tenri.' Yoko's voice began to falter. She knew little enough about the religious sect her mother had attached herself to, but was sure that Mr Nagai would think it beneath intellectual contempt.

Then she raised her head which she had lowered as she spoke, sniffed audibly and looked at him defiantly. 'My mother has belonged to Tenrikyo for some time. I think the people at the head temple must be very kind and generous. The telegram was sent in the name of the Patriarch himself. It said that my mother is in their care there. Their *loving* care, it said, and that we have no need to worry about her wellbeing until we bring her home to Tokyo.'

'I'm sure you haven't,' Nagai said. 'I have great respect for Tenrikyo. Members of Tenrikyo have been courageous and independent-minded since the religion was founded fifty years or so ago. Your mother is in good hands.' His calmness was comforting to Yoko, who hurried gratefully into the conclusion of her explanation.

'Thank you. We do feel somewhat reassured, but we have to fetch her now and take care of her ourselves. My father has already been away from his office for several days and can't ask for any more time off. And my elder brother is in the Army. So it's up to me, you see. I'm taking the night train to Kyoto tonight. Tenri is near Nara, so I can get there by mid-day tomorrow. I am so sorry to have bothered you with my selfish concerns at a time when you are so busy and have much anxiety yourself.'

Nagai looked around ruefully at the chaos of the room, then smiled at her. 'My problems are trivial. Laughable, really. Miss Shimada, I'm honoured that you have confided in me, and I offer you my sincere sympathy in your distress. I take it that the Chief Librarian has not put any difficulties in your way? If there is anything I can do to help, or anyone I can speak to on your behalf?'

Yoko shook her head violently. 'No. No, thank you. The Chief Librarian has been very kind.' She jumped up from her chair clumsily, knocking over the pile of books nearest to her, and knelt down with a little cry of apology to straighten them.

Nagai got up and dropped to his haunches facing her. 'Leave them,' he said. 'It's of no importance. Miss Shimada, please don't talk about resigning. I'm sure your mother will soon recover completely and that you'll be back before long. In fact I insist . . . you're far and away the nicest person in this place, you know.' Yoko looked up at him in amazement and sudden, flaring delight, and Nagai for his part felt the warmth radiating from her tear-stained face. Nagai reached out and took one of her hands, and Yoko felt her own heart pounding. 'I care for you, too,' Nagai said simply, and Yoko was kissed for the first time in her life.

She fell back out of simple dizziness and pulled Nagai off balance so that they were sprawling in a clutter of books and papers, but almost immediately Yoko's mouth blindly sought again the bruising pressure of his lips and she clung to him with all her strength, shaking with emotion for endless seconds. Then, breathing with difficulty and horrified and ashamed of her behaviour, she pushed Nagai away and scrambled clumsily to her feet. He lunged after her and caught her by the wrist before she could open the door. 'I do care for you,' he said quietly. 'Promise me you'll come back.'

Yoko's whole body was wet with sweat but it was as though ice water were trickling down her spine as she struggled to control herself and regain the power of speech. 'There is no excuse,' she muttered at last. 'I am ashamed of myself. Whatever happens, you must have nothing more to do with me.' Then all at once her voice rose shakily to a near-scream. 'What are you thinking of? MY MOTHER'S OUT OF HER MIND! I expect I shall end up like her. Are you mad too?'

Yoko was sobbing uncontrollably, but Nagai now had her by both wrists and he pulled her close to him again, his kiss this time no more than a soft brushing of her swollen lips. 'It's a mad world,' he said then as he released her wrists and put his arms round her trembling shoulders. 'But you've made me feel more sane than I have for a long time.'

## 23. *Kamakura, Sunday*
## *2 February, 1986*

'It was sheer coincidence,' Yoko Nagai said, her hand trembling slightly as she poured Lesli another cup of the delicately aromatic green tea, 'that Dwight should have been travelling to Kyoto that night. And if he had been a less conspicuous-looking person I might never have noticed him on the platform. There were quite a few foreigners travelling apart from him, after all: even in those days Kyoto was quite a tourist attraction, and the European and American diplomats and business people in Tokyo often used to go down there even when it wasn't the holiday season. I was certainly not in any state of mind to take in much that was going on around me. You see, it had been a very upsetting sort of day for me . . .' Her voice trailed off and Lesli waited patiently for her to go on, wondering when and how she ought to break it to the old lady that she had seen Dwight Rogers very recently.

'To this day I can't think what possessed me to go up and speak to him. I was so shy in those days, but after what had happened, I felt so strange and shaken . . . and then of course on top of everything else I was worried about Teruko. Ever since New Year she'd been talking to me as though she was head over heels in love with him, but lately she'd been sleeping very restlessly and looking quite terrible, with a kind of feverish glitter in her eyes and great dark patches under them. I knew she'd been out with Dwight and thought that something might have happened.'

Lesli was glad that Mrs Nagai had agreed to allow her to turn on the tape recorder, and that having done so she had apparently forgotten its presence. Her references to Teruko were interesting, but Lesli was hoping that something more might emerge about the 'upsetting sort of day' which had left her feeling 'strange and shaken'. Lesli had begun their conversation that day by asking about the Shimada parents, and had been surprised and fascinated by the candour of Yoko's revelations about her mother's gradual drift into a vaguely mystical detachment from the world, her disappearance to Kyushu and Yukichi's fruitless pursuit of her.

Lesli had already obtained so much unexpected and revealing information about Jiro Shimada's prewar family background that on the whole it seemed best to let Yoko run on with only the most unobtrusive prompting in the hope that one reminiscence would lead to another and that eventually there would be some clues to the fate of the brother Hideo, and of the sister Teruko who had died. 'You hadn't seen Mr Rogers yourself since meeting him at the Meiji Shrine, then?'

'No. No, I hadn't.' A rueful little smile crept over Mrs Nagai's face, and again it was as though she had all at once shed half a century of her age. The effect astonished Lesli, who realised for the first time how attractive she must have been, and remembered what Rogers had said about her. This in turn reminded her of the comparable impression the old man in the sunlit patio in Vermont had made on her with his occasional surges of disconcerting charm.

'Of course, he didn't recognise me, and when I explained who I was I'm sure he wasn't at all pleased to see me. Looking back on it, I realise that he must have already decided that he didn't want to get involved with Teruko in any serious way, and so it wasn't exactly a pleasant surprise to have her sister suddenly appearing at his side.' The impish expression faded from her face and she closed her eyes for a moment, then took up the story again.

'Anyway, he asked me very courteously why I was travelling, and was so kind when I said that Mother was ill and that I was going to fetch her from Tenri. I didn't go into details, but he must have seen how upset I was, and when they let us on the train he took the ticket out of my hand, went straight to the conductor and paid the extra so that I could travel in the first-class coach with him. He simply *ignored* my protests.'

'And that was how it all began?'

Mrs Nagai opened her eyes wide as though about to deny the implication, but then nodded. 'Fifty years ago. I've never talked about it, though. Not even to my husband when he was alive. It's funny that I should want to tell you, almost a stranger. I suppose it's because you're a woman. And in a strange way you're Japanese, but *not* Japanese, if that doesn't seem an impolite thing to say.'

Lesli shook her head with a smile. 'Of course not. It means I can hope to understand, but from outside. Please do tell me.'

It had been quiet in the tidy little house, but Lesli's words were almost lost as a waste-paper dealer's truck cruised slowly along the narrow street outside, its loudspeaker crackling over and over again a tape-recorded offer to exchange toilet paper and paper handkerchiefs for old newspapers and magazines. Lesli winced at the ugliness of the intrusion, but although Mrs Nagai instinctively waited for the sound to diminish before speaking she seemed unperturbed by it, re-living as she was her experience of half a century before.

'There weren't very many first-class passengers at all, and there was just one other man in our compartment. A middle-aged foreign man: he had a fur collar on his overcoat, I remember. Dwight didn't know him, and when the conductor came round it was clear that he didn't understand Japanese. He was going as far as Nagoya, about two-thirds of the way to Kyoto where I had to change. I was rather frightened and embarrassed to be the only woman, but the other man went to sleep as soon as the train started, and Dwight talked to me – oh, so quietly and gently in Japanese, and I soon began to feel calmer. It was so strange. Although I had listened to Teruko chattering about him we were really perfect strangers, yet after an hour or so of talking in that dimly-lit train it was as though we were old friends. Every time we stopped he got off and bought us tea, or noodles from the vendors on the platform, and I found I could even let myself doze off for a few minutes now and then.'

'I know the feeling,' Lesli said. 'A few hours travel in the company of a stranger, especially at night . . . and you find yourself coming out with all sorts of intimate things.'

Mrs Nagai nodded. 'Yes . . . he was so sympathetic and kind, that after a little while I lost my shyness and answered all his questions. And I found out a lot about Dwight, too. I remember thinking how lucky Teruko would be if he really did ask her to marry him one day . . . and warning myself not to say too much about Mother in case it might put him off her, and then wondering whether that was fair to him. It's hard perhaps for someone as young as you to understand how . . . unspeakably awful the idea of insanity in the family was in those days. Almost as bad as leprosy, or this new AIDS disease we read so much about. There was hardly any attempt to distinguish among different kinds of mental illness. People are a little more sensible these days, but here in Japan a whisper of mental trouble in a family is still quite enough to block a marriage, you know.'

Lesli looked at her with respect and a growing sense of affection. There could be no doubt whatsoever about Mrs Nagai's robust mental health, nor her intellectual vigour, even when she abandoned her professorial manner almost as soon as she had assumed it and smiled again with that shy impishness which made her look so young.

'It all comes back to me so vividly. It seemed almost no time before we arrived at Nagoya, though it must have been six or seven hours at least after we left Tokyo. The night train was quite slow, and even the fast express in the daytime used to take five hours or so. It was in the very early hours of the morning, anyway, with two or three hours still to go before we arrived in Kyoto. I was quite nervous again for a little while when the other man got off, even though he had done almost nothing but snore all the way from Tokyo. But then when we were alone together Dwight made me laugh by imitating him. I was helpless with laughter. I couldn't stop.' Mrs Nagai paused for a long time, her facial muscles working not with humour but with what looked to Lesli like remembered distress, then began to speak again very quietly.

'I was hysterical, of course. It had all been too much for me. Dwight soon realised that something was wrong. He didn't slap my face as they say you should with hysterical women. He took me by the shoulders and shook me until I stopped laughing and began to cry. Then he put his arms round me and just held me while I told him everything. About what was really the matter with my mother, and about my father wanting me to marry a man called Mr Sato in his office, and that I was in love with someone at the university, and . . . just everything. It was as though I couldn't stop talking no matter how hard I tried. And he just held me and listened, and didn't seem to mind anything I said. He comforted me so much by simply being there, and dried my tears with oh, such a huge white handkerchief.' She looked up and tried without much success to smile at Lesli.

'It's unseemly for an old woman like me to remember such things, but . . . after a very long time, Dwight kissed me on the forehead. And in spite of what had happened to me just a little while earlier, I wanted him to kiss me . . . you know, properly. But he didn't. Not that night.'

## 24. *Monday 3 February, 1986*

'Luck *and* judgment, in that order, Miss Hoshino. In my opinion all successful traders need both. And the judgment part is really no more than a combination of common sense and just a trace of imagination: enough to see fractionally sooner than the potential competition what people in general are going to want enough to pay good money for. Notice I say *want*, not *need*. Human needs are basic and unchanging, but wants . . .'

Jiro Shimada smiled. There was no chance of seeing Mount Fuji from his office that day: the huge windows were curtained with rain, and Lesli's boots had become spattered and filthy even during the two short walks between the International House and Roppongi subway station and between Shinjuku station and the STC Building. Even after she had cleaned them up to some extent with paper tissues they looked dirty, and she found herself glancing at the glittering shine on Shimada's shoes with embarrassment. His feet were surprisingly dainty, and he had a way of edging a toe forward from time to time as though testing the temperature of the water in a pool, then withdrawing it and tucking one foot demurely behind the other.

'I'm sure you're right,' Lesli said. 'But it can't always have been an easy matter to distinguish between the two at the end of the war when you got out of the Navy.'

They were speaking in English, which Lesli much preferred when in the company of Shimada. It was not that it gave her any significant linguistic advantage: when she thought about it, she supposed that Shimada might have trouble in understanding or making himself understood here and there in America, but his command of the standard speech of educated people was remarkable. The real reason was, Lesli knew, rooted in the cultural characteristics of the two languages.

When they were speaking Japanese the sharp disparity in status between them became so apparent that it inhibited her, and automatically made Shimada much less approachable. He was scrupulous to observe all the courtesies, but the polite forms of speech for women are much more self-effacing and deferential than those for men. It was second nature to Lesli to use them, though, and inconceivable to her to ignore them as some Japanese-speaking foreign women of her acquaintance did, making her wince with embarrassment. The result was that she unconsciously fell into Japanese attitudes when she spoke the language of her parents, and Shimada in particular instantly became a formidable figure of authority to her.

It was quite different when they used English together. Lesli was confident and sometimes even aggressive in her questioning, secure in her skills as an interviewer, aware of but not intimidated by Shimada's international reputation, wealth and power. Shimada for his part was strikingly more affable, friendly and forthcoming when speaking English, seeming to consider Lesli's questions with an open mind and taking his time over his replies, which often developed into quite interesting reflections on all manner of subjects. The difference was so marked that it was as though he were two different men.

The sexual signals Lesli received from him also varied according to the language they were using. She was no longer in any doubt that there were such signals, nor that in spite of his age Shimada was a virile and sexually attractive man. She had several times wondered to herself quite frankly what he would be like in bed, and arrived at two quite contrary conclusions. As she had put it when discussing the matter with Charlie, the 'American Shimada' adopted the soft sell approach, charming her gently, while she was often perturbed by a latent but none the less threatening animalism in his intensely Japanese alter ego. 'Good old Jiro would give me the best dinner in New York and hours of sweet talk before leading me into the bedroom, whereas given half the chance, President Shimada of the STC would grunt his instructions and knock me down if I weren't quick about it.' 'And keep his shoes and socks on like those guys in Japanese porno movies,' Charlie had replied sourly, thoroughly put out. 'That geriatric degenerate lays a finger on you, I wanna know.'

Shimada was looking at her quizzically. 'Of course you're right in one sense,' he said. 'Food, clothing and shelter were uppermost in the majority of people's minds, but there were still plenty who were provided for in those respects and who could think about desires rather than needs, both their own and those of potential customers. And even what we think of as needs vary a lot in different individuals. For example, I made a great deal of money and enjoyed all sorts of privileges during my years in the Imperial Navy simply because I didn't smoke. It was staggering what other men would offer in the way of cash or services for my cigarette ration.' He spread out his hands and smiled at Lesli, as though inviting her to join him in wondering at the folly of lesser people.

'I suppose it's inevitable that your archives are pretty scrappy for the first year or two after the war,' Lesli said carefully. 'But it's clear that by early 1947, when you were still only – what, twenty-seven or so? – you'd acquired some substantial holdings in real estate here in Tokyo. You must have gone without an awful lot of cigarettes in the Navy to have been able to afford it.'

Shimada's face darkened for a moment and Lesli wondered if she had gone too far, but then he chuckled. 'You're remarkably forthright sometimes, Miss Hoshino. Such remarks are startling, coming from a lady who looks in most ways so thoroughly Japanese . . . though now I come to think of it I suppose it's the sort of delicate impudence that experienced geisha specialise in. I like it.'

Lesli flushed, not with embarrassment but in annoyance at the man's patronising attitude to her. 'You've warned me off asking questions about your early life, Mr Shimada, but I wasn't aware that I had to skirt around anything concerning your wartime and postwar activities.' She noticed that her voice had coarsened with anger, and she reached for the coffee cup on the table in front of her to give herself time to calm down.

Shimada raised one hand in a conciliatory gesture and shrank back in mock terror. 'Don't be so fierce, Miss Hoshino. I apologise for offending you. That coffee must be cold by now. I'll have my secretary bring you a fresh cup. No? Very well, as you wish.'

The shiny shoe emerged again from behind his trouser leg and he stirred the carpet delicately with its toe. 'In the first place, I haven't "warned you off" my boyhood, as you put it. I've told you that it was very ordinary . . . of no consequence for the purposes of a biography. So there's really no point in your wasting time and energy by making private enquiries. If you're thinking of doing so, that is. And in the second place, I've no objection in the least to telling you how I raised the funds to buy land in the Tokyo area. In fact I began to speculate in real estate well before the war and continued to do so throughout the forties.' He looked around the beautiful room in which they were sitting.

'The land on which this building stands was my first acquisition. Shinjuku was little more than a suburb in my young days –

apart from a licensed brothel quarter around where the original post station stood. You remember I said a while ago that successful trading calls for luck *and* judgment. I judged accurately as a very young man – while still a boy, in fact – that within a decade or two this area would become a major commercial and entertainment centre and that property values would soar. And : . . well, I was lucky enough by the time I entered Tokyo University to have saved sufficient money to buy up some of the rice-fields still left hereabouts and still get an income by renting them out. It was obvious that war was coming, even though it was inconceivable to most Japanese in those days that this country would ever come under direct attack. I thought it possible, but reflected that although buildings might perhaps attract bombs, not a lot of harm would come to my smallholding, and that development could begin with the coming of eventual peace. This skyscraper is the third office building I've put up on this site since the forties. The first was just two storeys tall. Can you imagine? This present STC Building will probably outlive me, but who knows what someone else may replace it with one day?'

'I still don't see . . .'

' – where the money came from. I was just about to explain. It's a sad thing to have to talk about, but I must be honest. My first savings were a kind of inheritance from my mother. As a young girl in Kyushu she had been acquainted with a famous potter, towards the end of his life. To put it rather more accurately, he was respected in his lifetime but became really famous after he was dead. Anyway, he must have been fond of her, because he gave her a number of examples of his work, and she treasured them all her life, but had no idea of their value. The pots . . . came to me when my mother died in 1936. I showed them to experts and discovered that they were worth a small fortune. Well, Miss Hoshino, I was young and ambitious, I was tempted, and I disposed of them. That's how it all began.'

Shimada fell silent and stared at nothing, his face grim and set, and the silence between them was profound until Lesli shifted in her seat and spoke quietly. 'Have you ever regretted parting with them?'

Shimada rubbed his eyes and Lesli thought irrelevantly that he wouldn't have done that if he wore contact lenses. Then he looked at her with a distant smile. 'How could I?' he asked. 'I think my mother would be delighted if she could know what her few simple belongings had made possible.' He stood up and walked across to a low table against the far wall and came back with something in his hand which he passed to Lesli. 'I managed to trace and buy one piece back many years later. This little bowl. I shall never part with it again.'

Lesli looked at the bowl with unfeigned delight. The bamboo design seemed to dance before her eyes with a subdued grace, as though touched by a gentle breeze, and after a long moment she laid it down reluctantly and with reverence on the table, almost afraid to go on handling it. 'It's beautiful,' she said humbly, and Shimada nodded in agreement.

'Yes, it is,' he said. 'Actually, it's flawed, like the other pieces my mother possessed. That is possibly why the potter saw no harm in giving them to a little local girl. But paradoxically, that's what made them particularly valuable.'

'No, two fascinating conversations, and it's time I tried to straighten out my thoughts. I think I'm going to have the regular prime rib.' Goldfarb continued to study the menu for a moment, and then turned to the patiently hovering waitress. 'Make that two, will you? And a carafe of red California.' As the girl went away he put one finger against Lesli's lips. 'Not a word to the rabbi about this, you hear? Right, on your feet, woman. We have to go make up our own salads at the bar.' They were at the Victoria Station Restaurant in the basement of the Haiyu-za Theatre at Roppongi, American-style in spite of the antique enamelled English railway station name plates which decorated the walls.

'Thank you for taking me to the movie, Charlie,' Lesli said as he handed her a bowl from the chilled stack at the salad bar. 'Woody Allen makes so much *sense* even at his zaniest compared with some of the real-life drama I've been hearing about. It's reassuring that he's popular here. They can't be all bad, to use your own favourite phrase.'

Goldfarb put the finishing touches to the edifice of salad he had constructed for himself, and then assumed a shocked expression. 'Hoshino, I don't know what's come over you, saying such things. What would your folks back home think if they could hear you talking about the Japanese as "them"! Back to the table, and shame on you.' Lesli put out her tongue at him to the great surprise of a passing waiter, and they resumed their seats.

'Shoot,' Goldfarb said then. 'Two conversations.'

'Yes. Well, the fact is, I should have made some notes when I got back from Kamakura yesterday, but my head was spinning. It helped a little to tell you about Yoko's latest revelations when you called later on. What did you make of them? I suppose I never shall know for sure what in hell *had* happened to Yoko earlier on the day she set out to go fetch her mother, but it certainly seemed to have put her into a state to be turned on by Dwight Rogers. Mind you, her falling for a foreigner isn't in itself surprising. Especially someone who treated her gently and kindly. Japanese men can be such bastards.'

'If you say so, ma'am.' The waitress had brought the wine and filled their glasses, and Goldfarb raised his in salute before drinking. 'Maybe some other man had roughed her up or something, could be even tried to rape her. Pretty unlikely really, a nice middle-class girl like her, though it would account for her being in a hysterical state even without being worried half to death over her mother and wondering if she'd inherited a crazy gene herself.'

Lesli nodded thoughtfully. 'Could be. On the other hand she said she told Rogers she was in love with somebody at the university . . . more likely to have been some emotional scene, I suppose. Let's not get over-imaginative. Whatever it was upset her, having now met Rogers myself I can easily imagine how good he must have been for her. And having gotten to know Yoko so much better now I can also see why Rogers wanted to tag along with her on the local train to Tenri. But she wouldn't have it, and I don't blame her. Besides, I don't think I mentioned that he'd told her that the whole point of his going to Kyoto was to meet up with this tour group of members of the Hitler Youth organisation on their way back from a visit to Kyushu and write a story about their impressions of provincial Japan – and the impression *they* made on Japanese provincials, I shouldn't wonder.'

'You're kidding!'

'No, it's true. I think it's kind of weird, too. It wouldn't have occurred to me that by 1936 the German government would think it worth while to ship a bunch of well-scrubbed blond Nazi kids all that way for a propaganda tour, or that the Japanese would lay on all sorts of elaborate goodies in their honour. But they did. Including a trip to Kumamoto Castle, she said. I wonder if her father Yukichi saw anything of them while the poor man was chasing around trying to locate his wife?' Their plates of beef arrived, each garnished with a baked potato, and they fell silent for a while. Goldfarb seemed content to let Lesli make the running, and waited for her to begin to think aloud again.

'It must have been tough on Yoko to handle the Tenrikyo people and get her mother straightened out enough to go home to Tokyo, even if as Yoko claimed she was happy to see her daughter, and went along quietly enough with her. Poor Mrs Shimada. She told Yoko she felt secure and at peace there in the shrine complex, and it seems she was making herself useful too, wandering about with a cleaning rag and a duster between prayer and sacred dance sessions. They ought to have let her stay there, instead of dragging her back to face – what?'

'I guess you're right. Might not have looked like that at the time, though. Okay, that's one conversation. Tell me more about the session with Wonder Boy today.'

Lesli raised her eyes heavenwards. 'Believe me, Charlie, that was something else again. A real bombshell. Do you know that man was a successful capitalist while he was still in high school?'

Goldfarb shrugged. 'So what's new? Never heard of kids making a lot of money buying and selling before? And what about all these teenage computer software millionaires nowadays?'

'No, listen Charlie, this was real estate. He started buying up land in Shinjuku way before the war.'

Goldfarb was grudgingly impressed. 'Real estate, huh? Okay, you win. That does take balls at that kind of age.'

All at once Lesli shivered, and Goldfarb looked at her in concern. 'Something wrong?'

'No, no. I'm fine. I just remembered a slightly unnerving remark Shimada made. Sort of warning me off making what he called "private enquiries" about those prewar days. I can't think what prompted him to say that. I've been scrupulously careful about what I say to him and I'm *certain* I haven't let anything slip to make him suspect anything. Surely he couldn't be having me *followed*, could he, Charlie?'

Goldfarb shook his head reassuringly. 'That's a pretty wild idea, Lesli. I'd very much doubt it. You didn't say anything to him or Yamada or anybody else at STC about going to America, did you?'

'No, not a word. I just told Yamada I'd be out of Tokyo for a week or so. I told Yoko the same thing. Besides, she's so concerned that nothing should get back to Jiro that it's inconceivable she could have been in touch with him anyway. Though of course he must know all about her, possibly even gives her an allowance. Oh dear. I wish he didn't scare me so, Charlie.' She smiled at Goldfarb to soften the effect of what she had said and drained her glass, which he promptly replenished, his expression serious.

'He's a tough, successful man with a lot of influence. But you have no reason to be scared of him, Lesli. Unless you've uncovered something really bad you haven't told me about.'

'No. It was just that not-so-gentle hint that if I was thinking of digging around that particular area for myself I'd be wise to forget it, that's all. He was forthcoming enough in a way. For example, he told me his mother died that same year, 1936, and that he made what he called a small fortune by selling a collection of pottery he inherited from her. Seems she had no idea it was valuable. I can believe it though – he showed me one piece he bought back and it's one of the most beautiful things I ever saw. I still have no idea what his mother died of or exactly when, though. The trouble is, I know he's a liar, and he could easily be lying about that too.'

'More wine?' The carafe was empty and Goldfarb raised his eyebrows as he tilted it, making no attempt to press the point when Lesli shook her head. 'Coffee, then.'

'Mmm. Please.' When it arrived Goldfarb stirred his pensively, still unusually subdued. 'It's certainly a strange story, Lesli,' he said at last. 'Questions occur to me. For a start, I wonder if anybody else in the family guessed the value of those pots . . . or even knew he sold them just like that? Come to that, why should *Jiro* have inherited them? Seems an odd, rather un-Japanese thing to happen. I'd have expected anything like that to have just stayed in the family, wouldn't you? Kind of mysterious.' He shrugged and sipped his coffee as Lesli nodded, then went on. 'From the way you describe it, that must have been quite a setup when everybody was back in Tokyo, with Mom goofy on sedatives and Yoko at home taking care of her. And cool cat Jiro just quietly getting on with his school work, listening to Bix Beiderbecke records and scheming about buying up Shinjuku and making a fortune. I tell you something, honey, I'd hate to play Monopoly against that guy.'

Lesli smiled gratefully, feeling lighter in spirit without any particular reason. 'How right you are. It must have been some household. There's another thing: presumably Dwight Rogers started calling on Yoko within a very few days, when everybody else was out. It would have been easy enough for them to have time together while her mother was in a daze, poor soul. The neighbours must have had a ball speculating about him. One thing's certain, judging from what Yoko said before she shooed me away and made me promise to go back soon – it couldn't have been long before he kissed her "properly", as she put it, and they got it together.'

Goldfarb heaved a theatrical sigh. 'I can't persuade you to drop in at a love hotel on your way back to your highly respectable dorm, can I? There's one near here fitted up with the cutest gadgets you ever did see.' Lesli wondered what would happen if she said yes, which she was briefly tempted to do. She rather suspected that Charlie might be more embarrassed than delighted: Rachel must be wondering what was keeping him as it was. She smiled at him with special warmth as she shook her head slowly. 'No? I thought not. Face it, Goldfarb, you're no match for Lucky Dwight, with two good-looking sisters both horny for him.'

As they made their way to the cash desk Lesli kissed him quickly on the cheek. 'You're the greatest, Charlie. You know that. I hope you won't ever stop asking.'

He grinned and squeezed her round the waist. 'You should be so lucky. Yup, must have been great for Rogers. Not so hot for Teruko, though.'

## 25. *Thursday 6 February, 1936*

Mr Matsumoto was a thin, sharp-featured man whose hair had been parted in the middle of his scalp with mathematical precision before being plastered down and brushed to such a high gloss that it glittered under the lights of the Ginza Premier Ballroom. The quick, bird-like glances he cast in all directions around him as he spoke made Teruko fearful of his impatience, for the moment the cloakroom girl had taken her into the huge hall where shirt-sleeved members of the band were taking their instruments out of their cases, and waylaid him, the manager had said 'Two minutes, young lady. We open at six and I'm a busy man.'

Now she fixed her gaze on one of the pearl studs in the starched shirt front that looked even to her distracted eye uncommonly like celluloid, and repeated again the short speech she had rehearsed on her way from the Arden Beauty Salon. 'Yes, yes,' she heard him say impatiently in his strong Osaka accent. 'I heard you the first time. Well, let's have a look at you. Coat off. Look sharp, now, we open at six.' Teruko's heart sank as she fumbled with the buttons on her old cloth coat and opened it. She had no dress remotely as expensive and stylish as those she had seen on the taxi-dancers the night she had been to the ballroom with Dwight Rogers, and the one she had borrowed from Haru at the salon for the evening was not only the wrong sort of red for her but was also very tight round the bust.

She felt the colour rising up her neck as Mr Matsumoto looked her up and down appraisingly, and jumped when he snapped his fingers resoundingly. 'How old are you?' he demanded.

'Twenty.'

'Oh? Since when?'

'Since last month,' Teruko whispered.

'Ah. Can you dance?'

'Oh, yes, sir. I've been learning for ages.'

The skinny little man in the dinner suit looked round in momentary irritation as the drummer executed a smart tattoo on the snare drum and topped it with a clash on the cymbal, then somewhat to Teruko's surprise fixed his eyes on her for a long moment. 'Come over here,' he said then in a more thoughtful voice, and led her to one of the tables. 'I don't think much of your frock,' he said when they were sitting down. 'But I like your make-up. And you're well-spoken. Are you a student?'

'No, sir. I . . . I work in a hairdressers.'

'Ah. That accounts for it. I'm surprised you aren't at college, though. A girl like you. Not married, are you?'

His sudden friendliness put Teruko a little more at ease, and she found herself able to be a little more forthcoming. 'Oh, no, of course not. I was never much good at school,' she admitted. 'So my parents let me become an apprentice when I was fourteen. I'm a good beautician,' she added stoutly, 'in a very select salon. And if you let me work here I'll buy a proper dance frock right away.'

Mr Matsumoto nodded and consulted a smart wristwatch. 'Need the money, do you? Well, all right. I'll give you a trial. You can start tonight if you like. Six till eleven, tonight, tomorrow and Saturday. We'll see how you get on and then I'll let you know about next week. What's the matter?'

Teruko held the tears back with difficulty. 'I can only come by six o'clock on Thursdays, sir. I don't finish work till eight other evenings. I couldn't get here till a quarter past. I'm sorry I bothered you.'

Miserably she began to button up her coat, then paused as she saw the manager still staring at her. 'Well then, you won't earn so much the other nights, will you?' he said briskly. 'All right. Come over here and I'll introduce you to Miho. She's been working here a long time and she'll explain the system to you and fix you up with a number.'

He led the way back across the floor to where three or four girls were now standing about talking, then abruptly stopped and placed a hand on Teruko's arm. 'What's your name?'

Teruko stood as though stunned. 'I . . . I . . .'

'All right,' Mr Matsumoto said with surprising mildness. 'Don't want your family to know, I presume. Well, you aren't the only one. Just your first name will do. What was that? Teruko? Right. Now listen to me, Teruko. You look like a good girl. Nicely brought up. There are two ways to be a dance hostess. I advise you to stick to the first, however hard up you are. Pretty girl like you shouldn't do too badly at all. You'll hear the others talking about the other way. Don't be in too much of a hurry to listen. Not all of the girls do, and nobody's going to push you.'

After two hours Teruko was still puzzling over Mr Matsumoto's last remark. She had, however, been asked seven times to dance and was beginning to get over the hot embarrassment of being stared at. This had come close to making her take to her heels and run in the first half hour, when patrons had begun to arrive and lone males sauntered up and down the line of girls staring openly at their legs. She kept hers primly together and repeatedly tugged at the too-short skirt of Haru's dress in a vain attempt to cover her knees, but soon noticed the way some of the others languidly crossed their legs to afford a better view as the men approached, and even occasionally winked at them.

The stares of the other girls were bad enough in their way, though the one Mr Matsumoto had called Miho was pleasant, showing her where to leave her coat and helping her to fasten the big tin badge with '18' on it to her dress without leaving obvious pinholes. Teruko was relatively inured to the rough and tumble of mutual female appraisal, though, and soon found some small sources of satisfaction. For all the inadequacies of her dress she could see that she was easily the most expertly made-up: full marks to Mr Matsumoto. Her hair was also sleeker and better styled than that of all but one or two, and her legs were well above standard. Some of the girls were so bandy that Teruko wondered how they could bear to show their legs at all. She knew from frequent discussions at the salon that Japanese women were all too often unlucky in this respect compared with western or even Chinese girls, and gradually began to look the men who inspected her in the eye rather than keeping her head modestly lowered.

The first dance was the worst. The man who beckoned to her was corpulent and smelt of beer. He burped noisily from time to time as he blundered about the dance floor, and his face was glazed with sweat. Teruko had been held in only two men's arms before, those of Dwight Rogers and of her brother Hideo, and she danced rigidly, face averted, as she was bounced against the fat belly and tried not to wince when her partner trod on her toes.

Soon the hall was quite full, and the sound of the band mellower. She could smell the tobacco smoke collecting in her own hair and worried about its being noticed when she got home. Her second and third partners were less objectionable, and her fourth was a tall foreigner: not American, but German, he said. He did not smell so nice as Dwight Rogers but Teruko found herself able to smile at him through all her anxiety. As the music swirled about them and his warm hand pressed her back she forgot for a few minutes about Hideo and their two hours at the cheap inn in Yoshiwara, the contrast between his ignorant, brutal using of her and his dog-like obedience to her own demands and vulnerability to her scorn. For a blessed space she was free from the hopeless tumbling confusion of her own feelings for Hideo, and from the black oppressiveness of what she had now to undergo for both their sakes.

At soon after nine, feet aching and weak with hunger because she had eaten nothing since lunchtime, Teruko was back in her chair when the girl who had been sitting next to her came over to fetch her bag. She winked at Teruko. 'See you tomorrow, then,' she said. 'I'm off. Bought out for the rest of the evening. Not a bad-looking bloke, either.' Uncomprehending, Teruko smiled and nodded, and then watched the girl go over to a middle-aged man who put his arm on her shoulder in a proprietorial way as they headed for the door.

By the time the ballroom closed at eleven Teruko had danced with a total of fourteen men and her feet felt as if they had swollen to three times their normal size. In exchange for the tickets the men had given her she received from the cashier the sum of twelve yen sixty sen and an approving nod from the manager who was standing nearby. Of the twenty-three taxi-dancers on duty that evening at the Ginza Premier Ballroom, including herself, eleven had been bought out by ten o'clock, and as she slumped exhausted on the tram going home Teruko was no longer in doubt about what Mr Matsumoto had meant by 'the other way' to work as a dance hostess.

## 26. Tokyo, Monday
## 10 February, 1936

'There are several points in the March forecast that I am not perfectly clear about, Mr Shimada,' Director Nishi said, pushing the sheet of figures to one side. He then took out his watch and studied it for some time before replacing it in the pocket of his waistcoat, after which he looked up and smiled briefly and without warmth. 'Though that is not the reason I have asked you to come to see me. I have just been in conference with President Ikeda, and I am to meet him again later this afternoon.' He hesitated, and Yukichi was surprised to see an expression of embarrassment flicker over his normally bland features.

'It is, you will appreciate, unusual for the head of the holding company to concern himself directly and personally with the affairs of this department. To be perfectly frank with you, a matter of some delicacy has arisen. It was first mentioned to me while you were away, and again soon after your return. President Ikeda did not wish me to trouble you with it while you were personally distressed, but he now feels obliged to ask me to raise it without further delay . . . he is, I gather, under some pressure from Baron Mitsui himself.'

Again he paused, before baulking at his task and taking refuge once more in petty irritation over the reason for Yukichi's absence. 'It really was most unfortunate that your wife was taken ill in so distant a place as Kumamoto. We could not easily spare you for so long a time, especially . . . I must tell you frankly, Mr Shimada, that I have incurred a certain amount of criticism for having granted you several days leave to go to her. Needless to say I had to explain that you had led me to believe that her condition was a matter of grave concern. I must admit that I assumed she . . . but now you tell me that she is back in Tokyo and making a good recovery . . .'

His words hung on the air, and Yukichi tried to imagine how on earth the head of the Mitsui family had even come to know of the existence of a minor executive like himself. The Baron was not personally concerned with the day-to-day affairs of the vast network of industrial and commercial enterprises which bore his name. It seemed extraordinary that he and the astute, Harvard-educated Seihin Ikeda who as head of the Mitsui Holding Company was the chief executive of the entire enterprise, should interest themselves in anything which might involve Yukichi, and inconceivable that it could be in a petty administrative decision like granting him a few days compassionate leave.

So far as that was concerned, well, it was true that although he had chosen his words carefully when requesting time off to go to Kyushu it would not have been unreasonable for Nishi to have inferred that Chie was on her death-bed. Yukichi was unrepentant: though depressed he felt curiously detached, and quite without any inclination to try to justify himself. Nor was he anything more than puzzled by Nishi's mysterious references to President Ikeda and Baron Mitsui. The problems and anxieties associated with Chie's condition dominated his consciousness, and even as he stood there waiting for his superior to enlighten him a sudden recollection of his state of mind as he approached the waterfall near Kumamoto with the master potter made Yukichi's legs tremble: the Director had not invited him to sit down.

He reached out unobtrusively and grasped the back of the chair beside him, distressed to realise that with the immediate crisis over he found himself more and more often reflecting that it might have been for the best if they *had* found Chie's body in the cave. Chie was dying anyway, he realised, drifting away slowly and lightly like a leaf borne along by a sluggish stream. Neither he nor the old doctor who called to see her from time to time could find in her any trace of a will to live, and Yoko was unwilling to discuss the matter. He forced himself to speak briskly.

'Yes. A slow recovery, but I am glad to say that she is a little better now. My eldest daughter has left her work at Waseda University for a time to stay at home and take care of her. Provided you will excuse my wife's absence, though, there is no reason why the proposed *o-miai* should not take place at any time convenient to you and to Mr Sato.'

'Yes. Well, that is a matter which we can discuss at leisure. It might be wise to postpone the meeting between the young people until this other matter is dealt with.'

Nishi's obvious unease finally communicated itself to Yukichi. He no longer cared very much about what the Director thought or did, but this was the first time he had shown signs of modifying his insistence on bringing his assistant Sato and Yoko together as soon as possible so that serious marriage negotiations could be initiated. It came as something of a relief to Yukichi, but at the same time a sense of foreboding swept over him, and he now wanted to know what was going on, for his daughter's sake as much as his own.

For since bringing Chie back from Tenri Yoko seemed to have changed. She nursed her mother uncomplainingly and with loving patience, and kept house efficiently. With Yukichi, though, she was brisk and businesslike, speaking only about practicalities, and professing herself perfectly willing to go ahead with the marriage negotiations. When Yukichi himself had once tentatively referred to the question of Chie's breakdown and its possible bearing on her own prospects she was cool to the point of rudeness to him. 'Go ahead then, Father. It doesn't bother me. Tell him your wife's off her head and that your daughter might very likely go the same way one day. If I'm prepared to risk having children with horrible squints I don't see why your precious Mr Sato should object to the prospect of their being feeble-minded into the bargain.' She fumbled among the small pile of loose papers beside the wireless set which stood on a low table in a corner of the room, found the photograph of Sato which had been supplied, and thrust it at him.

'Look at him! He should think himself lucky, if you ask me.' Then Yoko had relented. 'But Mother's not mad, you know. She's tired, and a bit confused, that's all. I hope you realise I'm doing this to please you, Father. To make things easier for you at the office. It's just a meeting, after all, as you said yourself. Nothing may come of it. When he actually sees me he may not be at all keen.' Yukichi doubted that very much. Far from sagging under the burden of washing and ironing, cleaning and cooking, Yoko was the one member of the family who seemed to be blossoming.

His wife was placidly remote in her drugged world of dreams, but had lost much weight and was deathly pale. Yoko laid down separate bedding for him at night some distance from where Chie lay but he slept fearfully and badly, as though sharing a room with a corpse. Jiro was as usual self-contained and uncommunicative, but the effects of long hours of study were to be seen in the purplish smudged look of the skin beneath his eyes, and the boy was obviously tormented by a series of boils which erupted one after another on his neck and thighs. Teruko too looked far from well, and trailed round the house listlessly on the rare occasions she was there.

The contrast between Yoko and the rest of them was astonishing. Her skin glowed with health and there was a new, assured air of womanliness about her which even in his depression and anxiety Yukichi noticed and admired, aware that it was her strength and determination, not his, which was keeping the household on a more or less even keel. He was at a loss to know whether she would be pleased or annoyed to learn that the much-discussed *o-miai* between her and Sato was not, it seemed, to take place within the next week or so after all.

'Director, perhaps you would be kind enough to tell me what it is that is troubling President Ikeda. He has scarcely ever had occasion to speak to me, of course; and as for Baron Mitsui –'

'It's not you. It's your son.'

'My *son?*'

Coming to the point at last seemed to loosen Nishi's tongue, and he leant forward urgently. 'You'd better sit down. Why don't you sit down?' Yukichi lurched awkwardly into the chair, his legs all at once rubbery and his mouth dry. 'What do you mean, my son?' he croaked.

'Mr Shimada, I don't really know how to put this, and normally it's certainly not a matter to be discussed except at very senior levels and in strict confidence, but in the circumstances . . . you must be aware that an organisation as large and complex as ours must at all times maintain close and cordial links with the authorities, and perhaps more than ever at the moment, with elections pending, a certain amount of . . . political confusion, and even some outright public hostility to Mitsui and other *zaibatsu*. And of course our heavy industrial operations have an obvious and vital bearing on the national security. Several members of the Mitsui family have in recent years thought it prudent to distance themselves from the business by withdrawing from the Board of Directors or retiring from senior posts.'

'I know.' Yukichi had found his voice again, and anxiety made him speak with an uncharacteristic tart bitterness. 'The subsequent reorganisation is the reason why I am being obliged to retire several years before I would have wished to. I can assure you, Director, that what you are saying is common gossip among staff at all levels. What has it to do with my son? I presume you mean my elder son, by the way. My second son is just a schoolboy.'

'The army officer, yes.' There were beads of sweat on Nishi's forehead and pock-marked cheeks, and he seemed both taken aback and jolted into aggressiveness himself by Yukichi's forceful response.

'I was about to explain. And perhaps this is one aspect of Mitsui policy which is *not* a matter of "common gossip" among junior employees. Certainly I expect you to keep this information strictly to yourself. It is very much in your interest to do so.' They glared at each other across the desk. 'Obviously our directors openly cultivate highly placed individuals in the world of politics in the interests of normal good relations. At the same time and on a confidential basis we maintain links with well-disposed officials, not necessarily at the most senior levels – who are frequently in a position to pass on extremely valuable information.'

Yukichi's lips twisted. There seemed little point in saying that he knew about the paid informers in government departments, too; the Mitsui spies who probably took bribes from the Sumitomo, Mitsubishi and Yasuda *zaibatsu* as well and sold the same information to them all. 'As a matter of simple prudence we have similar arrangements with well-informed people in the Army and the Navy.' Nishi had recovered his composure, and the false smile drifted across the lower part of his face again.

'Information has reached us that a number of young officers are involved in a plan to try to overthrow the government and instal a military regime. A list of names has been supplied: it is almost certainly incomplete, but your son's name is on it.'

Yukichi heard what he said, but at first his brain refused to deal with the words and they spun round his consciousness as gibberish. Physically he felt quite calm and detached, and he looked across at the Director as though seeing him for the first time. Yukichi could not at first understand why Nishi's mouth was opening and shutting, but then the strange buzzing in his ears subsided and he heard words again.

'. . . as something of a shock to you. It wasn't taken very seriously at first. The court-martial of Colonel Aizawa began a week or so ago, of course, and is as we all expected generating a good deal of fuss. Predictably, a number of his hot-headed supporters have been making all sorts of indiscreet and vaguely threatening statements. But more recently additional information has come our way. There are indications that these other young men including your son have tacit support at a much higher level . . . I won't mention any names. If they go ahead and even perhaps succeed . . . well, we all know that the Imperial Way faction have swallowed the philosophy of that lunatic Ikki Kita and that they are no friends of the *zaibatsu*.'

Out came the watch again. 'I must go. It wouldn't do to keep the President waiting.' Yukichi looked dully at the other man as he returned the watch to his waistcoat pocket and prepared to lever himself to his feet, looking positively jaunty now that he had done what had to be done.

'But . . . I can't believe this is true. Anyway, what –'

'What does Mr Ikeda want you to do? Why, find out whether it really is true, of course. If it is, warn your son off, for a start. It might do no harm to let him know that Baron Mitsui has ways of communicating with His Majesty himself. I know you have only a few months more at Mitsui, but . . .'

Then he was gone, and Yukichi sat slumped in the chair for some time, grateful for the solitude.

'Well, how did she react?'

'Are you really interested, Charlie, or just being nice?'

Goldfarb settled back in his swivel chair cradling the back of his head in his linked hands and scowled at Lesli. 'Brilliant, good-looking, sexy: I have to admit it. But nice? No. Tell me.'

Lesli sighed. 'It's just that I'm afraid I'm beginning to get obsessed, and I don't want to be a bore.' Goldfarb raised his eyes to heaven and produced an inverted smile of mingled exasperation and despair.

'Listen kid, I don't recall you paying me fifty bucks an hour for analysis. Just answer the question, willya? How did the old dame react when you told her?'

'Well, I think she was all set to be furious with me for not saying sooner that I'd been to see him. Right after I got back from America, I mean. I felt bad myself; I'm fairly sure she wouldn't have come out with all that stuff about meeting him on the train if I'd come clean with her then. But then she seemed to sort of swallow her anger and went very quiet for simply ages. I sat there feeling ashamed of myself until quite suddenly she gave me that fantastic smile I told you about, and the questions just came tumbling out. How did he look, what did he say, how was he dressed, what was his house like, what did we eat for lunch . . . she was just like a starry-eyed teenager. It was –' 'Nauseating, by the sound of it. Little old Japanese ladies in Kamakura have no business carrying a torch for decrepit professors in Vermont. Toothless old goat. Hey, I've just had this great idea for a soap opera – a re-make of Madam Butterfly –' 'Watch it, Charlie. One of these days I'll be a little old Japanese lady myself, more or less. Might even go to live in Kamakura. Wouldn't you like to think of me going all rubber-legged if someone came to see me and told me you were alive and well in Superstition, Arizona?'

'Lesli, I think I love you,' Goldfarb said seriously. 'Tell you what, I'll convert to Islam and marry you. It's a big bed, and Rachel can move over.' He raised a hairy, cautionary hand as Lesli opened her mouth. 'No, no. You don't have to thank me right away. Finish telling me about Shimada's big sister first.'

Resisting a sudden impulse to go over and hug him, Lesli contented herself with a bow of the head and a flowery, mock-humble Japanese compliment, then grinned broadly at him. 'Okay. Keep me waiting, damn you. Well, to cut a long story short, I guess she decided to let it all hang out. She confirmed what we already knew, that young Mr Rogers of the *New York Times* was just as taken with our Yoko as she was with him. I was right in surmising that he came calling right after she got back to Tokyo with her mother, and in next to no time they were screwing each other like there was no tomorrow. The only snag – well, there were all sorts of snags really, but . . . Charlie, are you all right?'

'Sure. I was just thinking.'

'Oh. Yes, I see. I'm sorry, Charlie.'

'So'm I. Go on.' Lesli tried to continue, faltered as she felt the tears pricking her own eyes, and then made a fresh start, avoiding Goldfarb's steady gaze. 'So Yoko began this terrific affair with Rogers, but there were problems. Like younger sister Teruko, for one, of course. Yoko assumed that she was still in love with Rogers and had her heart set on marrying him. She knew they'd been out together at least once, but had no clear idea how things were between the two of them at that stage. I told you Teruko was a beautician?'

'You did. In the Ginza some place.'

'Right. Well, around this time – I got a little confused here – Teruko started working nights too, to earn more money. Either as a bar hostess or a dance partner or something like that, and the thing with Rogers kind of fizzled out, it seems.'

'Just as well. Family was hard up, then?'

'I haven't formed that impression from what I've heard from either Shimada or Yoko. Shimada said they weren't too badly off – his father was a Mitsui section head, after all, and with an army officer brother and both girls working until their mother flipped they were hardly on the breadline. And of course we now know that Shimada started to build up his fortune that same year after selling his mother's collection of pottery. No, Yoko made it very obvious by the way she talked that she thoroughly disapproved of her sister's moonlighting, especially as whatever it was . . . it was something Teruko definitely didn't want her parents to find out about, anyway. Yoko was having a great time with Rogers, but it must have been pretty rough for her all the same. She'd had to take extended unpaid leave from her job to stay home and take care of her mother, for a start. That might not have been such a bad thing at that, because of this traumatic relationship of some kind she had with a man at the university where she was working – I told you she was a library assistant at that time –'

'Hold it, I'm losing track. It really does sound like a soap opera. Who in hell is this other guy? He the one we thought might have raped her?'

'I wish I knew. But Yoko needed him like a hole in the head at that time, being all wrapped up in Rogers. Because at the same time her father was fixing up an arranged marriage for her with a young Mitsui executive. Maybe I forgot to tell you about that.'

'Ye gods. This would be Nagai, would it? The one she ended up marrying?'

Lesli shook her head as she flipped through the notebook on her lap. 'No. At least, I'm pretty sure not. I may be able to find out next time I go to see her. I don't have a lot of control over these conversations I have with her, Charlie. I'm curious about the elder brother, and I have a whole list of questions I want to ask her about Shimada himself of course, but I have a feeling that I'm not going to be able to get at the truth about Jiro Shimada until I find out what happened to everybody else in that family. I'm squeezing more and more information out of him, but it's on his terms and I'm not believing a thing he says without corroboration. So right now subject number one is Yoko. I believe her implicitly, and if I let her re-live those years, why, pretty soon I think she'll loosen up about the others the way she has done about herself.'

'Yeah. Maybe you're right. Well, I keep saying it: anything I can do.'

'You may not think it, Charlie, but you've helped me so enormously by just taking an interest. Talking to you straightens out my own impressions . . . helps me to hang on to the main outline. I wish I could do something for you.' Even as she said the words Lesli prepared herself for the inevitable suggestion, accompanied by a lecherous leer: she almost looked forward to it, as being something she could cope with cheerfully, unlike the fragile tension which had developed between them earlier when she had seen the strength of the emotion in Goldfarb's eyes, known that he still really did want her and felt a responsive confusion in her own heart.

'Maybe you can.' There was no hint of double entendre in Goldfarb's voice, and Lesli raised her eyebrows in some surprise.

'We've been putting together this piece about early 1936. The February Twenty-Six Incident. Know anything about it? With the fiftieth anniversary coming up it occurred to me that it might make a feature. Even a cover story if nothing world-shattering happens that week. The folk back at the ranch like the idea.'

'I've heard about it, of course. I'm pretty vague about the details, though. Didn't a bunch of government ministers get murdered?'

'Assassinated. Nice guys don't do murders, they do assassinations. And these were real nice kids. Just misguided. Hot-headed maybe, got a little carried away by their own enthusiasm. Besides, they turned out to be losers, and you know how the Japanese love a loser. Anyway, it struck me that your sessions with your ancient Professor Rogers and his fancy piece in Kamakura during these last few weeks seem to have given you a whole lot of eye-witness background stuff on that precise time. Care to look over what we have so far? Add a little atmosphere maybe about New Year's Day 1936 at – where was it – the Meiji Shrine? Something like that. Jun and Miyoko already interviewed some Japanese old-timers and got some quotes, of course, but the piece could use a little more colour before we let those illiterates back in New York loose on it.'

'Why, of course, Charlie. I'll be delighted. I'd like to see it anyway.' Goldfarb grunted his satisfaction, stood up and stretched, then crossed to the low bookcase against the wall and picked up a yellow-tinted translucent plastic folder containing a number of photocopied sheets of typescript. 'Great. I hoped you'd say yes. Had them Xerox a copy when you called to say you were coming in. Can you turn it around in two-three days?'

'I expect so. It's not like coming at a job cold. I sometimes feel as if part of me is living through that time.'

Goldfarb moved over to where she was sitting and handed the folder to Lesli. 'I'll see that your name goes at the end along with the fifty-six others. Kinda repulsive, isn't it? Used to be that somebody wrote a story over a beer and pastrami and it either got printed or spiked. Now a dozen eager beavers fall over each other's feet for two weeks to sweat out eight hundred words. *Newsworld* has editors the way some people – oh, never mind. Hey, have you noticed the delicatessen counter at the Kinokuniya supermarket since you've been back? It's not bad.'

'Not yet.' Lesli stood up and smiled at him. 'I'll take a look some time, though. I have to go now, Charlie. Sorry about lunch, but I have a session scheduled with Yamada-san over at the STC building in half an hour.'

'I'll kill him,' Goldfarb said cheerfully. 'Take care now, Lesli.'

'I will. I'll call you tomorrow to fix a time to return this with any ideas that occur to me. Bye, Charlie.' Lesli kissed him quickly on the cheek and then skipped away before he could embrace her. Her hand on the door-knob, she turned back with a dazzling smile. 'Thank you for offering to marry me, Charlie, I was beginning to think you'd never ask. I bet Rachel put you up to it.'

## 28. *Monday 17 February, 1936*

'Mr Shimada tells me that he was finally able to speak to his son yesterday,' Nishi said as he preceded Yukichi into the luxuriously furnished office of Seihin Ikeda, Mitsui's chief executive. 'I thought it better that you should hear directly what he has to say.'

Ikeda looked up at the two men and studied them, disengaging the wire earpieces of his glasses from his ears as his secretary withdrew and closed the door. 'Good morning, Director Nishi,' he then said pointedly. His voice was quiet, controlled and full of silky authority. 'Good morning, Mr Shimada. I am much obliged to you for coming to see me. Sit down, gentlemen, both of you. It's wretchedly cold again, but I suppose we must expect this kind of weather in February.'

Although the conversational cliché was not really intended to mean anything and it was relatively warm throughout the Mitsui building with its modern steam heating, Yukichi shuddered as he momentarily saw himself as he had been the previous day, following his son Hideo out of the shabby restaurant near Ueno Station and hunching into his overcoat as the wind lashed the fine rain against his face. At least it had been clean and fresh: the restaurant was heated by a single reeking parafin stove, and the pot of thin fish and vegetable stew they shared had tasted unpleasantly oily.

'Indeed we must. I fancy there is more snow on the way. It will make spring all the more welcome when it comes.' Belatedly aware that he had been overly crude and direct in plunging into the subject of their meeting while still half-way through the door, Nishi was now all graceful affability, and exchanged a few more remarks about the weather with Ikeda while Yukichi sat in silence, trying to stir his sluggish thoughts into some sort of order. Eventually he became aware that both the other men's faces were turned expectantly towards him, and focused on Ikeda, much the more sympathetic of the two. In his sixties now and apparently immune to the chill winds of the retirement code, he had been a legend at Mitsui for many years, having joined the banking side of the business before the turn of the century and risen remorselessly through the hierarchy. Yukichi had not had much to do with him for ten years or more, but for three years in the early twenties Ikeda had been Yukichi's departmental director before another promotion elevated him almost out of sight.

Ikeda laughed deprecatingly, a papery rustle of a sound. 'As I was saying, Mr Shimada, it was a little confusing for me at first, because I distinctly remember the birth of your son when I had the pleasure of your company in my department. No more than fifteen or sixteen years ago, surely. Then I remembered that he was your *second* son. How is he, by the way?' It took Yukichi a moment to redirect his thoughts from Hideo to Jiro, who so seldom made his presence felt in the house, and who alone gave him no cause for anxiety.

'Oh. Yes, quite well, thank you. You are most kind to trouble to ask after him, President. He is seventeen, as a matter of fact. Working hard at present in the slender hope of gaining a place at the Imperial University.'

Ikeda's eyebrows rose in admiring surprise. 'Indeed? Very praiseworthy. I am sure he will do well. And his elder brother already a lieutenant. You must be very proud of both your sons . . . and pleased that they are both here in Tokyo. Though I can quite see that it must be difficult for you to get in touch with the lieutenant. I expect you enjoyed a good chat with him over the New Year holidays, when he was on leave.'

'It seems a very long time since the New Year,' Yukichi said. 'My elder son manages to drop in and see us for a few hours once or twice a month, but it's not easy for him.' Nishi shifted impatiently in his chair.

Ikeda nodded gently. 'And of course we all share your distress at your wife's continued illness, though I was pleased to hear from Mr Nishi that she is on the road to recovery. I was so sorry to have to add to your anxieties by passing on this . . . disturbing rumour.'

'Anyway, you saw him yesterday, you told me,' Nishi butted in abruptly, ignoring Ikeda's sharp warning look.

'Yes. It was fortunate that it was a Sunday. My son had the whole day free, so we went out for lunch together. I . . . I do not know how it can be that his name came to your attention, but I am convinced that the rumour that he is involved with some sort of political group is groundless.'

At least they had come to the point at last, Yukichi reflected, remembering how alienated he had felt from his son as he fell into step beside him and they set out to walk home in silence in the grey Sunday afternoon chill. It had been hard enough, when Hideo turned up at the house unexpectedly in the late morning, to get him to go upstairs and see his mother, still harder afterwards to persuade him to go out with him for lunch and a talk: he seemed to be determined for some unfathomable reason to drag Teruko off to visit the Mitsukoshi Department Store near the Ginza, something she obviously had no wish to do. In any case, Yoko had gone out for the day and for once Teruko seemed bent on devoting herself to her mother, unexpectedly refusing point-blank to go with Hideo.

'You are quite sure, Mr Shimada?' Ikeda asked very quietly. 'I need hardly say that I am intensely reluctant to intrude into your private concerns, but the information we have been receiving from a very particular contact of ours who has, shall we say, a unique relationship with the leading figures in the Young Officers' Movement is very specific . . .'

Something in Yukichi seemed to snap. 'I know my son, Mr Ikeda,' he said harshly. 'He is not an intellectual. Indeed in many ways he is still naive and immature. He is proud to be an officer, and his sole ambition is to serve. He is no politician, and certainly no conspirator. He is a simple, conventionally patriotic soldier.' He had never before spoken about his view of Hideo's character to a living soul, and the outburst left him distraught and quivering.

'Yes, yes, but did you *ask* him –'

'I am sure the lieutenant is everything you say, Mr Shimada. Who is in a better position to assess a young man's character than his own father?' Ikeda's voice, though much quieter, cut icily into Nishi's attempted intervention. 'Nevertheless, I think that all three of us are sophisticated and realistic enough to acknowledge in the privacy of this room that this is precisely how such prominent activists of the Imperial Way faction as Colonel Aizawa like to describe themselves.' There seemed to be no hostility in Ikeda's manner. In spite of his obvious scepticism he gave the impression of allying himself with Yukichi against Nishi, who sat in glowering impatience.

Yukichi forced himself to be calm, and achieved something like a detached tone. 'Yes. I don't dispute that. I asked my son frankly what he thought about the current debate over the trial of Colonel Aizawa and the conflict within the Army between the Imperial Way and the Control factions. His reply was to the effect that he regretted that the generals were not agreed on whether the

Chinese or the Russians constitute the greater strategic threat to the security and prosperity of the Empire. I asked him whether he had thought about the domestic political implications of the disagreement. He had clearly not done so. Nor was he in the habit of discussing them with his brother officers, he said. I believed him. I further asked him whether he thought that elements in the officer corps might be contemplating any form of direct political action. He scoffed at the idea.' Yukichi took a deep breath. 'Finally I asked him if he might ever be tempted to emulate a man like Colonel Aizawa. It was perfectly clear to me that the notion had never entered his head.'

Yukichi listened to himself in a kind of wonder, and sat back when he had finished, reflecting that it could only be simple exhaustion that made him lie so fluently. He had almost convinced himself that he and Hideo had in fact had a reasoned and reassuring conversation the previous day, rather than an encounter which had left him frightened and full of foreboding, and Hideo red-faced and angry.

Evidently bored and frustrated, Hideo had been by turns haughty and petulant, and utterly deaf to the subtleties of what Yukichi tried to say to him over the meal. Far from expressing the opinions Yukichi attributed to him, he was loftily dismissive about the whole tribe of politicians and their big business allies, and spoke admiringly of men like Colonel Aizawa and Generals Araki and Mazaki as being the only public figures with the interests of the Empire at heart.

Hideo's manner became more heated when Yukichi murmured that he had heard rumours that some officers might be tempted to take the law into their own hands. 'And what if they do?' he snapped, and went on to make recklessly disparaging remarks about Admiral Saito and the Prime Minister, heedless of the curious, uneasy glances he was attracting from other customers. Real anger had erupted when Yukichi urged him to lower his voice, and said that he hoped very much that Hideo would never allow himself to be sucked into association with any seditious group. Yukichi shrank back in his chair as he remembered the scene and the shaking of his own hands as he paid the bill for their food while Hideo stormed out.

'Well, my informant could be mistaken, of course,' Ikeda said calmly. 'About the possible involvement of your son, I mean. There is no doubt that *something* is afoot, and whatever the results of the elections this week we must expect even greater unrest in the Army.' He sighed and smiled wearily at Yukichi. 'Thank you so much for speaking to the lieutenant, and for this helpful information. At least I shall be able to reassure Baron Mitsui that your son has not allowed himself to become involved with this group of rash young hot-heads who are said to be scheming some foolishness or other.'

'I certainly hope not,' Nishi said grimly as he and Yukichi stood up and Ikeda inclined his head in dismissal. 'It would be intolerable for someone with a family connection with us to get into trouble of that sort.'

'Unfortunate, certainly, Director Nishi,' Ikeda agreed. 'Thank you for joining us: I am sorry to have kept you so long. Mr Shimada, could you remain for just a moment or two longer?'

Nishi was so taken aback by his dismissal that he opened his mouth to speak, but Ikeda's eyes were fixed on him bleakly and after a second's hesitation he turned angrily on his heel and left the room. A mirthless smile fluttered over the chief executive's face as he watched Nishi go, to be replaced by an expression of great gravity when he looked up at Yukichi again. Then he stood, straightened his black jacket and went to the window overlooking the banks and other commercial buildings of the Marunouchi financial centre of Tokyo. He turned so that his back was to the light and Yukichi could no longer see his features clearly.

'Sit down again, please. There are a number of things Director Nishi does not know and has no reason to know, Mr Shimada,' he began. 'I have no business to confide in you either, but I propose to do so, because I have respect for you and it distresses me for you to be put in the position of having to be deceitful. Your son is an active member of the Young Officers' Movement. You may not have known this, but I am quite sure that he did not react yesterday to your questions in the way that you have reported. Mr Shimada, Mitsui has been handing over substantial sums of money to representatives of the radical officers for a number of years. This is partly because I personally believe that in order to safeguard Mitsui interests a genuine change of direction is needed. Others may call it protection money: I myself am one of those whose safety is bought. I hope.'

Ikeda came away from the window and Yukichi could then see his wintry smile. He found it hard to credit what he was being told.

'It is with some difficulty that arrangements have been made for my name to be struck off a list of potential assassination victims, and I am told that I am likely to be accused during the Aizawa court-martial of all manner of unpatriotic attitudes and activities. Ironically, by an officer called Colonel Mitsui. No relation, Mr Shimada. This last is I suspect because last month I rejected a request from one of your son's brother officers, a Captain Yamaguchi, for a donation of three thousand yen towards what he quaintly referred to as publication expenses. It does not do to be too obvious. Tell me, have you ever heard of Ikki Kita?'

'Yes, sir, of course.'

Ikeda sat down with friendly informality in the easy-chair beside Yukichi's.

'Yes, of course. But what you may not know is that Mr Kita lives in some style at Nakano with his wife and his adopted Chinese son. He affects the ascetic manner of the scholar and invariably dresses in a Chinese robe, but in fact he employs three maids and a chauffeur. He can do this, Mr Shimada, because for the past two years I have been paying him twenty thousand yen annually from Mitsui funds – oh, and I gave him an extra five thousand last year so that he could move house and have a telephone installed. You look rather surprised: I suppose it *is* surprising.'

Yukichi's reaction was not one of surprise, but sheer incredulity. That Kita, an arch-enemy of the *zaibatsu*, the philosopher and inspiration of the radical right and revered teacher of Mitsugi Nishida, should be in the pay of Mitsui was simply unbelievable – yet the President of the Mitsui Holding Company was not a man who made jokes.

'And you may well ask what we get in return for this considerable outlay – not to mention the three *million* yen I donated to the Tokyo Military Police last year, ostensibly to be spent on additional educational provision for young army officers in the district. Well, I have mentioned protection. It is to be hoped that any future military government, in consequence of Mitsui's generosity, will be reluctant to see our interests harmed. Mr Kita's views are also, I believe, coloured by our little arrangement, and they carry great weight with your son's friends. Quite apart from that, however, these payments ensure that I am kept fully informed about what is in the wind.' Yukichi buried his head in his hands.

'So you see, I know rather more about your son's current activities than you do, Mr Shimada. Please be assured that I have said no more to Mr Nishi than I did to you when he was here in the room. There could, you see, be some advantage for us in your personal link with the group who are quite definitely plotting a coup d'etat and who may well be instrumental in bringing about a change of government – but not if you are on bad terms with your son. There might be no harm in your letting him know of Mitsui's special relationship with Ikki Kita and of the extensive financial support we have given to the Young Officers' Movement in recent years – in spite of the assassination of our former chief director, the late Takuma Dan, in 1932. In case Kita-*sensei* and his disciple Mitsugi Nishida haven't thought to mention it, I mean.'

Ikeda rubbed his dry hands together and began to stand up. 'Well, I hope we understand each other a little better after this chat. Incidentally, Mr Shimada, I realise that you must be anxious about the future . . . your retirement, I mean. Well, please don't be. We do know how to express our gratitude for favours, as you will have gathered.'

Yoko had been drifting in a state of drowsy half-consciousness, but turned over in bed as she heard her sister's stealthy step on the stairs followed by the hissing whisper of the sliding *fusuma* foor. Then she relaxed completely in sensual comfort, eager to yield to the velvety embrace of deep sleep. After two weeks she had begun to accustom herself to Teruko's furtive homecomings at midnight or later, and once or twice had been sleeping so profoundly that she had been oblivious to her arrival in bed beside her. The physical demands of housework combined with almost daily bouts of ecstatic lovemaking left her languidly exhausted every night, and the fierce happiness of her love smothered her despairing anxiety over her mother, her realisation that there could be no long-term future for her relationship with Dwight Rogers, and her uneasiness about what she thought of as the deception she was practising on Teruko. In spite of everything, therefore, Yoko experienced no difficulty in sleeping.

She had no idea whether her mother had any awareness of what had been going on in the house, or whether indeed she had even properly registered the American's existence on the two or three occasions when he had arrived while Chie was wandering wraith-like through the house rather than sitting quietly or murmuring her long drawn-out prayers in the upstairs room she seldom left: on the whole Yoko thought not. During Rogers' first visit three days after the return from Tenri his manner had been stiff and awkward, while Yoko sat miserably, her face flaming in an agony of embarrassment as she tried to thank him for his kindness on the train and for the gifts of expensive chrysanthemums and Morozoff chocolates he had brought with him.

On that occasion she had been relieved to see him go; relieved also that he had come at a time when she and her mother were alone in the house. In a mood of solemn acceptance of her lot, and convinced that her career was at an end, she even began to compose a letter to Mr Nagai at the university, a careful matter of oblique apology and dignified regrets. Marriage to the squint-eyed and ambitious Mr Sato of Mitsui seemed inevitable, provided he did not learn of the nature of her mother's illness and back off. Yoko looked at the incomplete draft in a kind of disbelief after Dwight Rogers' second visit the following lunchtime.

After they had bowed to each other in the little entryway to the house, Dwight had, without a word, reached behind him to close the sliding outer door, slipped out of his shoes and stepped up to where she was kneeling in disconcerted welcome, raised her in silence to her feet and kissed her.

It was not in the least like what had happened in Mr Nagai's untidy office. Yoko's body did not take over as it had then: indeed she struggled, fluttering her arms weakly and pushing herself away from the American's bulk as he cradled her cheek and chin in one warm hand and gently but inexorably drew her face upwards. The kiss seemed to last forever, though, and by the time he released her she was in a daze. She offered no resistance as he led her into the main downstairs room, and they sank to their knees at the same time. Then he lowered her on to the *tatami* matting, pulling a flat cushion over to support her head, and kissed her again.

Kisses were enough, that first time. An hour later Yoko was clinging to him in a last embrace before he left, drunk with pleasure but still a virgin, her kimono scarcely disarranged. On the following day they made love, and Yoko whimpered with the pain of it but cherished the throbbing which continued deep inside her long after Rogers had gone. It saddened her to have to ask him not to come on Saturday or Sunday, but the following Monday's pleasure was all the more piercing, and by the fifth day she was trying shyly to please him both before and after giving herself up to the sweeping waves of delight which engulfed her. Thoughts of marriage to Mr Sato were obliterated and even Mr Nagai was almost forgotten, diminished and supplanted by the immediacy of the miracle which had raised her from near-despair to joy.

Teruko was noisier than usual as she undressed, blundering about the little room and once stumbling over Yoko's leg, jolting her into a stage nearer full consciousness. Yoko rolled over in momentary irritation as Teruko slumped into bed and pulled at the eiderdown-like coverings, and then for the first time became aware of the subdued sniffs and sobs coming from her sister.

'Teru-chan! Are you all right?' There was no reply, and Yoko propped herself up on one elbow and moved the hair out of her eyes, now fully awake. It was pitch dark in the room, for on winter nights they always closed the heavy wooden storm shutters outside the lath-and-paper *shoji* to keep the cold out, and left them in place all day as well if the weather was dull. The family had talked sporadically about having the upstairs *shoji* screens partially glazed, a luxury that some smart people were beginning to go in for; but the installation of the bathroom had been enough of an upheaval and nothing had come of the idea.

'Teru! What's the matter? Why are you crying?'

'I'm not. Leave me alone.' Teruko's denial was at once belied by another choking sob as she turned her back on Yoko, who shook her by the shoulder.

'Don't be silly. Tell me. What's the time, anyway?' Their cheap tin alarm clock with its double bells on top was reasonably reliable but did not have phosphorescent paint on its face.

'Quarter past one,' Teruko muttered. 'Leave me alone. It's bad enough having to get up at half past six as it is.' She sniffed again as Yoko burrowed back down into the warmth of the bedding.

'Father asked where you were this evening,' Yoko said. 'He doesn't usually seem to notice. I had to tell a lie. I told him you came in very tired while he was in the bath and went straight to bed. You're bound to be found out, you know. Even if you have talked Jiro into unlocking the front door again after Father locks it last thing. I think it's very unfair of you to involve him. Besides, what must the neighbours be thinking, with you coming home at all hours like this?'

Even as she whispered to Teruko, Yoko was uneasily aware that Mrs Toda and the other neighbourhood gossips were much more likely to have taken note of the comings and goings of Dwight Rogers in broad daylight than they were to have observed Teruko's discreet homecomings long after they were in bed. Foreigners were not only a rare sight in the quiet Hongo district, far from their normal haunts in Ginza or Hibiya, but were objects of the suspicious curiosity of patrolling policemen, and after Dwight's fifth visit to the house Yoko had shyly spoken to him of her fears. He sadly acknowledged that he was being unjustifiably reckless, and agreed that it would be wise to stop coming to see her there.

Yoko now went out on some weekdays as soon as Jiro arrived home from school and could keep an eye on his mother, and hurried to the Tokyo Station Hotel where Dwight would be waiting for her in his room: it was comparatively easy for her to slip up the stairs unobserved amid the general bustle at that time of the day.

On the previous Sunday she had boldly claimed a whole day to herself, leaving Teruko to feed Jiro and their father. She and Dwight had gone to Kamakura, where he had a share in a tiny weekend house, and made love so many times that for once they were both satiated: she had re-lived every moment of their long hours together since, feeding her spirit on remembered joy. Yoko had no idea how long she could keep up her complex double life. She knew that sooner of later they must be separated, but in the meantime lived for each day and thought endlessly about ways to contrive an hour or two with her lover. Dwight for his part seemed equally besotted, and was speaking of renting an apartment in one of the new blocks occupied by foreigners, who unlike Japanese took little interest in other people's activities.

'I don't care about the neighbours. They're enjoying themselves enough as it is wondering how mad Mother is. And don't waste your sympathy on Jiro. He's the last person to feel sorry for.' Although Teruko was whispering too, Yoko was taken aback by the bitterness of her words. She sighed and turned so that she was lying flat on her back. 'I don't know about Mother,' she said. 'If you won't tell me why you're upset, then I suppose you won't. I think *you* must be going soft in the head, though, wearing yourself out and coming home half-dead with exhaustion every night like this. You never used to be obsessed with money. I still can't understand how you can bring yourself to go to that place night after night and sit there being looked over and then dance with any man who cares to pay.'

'Shut up and mind your own business!' There was such savagery in Teruko's voice that Yoko physically recoiled. 'I'm sorry,' she whispered at last. 'I shouldn't have said that.' She reached out tentatively and took Teruko's hand in hers. Teruko began to snatch it away, but then gripped Yoko's hand in return with another stifled sob.

'It's your business, I know,' Yoko went on. 'And you have been able to buy some very pretty clothes already . . . it's just that I worry about Father finding out. He has a lot on his mind as it is, and I'm afraid of what might happen. Oh, come on, why are you crying, Teru-chan? Please tell me.'

'I can't. It's – oh, lots of things. I can't explain. Please don't ask any more. I simply must try to go to sleep.'

Yoko's heart missed a beat as she forced herself to put the question which had been drifting in and out of her consciousness ever since Dwight Rogers' first visit to the house. 'What about Mr Rogers, Teruko?'

Teruko made a sound halfway between a sigh and a sniff. 'I suppose he might come in one evening and pay a yen for a dance with me. I won't even be embarrassed now if he does. I'm not clever enough for him. I knew it really on that first evening he asked me out. Besides, everything's changed now. I've got no time for dates. Nothing to give away. I'm for sale now.'

She pulled her hand away and slumped on to her side. Neither girl spoke again, and within a few minutes Yoko realised that her sister had cried herself to sleep. A mixture of guilt and anxiety kept her awake a little longer, but then she too slid into unconsciousness.

## 30. *Wednesday 19 February, 1986*

'Good afternoon, Hoshino-san. Please have a seat.' Lesli sat down warily. It was the 'Japanese Shimada' who had greeted her, and he looked at his most formidable. He was wearing a dark blue pin-striped suit instead of his usual grey, and an STC company badge winked in his lapel. 'I have just returned from a long conference at the Federation of Economic Organisations and have scarcely had time to gather my thoughts. Forgive me.' He looked neither confused nor penitent, and brushed aside the courteous apologies that came so much more naturally to Lesli in Japanese than in English.

'Yamada-san tells me you've been concentrating on the Brandt Commission papers in the past few days. We hear precious little about the so-called North-South dialogue these days.' He looked at her keenly. 'Are you feeling quite well? You look pale.' Lesli was surprised he noticed. 'Thank you, yes. I'm all right. I didn't sleep well last night.'

'I'm sorry to hear that. I used to suffer greatly from insomnia when I was young. They say people sleep less well as they grow older; with me the reverse has been the case.'

'I envy you,' Lesli said with feeling. 'Yet you have taken the world's problems on your shoulders in the last twenty years. Previously you only worried about yourself.'

Shimada's head jerked up. 'That's a curious remark.'

She hastened to explain. 'Excuse me. I didn't mean to be rude. It's a simple matter of fact, surely? You began to lay down the foundations of your business success very young – as a schoolboy, in fact – and concentrated on that, so far as your war service permitted, right up till the nineteen-fifties. Then you began to involve yourself with international problems. I'd like to ask whether some personal experience around that time perhaps triggered off these new concerns.'

'I see.' Shimada did not sound as though he found Lesli's explanation entirely satisfactory. 'You always get back to my personal life, don't you? Is this a female characteristic, I wonder?

As a matter of fact my interest in the state of the world was not something which developed suddenly. Politics and money are inextricably linked. At every level, and in every country. Perhaps especially in Japan. When I was building up my business I needed politicians. Later on they began to need me, and I was often invited to go into politics myself. Japanese businessmen can in the long term only prosper in a stable and healthy economy. By the same argument, Japan as a nation has, or should have, a keen interest in helping to secure a stable and prosperous world order.'

'Yes. You've made the point in a number of your speeches. Why *didn't* you go into politics, then, President Shimada? You're one of the most influential individual businessmen in Japan, perhaps in the world, but you're still a private citizen. Could you not have exercised even more influence on the course of events if you had become one of Japan's political leaders, Prime Minister perhaps?'

'Perhaps. I chose not to,' Shimada said shortly. 'Let us turn to some of your other questions, shall we?'

## 31. Tokyo, Friday 21
## February, 1936

Captain Nonaka was in the chair. Although not one of the key leaders he was the most senior in rank among them, having held his captaincy the longest. There was no need for him to call for attention: all eyes were on him as he drained his *sake* and then nodded to the civilian Mitsugi Nishida who was placed in the seat of honour in front of the *tokonoma* alcove. Nishida cleared his throat and looked round, and then at last began to speak. 'Gentlemen, it has been an evening of comradeship, trust and expectation. We still have no specific news for you, but you may be assured that action is imminent. I think it most unlikely that the First Division will be going to Manchuria in April as some of our highly paid, *geisha*-fondling generals seem to think it might.'

A ripple of laughter went round the room. Captains Kono and Ando were seated on either side of Nonaka, and all three looked gravely at the other young men gathered in the upstairs room in the same Shinjuku restaurant the conspirators had used for their early meetings some months before. All were in civilian clothes and the waitresses had been banished from the room having cleared away the remains of the meal and supplying plenty of *sake*.

There were almost certainly police spies among the restaurant staff, and Nonaka and his colleagues knew that the civil authorities must be aware that a 'folk poetry appreciation society' of army officers met in the restaurant from time to time. It was not a matter of much concern: the absurd name fooled nobody, and there were a number of such political discussion groups in Tokyo and the provinces. 'No further details will be discussed at this time and in this place. Guard your tongues as always, and make it your business to consult with your individual briefing officers each day from now on without fail. We shall not all meet together again until success is assured.'

The atmosphere throughout the meal had been one of subdued excitement, and there had been none of the lively arguments which had previously characterised their meetings. As Hideo looked round at his brother officers he hoped that the same dignified dedication which he saw in their faces was apparent in his own. He was glad that the waiting was almost over, but contemplated what he was expected to do personally in probably less than a week's time as though watching a film in his head. The thought of meeting Teruko again for an hour or two on Sunday displaced and distanced the image of himself assassinating Viscount Saito: several times he had stood in his cell-like room pointing his unloaded pistol at the hard pillow on his narrow cot and trying to visualise the head of the old man he had seen getting out of the car and going into his house. Each time the picture melted, sliding out of focus and floating back as the face of his sister.

The image of Teruko was never far from his consciousness. As he sat there surrounded by his comrades, Hideo saw her in his mind's eye with a sharp physical immediacy which almost took his breath away as she had lain with him in the cheap inn on the fringes of Yoshiwara, the throbbing at the base of her delicate throat clearly visible to him as he traced the lines of her body with shaking hands. She would not look at him; kept her eyes tightly closed and her face averted, and denied him her lips even as she writhed in fierce, shameful ecstasy under him.

That he did give his sister intense sexual pleasure was obvious to Hideo, and it never occurred to him to consider her emotions. He was in a dreamlike, exalted state, and Teruko's refusal to go with him again to the inn the previous Sunday had left him quivering with uncomprehending frustration, a demigod with divine appetites which no ordinary person should dare to deny, least of all one who was a mere girl, a younger sister trained and conditioned in any case to defer to him even had he not been entrusted with a vital mission in the service of the Emperor.

Yet, although part of him did not want to remember, Hideo thought often too of that first night, when Teruko had stood scornfully over him and made him grovel in blind worship between her thighs, glorying in her power. The power to withhold herself was just as total, and he had seen the flash of contempt in her eyes when, later that Sunday, he begged her to meet him the following week instead and finally extracted a maddeningly inconclusive half-promise from her. He was tormented by the possibility that she might not keep it, and thought it intolerable that he should be distracted in this way.

Then there was his mincing, dandified old fool of a father babbling on about matters he could not hope to understand and had no right even to attempt to discuss with an officer of the Imperial Army. As a child, and even in his gangling, pimply adolescence, Hideo had admired Yukichi's elegance and sophistication, watching him intently as he tied his necktie with artistic precision of a morning and blushing at the harsh sound of his own voice and his inarticulate clumsiness when his father spoke to him in his polished way, using complex forms of words and referring with casual familiarity to all manner of intellectual mysteries. It was shaming for him that even at twelve or thirteen Yoko seemed to be able to keep up with their father, earnestly discussing the novels of Riichi Yokomitsu and Yasunari Kawabata and the 'new sensibilities' school of writing they both admired, while Hideo grimly struggled with the school textbooks which, with the exception of those concerned with mechanics and mathematics, were so much gibberish to him. His mother had been good to him during those painful years, for she too was shy, and as awkward in expressing herself as her eldest son. Yet they had seemed to communicate well enough, and in those days he had seldom been truly comfortable and relaxed except in her presence. He wanted to feel sorry for her in her present state, but it only made him angry and embarrassed to think about it.

It was different with his father, who had seemed contemptible in his timid presumptuousness as they sat over that disgusting meal in the restaurant. How dared he poke his nose into Army business, and even attempt to silence Hideo when he told him a few home truths about the corrupt politicians who were imperilling the Empire while feathering their nests with the help of the cigar-smoking capitalists who preyed on simple, honourable farmers and artisans who wanted none of the tinsel degeneracy of westernised ways. And it was these very capitalists to whom his father, for all his elevated cultural posturings, had sold himself body and soul as a young man, and towards whom he had become ever more servile since! Thanks to the inspiring lectures of the former officer Nishida and his fervent exposition of the writings of his master Kita-*sensei*, Hideo now saw his father for what he was, and he despised his pathetic attempts to understand the noble philosophy to which he himself was committed.

He had seen no reason to report the fact that rumours of some impending political intervention by the Army seemed to have reached the ears of people in Mitsui and presumably the other *zaibatsu*: let them scurry about in their stinking funk-holes until driven out to face the cleansing power of the new order represented by the fine men who had accepted him as one of them and whom he was privileged to call friends!

'So, gentlemen, it remains only to drink to that success, and to the health of our civilian comrades and above all to our teachers, Kita-*sensei*, who is not able to be with us this evening, and Nishida-*sensei*, who is.' Captain Nonaka scrambled up, seized the nearest *sake* flask and went over to fill Nishida's cup. Returning, he offered the same courtesy first to Captain Ando and afterwards to Captain Kono. Then he lifted his own cup as Kono returned the compliment and all the others in the room similarly offered and received *sake*. Satisfied that everyone was ready, Nonaka looked round the room and raised his cup. '*Kampai!*'

The toast completed, Nishida rose to his feet and surveyed the others. He was one of the few in the room to be wearing Japanese dress, and Hideo wished he had done so himself, Nishida-*sensei* looked so right in it. 'Gentlemen, I thank you on Kita-*sensei*'s behalf, on behalf of our other civilian associates, and on my own. I now ask you to kneel and face in the direction of the Imperial Palace and join me in an act of obeisance.' He made a half-turn and dropped to his own knees as the others hurriedly turned in the same direction and scrambled up from the cross-legged posture in which most of them had been sitting at the low tables on the *tatami* matting.

It was Captain Nonaka who barked the order. '*Ojigi!*' Hideo felt the goose-pimples rise on his skin as he bowed lower and lower until his sweaty forehead rested against the cool, fragrant smoothness of the *tatami*. A surge of great confidence and joy swept through him, so powerful that he felt that His Majesty must surely sense the emanation of devotion being directed towards him. The silence in the room was profound, and remained so until Nonaka gave the order to rise again, this time in a quiet reverent voice.

Hideo had little recollection of leaving the restaurant, and remained silent as he shared a taxi back to the barracks at Azabu with three of the others. It wasn't so very far, and took only twenty minutes or so. After they were deposited outside the gates he made his farewells to his friends there, and went for a walk before going inside. The stars were bright that night, and the *sake* he had drunk kept him delightfully warm. He turned back with a secret smile when in sight of the Prime Minister's official residence, and was still in such a good mood that he acknowledged the salute of the sentry on guard outside the Azabu barracks with an affable greeting, and chatted for a few moments with the orderly sergeant at the guardhouse.

Everything seemed clear, clean and certain, and he now had no doubt that Teruko would join him at the inn on Sunday. Their love-making would crown his preparations.

'I think he's asleep, dear.' Mrs Grew leant over and barely breathed the words into her husband's ear as the faces of Jeanette MacDonald and Nelson Eddy filled the screen which had been placed towards one end of the huge drawing room of the Residence, and Victor Herbert's music swelled from the speaker on a low table beside it. The American Ambassador glanced across her and allowed the merest suspicion of a smile to flicker over his disciplined features as he saw that the old man's eyes were indeed closed. He made no attempt to reply, but reached out stealthily and squeezed her hand.

Joseph Grew could see no harm in the fact that the guest of honour was taking a little nap. The dinner for thirty-six had been a great success, and the fact that the Lord Keeper of the Privy Seal and Viscountess Saito had stayed on to see the movie proved it, for it was well known that as a rule the Admiral liked to get home and to bed early. Just then the muffled sound of the ringing of the telephone in the hall interrupted his reverie and irritated him for a moment, but it soon stopped: one of the servants obviously got to it right away. The Ambassador soon relaxed in the comfort of his armchair in the front row and noticed that Viscountess Saito on the other side was nodding happily in time to the music and tapping her fan unobtrusively but rhythmically on her lap.

Grew smiled to himself again in the semi-darkness as he recalled the dubious expression on the dear old soul's gentle features when he explained to her over dinner that he had viewed the film in advance and that its title *Naughty Marietta* implied no impropriety, reassuring her that he had chosen it from several offered by the representative of the film company precisely on account of its wholesome nature and the charm of the musical score. He fished out his watch and consulted it by the flickering light from the screen. Ten past eleven and they were well over half-way through the last reel. The old couple would be on their way home by eleven thirty at the latest. The Ambassador knew that he could rely on dear Alice to wake the Admiral tactfully in good time.

In the Sanno Hotel Hideo wiped the sweat from his forehead as he put the phone down. It had been risky to ring the Ambassador's residence, and he would have had to break the connection at once if an American had answered it, but mercifully the Japanese butler had identified himself as such, and obligingly told the caller, who said he was a member of the Lord Keeper's staff, that the Admiral Viscount and his lady were enjoying a film which was expected to end within half an hour at most. And yes, it was snowing rather heavily, but the Lord Keeper's chauffeur had already started the engine of his car and it would be comfortably warm inside by the time they set off for home.

It was reassuring to know for sure where his target was, and more especially where he would be at five the next morning when the special groups were to strike. The fact that the Saitos would be unusually late abed that night made it all the more unlikely that they would be up and about before dawn the next morning. The unexpected snow was something of a nuisance, though. They couldn't afford any mechanical troubles, and Ando had just been making it clear to Hideo that as soon as he and his group had dealt with the Admiral, the other officers and men were to be shifted quickly to the strategic buildings they had to seize, while he himself was to return to the coup headquarters at the Sanno and concentrate on his vital responsibilities as principal liaison officer.

It had already been a day of furious activity, precipitated by the fact that Captain Ando was down on the roster as the Third Regiment's orderly officer of the week, that Captain Yamaguchi had consequently arranged to take the same duty for the First Regiment and that Lieutenant Nakahashi's company of the Imperial Guards was unexpectedly assigned to relieve part of the Palace guard with effect from the twenty-sixth.

General Mazaki had made his crucial appearance as a defence witness at the Aizawa court-martial earlier that day, when Hideo and the other eighteeen officers at the centre of the plan had been finally briefed and sent off to invite their NCOs to cooperate. It was gratifying that all those he addressed had agreed to throw in their lot with him and Yasuda, even though they had been left free to refuse. Hideo was honest enough to remark afterwards to Yasuda that the knowledge that the popular Captain 'Four-Eyes' Ando was behind everything had probably done the trick.

There were rumours that at the last minute Kita and Nishida had counselled postponement, but the die was cast now. Captain Kono would be off around midnight with a small back-up team of civilians in two cars to the Yugawara hot-spring resort, sixty miles west of the capital, to deal with Saito's predecessor Count Makino; and at two a.m. – in a few hours – it would be time for Hideo to rendezvous with his three brother officers and their NCOs, carry out a hurried roll-call of their companies, tell the men in general terms about the action, then get them quietly out of barracks and head for the Saito house at Yotsuya, a couple of miles away.

'It's time you were in bed, Jiro,' Yukichi said, looking at the clock near the wireless set in the corner as Jiro passed through the room again on his way back from the lavatory, and he realised that his younger son was still fully dressed, with only the two top buttons of his black student tunic open. 'It's no good working *too* hard, you know. Making yourself ill.' Yukichi kept his finger in his book to mark the place, but had absorbed nothing of what he had been trying to read since Yoko had given him his supper, cleared away and gone up to bed.

'I'm all right. It's still snowing quite hard.'

'Yes. It makes everything so quiet, doesn't it? Your mother's sleeping very well: the quietness must be helping.' Yukichi looked again at the clock. 'I can't think why Teruko isn't home yet. She should have been back long ago.'

Jiro rubbed a hand over his bristly scalp and stifled a yawn. 'If it comes to that, Yoko didn't get in until about ten minutes before you. She went out as soon as I got back from school. I don't know where.'

It was true, and Jiro resented the fact. He had every intention of following Yoko the next time she went out on one of her mysterious late afternoon expeditions. She was sufficiently evasive whenever he made any comment about them for Jiro to have become convinced that she had something to hide. Her absence for the whole day the previous Sunday but one bothered him, too.

'Yoko is having a very hard time at the moment with Mother so ill. She needs to get out of the house now and then,' Yukichi said as the front door rattled, and they both heard Teruko's voice as she off-handedly called 'I'm home.' Then came the stamping of feet as she knocked the snow off her shoes, and after a moment she came into the room rubbing her hands.

'Ah. There you are at last. Yoko's already gone to bed, and Jiro's just going. I was getting quite worried about you.' They both stared at Teruko. The cold air had brought a little colour to her cheeks and a few melting snowflakes in her hair where her hat had not covered it glittered under the electric light.

'It's half past eleven,' Jiro said evenly, and Teruko snapped at him, 'I'm perfectly well aware of the fact.' Then she turned to her father. 'The snow held you up, I suppose,' Yukichi said wearily. 'Unusually heavy. It took me longer than usual to get home myself, and it's much worse now. You'd better clear the path in the morning before you go to school if you don't mind, Jiro. We don't want anyone slipping and falling. Yoko said that the doctor would probably look in tomorrow.'

Yukichi did not press the point of Teruko's late arrival home. Now that she was there, and had more or less answered his own implied question, he forgot about it. It was, after all, the least of his worries. The most pressing one at the moment arose from the fact that there was gossip at Mitsui to the effect that President Seihin Ikeda had come to the office as usual on Monday and then, after receiving and making a few telephone calls, abruptly left Tokyo for an unspecified destination. His secretary had been obliged to cancel several important meetings. Yukichi had not been able to do more than write a careful letter to Hideo following his talk with Ikeda, and now feared the worst.

Getting into the Saito house was simplicity itself. Hideo's only worry had been that there were so many of them that it might be difficult to achieve it quietly enough. He had therefore placed each of the three other lieutenants assigned to his force in command of fifty of the total of nearly two hundred men, and had kept them well back. One detachment, indeed, was seizing the neighbourhood police station to block off any possible intervention from that quarter, while the others sealed off the approaches to the house and the back entrance. Only Hideo, his sergeant and a dozen or so men walked up to the high gates, the blanket of snow muffling the sound. The smallest and lightest trooper scaled the gates with the aid of a leg-up from two of the others, dropped quietly into the snow inside, and unbolted them.

Although they had made little noise their arrival did not go completely unnoticed. As they approached the house a downstairs light came on, and the front door was opened by the little maid whom Hideo had last seen wriggling in the embrace of the local policeman. Her *yukata* crumpled and her eyes puffy with sleep, the girl's mouth hung open slackly as she gaped at the menacing shadows in the snow, then she shrank back frozen with terror as the sergeant shone the beam of his torch in her face. 'So long as you don't make a sound nobody will hurt you,' Hideo said as he pushed past her into the entrance hall, his service revolver in his hand.

Then he hesitated, not because a frightened look of recognition came into the maid's eyes as she cowered against the wall, but because he found himself instinctively wanting to take his boots off. It was only the pressure of the men crowding in behind him which forced him up on to the glossy, silky wood of the step and over the yielding *tatami* matting, and even then he winced as he heard the scraping of the heavy nailed boots of the others as they violated the austere beauty of the entrance.

The sergeant by his side, Hideo strode swiftly through the empty downstairs rooms. Having whispered an order to post two men down there to search the kitchen, lavatory and bathroom, he made his way as quietly as he could up the stairs. The house was somewhat larger than his own home, but its layout was not greatly different. It seemed that the Saitos, for all their status, did not live in any great luxury, though there may well have been priceless art objects in the alcoves, and in the fireproof storehouse which adjoined the main building.

There was little doubt in Hideo's mind which was the room they would be sleeping in, and although his heart was pounding and the blood roaring in his ears, none about what he had to do. He beckoned the sergeant as he slid open the *fusuma* screen door and the beam of his torch wavered only for a moment before it picked out the startled face of the woman struggling to sit up, and the recumbent man beside her. Hideo had time to fire two rounds into the body of the Lord Keeper of the Privy Seal before the old lady flung herself protectively over him and the other men thrust their way into the room.

On the other side of Tokyo Yukichi Shimada woke from his uneasy half-sleep as his wife Chie cried out in seeming pain, and then almost immediately began to babble one of her gibberish prayers as he dragged himself out of bed and went over to try to calm her.

'I couldn't help it,' Hideo said to Lieutenant Takahashi during a hastily snatched meal of rice balls and green tea several hours later. The rice tasted of nothing at all and his whole body felt as though it were anaesthetised; so much so that his emotions were numb too, and he could speak quite dispassionately about the affair. 'She took a bullet in each arm and one in her shoulder, even though I stressed to them all that we didn't want to harm anybody except her husband. The trouble was, she wouldn't get out of the way, so we had to shove her about to get our guns underneath her to hit him. Then of course we had to make sure we'd finished him off. One of the soldiers downstairs came in and said he'd like to have a go so the sergeant let him fire a few rounds: I didn't like to interfere. The sergeant wanted to cut his throat to make absolutely sure, but he was definitely dead and the old woman wouldn't leave the body, so we left. Then I don't remember much except you and the others forming the men up outside the front gate. That was a fine sight, wasn't it? I suppose it was your idea to call for a triple *banzai* for His Majesty before we all went off?'

'What do you think? Anyway, you did better than some of the others,' Takahashi said. 'So did Yasuda and Tanaka and me. We didn't stand any nonsense from General Watanabe. Or his wife. She had the impudence to ask us whose orders we were acting on. Yasuda told her straight, we weren't her old man's private army, we were His Majesty's soldiers. Then we found him skulking behind a heap of bedding and Yasuda let him have it. Then Tanaka told them to machine gun him, of all things. The others seemed to have made a hash of things. The idiots after Grand Chamberlain Suzuki practically finished him off and then they say *his* wife interfered. Demanded the right to give her husband the *coup de grace* with a dagger herself and the fools left her to it. Now he's been taken to hospital and might even pull through.'

'Group Four got the Prime Minister, it seems. Had to kill four policemen who got in the way, though,' Hideo said. 'And Naka-jima and the others in Five made short work of the Finance Minister. We shall know more when Nonaka gets back from the War Minister's house. That's definitely under our control. Keep an eye on things here. I'll be back in a minute.'

Hideo's legs felt like lead as he left the hotel manager's office which had been commandeered to serve as a communications centre, and his head began to ache as he emptied his bladder in the ground floor toilet. Then he gagged, and was soon vomiting helplessly.

## 33. *Friday 22 February, 1986*

Charlie:                                    11.45 or so, in a rush

I called to try to talk to you but you were out of town, so I stopped by to return the February 26 Incident piece, admired the swans and borrowed a typewriter to leave you this note.

Basically, I think the piece is great, and should fascinate readers. It must have been ghastly that night – those poor people, whatever they may have done! Just slaughtered in their beds. And how brave the women were, especially Count Makino's young grand-daughter Kazuko, helping the lame old man to get out of the inn at the hot-spring resort outside Tokyo when that crazy bastard Kono had his men set fire to the place. After all my years in this business I still can't image what sort of 'idealists' can *do* those things. At least the police managed to wound him . . . and I guess it took guts for him to commit suicide in the hospital. And imagine the War Ministry on the evening of that day putting out an official statement calling them 'a party that arose to uphold and clarify the national constitution'! Dictated by this Captain Nonaka, no doubt, or maybe one of their weird civilian gurus.

That's a great photograph you dredged out of the archives of the soldiers standing around in the snow with their rifles propped up in pyramids against each other like wheat at harvest time in old-fashioned pictures. And all the time the generals running around like a bunch of headless chickens wondering what to do about the naughty boys. I wish there were time to write to Dwight Rogers and ask him what he thought was going on at the time. I could call him, I suppose, but I doubt if he'd make a lot of sense on the phone. He's probably forgotten who I am by now, anyway. In any case, I don't see how I can possibly improve on the draft, even after I see Yoko tomorrow morning. Jun and Miyoko may have done some good leg-work, but it has your signature all over it. I really hope they use it as the cover story – it deserves to be.

I can see now why the Japanese have this thing about the affair.

Murder in the snow and all – it's almost as good as their favourite story of the forty-seven *ronin*. What I never realised before is how much depended on the Emperor personally, though. And him only in his early thirties. He was pretty tough when it came to the point. As I was reading I began to speculate that having had a son at last a couple of years before might have made him feel more secure . . . I seem to remember some story to the effect that there'd been a move to have him step down in favour of his brother Chichibu. It might be worth checking it out. Anyway, all I've done is just pencil in a couple of sentences which might help to bring out the Emperor's role more strongly, though I'm really very diffident about doing even that. What a life that old man with the pebble glasses has lived! It's kind of nice he still likes to wear the Mickey Mouse watch they gave him at Disneyland, or so they say.

Oh, just one other thing. I wonder if you shouldn't highlight a little more the fact that the insurgents had a lot of support high up in the Army at first . . . even though those two generals Mazaki and Araki didn't work too hard when it came to the point, did they? I like that quote you have from the other general who said Mazaki was like a man with matches in one hand and a fire-hose in the other. What a creep. I'll ask Yoko what young intellectuals like her thought about it all. And big brother Hideo, of course. There'd be no harm in asking the man himself too next time I see him I suppose, but the idea scares me somehow. He might just begin to suspect that I know he had a brother in the Army. All that would take me way beyond your deadline, in any case. Maybe I'll just leave it that I'll call you if I get any brilliant ideas within the next twenty-four hours.

By the way, the subject (as they say in private eye novels) was in a pretty tough mood last time we met. I'll buy you a drink some time soon and tell you about it if you have time to stop by the International House. Put this note in your shredder when you've read it, will you? Okay, so I *am* getting paranoid, but at least I admit it.

Love, Lesli.

## 34. Wednesday 26 February, 1936

Their heads bent, War Minister General Kawashima, General Honjo the chief aide-de-camp, Deputy Chief of Staff General Sugiyama and the Home Minister stood quivering before the wrath of the slightly-built, glaring figure in military uniform facing them. The Minister of the Navy was out of the firing line, watchful and amazed in his place to one side beside a frightened chamberlain. The chamberlain and the Home Minister were the only people in the room in civilian morning dress, though they too wore white gloves like the military men.

They were all accustomed to inferring the meaning of Imperial utterances from vague, allusive hints which now and then drifted near the surface of the archaic Court Japanese the Emperor habitually used, like magnificent multi-coloured carp deigning for a tantalising moment to come into view before returning to the murky depths of an ancient pool. Most of those present had often enough seen the Emperor listless and depressed, especially when he had been nagged yet again by his advisers to spend less time in his marine biology laboratory and at the Imperial Villa at Hayama on the Bay of Sugamo. They had also seen him irritated, even petulant, when chafing against the myriad restrictive rules of protocol which governed almost all his waking hours. But this was totally, amazingly different. The mild, scholarly Son of Heaven was imperially angry. Although his manner of speaking was still choked and stilted, the words were plain and unvarnished, their meaning clear beyond the slightest doubt. Three of his closest and most cherished courtiers had been attacked; the Lord Privy Seal murdered in the most cowardly fashion, Grand Chamberlain Suzuki lying near to death and Count Makino spared only through the courage and resourcefulness of his grand-daughter. Finance Minister Takahashi and General Watanabe had been slaughtered too, and the Prime Minister's fate was still obscure. Not to mention the casual murder of several loyal policemen who had sought to protect the victims of these . . . *traitorous* mutineers.

How *dare* the generals speak of this cowardly rabble as 'misguided', 'over-zealous', 'concerned for the Constitution and the security of the Empire'? How dare they even *hint* that the disgraceful, impertinent so-called 'demands', which the War Minister had taken it into his head to bring to the palace after actually *meeting* the criminals whom he had *invited* into his own offical residence, might be considered for a single moment? How could he have cravenly listened to such treasonable rantings?

General Honjo hung his head in a degree of shame even greater than that of the War Minister. To him had fallen the lot of breaking the news of the uprising to the Emperor at six that morning: he had not yet dared to say that the news had come to him by means of a telephone call from Captain Yamaguchi, not only one of the ringleaders, but also his own son-in-law. He had not known.

*He had not known!* Honjo burrowed for security in that thought. The nerve-centres of the capital were in complete chaos. The headquarters of the Tokyo Metropolitan Police had been handed over to rebel officers without even a show of resistance – at that very moment they must have been browsing at will through the files. No attempt had been made to evict the mutineers from the Prime Minister's residence, even though rumours were already circulating in the Palace to the effect that the assassins had not known what Premier Okada looked like and had killed his brother-in-law by mistake: it was conceivable that Okada had escaped. Even at that early hour Generals Mazaki and Araki were busy lobbying the other members of the Supreme Military Council and getting support for a draft submission to the Throne approving the political aims of the activists, and it was by no means clear that even after his angry reaction of personal outrage the Emperor would be able to make his views prevail.

The Emperor wheeled round and addressed himself to the Navy Minister, like his war ministry colleague a serving officer. 'We see the Army in pitiful confusion,' he snapped, 'What of the Navy? Lord Keeper Saito, Grand Chamberlain Suzuki and Prime Minister Okada are all retired admirals. How does the Navy feel about that?' The Navy Minister made a helpless gesture. In the presence of the generals he was determined to say nothing: he hoped to secure a private audience with the Emperor before the Cabinet was due to meet later in the day and assure him that warships were already being prepared to sail from their base at nearby Yokosuka and take up station in Tokyo Bay. Although both Mazaki and Araki had brothers high in the Navy, there were few young Turks in its officer corps of the kind that made so much noise in the Army, and little sympathy in the Fleet for the inveterate politicking of the military.

General Sugiyama was the only one bold enough to look his quivering sovereign in the eye. 'The General Staff humbly shares Your Majesty's displeasure. Although the Chief of Staff, His Imperial Highness Prince Kan'in is, as Your Majesty is aware, unfortunately indisposed and not in Tokyo, I am confident that he will endorse my intention to take firm action. Your Majesty will wish to know that the Imperial Guard detachment here at the Palace is unwavering in its loyalty, thanks to the prompt action of duty commander Major Homma and Lieutenant Otaka, who frustrated an attempt by a Lieutenant Nakahashi to seize control of the Sakashita Gate and admit insurgent troops, and ordered him from the precincts.'

The War Minister glanced at Sugiyama in furtive surprise. This was the first setback to the rebels that he had heard about, and Sugiyama's own firm attitude complicated matters more than a little. It began to look as though it might be more difficult than he had at first supposed to calm the Emperor down and smooth things over to the advantage of the Imperial Way faction among the senior Army men.

For the first time during the audience the Emperor gave an indication of slight satisfaction. Then he spoke again. The officers Homma and Otaka were to be commended. So far as the general situation was concerned, there was to be no shilly-shallying; no truck with mutineers who had monstrously presumed to invoke the imperial name in support of their criminal actions.

There was no formal end to the proceedings. The Emperor gave one last withering glance round the room, then turned on his heel and disappeared behind the gold and green screen which concealed the door to his study, the chamberlain scurrying after him. The men he left behind remained in their places for a moment, frozen as though taking part in a *tableau vivant*. Then the Home Minister sidled up to the Navy Minister, who exhaled with care as he looked across at the generals.

'You shouldn't have come here,' Yoko whispered as she clung to Rogers, elation and apprehension mingling in a sweet agony of desire for him. 'We agreed . . .' He disengaged himself in silence and she suddenly felt very cold as he stood there looking at her, an expression on his face like none she had seen there before. 'Dearest, what is it? What's wrong?'

'I had to come, Yoko. The Army uprising – you've heard about it, of course?' The look on her face was almost comically blank, and Rogers felt rather as he did when one of Tokyo's frequent earth tremors made him doubt the familiar dimensions of the material world. Conceivably she really hadn't heard. Certainly trams and buses were running normally, shops were open and he had found a taxi without too much trouble. People seemed to be going about their business much as usual, though with a few curious glances at the soldiers who were very much in evidence on the streets in the administrative and political centre of the city north of the Imperial Palace, and the barbed wire entanglements which were being put in place around a number of official buildings. Only the bolder spirits among them stopped to take one of the leaflets the soldiers were rather sheepishly proffering.

'No. What do you mean? There was nothing on the wireless news bulletin, and Father didn't say anything had happened when he came home last night. He's been so tired and worried lately that he doesn't talk to me much . . . and I hardly saw him this morning. He went to the office earlier than usual.'

'Has your younger brother gone to school?'

'Yes, of course. Why not? And Teruko's at work. Please, Dwight, what is it? Why do you look so sad?' Yoko reached up with a timid hand to caress his cheek and he caught it with his own and held it there.

'Yoko, it's very serious. I've just come from the Foreign Press Club. You're right, there's been no official statement yet, but the rumour is that several ministers have been assassinated. The insurgents have control of the War Ministry and several other important buildings in Tokyo and have been negotiating their demands with the War Minister. They want to instal a new government headed by General Mazaki and . . . well, it's all very confused. But there's something more important, Yoko. One of my best-informed contacts is a German reporter called Richard Sorge who's friendly with a German general attached to the Japanese army as an adviser. Sorge told me who's behind it all. A group of young Imperial Way faction officers. He even knew a lot of their names . . . Yoko, I believe your brother is one of them.'

'Yoko-chan. I think I know this gentleman.' They both spun round at the sound of the faltering voice, to see Chie lowering herself painfully to her knees. Her *yukata* was very loosely belted and her hair hung down straight on either side of her deathly white face. It was the first time Rogers had seen her since New

Year's Day and as he dropped hurriedly to his own knees he thought she looked like nothing so much as the tragic, demented figure of the mother searching for her lost child in the Noh play *Sumidagawa*.

Yoko's own face was pale with shock, but she gently raised her mother from her profound bow and beckoned Rogers to help her. 'Yes. It's Mr Rogers, Mother,' she murmured. 'You met him at the Meiji Shrine. He has come to ask how you are. But it's cold down here. Let me help you back up to bed.'

On her feet again, Chie looked up at Rogers as he supported her on one side. The skin of her face was waxy but there was a flickering intelligence deep in her eyes and he was conscious for a moment of subtle communication. 'I must apologise for my elder son's ungracious behaviour, sir,' she said, and then began to weep as Yoko led her away, avoiding Rogers' eyes.

The police arrived while Yoko was still upstairs.

'I suppose you're going out again,' Jiro said sourly when he arrived home that afternoon.

'Yes. You must take care of Mother until Father or Teruko get back. Listen, Jiro. Something terrible has happened. The police were here earlier, searching the house.'

Jiro had gone straight over to switch on the wireless set and had his back to Yoko as she spoke. He stood stock still for a long moment and replied without turning round. 'The police? Why? What were they looking for?'

'Jiro! LOOK AT ME!' Yoko screamed the words as she flung herself at the boy and grabbed him by the shoulders. 'Hideo's in terrible trouble! He's involved in this army business. The police say he's a rebel. I've got to go to the police station to answer more questions. I don't know when I'll be back, they only let me wait here for you because they could see Mother couldn't be left.' Weeping and distracted, Yoko began to struggle into the coat she had put in readiness by the door.

'If you've got to go, I expect they'll have picked Father up too. From his office. He'll probably be late,' Jiro said. 'And I expect Teruko will go to the dance hall as usual. Never mind. I'll be here.'

He watched coolly as Yoko put her shoes and galoshes on and with a speechless last look at him left the house. Then he went quickly into his own room and was relieved to find that the money was still under the *tatami* where he had hidden it. The police couldn't have searched very thoroughly; but they might well come back. Jiro devoted some time to thinking of safer places before going upstairs to look in on his mother.

'You'd better go over some of this again, Mr Rogers,' Ambassador Joseph Grew said to the tall young man sitting near him in the spacious drawing room in which *Naughty Marietta* had been shown the previous evening. 'It may be that George here has followed it all, but you lost me some time back. The police held you for five hours, and you came here as soon as they'd finished with you. So they picked you up at two, two-thirty or so at this Miss, er, Shimizu's house –'

'Shimada, sir. Miss Yoko Shimada.'

The Ambassador made an irritated gesture. 'Yes, yes,' he said testily. 'And they were there because her brother is one of the ringleaders of this, this uprising. Now did you *know* this? That's the point, surely.' Rogers rubbed his eyes. He was exhausted and sick at heart. 'Yes, sir,' he said again heavily. 'Like I said before, that was the whole point of my being there. I'd been running around the whole morning talking to various contacts about the political assassinations and picked up a few names of some of the officers who are seemingly behind it. One of them is apparently Lieutenant Hideo Shimada. I'm ... well, pretty fond of Miss Shimada, sir, and I went to the house to see if she knew anything about it, and, well, to warn her, I guess.'

'Did you tell all this to the police?' It was the watchful man the Ambassador called George; the duty officer the US Marine guard at the Chancery had called when Rogers arrived and asked to speak to someone in authority.

'Yes. At first I thought of bluffing it out by telling them that I'd heard Lieutenant Shimada's name mentioned in the course of my work, traced his family's whereabouts and gone there to try to get an exclusive interview with someone in the family. Then I realised that they'd be certain to ask Miss Shimada about me and that she'd surely tell the police something different, which could put us both in bad trouble. So I told them exactly what I've told you. How I came to meet the Shimada family quite by chance on New Year's Day and how that was the first and only time I ever set eyes on the lieutenant. How my friendship with the young lady dates from when she happened to recognise me again three weeks or so ago when we were both taking the same train to Kyoto, and I heard about her mother's illness, and ... how I'd called at the house a few times to see her back here in Tokyo.'

George nodded. 'Uh huh. Probably the wisest course. And no doubt you told them a whole bunch of stuff about your own family background, education and favourite reading matter because they were real curious about it. Right?'

'Yes, sir. I guess we all know how enthusiastic the police can be when they get started.' The Ambassador intervened, his voice sharp. 'You haven't been mistreated in any way, have you, young man?'

'No, sir. They were persistent, and none too friendly. You know how it is: they don't seem to be able to distinguish between a journalist and a spy, and in any case hate the idea of foreigners interesting themselves in the crisis. I got the impression they don't know who's in charge of the government right now, which may have made them careful. Anyhow, nobody laid a finger on me.'

'On the other hand,' George said thoughtfully, 'I'd think it more than probable they had him followed, Mr Ambassador. It might not have been too smart on your part to come here, Rogers.' Rogers went hot and cold at the thought. How could he have been so callow as to have come rushing straight to the American Embassy after spending hours denying that he had anything but very occasional and purely social contacts with American diplomats except for the Press Secretary? Yet it had seemed the most natural thing in the world to report his temporary detention at once, if only as a matter of ordinary prudence in case he should be picked up again. Dispiritedly he faced the plain fact that he was frightened, both for himself and for Yoko, and had come running like a kid for reassurance and protection. It was deeply shaming, and would be infinitely worse if his thoughtless reaction had the effect of creating even more serious trouble for the Shimadas.

Ambassador Grew had finished filling and lighting his pipe, and raised a luxuriant eyebrow at George. 'Yes. Well, be that as it may, George, now that Mr Rogers *is* here it would be interesting to know what he makes of this tragic affair. At the very least he can tell us something about the background of one of these blood-thirsty young officers.' He looked round the splendid room gloomily. 'I can't stop thinking about poor Admiral Saito. Darn it, it was just yesterday evening he was sitting right here so contentedly dozing off, and then a few hours later he was dead. They say the Emperor is beside himself with grief . . .'

## 35. *Thursday 27 February, 1986*

'I can't tell you how awful it was, Charlie. Or how utterly *stupid* I felt not to have realised it sooner, before shooting my big mouth off.'

Goldfarb looked at the red-rimmed eyes of the woman sitting near him in the downstairs lobby at the International House, and noted the concerned but curious glances of other people as they passed by or hovered near his own chair to reach for one of the newspapers suspended in their wooden holders from the rack behind him. 'You couldn't have guessed. Go on up to your room, Lesli,' he said quietly. 'It's 302, isn't it? I'll join you there in a couple of minutes. I know you aren't supposed to have visitors up there, but we need a little privacy.'

Lesli looked at him for a moment, hardly registering what he was saying, then dumbly stood up and went over to the lifts. Goldfarb walked briskly towards the main entrance, then carried on to the men's room, returning afterwards through the lobby towards the library but not entering it. Instead he took the stairway opposite. The door of Room 302 was ajar and he went in, closing it behind him. Lesli was sitting on the bed, but apart from squeezing her shoulder briefly, Goldfarb made no attempt to join her there. Instead he crossed to the easy-chair in the corner by the window and sat down without a word. 'Fix yourself a drink, Charlie,' Lesli said at last. 'There's only Suntory I'm afraid. Ice water in the thermos jug.' Goldfarb shook his head. 'Thanks, but no thanks. Only in extremis, sweetheart. You could probably use one though?' Lesli shook her head as she blindly reached for a Kleenex from the box at the bedhead and blew her nose.

'Okay, begin again. You went to see Yoko this morning, all hopped up about the February 26 Incident and wondered why she didn't seem keen to talk about it.'

'I bullied her, Charlie.' Fresh tears had begun to flow. 'Nagged at her to tell me what she was doing that day, whether ordinary folk even noticed much what was going on during those three days.'

'Four really,' Goldfarb said quietly to give her a chance to get her voice under control. 'There was a time when the rebels thought they had it made, when they were actually made *part* of the martial law command, and things stayed real confused through the twenty-seventh until Sugiyama and the other tough guys finally persuaded the others that the Emperor meant business. That became clear when brother Chichibu turned up in Tokyo with the idea of lending the rebels a hand and big brother made him stay right there in the Imperial Palace out of harm's way. When the Emperor put his seal to the order instructing the martial law command to move in on the twenty-eighth and the Navy had warships in position in Tokyo Bay it was pretty much over. But they didn't want any more bloodshed, so the twenty-ninth was psychological warfare day with the tanks moving in on the rebel positions but not firing a shot. Boy, must have been something to see planes dropping leaflets all over and the banner hanging from the advertising balloon over the Aeronautical Association building telling the troops to defy their officers in the name of the Emperor. And the general commanding Tokyo District who broadcast along the same lines. Hey, do you know the poor sap got court-martialled later on for telling his boys there was still time to obey the Emperor? Prosecution argued that suggesting anything less than *instant* obedience was treasonable. He got off.'

Lesli nodded gratefully as she sniffed. 'Thank you, Charlie. I'm all right now.' She even managed a small smile. 'I did read the article, you know.'

'Sure you did. And after a night's sleep you'll change your mind about not wanting to add anything. At what point did she tell you about Hideo?'

Goldfarb watched as Lesli slipped her shoes off and eased herself fully on to the bed, eyes closed. 'My head aches, Charlie. Don't get the wrong idea. Insensitive cow that I am, I actually asked her whether the crisis had affected her elder brother personally. I was *still* too dumb to even consider that he might have been involved. Yoko said in a very dignified way that she didn't care to talk about it, but that her brother had been associated with the Imperial Way faction. That he had played a part in the rising and that he had accepted responsibility for his actions . . . then she broke down, Charlie. I felt . . . I can't tell you how terrible I felt as I tried to comfort that poor old lady while she pushed me away as though she hated me. I've been tormented about it ever since I came away. Her reaction was so violent, so distraught that I can only think he must have committed suicide or something, unless . . .'

'Say it, Lesli. It'll help. Unless he was one of those who were shot after the court-martial. I don't think he could have committed suicide. The troops had all drifted back to their barracks by two or so on the afternoon of the twenty-ninth. Only the officers were left. They'd all *offered* to commit suicide provided the Emperor was informed of the fact, and actually when he realised the jig was up Prince Chichibu sent a message to his pal Captain Ando suggesting they do just that. But the martial law commander refused even to try to get them the Emperor's endorsement, and in the end only two of them actually killed themselves. Captain Nonaka after a confrontation with an old commander of his at the war ministry, and Captain Kono in the hospital where they'd taken him after the attempt on Count Makino. Oh yeah, I just remembered, there was one other – a lieutenant who killed himself early on. Yukio Mishima wrote a short story and made a movie about him. But he had nothing to do with the coup. Just went out of his mind when he heard about it, poor guy. Besides I recall Miyoko mentioning that he was married and quite old. To that kid "quite old" probably means around forty. Not Yoko's brother, anyhow.'

Lesli raised herself on one elbow and opened her eyes as she stared at him. 'We must check, Charlie. We have to know.'

'Easiest thing in the world. We didn't put all the names in the article, you know how it pisses people off to read a whole bunch of jaw-breaking foreign names. Either Miyoko or Jun's sure to have them all some place among the photocopies from Japanese source material though. I'll have them turn them up first thing tomorrow –'

'No. Tonight. I must know tonight.'

Goldfarb scratched his head. 'Gee, Lesli, that's kind of un-reasonable. Jun and Miyoko have long since gone home . . . I guess I could ask one of the *Mainichi Shimbun* night staff to look through the file, but –'

'Charlie. Japanese is my second language. I can look for myself. Please take me there.' Goldfarb sighed, then hauled himself out of the chair and stood looking dubiously down at her. 'You sure you're really okay, kid? Is there really such a hurry?' Then he shrugged and smiled. 'Okay. I know when I'm beat, and I'm sure not about to get suicidal. Let's go.'

Puffy-eyed, Lesli held out her hand and Goldfarb took it,

supposing she wanted him to help her up, but she pulled him down towards her and he crumpled into an awkward sitting position on the edge of the narrow bed. 'Hold me, Charlie,' she whispered. 'I feel so bad. I should never have gotten into all this.' She began to sob as he raised her and cradled her in his arms, and clutched at him fiercely.

'Well, I'll say this, Lesli. If what we think is true, it makes me feel a certain sympathy for Shimada. No wonder the guy's so cagey about those days. What was he, sixteen or seventeen? Must've been a hell of a trauma for a kid that age. Sure we'll go to the office and check it out.' He kissed her forehead gently. 'Better fix your face first.'

## 36. *Sunday 2 March, 1936*

Yukichi shifted uncomfortably on his knees, shocked to find that even at such a time he could be prey to such trivial and unworthy reactions as satisfaction over having decided to wear Japanese dress after all. The striped trousers of his morning suit would have been disagreeably tight round his thighs and knees, and the waistcoat and stiff collar would have constricted his movements as he bowed mechanically and accepted the condolences of those who passed through the room. He had worn clothes like them almost every day of his adult life and as a younger man had cut something of a dash in the eyes of his contemporaries with his eye for a smart necktie and the suits he went to a Chinese tailor in Yokohama to be measured for, but all at once the fussy and convoluted tubes of western male attire seemed to him to be alien and ludicrous, absurdly inconvenient compared with the graceful but practical simplicity and flowing, generous folds of kimono and *haori*.

Not very many people had come to bow and offer a pinch of incense before the black-draped photograph of Chie which stood on the improvised altar in the little entrance hall. It was out of the question for her Kumamoto relatives to come. They could not afford it, and the fact that the old woman was much too ill and frail for Chie's brother and his wife to leave her provided a satisfactory concealment for any embarrassment. They had sent a telegram of condolence and a postal order for ten yen by way of 'incense money', a handsome gesture on the part of people in their circumstances. Yukichi's family were represented by a cousin of his, a schoolteacher from Shizuoka who had made the three-hour journey with great good grace considering the circumstances.

Apart from him and a few neighbourhood women who came through the black and white drapes at the gate, approached the entrance whose sliding doors had been lifted out completely for the occasion and went through the motions of dignified grief with their eyes glittering with respectable malice, the mourners had consisted mainly of local tradesmen, interspersed with a handful of acquaintances of Yoko, Teruko and even Jiro. Jiro himself was outside the gate in his black student uniform, helped by a school friend, as one by one the callers took up the brush provided and entered their names in the book he had bought from the stationers the previous day and handed over their gifts of money in special mourning envelopes, receiving from Jiro the necessary token return gift, in this case a handkerchief in a flat box of thin grey and white cardboard.

It was Jiro who had shouldered the burden of making the practical arrangements for Chie's funeral after Yukichi had come home from the police station on that dreadful night to find that she had cut her throat; Jiro who had pointed out that it would be much simpler to set up the altar in the entrance hall so that people would not have to take their shoes off in order to come right into the house; Jiro who had summoned the undertaker and later personally cleaned the room in which his mother had finally and irrevocably retreated from the world which so oppressed and confused her. Jiro had been a tower of strength to them all.

Those of the visitors who ran to such things not only entered their names in the condolence book but also left their name-cards: one such was Director Nishi from Mitsui whose murmured words of sympathy had a quality of icy hatred about them. Yukichi was too numbed by the events of the past few days to care. It was as though he saw himself from the viewpoint of a dispassionate critic, wondering how this son of a samurai could ever have been so despicably craven as to have contemplated selling his daughter to an ambitious functionary to please this polished sadist and secure a few years of financial security for himself. He would manage somehow, and at least he would be able to look Yoko in the eye in the years to come.

Yukichi allowed himself a bitter smile as he reflected that he was in no position to help Mitsui now. President Ikeda's sources of information had indeed been reliable, and he had kept well under cover, out of range of potential assassins until both Kita and Nishida had been arrested and it was clear that the rising had failed. There was nothing Yukichi could do to be of service, even if he had wanted to. It was a relief to him that he would no longer even have to resist the temptation of a bribe.

For years Yukichi had, tolerantly on the whole, regretted that his wife Chie had never been able to rise to his level. Before Yoko had reached the age of reason and become his intellectual companion there had been many times when he bitterly regretted the timid indecisiveness which had lost him the regard of Fujiko, the medical student who would surely have led him to a way of life far removed from the humdrum scrimping of his marriage to Chie. Now as he looked at the photograph of Chie on the altar, enlarged from a family picture taken to mark their son Hideo's graduation from the Military Academy, the detached observer dominating Yukichi's consciousness pointed out that he had it all completely wrong.

It was Yukichi who had failed to rise to Chie's level of sensitivity and insight; Yukichi who had callously watched her over the years being starved of grace and beauty, wrenched from her dancing world of dreams and turned into a meek, uncomplaining drudge. The resigned but somehow fearful expression on the face in the photograph became blurred as tears obscured his vision, and Yukichi bowed his head in remorse and shame.

From her position between her father and stony-faced Teruko, Yoko watched Dwight Rogers retreat towards the gate, her emotions in turmoil. He had behaved with perfect, sensitive courtesy; but he should not have come. He must have known of Hideo's arrest late on Friday 29th, but how could he have learned of her mother's death? There had been no contact between them since the police had taken him away from the house, much as Yoko had longed for the comfort of his presence in her bewilderment, grief and terror. And now, on top of everything else, Yoko knew as surely as if Teruko had spoken that her sister had seen the look on Dwight's face before and after he bowed to the three of them; seen that it was directed at Yoko alone, and intuited at last the truth about their relationship.

For Teruko it was no more than bleak confirmation of what she had guessed a long time before, and she was not resentful towards Yoko. She had little room for any emotions other than the savage hatred which alone kept her from complete despair, and the sight of Dwight Rogers more than anything else made her think with helpless incredulity how long it seemed since she had no real worries, just silly frustrations more than compensated for by the exciting daydreams which chased each other through her head. Yet it was less than two months since she had walked on air at the American's side and boldly kissed him in the taxi; and now she was a whore.

The first time she screwed up her courage and went with one of

the men who asked to buy her out, to the discreet inn at
Nihonbashi of which the other girls had told her, the prospect was
frightening but the actuality was more ridiculous than anything
else. The man was too drunk to do much, but paid up like a lamb
before taking himself sheepishly off, and receiving so much
money made Teruko almost light-hearted for a day or two.

Since then there had been a few foreigners as well as many more
Japanese; Teruko had begun by keeping count but had then given
up. It must be nearly thirty by now, and the hairy bodies of
western men were no longer mysterious to her. It wasn't so bad
once you got used to it. Especially with the ones who seemed to
enjoy being degraded and reviled. She had made more money in
the past three weeks than in the whole of her previous life, but it
was not enough yet to lift the awful burden from her. Worse, now
that Hideo's name would inevitably be widely publicised a
sickening realisation was dawning in her that her punishment
would be all the more crushing and protracted. Jiro would never
be satisfied with the sum he had originally stipulated as the price
of his silence.

The allotted hour and a half came to an end at last, and Jiro's school
friend came to make his farewells as Yukichi was wearily rising to
his feet with Yoko's help. The undertaker's men were already
taking away the mourning draperies from the outside gate, and
Jiro was on his way through it carrying a lacquer tray with the
envelopes containing the incense money piled up on it when a
drab army lorry pulled up outside.

Yoko unconsciously clutched at her father's arm and Teruko,
who was still kneeling on her cushion, a slight figure in her formal
black kimono swayed slightly as an army captain in uniform
pushed peremptorily past Jiro, followed by Hideo, also in uniform
but hatless. A sergeant brought up the rear. The captain brought
his high boots into meticulous alignment and bowed formally to
Yukichi. 'Captain Iwaya,' he said. 'On behalf of the martial law
commander, Tokyo District, I offer condolences. In the exceptional
circumstances permission has been granted for Lieutenant Shimada to offer incense. The sergeant and I will withdraw to the gate
out of respect for the departed, and wait for ten minutes. The
prisoner is required to remain in plain view throughout.'

Captain Iwaya saluted Chie's photograph and then made as if to
turn away, but hesitated and then swept his cap off, took a pinch
of incense from the container and dropped it on the dying embers

of the charcoal in the burner and bowed low. He then turned about and gave way to Hideo, retreating to the gate with the sergeant as he had promised.

Teruko made no attempt to check her tears as warmth flooded through her at the sight of her brother standing there bareheaded but proud. At that moment she acknowledged to herself that she loved him and knew that she must find the strength to bear her burden.

Yukichi looked intently into Hideo's eyes, and saw arrogant self-confidence in them, tinged with a kind of serenity. His mouth worked as he tried to find words to speak to this stranger who was his son.

## 37. Kamakura, Tuesday
## 4 March, 1986

Yoko Nagai clasped her hands tightly in front of her and spoke in a voice so quiet that even in the stillness of the small room it was not easy for Lesli to make out what she was saying, but she dared not interrupt for fear she might, through some clumsiness, shatter irreparably the eggshell-thin bridge of reconciliation across which the old lady was reaching out to her. 'It was the fiftieth anniversary of my mother's funeral the other day which made me realise how silly I had been last time you came here. There is no excuse for my childish behaviour. I am so glad that you were not too angry with me to come back.'

Lesli began to murmur her own apologies, but Yoko brushed them aside with a small but oddly graceful gesture and continued to speak. It was the first time that Lesli had seen her in a kimono: she looked much smaller, and more vulnerable than the clear-eyed, vigorous former academic who had always previously greeted Lesli in woollen skirts and jumpers, or blouses with cardigans. 'We laid her ashes to rest in the big cemetery by Nippori not far from Ueno. My mother had always loved to wander about there, and we were able to get a plot not far from her favourite temple. There are several round the edges of the cemetery. I expect you know. It's the family plot now. My father's ashes lie there. And part of Hideo's, even though the authorities did not permit a proper funeral . . . I buried a lock of Teruko's hair there too.'

Yoko dabbed at her eyes with a miniature handkerchief, then sniffed and held her head high. 'You have been very kind to indulge a foolish old woman during these last weeks, Hoshino-san. I know I have not been very helpful, and I realise that you have found out very much more for yourself than I have seen fit to tell you so far. I think I must be more honest now, and tell you the rest of the story. After all, it was I who first invited you to come here to talk about my younger brother, and you cannot understand him without knowing about the rest of us. And besides, the time has come for me to tell you why I sought you out in the first place and why I have taken up so much of your time.'

The old lady stood up and went to the tiny *tokonoma* alcove in the corner of the room. It was too small to contain more than a simple flower arrangement, and Yoko's consisted of a twig beaded with plum blossom in bud and a delicate froth of greenery. 'The plum blossom was very late that year,' she whispered. 'It had been such a very cold February.' Then she turned round to face Lesli again.

'My elder brother Hideo was placed under arrest on 29th February along with about a hundred other officers and non-commissioned officers. The ordinary soldiers were not punished when they laid down their arms and returned to barracks in obedience to the Emperor's order. Mother had . . . had done away with herself on the evening of the twenty-sixth, after the police came to the house and questioned me about Hideo.'

Yoko closed her eyes and bowed her head momentarily, but soon continued. 'Dwight was there. He had heard somehow that my brother was one of the ringleaders and came to warn me, and the police found him there. My mother happened to be up and about that day, and though we never knew how much she was aware of what was going on around her, she must have heard Hideo's name mentioned and somehow understood that he had done something dreadful. It must have been that. It must. The alternative is too horrible to believe, even now.'

'I know what the lieutenant did,' Lesli said quietly as she saw his sister's face working. 'Don't try to say it. I'm familiar now with the details of the court-martial.' Yoko nodded at her gratefully. 'Yes. Yes, I suppose you are by now. Much has been published in Japanese about the subject. It was terrible, frightful. But that is not what I meant.' She seemed to be fascinated by the plum blossom and fingered it delicately for a few seconds before turning away and sinking down again on to her flat *zabuton* cushion. 'The even greater horror that I have lived with all these years is that Jiro may have killed our mother. He immediately stole her most treasured possessions, you know.'

'Oh, my God. The pots.' Lesli had unconsciously reverted to English, but it seemed that Yoko understood what she said, for she looked up at her with a kind of tired surprise, then bowed her head. 'So he told you about them. Yet I see that you find it unbelievable that he might have . . .'

'Quite, quite unbelievable. He is a hard, ruthless man, that I know. But surely not a murderer.'

Yoko looked up again, tears in her eyes. 'I wish so much that

before I die I could know without any doubt at all. He is a wicked
man, Hoshino-san. He has offered me huge sums of money over
the years – I have always refused to accept a single yen from him. I
know such bad things about him, and he realises it. My sister
Teruko wrote me a letter, you see, with instructions that it was to
be sent to me only after her death. In it she told me how Jiro had
blackmailed her because he had discovered that she . . . that she
and Hideo loved each other in a forbidden way. It was to pay Jiro
the money he demanded that she went to work as a dance partner
and later . . . worse. I am so ashamed to tell you this. I have hated
him ever since the day I read that letter, and I never wish to see
him again. But I could find a little peace if I knew that at least the
other thing was not so. I had the foolish notion that you might be
able to find out. It was Mr Yamada who is taking care of you at my
brother's company who suggested it. He is my friend, a former
student of my late husband. He has for years kept watch on my
brother, but has discovered no more than I already knew. I see
now how hopeless it was . . .'

There was nothing that Lesli could say. She reached out and
took the old hand in hers as she had done with Dwight Rogers in
Vermont, and waited until Yoko was able to speak again. It was a
long time before she did, and then Lesli had to force her mind
back to the other horror, the one Yoko *had* somehow contrived to
reconcile herself to.

'It was good of them to bring Hideo to the house on the day the
mourners came to offer incense. The captain who escorted him
was very kind. He went out of earshot and let us talk to my brother
for several minutes.' Lesli bit her lip but couldn't hold back the
thought. Besides, it might help to prevent Yoko from reverting to
the astonishing charges against Jiro which Lesli would need time
to assimilate and consider.

'It must have been terrible for you all. How did he –'

'How did he seem? Strange. Remote, but somehow deeply
happy. He expressed no regrets for what he had done – that was
what shocked me most, I think. Indeed he said to Father "I want
you to tell your privileged capitalist friends to reflect upon their
conduct and be more prudent. My friends and I will be making
this point at the court-martial." I shall never forget it, it seemed so
. . . well, *unbelievable*.'

'Did any of you at that time have any idea what would happen?'
Lesli feared that she might have put the question with an excess of
tact, so delicately as to render it incomprehensible, but Yoko
shook her head at once.

'No, I'm sure we didn't. Certainly Hideo seemed to be expecting a demotion and disciplinary transfer to the provinces, perhaps even dishonourable dismissal from the Army.'

Lesli was incredulous. 'Surely in view of what had happened. . .?'

'No. You see, there had been incidents before involving army officers, and most of them had been dealt with very leniently. Colonel Aizawa had been on trial almost a month for killing General Nagata and had been allowed to make long political speeches. Hideo told us that some of the most important generals had supported the rising. Openly at times. Two of the more senior of the young officers had committed suicide anyway –'

'Captain Nonaka and Captain Kono.'

'Yes, I believe that was their names. The others thought that since their leaders had accepted responsibility in that way their own trial would be a formality. I got the impression that my brother was even contemplating taking part in another attempt of the kind when what he called "the fuss" was all over.' Yoko's face softened and she gently withdrew her hand from Lesli's.

'I make it sound as though he was intolerably hard and arrogant, but it wasn't really like that. Father was angry and upset at first – we all were – but for the rest of the time Hideo talked about Mother, so gently and lovingly. Then, when the captain called out from the gate that it was time to go, he bowed to Father and asked his forgiveness. Then he and Jiro bowed to each other. And the strangest thing of all, just before leaving he kissed me, and then Teruko. Such an unusual thing for a Japanese man to do. It was not until many years later that I understood the reason.'

## 38. *Thursday 6 March, 1986*

Lesli picked up the last few sheets of paper and tapped them into alignment on the desk top, then clipped them together and put them into the already bulging folder. There were three more like it in her room at the International House. The grey-green plastic dust-cover was already in place over the IBM, and Lesli wondered whether it would now be consigned to limbo in some basement storage area and rediscovered only when the time came to tear the building down and replace it with a new and even more lofty Shimada Trading Corporation skyscraper on the site the young Jiro had so cannily bought as a schoolboy. Mr Yamada would no doubt have plans for it.

She would miss Mr Yamada, and all the more now that she knew of his loyal friendship for Yoko. He had been so eager to please, so ready to dash into the filing room to check a date for her, or to run off photocopies himself rather than letting Lesli or one of the secretaries do it, even though as head of the sizeable international liaison department he must have plenty of work of his own to do. His discretion had been perfect. Lesli had not for a second supposed that he had been willing her on Yoko's behalf to unlock the innermost safe of Jiro Shimada's heart and mind. She would have given a great deal to have been able to answer Yoko's agonised question before she left Tokyo.

She looked round the tidy, well-planned, impersonal office and sighed. She could not help Mr Yamada to help Yoko, and there was nothing more that he or the lavish resources of the Shimada Trading Corporation could offer her. No file had been closed to her, and she probably knew as much about the history of the company and the steady development of Jiro Shimada's international contacts, commitments and reputation as anyone apart from himself. She knew which senior Japanese politicians and officials he had cultivated over meals and golf in the early years, and which ones had quite soon learned to cultivate him, to be joined in more recent years by an ever increasing number of the great and good who sought his discreet personal support or wanted to boost some project or other by adding to it the lustre of his name.

Lesli had seen fulsome letters signed by American politicians from several Kennedys through Johnson, Kissinger and Nixon to Carter, Schultz and Reagan; friendly messages from Willi Brandt and Edward Heath, Pompidou, two Popes and three Secretaries-General of the UN, and dozens of photographs of Shimada in the company of these and similarly grand personages.

The book was more than just sketched out. Lesli had so much meticulously organised material that it would, as she had re-marked what seemed like aeons before to Charlie Goldfarb, write itself. Yet the *other* book, the real story of Jiro Shimada, would never be written; and this was the one, undreamed of three months before, which now obsessed her. She shuddered briefly as she wondered how Shimada would react if he were ever to discover how much she now knew about him. About the brother who had in the company of others murdered an old man in his bed, and the mother who killed herself when an awareness of her son's awful deed pierced the clouds of her drugged consciousness – or conceivably whom he himself, as a coldly amoral teenager, had killed for gain. About the father whose ashes lay also in the family plot at the Nakano cemetery in Nippori, beside part of the ashes of a disgraced army officer, the remainder having been consigned with those of his comrades to a common, unmarked grave. About the pathetic little reminder of Teruko which reposed beside them: a lock of the hair of the sister Shimada had blackmailed into prostitution and who had died – how? where? And above all about his elder sister Yoko, alive and consumed with anguished hatred towards him, yet gentle in her pain and cherishing the memory of the love of an American, himself one of Lesli's informants.

Then, as Lesli was gathering up her belongings after checking that she had left nothing of her own in the desk, there was a tap at the door. '*Ohaeri nasai!* Come in!'

'Hoshino-san. Sorry to intrude. Yamada-san tells me you are moving out today. So soon?'

'Oh. Mr Shimada. Yes, I have everything I could possibly want or need from your archives. Mr Yamada has been incredibly helpful . . . but it's better for me to leave now.'

'You're not forgetting the interview I have scheduled with you for next Monday, I hope?' Although Lesli had responded in English he continued in Japanese, peremptory and intimidating as always in that language.

'No, sir, of course not.'

Shimada looked round the room appraisingly. 'Good. Good. I

hope you've been reasonably comfortable in here . . . I haven't
been into this room for a long time. I should get about and talk to
people at their desks more often. Good management practice, they
say. Not that I would presume to try to manage you, obviously.
Unless – it's just occurred to me – unless I could persuade you to
take a job here? You'd be very welcome if you ever felt inclined.
Yamada will be moving on soon. We're giving him a promotion
before his retirement in a couple of years, and the international
liaison department could use a director like you.'

Shimada stood foursquare in the doorway in the attitude of a
much younger man, helped by his expensive tailoring but looking
essentially fit and alert, his eyes alive with the new idea. Lesli
worked hard to produce a smile as she stood up.

'That's a flattering offer, sir, even if you don't mean it.'

'I mean it, Hoshino-san. I'm not in the habit of saying things I
don't mean. Think about it. We could arrange timing to suit you,
you have the book to finish and then you'll want a vacation. Think
very seriously about it, and let me know on Monday. You're quite
set on doing the actual writing of the book in America?'

'Yes. It's a book about an international man. I need to get the
international dimension right and Japan is too busy being
Japanese.'

Shimada made a sound that might have been a laugh and finally
switched to the English which Lesli had doggedly stuck to
throughout. 'I think I see what you mean. Anyway, you know all
about me now. The subject isn't supposed to look at the portrait
until it's finished, but tell me, am I going to be horrified and toss it
in the lumber room like Winston Churchill did with his?'

'I know almost nothing about you, Mr Shimada, and the more I
find out the less sure I am that I mind,' Lesli said steadily. 'I don't
even know where you live.'

Very slowly, Shimada straightened himself up and unfolded his
arms. 'That's a strange and provocative thing to say. But then
you're good at coming out with the unexpected, aren't you? At the
very least, where I live is no great secret. Yamada would have told
you if you'd bothered to ask. So would I. I live here. In this
building. As for knowing almost nothing about me, I can't believe
your researches have been so unproductive. It's all there, in the
files.'

Having managed to say something which had obviously nettled
him, Lesli persisted. 'I ask myself what kind of man keeps all his
personal files at the office, not even under his own direct control,

but handed over to the care of a professional archivist. All his various certificates, awards and decorations. Now that I know you live in the building, it seems to me to be all the stranger.'

'Not strange. Convenient. I'm not a young man, Miss Hoshino. The only thing any of us knows for certain is that he – or she – ' He interrupted himself to make a graceful little bow in her direction ' – will die. My affairs have been in order for a good many years now. I plan to keep them that way.'

'You must surely have kept back *some* papers, photographs, keepsakes, whatever.'

'You're positively aggressive today, Miss Hoshino. Don't misunderstand me, I like that characteristic. But I've told you before and I'll tell you once more. Everything relevant to your work has been made available to you.'

Jiro Shimada rubbed his chin pensively and seemed to be on the point of turning away before changing his mind. 'We are due to meet quite late on Monday, I think, four-thirty or so? Yes. Well, I shall look forward to welcoming you to my office in the usual way, if that will be convenient for you. Then afterwards, if you're not busy, I should like to invite you to join me for drinks in my apartment – dinner too if you have time. If it will satisfy your curiosity, I shall be glad to show you the few purely personal mementoes I keep up there. You've no need to be nervous, Miss Hoshino. I live alone, but I'm more than old enough to be your father.'

For the first time ever in his presence, Lesli laughed scornfully and loud. 'And you think that's reassuring? I could tell you some things about men old enough to be my father, Mr Shimada, and I don't believe they'd surprise you in the least. All right, I accept your invitation for drinks –' She hesitated, looking up at the now familiar but still unreadable expression on his face. 'And dinner. Thank you. And I'm not nervous.' She took a deep breath and plunged on, wondering how he would react. 'What I have been able to find out about you makes me certain that you're a cold, heartless and totally ruthless man of whom any sensible person ought to be scared. But I'd like to believe that no woman has ever had cause to be physically frightened of you.' Her lips settled into an insincere half-smile. She heard her own voice and was ashamed of the mixture of aggression and incipient hysteria in it. Lesli was in fact already regretting her decision, and perfectly sure that Shimada could see how jittery she was.

He just stared at her for a long moment, while Lesli found it difficult to breathe evenly. 'An interesting piece of character analysis. It makes me look forward with special pleasure to next Monday,' Jiro Shimada said before disappearing into the corridor.

## 39. *4 March, 1986*

Route 3,
Alderton,
Rutland, Vt.

Dear Miss Hoshino:

I can't really say that I enjoyed your letter, it brought back too many painful memories for that, but thank you for it anyway. I'm not sure you were telling the truth when you wrote that our conversations were helpful to you in your work. It was kind of you to spend time visiting with an old man, and I hope you enjoyed the chance to be with your folks again, so maybe all that money it cost to come clear across half the world from Japan wasn't wasted after all. I'm sorry I never got around to writing to you sooner as I seem to recall I promised. It's quite an effort for me these days.

It's a real joy and comfort to me to know that Yoko is well and thinks kindly of me. I wasn't quite truthful with you when we talked – to be honest, my memory isn't what it was and I don't recall exactly what I did tell you, but I rather think I gave you the impression I was like Lieutenant Pinkerton in Madam Butterfly and just sailed away and never tried to make contact with Yoko again. The truth is, I made enquiries through a friend of mine in the State Department who was assigned to the Tokyo embassy in 1938 and learned that she'd married a lecturer at one of the big private universities – Keio or Waseda, I can't recall which. Waseda I guess because that's where Yoko worked. A fine man called Nagai who'd been jailed for a couple of years for speaking his mind. So naturally it wouldn't have been right for me to bother Yoko again.

When I got back to Japan myself after the war I asked around and discovered that this Mr Nagai had been in trouble again with the wartime regime. After another spell in jail they drafted him as a buck private into the infantry and he was badly wounded in Burma. Yoko herself was dismissed from her job at the university and had to go to work in an airplane factory or something like that.

Well, in those early postwar years I had friends in useful places on MacArthur's staff and with their help I was able to locate Yoko and her husband. They were living quietly in Shizuoka where I understand she had some family connection, a cousin of her father or something like that. Yoko was teaching librarianship in a junior college and her husband was working on some two-bit newspaper. Perhaps I should explain that it was acceptable to be left-wing by then. Well, meantime I'd gotten married myself, and so I left them in peace, and I sincerely hope with all my heart that they were happy together. I'm glad I resisted the real temptation to get in touch with Yoko at that time, and even though we're both on our own in our old age I reckon it's too late now for me to think of seeing her again. I've drafted so many letters to her since you came to see me you wouldn't believe it. I doubt that I shall ever send one though.

Well, I read the article in Newsworld about the February 26 Incident and most likely would have done anyway, even if you hadn't asked me to. Speaking as an old newspaperman and a kind of eye-witness to some of what happened I'd say it was pretty good, even if it did take all those people to write it. Saw your name among them and tried to figure out which bits might have come from Yoko. It did more than refresh my memory, it took me right back to those amazing few days.

You asked me to fill in more about the lieutenant and Yoko's sister Teruko. Well, I never saw him again, of course. Yoko told me after her mother's funeral that her brother had turned up at the house with a military escort, all full of piss and vinegar if you'll pardon the vulgarity. Expected to be tried and found guilty, of course, but seemed rather pleased with what he'd done and reckoned he and his friends would get a slap on the wrist. Early March that would have been, just about fifty years ago today as I sit here at my old typewriter.

I think it would be true to say that most people would have shared his expectation for a while, myself included, but we were all completely wrong. The special court-martial they convened to try around a hundred of those fellows wasn't a bit like the others had been. It moved fast and efficiently, there was no publicity, and no long speeches by the defendants allowed. In fact they weren't even permitted to have defence counsel. And of course as you now know Yoko's brother Hideo and a dozen or so of the others were condemned to death, including some civilians like that strange visionary Ikki Kita and a man called Nishida, I remember. I had to report it all, and it was no secret that even after sentence those young army men still clung to the belief that they'd be given the officer's privilege of being allowed to commit suicide. But they reckoned without the Emperor. He was *implacable*. They were mutineers, and that was that, according to him. So they were stripped of their military rank and shot.

Well, Miss Hoshino, I just wish I *could* tell you what became of Teruko. She was a very pretty young woman, and I once had a date with her. I soon realised that we really hadn't a thing in common, so I never asked her out again. Nothing would ever have come of a relationship with Teruko even if Yoko and I hadn't become close. I saw her just once after I took her out, and that was when I went to the house to pay my respects after Mrs Shimada died so tragically. Although it was only a few weeks later Teruko looked much older and somehow more cynical, I thought. I suppose it was the strain they were all going through and being dressed in mourning. If you do ever find out what became of her I'd appreciate your letting me know.

I'm glad you have all the material you need for your book about Jiro Shimada, and look forward with special interest to reading it when it comes out. I still find it hard to credit that he is Yoko's younger brother, but of course I will respect her wish that this should remain confidential. Who in the world would I want to tell it to, anyway? Please give Yoko my – darn it, yes, my love, and you might let her have my address just in case.

And come see me again when you get back to the States. I hope to be around for a year or two yet.

Sincerely,
Dwight A. Rogers

## 40. *Monday 10 March, 1986*

'Feel quite free to look around, Miss Hoshino. It's a perfectly ordinary apartment.'

'On the thirtieth floor? Hardly, Mr Shimada. An ordinary millionaire New Yorker's perhaps.' Glass in hand, Lesli wandered over to the window and looked out over the jewelled carpet of lights far below.

'I wonder . . . no, you're too young.' The voice was disconcertingly close to her ear, and Lesli drew away a little.

'What were you going to say?'

'I was going to guess that you were gazing down and remembering the famous scene on the Ferris wheel in *The Third Man*, and likening me to Harry Lime, but I don't suppose you ever saw the movie.'

Lesli turned and looked him in the eye. 'I did, as a matter of fact. But no, Mr Shimada, I don't think of you as someone who looks down on the mass of ordinary people as insects. Besides, why should you care what I think?'

It was more like being in a private dining room at a luxurious hotel than in a man's home. Two places had been laid at a table large enough to seat at least eight, and a white-jacketed waiter fussed professionally over an array of food set out on a side table against a wall. Some covered dishes were kept hot in *bains-maries* over spirit lamps, while he was removing cling-film wrap from others. Following the direction of Lesli's glance, Shimada waved a hand airily. 'I hope you like Chinese food. As you've no doubt already found out for yourself, there are all manner of restaurants in this building. I use them all from time to time. The coffee shop in the basement sends up my breakfast, but I tend to get my dinner from either the French or the Chinese restaurant on the floor below us.'

'You might just as well live in a hotel,' Lesli said. She heard herself being taut, prickly and disagreeable and wished she were a better actress. 'I'm sorry. I don't mean to be discourteous or ungracious. You have a fantastic apartment and I'm very grateful to have the opportunity to see it.'

Shimada spread his hands. 'I enjoy most of the facilities of a good hotel, it's true. But I spend quite enough time in hotels as it is, without wishing to live in one. Although this room may seem impersonal to you, it has many pleasant associations for me.'

The waiter had finished his preparations and moved soundlessly across the room to them carrying a tray with two fresh drinks on it. 'Oh. I've hardly started this one, but . . .' Lesli allowed the man to deprive her of her glass and took the new one, angry with herself for her unsophisticated jumpiness.

It was not as though there was any specific justification for it. On the contrary; the interview in Shimada's office had gone quite smoothly. Her questions had related to recent years, were factual and had been answered in a straight, businesslike fashion. Although she had not been able to put her preoccupations completely out of her mind, Lesli had felt comfortably in command of herself and of the situation in the setting of Shimada's office, which had over the weeks become reassuringly familiar to her. He for his part had been at his most effortlessly charming, and Lesli had not sensed anything like the faint air of menace which had disturbed her on the previous two occasions they had met.

Lesli could not have said what was so different about the atmosphere up in the penthouse apartment, but whatever it was made her feel ill at ease. The furnishings and decor were luxurious, but not in the discreetly tasteful manner of Shimada's office. There was a blatant extravagance about the heavy gold fringes on the olive-green velvet curtains at the windows of the penthouse, and the opulence of the cushions on the massive sofa contributed to an effect which was both oppressive and slightly ridiculous. Half an hour's conversation over drinks would have been quite enough: as she worked at her smile Lesli wished very much that she had not impulsively accepted Shimada's apparently casual invitation to stay on for dinner.

'Good. I'm glad you don't see me as a Harry Lime.' Shimada too seemed slightly uncertain in his manner, but this Lesli found all the more disturbing and she had to control a shiver as she looked at his carefully tended face and was visited by the ludicrous but stomach-turning idea that he might literally be wearing a mask, one of the realistic rubber kind she had seen used to terrifying effect in films. Shimada raised a hand towards his face and Lesli's heart missed a beat: it was as though he had read her mind and was about to rip off his disguise to reveal some unspeakable deformity before advancing on her with murder in his eyes. He did no more than rub his chin though, smiling with a hint of shyness, and Lesli felt her shoulders sag in relief. When Shimada spoke again it was with a certain defensiveness quite uncharacteristic of the man she had by now spent many hours in conversation with, and in a manner sharply different from that of even an hour before.

'I hope you found our last . . . how shall I describe it, formal conversation this afternoon helpful.'

'The last sitting before the portrait is unveiled? Yes. Thank you. But the analogy isn't really a good one, because I haven't actually started to paint it yet. What I have at this stage is a whole mass of sketches of my own to work from, and of course a lot of other people's views of you. Some of them flattering.'

'Only some of them?' Shimada looked at her over the rim of his glass of Scotch and water, and then turned his lips downwards ruefully. 'But of course. Judging by your outburst on the subject of my character last Thursday you must have been briefed by one or two people who dislike me cordially.'

His tone gave Lesli the confidence to deny him the aid and comfort he seemed to be seeking. 'Yes, I have. I've spoken with a number of people myself during the past couple of months, Mr Shimada, and then of course you must have realised I've also had the benefit of access to an enormous amount of interview material gathered in the latter part of last year by *Newsworld* magazine staff here when they were researching the cover story on you.'

She took brief refuge from his gaze in her drink, then faced him again. The alcohol was helping Lesli to relax, and she found herself able to simulate straightforward candour with increasing ease. 'You shouldn't be surprised. Nobody could have had a career like yours without making other people – politicians, competitors in business and so on – jealous of you. Suspicious of you. Scared of you. Bitterly hostile to you.'

'No. I realise that. I'm a little taken aback to hear you imply that people have been quite so forthcoming, though. I know you wouldn't tell me if I asked, but I'd give a lot to know who these informants of yours were. It's not the Japanese way to admit to such feelings openly.'

'Oh, they didn't. Not all of them. But you're forgetting, Mr Shimada. I'm Japanese by blood. I know all about *tatemae* and *honne*, image and reality, the true feelings behind the impassive face and the carefully courteous words, thinking with the stomach. I can read between Japanese lines.'

Being on the offensive made Lesli feel better and better, and she looked at Shimada boldly, in a growing awareness that it was enjoyable to be delicately taunting this powerful man. She knew that she looked her best, having changed after the earlier interview into the most elegant of the dresses she had brought with her to wear if she should find herself invited to smart evening occasions. It was of clinging silk jersey in a subtle mulberry colour, which worn on previous occasions had usually helped her to feel simultaneously poised, sophisticated and slightly daring. She concluded that it had simply been a case of delayed action this time. Anyway and whatever the reason, Lesli was beginning to enjoy the conversation, and rather surprised herself by realising that it was by no means disagreeable to be conscious of Shimada's glance flickering over her body.

'Yes. Yes, I suppose you can. As I've said before, you can be a disconcerting woman, Miss Hoshino. I see that it was very foolish on my part to have underestimated you. Perhaps we'd better have something to eat before you spoil my appetite.' He took her gently by the elbow and led her over to the table. It was the first time he had touched her since their initial introductory handshake early in January, and Lesli found the sensation both pleasant and disturbing.

The food was delicious, and the sense of the absurdity of sitting there being waited on as though posing for an American Express advertisement diminished slightly as Shimada again switched on his formidable charm, changed the subject and talked interestingly and amusingly about the impact on Japanese officialdom of Prime Minister Nakasone's forthright and individualistic style, and a conversation between Nakasone and Margaret Thatcher at which he had been present. Shimada was a competent mimic and made Lesli laugh several times, though she was still enjoying the idea of having held her own in the conversation earlier, and felt secure in the deep female strength which flowed from the awareness that he found her physically desirable as well as both outspoken and enigmatic. All the same, she was cautious enough to refuse the warm Chinese wine offered with the food, for fear of becoming indiscreetly talkative.

'It's unorthodox after food like this, I know, but I'm going to have some coffee,' Shimada said at last, laying down his napkin. 'What about you? Or do you have room for another crab claw?'

Lesli shook her head. 'I've eaten far too much as it is. Coffee would be very good.'

'Right. We'll have it in the study, so that the waiter can clear up in here and leave,' Shimada said, and rose to his feet as the waiter approached Lesli and pulled her chair back for her. She stood up while keeping her eyes fixed on Shimada's face, assessing the possible significance of his apparent eagerness to dismiss the waiter and wondering what she would do if, as now began to seem possible, Shimada were to make a sexual approach to her; but could read nothing but hospitable courtesy in his expression. As they made their way out of the room his hand was again at her elbow, though, and its warmth made the flesh of her upper arm tingle.

Shimada's habits must have been well understood because the coffee was ready and waiting for them in the study, which had a very different feeling from the huge formal living room which looked as if it had been fitted out complete by a pretentious but insecure interior designer. The books on the crowded shelves were not in fine leather-bound sets but a jumbled miscellany in Japanese and English, and magazines were scattered over the desk, television set and armchairs. Shimada scooped some of them up to clear a chair for Lesli, looked round rather helplessly and then dropped them on the carpet. 'The only room the cleaning woman isn't allowed to touch,' he said. 'Will you pour the coffee, or shall I?'

'I will. This is a good room,' Lesli said as she reached for the pot.

Shimada grunted as he bent over the desk, opened a drawer and shuffled through its contents. 'Here,' he said then. 'I made you a promise. My late wife.'

Lesli studied the photograph which he came over and handed to her, standing beside her chair to look down at the picture as she studied it. 'Why, she was *beautiful*,' she said.

'Try not to sound so surprised, Miss Hoshino. It's not very flattering to me. Yes, she was. That's a studio picture, of course, and they have ways and means of making women look their best. But a lot of people besides you and me used to think her beautiful. That was taken just before her last film was released: she was never photographed again, and she died less than two years later.' Shimada went to his own chair and lowered himself heavily into it.

'But . . . but you said it wasn't a love match.'

'It wasn't. We were in a position to help each other's careers. I became very fond of her though.'

'And she of you.'

'No. I think not. I am not a lovable man, Miss Hoshino, as you have gathered.' He cleared another chair and sat staring at her expressionlessly. 'You don't dispute my statement,' he said after a while. He seemed again to Lesli to be fishing for reassurance and she shrugged, finding it childish and distasteful.

'How can I possibly do that? I'm sorry if I was discourteous to you last week and again this evening, but I've already explained that whatever information and impressions I've been able to gain from others, personally I don't know you at all. I don't know what drives you, what began to drive you all those years ago. Nor do I know what you might have done to get where you are today.'

Lesli tried to rein in a growing sense of exasperation, finding it hard to cling to the cliff-edge of discretion from which Shimada's apparent mood of self-pity was threatening to dislodge her. She sensed her mental fingertips slipping: it would be so easy and satisfying to let go and plunge down on him from the height of her knowledge and force him into admissions, evasions, even blazing anger, yet this would bring her perilously close to making her acquaintance with Yoko obvious, and Lesli was still frightened enough for Yoko, and indeed herself, to want to pull back. She therefore said no more, but picked up her coffee with a hand which trembled slightly.

She was glad to have left it at that when Shimada replied, for he was once more confidently authoritative, the president of the corporation condescending to be interviewed. 'Can you really be in any doubt about what drives me, as you put it? You've come across the phenomenon of ambition often enough before, haven't you? Combine that with some strong convictions about where we Japanese have gone wrong in the past and the way we need to go in the future, and you have a psychological explanation of me and my actions which should suffice.'

It was with a sense of relief that Lesli felt firmer ground under her, but it seemed ironic that only now, when she was on the point of leaving Japan, the no-go barriers were being dismantled and for the first time Shimada seemed to be positively inviting the personal questions he had side-stepped so deftly in their many set-piece conversations.

'That's *your* explanation, Mr Shimada. I still have to arrive at my own.'

'And you expect to do that in the process of writing this book?'

'Perhaps. More in the process of writing the one in my head; the one that won't be published.'

'You speak in riddles, Miss Hoshino. Cognac?'

'No. Thank you. I'll take another cup of coffee if I may, though.' Shimada nodded as Lesli offered the pot in his direction and as she refilled their cups helped himself to a generous measure of cognac from the bottle on another tray nearby. 'You won't mind if I write to you from America with supplementary questions as they occur to me? And of course I shall send you a copy of the manuscript when it's ready. For your comments and corrections as to matters of fact.'

'That was the understanding. And I shall be pleased to receive any further questions you may wish to put to me by letter. Provided you will enlighten me as to what you mean by writing another book in your head.'

Lesli tried to laugh lightly, but was annoyed by the effect: she thought she succeeded only in sounding silly and girlish. 'Oh, that? That's the one I call *The Real Jiro Shimada*. Let me ask you a personal question now. May I?' Shimada stared at her fixedly and then nodded gravely, swirling the oily liquid in his glass.

'Your father died in 1940, you said. What of?' The silence was so protracted and Shimada sat so still that Lesli found herself beginning to formulate an apology in her mind. Then her mood veered abruptly towards one of exasperated disgust. She had had enough. It was time to pull back decisively from the brink, time to leave, time to go away from Japan and its bottomless layers of hypocrisy, deceit and complacency. The monstrous Shimada who had been prowling through her mind for weeks seemed to shrink as he remained silent, and Lesli felt flat, almost bored, and dully ashamed of her earlier burgeoning sexual excitement. There was no longer anything frightening or impressive about the lonely, ageing man across the table, with his artificial tan and his retinue of waiters and cleaning women. She expelled her breath with a sound of irritation and moved in her chair, about to get up. Then at last Shimada spoke, parrying her question with another.

'This book in your head. Did you mean what you said about its never being published?'

Lesli glared at him coldly. 'I don't see how it can be, do you? I couldn't write it without your full personal cooperation, and you certainly can't. Autobiographies are inherently flawed.' Then she shrank back a little: the look on his face was again arrogantly self-assured.

'I don't need therapy, Miss Hoshino,' he snapped. 'I'm not sick. Psychoanalysis is a bogus science which flourishes by gulling the feeble and the self-important. And I'm not religious, so I have no urge to make confessions. In short, I see no reason why I should satisfy even your own curiosity by telling you things about people other than myself, still less that of your readers.' Without warning he stood up and went to the window, then spun round and confronted her. 'I agree with you. You can't write my personal biography, and I forbid you to make the attempt.'

Lesli reacted at once. Splendid, satisfying anger suffused her consciousness as she uncoiled herself from her chair, stood and looked Shimada in the eye. 'You *what*?' she enquired, coldly incredulous. 'Did I hear you use the word "forbid"?'

'You did.' They both stood stock-still, staring at each other across a distance of several feet, lobbing sentences to and fro like wary, well-matched tennis players.

'Mr Shimada. You seem to have forgotten that downstairs in your office two or three hours ago I turned down your offer of a job here. I gave you some reasons. One I didn't get around to mentioning is that I didn't like the idea of taking orders from you. I still don't, and I'm not planning to.'

'You'll take this one.'

'On the contrary. In fact, you just got yourself a different kind of biographer.'

Shimada relaxed his stance very slightly, and when he spoke again his voice was silky and full of menace. 'No, my dear Miss Hoshino, you're mistaken. I might as well explain. I finally decided some time ago – last week, as a matter of fact – to do without a biographer altogether. The project is cancelled. Abandoned. Off.' He raised a hand gently as Lesli opened her mouth in renewed outrage. 'Wait. I have something else to say, and I will then explain why I have arranged that you will not seek to overturn my decision. I realised several weeks ago that, as I said before dinner, at first I seriously underestimated not only your persistence but also your resourcefulness. I also overlooked the fact that certain things are matters of public record. I admit all that, but on the other hand you for your part made a big mistake in taking me for a fool.' Shimada's eyes were glittering, and Lesli found it difficult to breathe. Her fury was now tinged with apprehension, and she felt a physical desire to run away, but was unable to move.

'It took me some time to find out what your purpose was in going to America.'

The blood rushed to Lesli's face and she faltered when she tried to speak. 'How –?'

'Oh, you foolish, self-righteous woman! Of course I knew you went: indeed that was what first sounded the alarm bells for me. I knew also of most if not all of your visits to Kamakura. You look not only embarrassed but surprised, Miss Hoshino. You shouldn't be. Do you seriously think I would permit you or anyone else to have access to my papers without making it my business to know what other sources were being tapped?'

'You . . . you *bastard*! You've been *playing* with me! All that stuff about checking the manuscript . . . offering me a job –' Lesli looked round wildly, and Shimada shook his head.

'No. Don't throw anything at me. It might make me angry, and you wouldn't like that. Perhaps I do owe you an apology. I have indeed enjoyed – how do you put it – stringing you along this evening. But the job offer was genuine as a matter of fact. And had you accepted, my plans would have been very different. I've considered various contingencies, you see. For instance, you may be interested to know that over the past few days I have also toyed with the idea of proposing marriage to you. You're an extremely attractive woman, and though I'm an old man I *am* very rich, after all. That combination has been known in the past to have a certain appeal.'

Lesli was almost choked with outrage. 'You have the goddam gall to imagine that you can *buy* me? *Marry* you? Marry *you*? I'll see you in hell first.' Shimada shrugged insultingly, then easily caught Lesli's flailing arm by the wrist as she tried to hit him.

'*Anyone* can be bought, Miss Hoshino. Believe me, I know: I'm a very experienced purchaser. It's just a question of fixing upon the right price. Oh, I'm not just talking about money in your case, though my American attorneys will I'm sure arrive at an amicable settlement with your publishers, and when you calm down I believe you'll consider the arrangements quite generous. There will be no problem there. If necessary, you see, I would simply buy the publishing house up. I realise though that this kind of settlement will not necessarily ensure your permanent silence, which is essential from my point of view.'

Lesli furiously wrenched her imprisoned wrist free and stepped back, her face flaming. She found it hard to believe the words she was hearing. Shimada's talk of marriage was as insidious as it was arrogantly outrageous, and it was as though the gears of her mind were stripped and her thoughts were careering out of control. She was terrified by the threat behind Shimada's words, believing him now not only to be a blackmailer but also a murderer. She tried to grasp the huge idea that her own life was in danger from him, yet at the same time she was astonished and horrified to find herself excited by his coldly merciless strength. For an insane moment as his eyes met and held hers she could feel her anger, fear and revulsion merging into a disgusting kind of lust, a blind, consuming passion to possess and to be possessed. Then terror was again uppermost as he smiled briefly and spoke again. He had not moved, but Lesli was sickeningly convinced that he had read her mind. She felt as if her legs were about to give way under her, and crumpled back into her chair, emotionally exhausted.

'I'm sure you understand. So naturally, I have given a lot of thought to ways and means of silencing you effectively. The simplest method would of course be to have you killed,' he said with a gentleness in bizarre contrast to the words he used. 'It wouldn't be any problem for someone with my resources and influence to arrange. I've contemplated doing so more than once during the past few days, particularly when I read the piece in *Newsworld* magazine about the February 26 Incident, you see. Your name was there. As soon as I saw it I realised that you must have been told about my brother. Probably by the American, Rogers. I'd be surprised if Yoko had talked about him in that connection.'

Shimada faltered over the last few words and unaccountably, Lesli felt tears welling up in her eyes. 'I'm sorry,' she said. 'Yes, I did find out. But I never had any intention of referring to him in the book.' Shimada nodded slowly as Lesli gazed at him with a new timidity, less harrowing than her earlier fear.

'Would you really have me killed? If I plan to go ahead with the book?' She waited for his reply with an almost academic interest, and Shimada shook his head.

'Not now. It would be crude, and rather cowardly on my part. Besides, I'm prepared to pay a different price, you see. I don't think you'll refuse it.' He sat down and sipped his cognac.

Lesli waited for him to go on, and when he did not, found herself unable to ask him 'What different price?' He had become very still, as though he were alone in the room, and questioning him suddenly seemed less urgent than watching him. Their silence lasted for almost half a minute, Shimada apparently so far away that he was unaware of the intensity with which she was studying him. When he gave his head a little shake and met her eyes, she held her breath.

'You asked about my father,' he said quietly. 'I suppose you could say he died of sadness, though in fact he died in prison. After my brother . . . was executed and he was retired from Mitsui he threw himself into political activity. He had always harboured leftish ideas, but was amazingly discreet about them until the last few years of his life. Then he made up for lost time. From the summer of 1936 until he was jailed he devoted himself to open anti-militarist activism. It doesn't sound much these days, but at that time he was one of a very few. I suppose he felt he had nothing to lose, and perhaps . . . a certain dignity to gain. So he faced the thought police. A matter of his own choice, I think, rather than of "being caught". Just as it's by my own choice that now I am facing you.'

Shimada's stillness had not been broken by his deciding to speak. Lesli had never seen him so apparently tranquil and relaxed. Now, at her expression of dismay at being compared with the thought police, a flicker of amusement crossed his face.

'Don't look so disconcerted. It's not an inapt comparison, you know. You have been arrogant in your presumption that you have a right to know things which were no concern of yours. You have been prying and conspiring, you have blundered into private places, smug in your sense of moral rectitude. Still – that's done with now. It's too late for resentment on my part or regret on yours. I'm not in fact going to *buy* your silence – but I am a man who has achieved all he can hope for in his lifetime, so it seems to me that I'm in a position to *compel* it.'

Lesli felt herself becoming almost as still as he was – and cold. . . . 'to compel it'? Instantly, before she had time to name to herself the nature of this 'compulsion' which he was substituting for a 'price', she was beginning to feel the terror – indeed, the awe – that was going to come with full understanding.

'No,' she whispered. 'No. You don't have to do anything – anything at all – for my silence. Of course you don't. You can have it. Look – you could have it anyway for Yoko's sake, even if not for yours.'

Shimada looked at her steadily for a long moment before shaking his head slowly. 'I believe you, and I thank you. You must not be offended, my dear, when I say that what you intend to do has become irrelevant. I've done all I can, and I am tired – my mind is made up.'

Unreality; inevitability – it seemed to Lesli that she had strayed into a dream where the two were blended, and anything she tried to say to this man would emerge as a meaningless twittering. At the same time everything competent in her – all that part of her which had given her control of her career – was insisting that of course she could find the right words, could hit the right tone, could restore reality and controllability. If she could only think quickly and shrewdly enough, she must be able to bring this man back out of the distance – the crazily *Japanese* distance – into which he seemed to be vanishing. 'Keep him talking,' she thought, 'that's what I must do,' as though she were a policeman playing for time with a lunatic perched on a windowsill. Drawing a deep breath, she made her voice sound cool as she said: 'You do realise, don't you, that if that's the case you have to tell me everything?'

Shimada nodded, as though her words had been perfectly logical. 'Yes. You want to know about the sister who died in the war. Her name was Teruko.' A wincing contraction of his brow disturbed his calm for an instant, and Lesli thought 'Oh my God, this is going to make it worse.'

'Teruko,' he repeated. 'She was a pretty girl . . . she was a whore. She began while she was a hostess in a dance hall in the Ginza, but after my mother died she soon went to work at a place in Shinjuku, an actual brothel. Not far from here. Not far at all. In the autumn of 1936 she found her own place to live and we lost track of her. She "evaporated" as people say here. Then in 1938 she wrote from Shanghai. She had become what they used to call a "comfort girl" for the Japanese troops, and remained one until her death. The notification spoke of tuberculosis, but a rumour reached me that she was strangled.' In the few seconds since he had uttered Teruko's name his face had become sallow. 'Now you know it all.'

'No, not quite all.' His attempt to claim that they had reached the end of the story re-awoke Lesli's indignation. 'You forget, Mr Shimada, that I already know why Yoko hates you.'

He answered wearily. 'You know why *she thinks* she hates me. Do you really imagine I could forget that? She thinks I killed our mother. It took her some years to conceive that idea – we were quite close for a long time after my mother died. It was no more than a few months later that my brother . . . and then my father was taken away. Teruko had gone and we had only each other . . . It was the news of Teruko's death that did it. It was the last straw for Yoko. She had a sort of brain-storm, ranting and raving and accusing me of killing Teruko – which was mad, of course. Then – I shall never forget this – she suddenly stood stock still, her eyes fixed on my face, and said – whispered – "Of course – *you killed Mother too*. Now I understand everything." And then she fainted.

She has never spoken a word to me since. When I tried to talk to her – I did to start with, very often – she took refuge in hysterics so I used to be afraid of driving her into a breakdown, and later, whenever I wrote to her the letter came back unopened. She didn't *want* to believe me . . . she'll be thankful when I'm gone.'

'And did you kill your mother?'

Shimada closed his eyes. 'No, I did not.'

'Why should Yoko believe that? Why should I believe it? You stole your mother's pots, you blackmailed Teruko. It wasn't out of the blue that suspicion came to Yoko, it was because she found out about the blackmail from a letter which Teruko wrote her. You're lying even now, trying to conceal that, so why should I believe you about your mother? You're capable of murdering for your own advantage – you admitted as much just now when you said you'd considered having me killed. You might still, for all I know.'

'No. You know better now.' Shimada held her eyes with his own. 'Don't you?'

Lesli glared at him, silenced. She did know better, but it did not diminish her anger; nor did the knowledge that he was going to drive her, finally, to respect.

'All right – you may not be going to kill me, but how could anyone not hate you for what you did to Teruko? That was vicious and pitiless – what reason could you conceivably have for hating her so bitterly?'

'Listen: I did not kill my mother and I did not steal her pots. She gave them to me a few days after Yoko brought her back from Tenri. It makes no difference whether you believe me or not, it's the truth. And it's also, alas, the truth that I did hate Teruko. I hated her for turning her back on Japan. For aping western ways. For her triviality, and for hideously corrupting the one man I ever truly loved and respected – my brother.' Shimada's eyes were closed again and his head was swaying slightly, as though he were in physical pain. 'At that time, whatever my brother believed, I believed. Teruko defiled him. In my arrogance I took it upon myself to be the instrument of justice and punish her for her evilness. At that time I was deficient in respect for my father, I had not seen through the modest front he kept up, to his great strength, so I had given to my brother the feelings I should have given him. It was when at last I understood my father's true courage that my eyes were opened to the horror of what I had done, and I also saw the enormity of what my poor brother stood for and had done in his romantic fever – his insanely Japanese folly. I could never undo what I had done to Teruko. I have lived with that guilt for half a century. But I have tried to . . . make amends. To use the product of the money I extorted from her to work for a different sort of Japan, not self-obsessed but open to light. A garish light, often, but it once made Teruko's eyes sparkle . . . before I . . . did what I did. There have been times when I thought I was exercising considerable influence, but I had to be careful not to look into my heart. That is what you have done: forced me to look into my heart. But what I saw there was always there – the knowledge that nothing I'd achieved was worth what my sister had to pay for it. It's a criminal account, and it's time it was closed.'

He finished off his cognac and then stood up, looking at his watch. 'So. It's getting late. My driver Hatano-san is waiting to take you back. You'll find him in the car in the usual place in the garage,' he said. His manner was equable and friendly as he approached her and offered her his hand: the evening's exchanges between them might never have taken place. 'Well, goodbye, Lesli.'

She took it in hers and looked at him. 'I believe you now,' she said quietly. 'And I may be able to stop hating you one day. I don't know about Yoko, but you have my promise that I'll try to explain to her. Goodbye, Jiro.' Except for a brief pressure on her hand before releasing it he made no response, but Lesli turned back when she reached the door and saw him looking at her with a twisted smile on his face. She hesitated, battling with the desire to return to him, beg him to change his mind, even try to comfort him in his last loneliness; but then shook her head sadly.

'*Sayonara,*' she said, her voice husky with emotion. Then something made her bow low to Jiro Shimada, in farewell and to honour his decision. There was both dignity and grace in his immediate response, and as Lesli left the room to find her coat she knew that he had chosen the right course.

It was the Japanese way, after all.

Although the season of the heavy 'plum rains' was officially
almost over, the air in the cell was humid, the painted steel of the
door beaded with condensation; and the clean shirt they had
given to Hideo stuck to his skin as he pulled it on. Then one of the
guards came with a little pot of paint and carefully dabbed the
sweaty skin of his forehead dry with a pad of cloth. Hideo felt the
cool slippery prickle of the brush against his forehead: he
imagined the tongue of a snake might feel like that, flickering in
exploration.

It was quite a relief to get outside into the open air, even though
the sky was the colour of lead, it was drizzling and even at that
early hour almost as hot as it had been inside. A gingko tree grew
just outside the execution yard and Hideo could see over the top of
the wall that its leaves were ruffling and stirring as each periodi-
cally shed its accumulated burden of rainwater.

Hideo realised that he must be the last out. The lieutenants of
the First Division who, against all normal procedure, composed
the firing squad were already in their positions of near-
concealment behind an earthern rampart, but Hideo could see
enough of them to notice dark patches of sweat already visible and
distinct from the drizzle beading the shoulders of their shirts. The
major in command was supervising the tying of Yasuda's wrists
and ankles to the frame.

Three more of his friends were already trussed up, and there
was only one space left. 'Good morning, Comrade Shimada!' one
of them called out, and Hideo smiled over at him. The four of them
looked rather comical with their bull's-eyes painted on their
foreheads, vaguely like the grotesque Daruma dolls people bought
blank-eyed as bringers of good luck, painting in one black eye at
the outset of a project and filling in the other only on its successful
completion. Soon they had finished with Yasuda and the guard
led Hideo to his place at the end.

'Are we the first batch, Major?' Hideo asked. 'Three lots of five,
is it?' and the major nodded as he watched the two soldiers at

work on his wrists. Hideo allowed himself to droop a little when they were done. He felt much too unreal to be afraid, and besides, the others were exchanging brave, hot words almost as they had during those strange days at the Sanno Hotel. The one who had greeted Hideo was now singing a little song, and when he had finished Yasuda shouted out to the detail of officer-marksmen 'The people trust the Army! Don't let them be betrayed! Don't let the Russians get the better of us!' and all five of the condemned men cheered. Then an oppressive silence fell as the major brought the firing squad to attention and then ordered them to present arms in the final compliment of a general salute.

Then the blindfolding began, beginning with Hideo. In the sudden private darkness of his head Hideo gazed on the image of Teruko which flooded his consciousness with beauty as he sagged against the bonds which held him to the rough wood behind him. She, Yoko, Jiro and his father had been permitted to visit the military prison at Yoyogi the previous evening to make their farewells. Hideo remembered little of what had been said, but felt the depth of Teruko's gaze still searching and sustaining his spirit.

Then the crisp sound of boots on gravel and the metallic rattle of the rifle-bolts roused him and he straightened up, aware of a scream of terror burgeoning within him, seeming almost to struggle physically up through his throat. Hideo could not silence it: all he could do was transform it, and tears of triumphant relief stung his eyes as he heard his own cracked voice cry out 'For His Majesty and the Empire!' and the ragged chorus of his comrades joining him in the last threefold *Banzai*!

Yoko knelt in silence beside Teruko and Jiro as she watched her father bow, take up the letter from the plain lacquer tray she had placed before him on the *tatami*, and open it. She had herself received it at the door from the military despatch rider who saluted her respectfully before turning away, and turned it over and over in her hands until the sound of his motor-cycle had faded into the bustle of mid-morning. They were all in formal Japanese dress, even Jiro who was wearing one of Yukichi's *kimonos*.

Yukichi first read and then set aside the offical notification of the execution of the sentence of the Special Court-Martial upon former Lieutenant Shimada, and then unfolded the enclosure, Hideo's testament and 'after-life' poem. He read them through in silence once, and then aloud to his children in the calm, polished voice they all knew so well. Then he looked again at the notification with its profusion of official seals, replaced all the papers on the tray and laid it in the *tokonoma* in front of the framed photograph of Hideo which stood in the place of honour. They all bowed in obeisance.

After a long time Yukichi straightened up, then stood and looked down at his children.

'I must go to the prison now,' he said quietly. 'To make the arrangements.' Jiro bowed again to Hideo's photograph and then stood up too, his face pale and set. 'I'll come with you, Father,' he said.